Jonny Nexus is a Lancashire based ↙
in his spare time. When not doing t﹍
daughter, and dog; reads; watches TV, ﹍,
of theatre; and plays the occasional board game.

Jonny began his writing career by launching the cult gaming webzine *Critical Miss* (criticalmiss.com), before moving on to write regular columns for the roleplaying magazines *Valkyrie* and *Signs & Portents*, as well as penning the *Slayer's Guide to Games Masters* for Mongoose Publishing.

The Sleeping Dragon is his third novel. His first novel, *Game Night*, was shortlisted for an ENnie award in 2008, and was followed in 2015 by his second novel, *If Pigs Could Fly*.

The Sleeping Dragon

By Jonny Nexus

To Aby,
Hope you like it!
Jonny Nexus
DWCon 2018

First published in the United States and the United Kingdom in 2018 by Wild Jester Press.

All contents copyright © 2018 Jonny Nexus.

The moral rights of the author have been asserted.

This is a work of satirical fiction. All characters and events are fictitious. Any resemblance to real persons, either living or dead, is entirely coincidental.

ISBN 978-1979419086

10 9 8 7 6 5

Web: www.jonnynexus.com
Email: jonny@jonnynexus.com
Twitter: @jonnynexus

Wild Jester Press
Littleborough
Greater Manchester
United Kingdom

www.wildjesterpress.com

Cover illustration & design by Alex Storer: www.thelightdream.net

Map of the Empire by Jacob Rodgers.

Thanks to Jules for the love and support over the ten years it's taken to get this one out of the gate;

to Amanda and Ro for their help shepherding this book into the world;

to Jean, Angela, David, and Richard for the kind words and encouragement;

to Mooch, Rebecca's, the Cherry Tree, and the Wine Press for the rocket fuel;

and to Violet, for being the best daughter a man could have.

Prologue

Five figures sit around a table. In a heroic age, these men are heroes. They have humbled tyrants, slaughtered dragons, and reduced entire tribes of rampaging orcs to tears. Occasional difficulty with taxes aside, no man or beast has bested them, and no challenge have they feared.

Until this day.

For even they feel stunned disbelief at what has just been revealed.

One of them, a priest, clears his throat before breaking the awed silence created by his previous announcement. "And so that, gentlemen, is that. In a little over five hundred years our world as we know it will be destroyed. Civilisation will fall. Starvation and plague will stalk the land. All that we value, all of our learning, all that we hold dear: gone. Nothing left save dust and ashes."

At the far end of the table sits an armoured warrior, his sword and shield placed on the table before him. The sacred symbol painted on the shield testifies to his faith and piety; the bloodstains and nicks on the sword bear witness to the fury and vengeance with which he has recently expressed that faith and piety. "Are you sure?" he asks.

The priest nods, his face a solemn mask. "The runes do not lie, Sir Ethelded. Nor the stars, nor the cards, nor the numbers. I have consulted them all, and it is certain: in five hundred years the sleeping dragon will wake and bring forth an apocalypse upon our world."

The figure who sits beside Sir Ethelded stirs, thinking. He is Halen Fleetfoot, the greatest thief who has ever lived. At his feet sit the tools of his trade: picks for a lock; a grappling hook for a wall; a cosh for a guard, and for when subtlety's lost.

He starts to speak, then stops. He slumps down in his chair and lets out a long sigh that mixes disbelief with horrified incredulity. "Wow. That's, erm... Really?"

The five fall silent again.

Here they sit, facing each other across a marble slab of polished perfection, flanked by pillars of flawless granite and topped by a roof of burning bronze. Beyond, green hills roll gently beneath a clear blue sky, white unicorns grazing upon their slopes. This is an oasis where the gods themselves might dine, or at least take afternoon tea. What could destroy such wonders? Surely a world such as this should endure forever?

Beside Fleetfoot sits an impossibly beautiful man clad in bardic robes and holding a miniature harp. He lifts it now and looks around at his four comrades. "Perhaps I should write a song that expresses how we feel?"

Withering looks give him his answer. He puts the harp down.

Fleetfoot is still slumped in his chair. He shrugs, a wry smile on his face. "Oh well. It's not like it's going to happen tomorrow, right?"

The priest bangs the table in a manner that isn't terribly priest-like but which is understandable given that he is several hours into a very bad day. "With respect, Halen, that is not the point. This tragedy may not befall us, but it is still a tragedy."

The thief considers this for moment, before delivering another in what is clearly a practiced repertoire of shrugs. "A single death is a tragedy. A hundred million deaths of people whose great-great-great-great-grandfathers haven't yet been born is a concept, and an abstract one at that. Anyway, what does it matter? All's lost, right?"

Only one of their number has yet to speak. The ebony wand before him and the prematurely aged eyes set into his face both speak of what he is. A wizard, and a good and daring one; a man who has ripped through the skin of the universe and looked at its soul, and lived to tell the tale. "All is not lost," he says.

Four pairs of eyes swivel towards him.

It is Sir Ethelded who speaks. "Are you deaf, Kellen? Did you not hear what Archbishop Idenn has foretold?"

The wizard smiles. "I heard."

"Then why do you say that all is not lost?" asks the priest. "Do you doubt what I say?"

"Of course not, Father Idenn," says the wizard. "I would never do so. Have we not stood shoulder to shoulder against both fury and storm? I say that all is not lost because all is not yet lost."

"How?" asks the thief. "Why?"

"Because prophecies are not what will happen, only what may happen should men of action not intervene. They reveal the challenges the SkyFather is setting us, rather than an end that he's decreed."

"But we are talking about events more than half a millennium hence!" splutters the priest. "In the name of all, Kellen, what we can do?"

"We? Nothing."

"Nothing?" says Sir Ethelded. "But you said all is not yet lost?"

Kellen smiles. "Gentlemen, we are heroes, the best of our age. But we are not the only heroes that ever were, nor the only heroes that ever shall be. When the events that Idenn has prophesied arise, the heroes of that future age will be there to face them."

The other four ponder on this for a moment.

Archbishop Idenn raises a questioning finger. "But what if they know not of what is to befall them?"

"We could leave a testament of what we have found!" says Sir Ethelded. "A story to be passed down from generation to generation."

The wizard shakes his head. "Stories fade. After one generation, they're conjecture. After two generations, legend. And after three generations, they're nothing more than a child's fairy tale. Such will be the fate of any testament we might leave."

The bard breaks in: "I could encode the message in song?"

More withering looks give him his answer.

"We could tell the elves?" suggests Fleetfoot, hesitantly.

"Bollocks to that!" shouts Sir Ethelded. "I'd rather the bloody world was destroyed than talk to those pointy-eared, no-souled bastards!"

He receives in reply a half-hearted chorus of vaguely affirmative mutters.

Kellen shakes his head. "We need not talk to the elves."

"Good," says Sir Ethelded. He looks at the priest. "And my apologies for my blaspheming, Your Grace."

The priest holds up a forgiving hand.

"Nor need we write our testament," says Kellen. "Nor encode it in song."

"Well, damn it all then, Kellen," shouts Sir Ethelded. "What exactly are we supposed to do? Nothing? Are we to hope that these heroes of the future discover for themselves the danger they face?"

The wizard shakes his head. "No. I have something in mind, have no fear. When the sleeping dragon awakes, the heroes of that age will be aware of its threat."

The warrior nods hesitantly, but concern returns to his face. "But how can you be sure that there will still be heroes in that age so far away?"

The wizard smiles a long, confident smile. "Because however much the world may change, one truth shall endure: there will always be heroes."

3

Five Hundred Years Later

bolt *noun*
A ranged weapon firing a beam of pure mana. A modern refinement of earlier wands enchanted with lightning bolt spells, bolts are available in small one-handed versions and larger two-handed versions.

broomstick *noun*
A small personal flying vehicle for one or two passengers. Originally a broom magically enchanted with a levitation spell, now a metal spine equipped with handlebars, seat, and footrests, and propelled by a mana-powered lift/repulsion unit.

buggy *noun*
A wheeled ground-transportation vehicle, typically seating two to five persons, controlled via a steering wheel and pedals, and propelled by a mana power unit turning a rotating drive shaft.

carpet *noun*
A personal flying vehicle carrying two to five passengers. Originally a rug magically enchanted with a levitation spell, now a metal monocoque shell propelled by a mana-powered lift/repulsion unit.

crystal *noun*
A round, flat-screened device used to broadcast entertainment and informational programming via ethereal plane transmissions, originally derived from crystal balls used for communication.

dial *noun*
A timepiece, either wall-mounted or free-standing, or worn on the wrist (a wrist-dial). Originally passive outdoor devices requiring sunlight to operate, dials now use chronological spells to track the time and a magical face to display it.

guard *noun*
A law enforcement officer, often a member of a city or town guard.

herb *noun*
Collective term for plant-derived psychoactive substances. Herb is often ingested in powdered form via the nose and is illegal in most jurisdictions.

mana *noun*
The fundamental energy force that powers all magical spells and devices.

oracle *noun*
A mana powered device incorporating thinking spells. Used for data calculation, analysis, and storage. Smaller models typically incorporate a crystal screen for display and a keyboard for input.

pictograph *noun*
Image of a person, scene, or object, taken by a camera. Originally saved on paper magically sensitive to different wavelengths of light, pictographic images are now usually downloaded to oracles in informational form.

pictographic memory *noun*
The ability to remember or recall information, particularly visual information, in exact detail.

wagon *noun*
A larger wheeled ground-transportation vehicle, typically used for the transportation of cargo, controlled via a steering wheel and pedals, and propelled by a mana power unit turning a rotating drive shaft.

whisper *noun*
A personal communication device used for person to person voice communications. Originally derived from the use of whisper spells for long-distance communications.

whisper *verb*
To contact someone using a whisper.

worm *noun*
Colloquial term used for Empire City's underground rapid transportation system.

Chapter One

The statue of Sir Ethelded had stood at the heart of Empire Square for nearly five hundred years. Built to honour a man who'd protected the city in its darkest days, it was now protected in turn by the combined efforts of the square's many pigeons and a phalanx of sash-wearing old women wielding furled umbrellas. The pigeons' excrement protected the elderly edifice from those who might use its plinth as a seat, while the sash-wearing old women attempted – largely unsuccessfully – to guard the statue from the pigeons.

The mark had chosen a new and exclusive coffee shop on the southern edge of the square as the place for them to meet. It was a ruinously expensive tourist trap, but that didn't bother Dani. It was just part of the cost of doing business, and the pavement table she'd sat at did enable a reassuringly good view of any events that might unfold. Besides, if the mark went for the bait, it would pay for a hell of a lot more than a cup of over-priced coffee.

The waiter finished fussing with the milk, the sugar, the linen napkin, and the various other pieces of crap such places use to justify their prices, and straightened up. "Will madam be requiring anything else?"

"Madam's fine for the moment," she told him.

The waiter flounced away. Dani took a sip of the coffee – which was actually damn good – and cast a deliberately calm and casual glance across the square. Expensive shops. Tourists, some elegantly dressed but most not. Suited, booted, and urgent-faced businessmen and businesswomen heading for lunchtime meetings. Street sellers peddling tourist tat and counterfeit goods.

No mark.

She took a few more sips, and tried to resist the temptation to play with the spoon.

Then, she saw him. The mark gave a smile and a wave as he caught sight of her. He stepped briskly up to the table and sat down, hand outstretched. "Ms Smidt," he said to Dani, smiling. "Good to meet you in the flesh at last."

Dani took the hand and gave it a good, firm shake. "Call me Johanna." She tossed a twenty gold piece note onto the table and pointed towards the statue of Sir Ethelded. "How about we go and take a look at the goods?"

"You're reading my mind," said the mark, smiling. They walked across the paved expanse to the statue, stopping just in front of its polished marble plinth. Dani gave him some time to admire it. After a few seconds, the mark spoke. "It's quite a sight, isn't it?"

Dani nodded. "It is." And to be fair, even covered in pigeon shit, it was.

"Hard to believe your bosses want to get rid of it."

Dani leaned in, looking first left, and then right, as though checking that none of the sash-wearing old ladies could overhear. "Which is why the City Council is insisting on absolute discretion. There are still too many who don't understand progress, who can't see this statue for what it is: an obsolete symbol of a bygone age. They don't see the shame in honouring a man who ethnically cleansed the East of orc, goblin, and beastman."

The mark paused again, the expression of oily covetousness upon his face showing clearly that it was the vision of the statue set upon the front lawn of his new-money mansion that currently occupied his mind, and not the fate of any orc, goblin, or beastman. "Ms Smidt."

"Please, call me Johanna."

"Johanna. I want this statue. Now."

Biting at the bait, thought Dani, time to start reeling him in. She waved a protesting hand. "This is a discreet process, not a secret one. There will be an auction. Sealed bids."

The mark snorted. "Auctions can be talked about. Bids can be leaked. Do your bosses want this to happen or not?"

Dani tilted her head. "Well, yes."

"And of course, Johanna, I could reimburse you for any, let's call them… expenses, that you might incur."

"I suppose, if you put it like that," said Dani, trying to project the air of a mid-level bureaucrat torn between greed, fear, and uncertainty. The hook might have been taken, but she still had to play it right. This was a con that was still very much blowable. She paused and smiled – but the mark wasn't smiling anymore. The man's face now wore a mask of shocked, awed horror. The air around Dani was shimmering, tendrils of energy swirling around her, pulsing through her, holding her. Dani had time for only one thought: *what's happening?*

And then she was gone.

The Storm looked at the dial on the dressing room's far wall, inwardly cursing when he saw the time. They'd been due on stage ten minutes ago, but the row that'd erupted ten minutes before that showed no signs of ending this side of the interval.

"Who do you think writes the bloody songs, eh?" Gekk was shouting.

"Who cares?" screamed Beffan, presumably at Gekk. "Newsflash, mate: it's the singer they come to see, not the short-arse behind the aurabox who thinks he's better than the rest of us on account of him writing a few crappy songs."

"Crappy? Crappy? I've won fucking awards! And I'll have you know I'm five foot eight, you slandering bastard!"

"Five foot eight? In your dreams! And only then if you're wearing platforms!"

The Storm ignored them, choosing instead to mentally tune into the background roar, a roar so huge that it was penetrating through several feet of concrete. A chant, rising over and over, again and again: "Northern Fire! Northern Fire! Northern Fire!"

Their audience were waiting. And they were late.

His lute was still plugged into the portable amp he'd used to tune it. He picked the instrument up and played a few random chords, the box's magic pumping them out with a rich vibration an old-fashioned acoustic lute could never hope to achieve.

Gekk looked over at him, a sneering smile on his face. "What? Trying to say you can write the songs instead of me? Dream on, mate. You've either got it, or you ain't; and you ain't." He didn't wait for the Storm to answer, but instead tapped out a line of herb on the dressing room counter and carefully snorted it up one nostril. He sniffed twice, and then smiled. "Stick to lead lute, mate. It's what you're passably good at." He looked around at the others, an unnatural shine in his eyes. "We going on then, or what?"

One by one, the band rose and walked through the dressing room's open door. It was only a short walk down a bare corridor to the stage; much shorter than some nightmarishly maze-like arenas they'd played at – although contrary to legend, and a few close calls aside, they'd never actually got lost on the way.

Then they were there, on stage, plugging in their instruments and launching straight into the first song, "Warriors of the East". The Storm crashed into the intro with Eddie's drums backing him up and Gekk coming in on the aurabox; all of them feeling more than hearing, sensing the change in the crowd. As always, the Storm found himself in awe at the effect music could have: uplifting, transforming, empowering. Fifty thousand faces were lifted towards them, a hundred thousand entranced eyes. A sea of waving hands that soothed nerves and fired the soul.

Arguments. Addictions. Money. None of it mattered when they were together on stage. This was what they did, and damn they were good.

And then it was better. Better than any gig. Better than any herb. A feeling that tore through every nerve: building, rising. He sensed a change in the crowd as the music faded. Beffan had stopped singing, was standing instead. Staring. At him. Pulsing energy sheathed the Storm, enveloping him with its soothing touch.

And then he was gone.

Men said many things of the Great Cathedral of the SkyFather. Some declared that the scale of its architecture taught an individual humility, and that the glory of its finish taught them awe. Some called it a place of spiritual cleansing in which life-damaged souls could shine once more. The Central Tourist Board of Empire City's municipal council described it as "an indispensable visit" that was "the perfect preliminary to lunch in the Cathedral District's many and varied high-quality eating establishments."

Right now, Father Darick would have described it as the last place in the universe he'd ever want to be. The man sitting on the other side of the large and impressive desk – Archbishop Ulfred, priest of the Great Cathedral, leader of the Empire City diocese, ultimate controller of a number of extremely wealthy investment portfolios, and Darick's boss – leaned back, stroked his chin, and finally spoke. "Darick, Darick, Darick. What are we going to do with you?"

Darick said nothing. It sounded like a rhetorical question, and since, if it wasn't, he hadn't a clue as to how to answer it, he figured he might as well treat it like one.

"I do have other things to be worrying about, you know," said the archbishop, waving a hand at the oracle that sat at one end of the desk, its crystal screen currently blank. "There are a few hundred messages sitting on that thing waiting to be answered, and they're not getting answered while I talk with you."

"Is this about Mrs Torden?" ventured Darick.

"Of course it's about Mrs Torden!" the archbishop exploded. "You think I've called you here to offer you a promotion?" He took a deep breath, trying visibly to calm himself, and then leaned forward, a smile on his face. "Why don't you give me your side of the events?"

Darick took a deep breath that turned into a gulp. "Mrs Torden came to me one day after the midmorning blessing. She'd had a row with her daughter. They weren't speaking, and she was very upset."

"And what was this row about?"

"Well, she'd found out that her daughter had recently begun a career in crystal, erm, skin-flicks. You know, those are the ones where you get to watch a man and a woman, and sometimes quite a few men and quite a few women, where they, well…"

"Thank you Darick," the archbishop interrupted. "I am aware of what a crystal skin-flick is."

"Yes, of course. Sorry. Anyway, Mrs Torden had told her daughter that she was…" Darick paused, coughed, and continued. "A whore and a tramp, and the daughter had stormed off."

The archbishop thought for a moment. "I see. And let me take a wild guess at what you didn't do. Did you suggest that she try to see things from her daughter's point of view?"

"No."

"Did you point out to her that she needs to be more accepting of other people's life choices?"

"No."

The archbishop wound up to what he obviously considered to be a conversational coup-de-grace, readying a sarcastic expression to accompany his querying tone. "Did you suggest that she pray to the SkyFather?"

"Well, yes. Should I not have?"

"Of course not, you idiot! This is the modern day, Darick. Now. The Second Millennium of the Third Age. The only people who still believe that the SkyFather actually exists are children and idiots."

I believe in him, thought Darick sadly.

"And you!" shouted the archbishop, as though reading Darick's mind. The older man made a visible effort to calm down. "When we talk about belief and faith, we're not talking about actual belief and actual faith – not like a belief that the sun will rise each morning, and a faith that the taxman will remember to apply our exemptions." He waited for a moment, presumably giving Darick a chance to laugh at his joke, and continued grumpily when he didn't. "We're not actually trying to imply that there's an old man in the sky with a big white beard watching our every move."

"We're not?"

The Archbishop's attempt to calm down ceased, abruptly. "For pity's sake, Darick, it's a metaphor!"

The older man carried on speaking, or at least his mouth kept on moving and his finger kept on jabbing, but the sound was suddenly gone – as though the SkyFather above had pressed the mute button on his crystal's control-wand. A feeling was flowing over Darick from both within and without. Warm. Comforting. Insulating. A shimmering enveloped him, glowing particles flowing past and around him like the plasma sheath created by a re-entering spacecraft. The archbishop was frightened now, he could see it in the man's face and in the way his mouth stuttered and closed.

SkyFather, thought Darick. *Is this you?*

And then he was gone.

Blade checked his wrist-dial. Quido was late, as he'd already been when Blade had last checked the time some five minutes earlier.

Hanging around the locker room like this made him very nervous. Anyone might enter, at any time. What would they think? One of the most famous AdventureSport warriors of all time hanging around the changing rooms of a dodgy back-street gym? If he was lucky, then maybe they'd figure he was hoping to indulge in what the news-slates still euphemistically termed "Elvish practices".

Or if he was unlucky they might just guess the truth.

On the wall opposite, a yellowing and torn poster stuck to a notice board taunted him with its message. "Taking illegal, performance-enhancing potions is cheating and may endanger your health. Just say no!"

A man entered the changing room. It wasn't Quido. In fact, it wasn't anyone Blade had ever seen, and that made him even more nervous, because from the way the bloke was looking at him, he'd sure as hell seen Blade before. But then again, who hadn't? The man stopped in front of him. "Quido sent me." He reached into his pocket and pulled out a plain grey plastic vial. He held it palm up for Blade to take and smiled. "Never figured you for something like this."

Blade wasn't in the mood for conversation. And he wasn't sure he was in the mood to talk to this bloke at all. This smelled of a dodgy set-up. What if that scum-bag Quido had turned him in to the game's authorities? Or maybe sold his story to some trashy news-slate? The guy could be a tester, or a journalist, or plain damn anyone. He took a step forward, ignoring the offered vial, forcing the guy to take a step back in turn. "Quido's the bloke I deal with and you ain't him."

Quido's man – if that was who he was – raised his hands in protest. "Hey, mate, Quido was busy and asked me to do him a favour. Now do you want the stuff or not?"

He held the vial out again. Thoughts tumbled inside Blade's head. Fear. Doubt. Guilt. How the hell had it come to this? Right now could be the moment it all ended, and ended badly at that. But he was in too deep for a U-turn. He started to reach, but the reach never came. Something had him, something he'd felt before, but never for real, never outside the arena. He looked at the guy, but the fear upon the man's face told its own story. Whatever this was, the guy wasn't part of it. Sensations swirled through Blade, faster than even he could react.

And then he was gone.

The crystal had broken three days ago. Three very long days ago. Or was it four? A sharp crack and a spark of mana and that had been that. No matter how hard or how often Presto had jabbed the on button, nothing had appeared on its gently-rounded screen. No crystal.

Dead.

Presto took a look around his apartment, and wiped a finger along the arm of his chair. Dust. An opened bottle of beer sat beside him. It was already a quarter empty and it wasn't yet ten. Was this what his life had come to? Destined for glory, now rotting in the slums? He grabbed a cigarette from the pack that stood beside the bottle, shoved it into his mouth, and brought his finger to its tip.

Flame, he thought.

A small jet of fire erupted from his fingertip. He sucked gently on the cigarette, until the tip glowed. The smooth smoke in his lungs merged with the ecstasy of magic cast and a universe tamed. But then the bitter sting of realities remembered came crashing back in. *I once commanded the forces of creation*, he thought. *Now I light my cigarette.*

Across the room the crystal stood, its blank screen mocking him.

He reached for the whisper and tapped in the number printed on the back of the crystal's control wand. A voice answered, synthetically cheerful, authentically fake. "This is the repairs and warranty department. We are currently experiencing high call volumes. Your call is important to us. Please wait."

    He waited. Music played. He waited some more, lulled almost to sleep by the soporific effect of the music and the periodic announcements of the importance of his call.

    Then he was awake. Suddenly awake. Very awake. A spell had him, was focusing, targeting. He stood, and took a staggering step forward, feeling the mana surging strong within him like a lost-but-grieved-for friendship now warmly renewed – except that it wasn't him who'd invited it in. The mana vortex built up around him – a big one, so big that it was warping space and scattering light.

    Whatever it was, it was going to be huge. He hadn't felt a rush like this since–

    And then he was gone.

The room was dark, the light unlit. Behind a plain and uncluttered desk sat a man, a lit cigarette smouldering in his fingers. He took a long drag, then put it down in a glass ashtray.

    What he had just seen written on his oracle's crystal screen pleased him. He picked up the whisper and dialled a number, not waiting for the person at the other end to speak when they answered.

    "It's started. Begin preparations to activate Amethyst."

    He put the whisper down and took another long drag of his cigarette.

    It had begun.

Chapter Two

The vortex swirled around Presto, like liquid sunlight. Then it faded to a nothingness – and he found himself sitting on an uncomfortably hard seat beside a table of once-polished marble. Six graffiti-marked pillars encircled the table, framing a set of views across a rubbish strewn park to grimy slums beyond; above was a dome of tarnished bronze.

Four others sat around the table.

A robed, earnest-faced priest.

A young woman in a dark, tailored jacket and skirt, her blonde hair cut in a neat, short style.

A guy in a ludicrous multi-coloured jumpsuit.

And a strangely familiar, powerful-looking bloke dressed in canvas trousers and a smock shirt.

All wore the stunned expression he suspected he too wore – although in his case, it would be a stunned expression soon to be replaced by one of anger. Teleportation was a spell so dangerous that it had been declared illegal more than three centuries ago, and that was before you added in the manipulation of the body during the process. Anyone who would attempt to perform such an insanely dangerous and illegal act five times simultaneously was either mad, bad, or brilliant. Or most likely all three of those combined.

He tried to push the chair back, but it wouldn't move – no, it was his legs that wouldn't move, the whole lower portion of his body pinned in place by a force unseen.

And then something was inside his head, a voice resonating across his mind, clear and authoritative, sparkling and pure: "The sleeping dragon will awake beneath Craagon's Reach."

As the final syllable settled across Presto's thoughts, he felt the invisible bonds that held him in the chair release. Standing up and looking around, he realised where he was: the Park of Pillars in the South Central district. He'd come here twenty years ago on a school trip to see a slice of the past conveniently set within a view of how the other half lived, history and social geography in one handy lesson plan.

Around him, the others were standing, their faces all showing a swirling mixture of fear, anger, and confusion. The man who wore the bizarre multi-coloured skin-tight jumpsuit shook his head and spoke. "What the fuck just went down? And where in hell is this joint?"

"The Park of Pillars," Presto told him, trying to keep his own fury under control. "In the South Central district."

The guy in the jumpsuit seemed to be having difficulty taking this in. "Sorry, which city did you say?"

"I didn't. But I'm talking about *the* City, Empire City."

"Like, what?"

Presto looked at him, considering. "Should we take it that the City is not where you were?"

"No. I was in..." The guy thought hard for a moment. "The Empire of the Sun."

"That's about eight thousand miles east of here!" the suited young woman blurted out.

It was the familiar-looking bloke who spoke next, looking straight at Presto as he did. "How about we leave the geography out of it and talk about what in the living shit just happened? Any of you people know what the sodding hell's going on?"

"Hey dude, don't look at me!" the man in the absurd jumpsuit fired back. "I'm as much in the fucking dark as you!"

"I'm a tad bewildered myself," said the priest. "One moment I was talking to my archbishop and then I was here."

The young suited woman leaned forward. "Same here," she said in a measured tone.

The familiar-looking man held up a placatory hand, and while it was clear from his tensely coiled body language that he was still only a couple of ticks away from a rage-fuelled explosion, his next words were spoken with a forced civility that had previously been lacking. "Okay, fine. Sorry. Seems like we're all victims here. Question is: what of? Anyone got any idea what in the seven planes of hell just happened?"

Presto had several such thoughts, but he didn't particularly care to discuss them with a bunch of complete strangers whose only connection to him was that they shared his current predicament. "Yes," he replied, leaving it at that, despite the resulting, awkward silence.

The other man considered that abbreviated reply for a moment, and then spoke. "That was a teleportation spell."

"Yes," said Presto. "It was. And pardon me for saying this, but you don't look like an individual who's studied the magical arts."

"Neither do you!"

Touché, thought Presto, smiling despite himself. The familiar-looking man relaxed slightly, and spoke. "In the arena, during AdventureSport matches. I know what it feels like when you're targeted by a spell."

The guy in the jumpsuit clapped his hands together and then pointed at him, smiling. "I knew I'd seen you somewhere. You're Blade Petros!"

Blade raised his hands. "Yeah, that's me." He frowned. "And ain't I seen you somewhere before?"

The young woman cut in. "He's lead lutist with Northern Fire. The Storm, right?"

The guy in the jumpsuit smiled a half-embarrassed smile. "Yeah, that's me."

The man wearing priest's robes extended a hand to the preposterously named rock star. "I'm Father Darick."

The Storm reached over and took his hand. "The Storm."

"I'm Dani," said the young woman.

They all looked at Presto.

"And I'm leaving," he told them, tipping them a fingertip salute before setting off towards the park's exit. He'd learned the hard way that trust freely shared was trust freely abused.

"But what about whatever it was that just went down?" the Storm shouted after him. Presto didn't answer, choosing instead to engage in a more immediate task: that of searching for the park's exit. Now where in the name of the gods was it?

A few minutes into whatever the hell this was, Dani's initial fight-or-flight reaction was beginning its transition into a post-adrenaline crash. She sat down, trying to get her breathing under control in the hopes that her heart might stop thumping. Then she looked back at her three remaining co-victims. But they all seemed as nonplussed as she currently was.

Control wasn't just important to Dani – it was essential. This, now, what had just happened, was so far beyond anything she'd experienced that she was at an utter loss about what to do, or even how to react.

And utter loss was not something she did.

She shook her head to clear it, watching as her fourth co-victim's back disappeared down a winding path. "Strange bloke," she muttered.

"Yeah," agreed Blade. "Definitely weird."

The priest, Darick, had the face of a man searching for meaning. "He has just been through a very strange and disturbing experience. As have we all."

Dani had to agree with that. "What do you think it all meant?" she asked.

"It?" queried Blade.

The Storm banged the table. "There was a message. It like, played in my fucking head."

The warrior nodded. "Oh, yeah. That."

"It's my head," the rock star continued, clearly angry. "Mine. I ain't that wild about someone else stomping around in there."

"I heard something about a sleeping dragon waking," said Darick. "And there was a place mentioned. Did anyone else get that?"

The Storm sat back down, his breathing ragged. "I got the line about a sleeping dragon. But the name of the place, that's gone."

Dani was drawing a blank on that one, and from the way Blade and Darick were shrugging, it looked like they were too.

Darick tried again. "We surely have to do something about it? Don't we?"

The priest's call to arms found a response of sorts in the Storm. "Screw this!" he announced. "I'm calling the guards." He reached down, as though searching for a pocket, but his skin-tight, one-piece jump suit had no pockets. "Dammit!" he muttered. "Stage clothes." He looked back up, an embarrassed half-smile on his face. "When I get back home."

Blade too was nodding. "I might make a few calls myself. But maybe we should get out of here first if we don't want to get taken again – or just plain mugged." He pulled a gold coloured card from his wallet and pressed a thumb onto its surface.

"Your carpet will be with you in three minutes!" it announced brightly.

"I've got an executive gold account," Blade explained. "You guys want to share a ride?"

Dani stood beside Darick and watched as the sleek carpet rose into the air and then accelerated away, its smooth metallic bodywork glinting in the rays of the afternoon sun. She'd declined Blade's offer, as had Darick. A ride in a chauffeur-piloted executive carpet was a bit too rich for her, even when offered for free, and she guessed Darick felt the same.

"Perhaps we should catch the worm?" Darick suggested, catching Dani still brooding about what the hell it was that had just happened, and more importantly, who the hell had just done it. She didn't really have any ideas and frankly, that was what was worrying her. She shook herself back to awareness.

"Sounds good to me," she replied. She looked around, but could see only trees and rolling landscaped hills, surrounded by slums on all sides. "Got any idea where the nearest station is?"

Darick pointed a hesitant hand in the direction that the arrogant intellectual type who'd declined to give his name had headed. "That way?"

Dani gave him a smile. "Good as any other."

The two of them caught up with the intellectual at the worm station, finding him begging for the fare from random passers-by. "I was at home when the spell took me," he explained, embarrassed. "I haven't got any change on me."

"No problem," Dani told the intellectual. "I can cover it." She shoved a twenty gold piece note into the ticket machine and asked it for three all zones tickets, which it produced one after the other, click, click, click. She handed one to the intellectual and one to Darick. "Pay me back whenever."

They headed down the moving steps towards the poorly lit platforms. "By the way," Darick said, "I don't think you gave us your name?"

The intellectual looked at him for a moment, as though considering whether or not to reply. Finally, he spat out an answer. "Presto. Presto Tannarton."

Darick grabbed Presto's hand and gave it an enthusiastic shake. "It's very good to meet you, Presto."

The Storm owned many homes, although he wasn't sure quite how many. That was a detail, and he didn't do details. He employed an accountant to keep track of petty financial matters, and a manager to keep track of everything else. He knew he had an apartment in Empire City's plush Westgate district and another somewhere by the old docks, together with a sprawling mansion out in the commuter belt. He remembered once telling his accountant to get him a ski lodge in the mountains in case he ever felt like taking up skiing, and he was pretty sure he had a ranch out on the Eastern plains – unless his accountant had sold it for some kind of obscure tax reasons.

But wealth – or at least wealth of a size both ridiculous and obscene — brings many paradoxes, one of which is that the more houses one owns, the less each one of them feels like a home. Other rich people understood. Blade certainly appeared to – or at least, he hadn't shown any apparent surprise when the Storm asked to be dropped off on the roof of the Envoy Hotel in Empire Boulevard, where he kept a semi-permanent room.

The Storm watched the carpet lift skyward and accelerate away, then headed off down the stairs. He had one goal in his mind right now – calling the guards. Whatever this game was, what had just happened was way out of order and he was going to make damn sure someone paid. He took four flights of stairs three steps at a time; bashed through the fire door into the plush, carpeted corridor; and started fishing in his pocket for his keycard.

At least he would have, if he'd somehow managed to acquire a pocket in the last half hour. Which he hadn't.

Dammit, he thought. Still stage clothes. He thought about the gig, and wondered what Gekk and the guys had done after his disappearance. He should probably whisper them after he'd talked to the guards. Then again, it was the last show of the tour and it wasn't like he could get back in time to do anything about it. Not when he was eight thousand something miles away. And hell, the way things had been going, he didn't particularly care if the crowd had rioted, rushed the stage, smashed the equipment up, and forced Gekk into the sort of intimate encounter with a mike-stand that makes a man stage strut when he's merely walking to the fridge.

No, at the moment it was what had just happened that needed to be sorted.

A woman came out of the lift, headed his way. She was attractive, young, and had that cute frowning look on her face that meant she knew he was someone but couldn't quite remember who. Which was exactly how the Storm liked them. He had a smooth line in modestly claiming to be no one, but that only worked because he was actually someone.

The phrase "sex addiction" was often bandied around by those in the Storm's social circle. It was not an affliction he'd ever claim to suffer from, but it was probably true that he had something of a weakness for the female sex. Just thirty seconds ago, the Storm had been a man on a mission, that mission being to get the guards to find the joker who'd both kidnapped him and violated his brain space, and then nail said Joker's ballsack to a roughly rendered wall. But that was then, and this was now.

The girl raised a querying finger and pointed at him. "Aren't you…"

He took her hand and gave her the full, thousand Kellen smile. "Why, yes. Yes, I am."

Chapter Three

The carpet dropped Blade off on the rather extensive lawn that stretched several acres behind his house, in between the modern art statue of a hole that his most recent girlfriend had blown a quarter of a million gold on and the flower beds that were, by comparison, remarkably good value for money, needing only the services of a head gardener, his assistant, and a haemorrhaging account at the local garden centre.

Blade took the quick route into the house through the kitchen back door. He was greeted by a silence broken only the sharp tap-tap-tap of his dwarven housekeeper, Magda, chopping carrots, keeping her head, and beard, down. He tried to sneak past her, but she spotted him.

"Where've you been, Mr Blade?" she asked. "You snuck out this morning without breakfast!"

"I had something to do," Blade protested.

"You've got too many things to do. You need to get some of my good home cooking inside of you."

"I will, promise," he told her.

Blade gave her a moment to glower at him, and then grabbed a carrot from under her knife before retreating to his study, a cosy little nook that commanded a view over the grounds from the third floor of the house's tower. This was his haven. Framed pictographs hung between one set of windows; antique weapons faced them. He paused before a picture of his father. He'd long since surpassed everything the old man had ever achieved in the game, but he doubted even that would have been enough to make the bitter, judgemental sod finally concede that maybe his son wasn't the disappointment he'd always claimed him to be. Of course, that was before he'd found himself the wrong side of thirty, and before he'd started down the route of illegal, performance enhancing potions. If his father was looking down on him now, from whatever plane of the afterlife he'd ended up at, he'd no doubt be feeling a sense of perverse vindication at the way his ungrateful son's glittering career was starting to lose its lustre.

He sat down at his desk, picked up the whisper, and tapped in a number he knew by heart. Tenny answered on the first ring. "Yes?"

"I just got kidnapped!" Blade blurted out.

Tenny, as always, was calm. If there was anything that fazed the veteran agent, Blade had yet to encounter it. "How much do they want?" he asked.

"What?"

"They've let you call so you can tell me their demands, right? And assure me that you've still got all your fingers, toes, and ears, for now, etc. etc. right?"

"No. I mean, they let me go. I'm back at the house."

"Then why are you calling me?"

"I want something done about it!"

"Gods, Blade, I'm your agent, not the Empire City Guard. What do you expect me to do about it?"

"I thought maybe you could call the guards for me."

There was a pause which, given that Tenny chain-smoked so badly you could practically smell it down the whisper, probably involved a cigarette, a lighter, and a little dancing flame. "Fine," he said eventually, presumably once he'd got the tip glowing. "I'll call them, get them to send someone around. But listen, you've got bigger problems than this."

"Bigger problems than being kidnapped?"

"Hell, yeah, I mean that's something we can work with. Did they do anything kinky? I could probably get you a two page spread in the Chronicle if they did."

"No. I just got magically teleported away to some dump part of town, and that was pretty much it."

"Shame. Anyhow, I've had the rest of the team bending my ear. They're not happy. They're talking about quitting."

"Why?"

"Why! You guys got yourselves totally creamed the last three matches and you have to ask why? Bron got himself toasted by a trap, Faran damn near got his flute shoved where Uncle Sunshine's never shone, and Denbi got so badly beaten up by the final monster that he's thinking of suing the league for specieist discrimination!"

"He's claiming a magically animated collection of wood and metal was specieist?"

"No. He's claiming the league is. He says they wrote its main control spell to prioritise attacks against halflings."

"Why would they do that?"

"He says they're trying to improve ratings by creating storylines in which weak halflings get into trouble and brave strong humans have to rescue them. You know, on account of humans making up ninety-five percent of the viewing audience."

"You really think the league would do something like that?"

"You really think they wouldn't?"

"But even if he wins they'll never let him play again!"

"He's looking to retire Blade, and... I'm saying this as your friend – maybe you should too."

Blade felt numb. Tenny wasn't the first to suggest it, but he was the first to say it so bluntly. An icy fear gnawed at his stomach. "Look, Tenny, I know things have been bad, but–"

"I've had Pete's Adventure Warehouse on the whisper. They're thinking of pulling the plug. And no sponsorship means no team."

"Tenny, it will just be some mid-level marketing flunky throwing his weight around ahead of contract renewal." He caught a note of desperation in his voice and hated himself for it.

The reply came back flat. "It was Pete who called."

Blade thought of Quido, and the potions. "I can pull it back. I know I haven't been performing, but I've got some new ideas about conditioning and I really think they're going to work."

"They'd better."

The line clicked dead. Blade replaced the handset and looked around the room. On the far wall his father smiled down upon him, sword in one hand and trophy in the other.

"Guess you're happy now, Dad," he muttered.

Magic touches, and when it does it leaves a part of itself behind. Only the ignorant think of magic as an invisible and intangible force. The truth is that magic leaves a residue, a residue that can be examined, analysed, and sometimes even identified. Presto didn't have much in the way of tools in his flat. Just a few scraps of second hand equipment he'd managed to save. But he figured it might be just enough to make a start. He bounded round the corner into the dank alleyway he called his street and–

There was a pile of stuff sitting outside the apartment block's front door. Stuff that had still been sitting inside his apartment when he'd been teleported out of it earlier that afternoon.

A couple of heavy-set and dim-looking goons stood beside the pile, wearing expensive suits in a manner reminiscent of the way in which a sofa wears its leather. "What the hell do you think you're doing?" Presto barked at them.

The marginally less stupid-looking one spoke, his tone sneering. "Evicting you. It's what happens when you don't pay your rent." He leaned in close to Presto and delivered a mixture of threats and bad breath. "And we've sealed the door. I wouldn't try breaking in if I were you. Not if you like having a working finger count in double digits."

Presto could have incinerated the guy on the spot, with just a few hand motions and some muttered incantations, but amusing as the thought of that was, both legality and basic morality ruled it out as an option. So instead, he just watched the goons walk down the alley and around the corner. A bright orange plastic bag skipped across the tarmac, caught by the wind.

He grabbed it and started salvaging what he could from the pile.

The Storm had a simple rule of thumb when it came to herb users: if they had a bigger habit than him, then they were probably bad news. Given that the girl had suggested a break for herb within thirty seconds of entering his hotel room, had snorted three long rows there and then, and had followed that with another three just a half hour later, she was almost certainly very, very bad news. But she was cute and willing and if she turned out to be a psycho he could always get the hotel to switch his room. (He was pretty sure that they'd have forgotten the unfortunate incident that had occurred to the last guest to take over his old room after just such a psycho-triggered room switch.)

The girl rolled over and blinked sleepy eyes at him. "Hey lover boy, you want to do it again?"

Why, yes. Yes, he did.

He gently stroked her cheek and gave her a long, lingering kiss that turned into an urgent embrace. When it came to sex he couldn't claim to have had no complaints, because he had. Plenty of them. But he was pretty sure he'd never had any complaints when he'd actually been trying, and right now he was firing every move he had at her and then some. Worries over herb usage aside, there was actually something about this girl. Something different. Something that might even have been special. Something that made him want to ask a question he very rarely asked.

But he could find out what her name was later. Right now, as seconds became minutes and minutes became a length of time that was quite impressive considering the day he'd had and the quantity of herb he'd consumed, he cared only for the sensations erupting in his body and hers. The urgency was building, boiling, spreading through him. A voice was shouting – his, he realised. "Yes, yes, yes!" His voice and hers, his shouts, her moans, merged, a chorus that echoed off the ceiling and set the furniture rattling.

Still the ecstasy rose, driving him toward a tingling pitch rendered agonising by its perfection. This was incredible. This was more than incredible. He'd made love to hundreds of women, but none had ever made him feel like this. He hadn't felt like this since–

This afternoon.

He heard the voice again, and realised it was still his. "No, no, no!" it was shouting.

And then reality blinked again.

Chapter Four

Knowing what was happening didn't make it feel any less of a violation. One moment Dani was sitting in an anonymous cocktail bar, trying to get her head back into something approaching working order, and the next she was back at the sodding place she'd been taken to that afternoon. The park was cold now, under a twilit sky, and the marble of the chair was sucking every ounce of warmth out of her. Then the voice from the afternoon was inside her head, speaking the same words as before in the same emotionless tone.

"The sleeping dragon will awake beneath Craagon's Reach."

The bonds holding her released, and she sprang up, rubbing warmth back into her frozen thighs. The four men with whom she'd shared the earlier kidnap were there too. Three of them – Blade, Presto and Darick – were also springing to their feet, spitting out a collective stream of words long on anger and confusion, but short on actual coherence.

The Storm did not rise. He was breathing heavily, panting, groaning – and was he naked? The musician arched his back, let out a long agonised moan, and then collapsed over the table. A shocked voice broke the resulting silence.

"Are you naked?" asked Blade.

"Have you had some sort of reaction to the teleporting?" added Darick.

The Storm said nothing for a while, then dribbled an answer out of the corner of his mouth. "I'm fine. I, I wasn't prepared to travel."

"Clearly," declared Presto.

Somehow, the absurdity of the Storm's situation punctured the emotional storm this second kidnapping event had plunged them into. Dani grabbed for the edge of the table, took a deep breath, locked her shaking knees, then risked sitting back down. Across from her, Blade looked to be in a mood to maim someone, while Darick seemed utterly bewildered. But Presto was up and moving, prowling around the edge of the plinth upon which the table sat, sniffing. A plastic carrier bag dangled from his fingers, a stray sock poking out the top.

"What's with the sniffing?" Blade growled.

"Magic leaves a discharge, and discharges of all kinds tend to share one common attribute. They smell."

"So what can you smell?" asked Dani.

"Ozone. Which is usually associated with a sudden high-mana discharge. Beyond that, I couldn't really say. If I had access to a half-decent magical laboratory with which I could analyse the residues on our clothing, I could–" He broke off and shrugged, embarrassed.

"But I don't."

Blade let a half-smile slide onto his face. "What would you say if I told you I had access to a modern state-of-the-art magical laboratory with a quarter-million gold's worth of equipment?"

"I'd ask you where it was and then suggest we head straight there. Do you have such access?"

Blade nodded. "Wouldn't have said it if I didn't." He took out his gold carpet contact card. "Shall I call us a ride?"

Presto waved him forward. "Please."

The two of them headed out into the park, followed by Dani and Darick. A voice called out from behind them.

"Guys!" It was the Storm. They looked round, and saw him still sitting at the table. "Any of you people got a spare jacket I can borrow?" he asked plaintively. "And maybe some tissues?"

Blade pushed the door open with a flourish that magnificently failed to express the nervousness he felt and waved a hand at the room's expensive looking contents. "There you are, guys. The best magical equipment money can buy. Well, that's what the salesman told me."

Presto followed him in, casting what Blade hoped were appraising glances, and muttering the names of each machine he passed. "Potion centrifuge. Full spectrum aura analyser. Spell containment device."

"Is it okay?" Blade asked hesitantly.

Presto paused. "It's not bad." He pointed at the console that sat in the room's far corner. "Is that oracle hooked into all the equipment?"

"Yeah, yeah. It's all linked together. Salesman reckoned you can monitor the whole lot from there."

The wizard said nothing, continuing with his inspection of the room. Dani leaned in close to Blade. "Pardon me for asking, but why exactly has an AdventureSport player got a fully equipped magical laboratory?"

Blade gave her an embarrassed smile. "I had this girlfriend a few years ago who fancied herself as some kind of progressive witch. Got all this installed for her."

"And did this erstwhile girlfriend of yours ever use it?" asked Presto, who'd apparently been listening in despite appearing to be fully engaged in checking out the oracle's main control program.

"No. Said the equipment interfered with her creativity." He took a few steps towards Presto. "So is it okay? Will you be able to figure out what's been happening to us?"

The wizard thought for a moment. "I can't make any promises. But if I can't find anything it won't be the lab you should blame. I'll need a lock of hair from each one of you, plus your jackets and your shoes. Those of you that have them, that is."

The heavy door shut behind them and then reopened, Presto's head appearing round it. "I'll come and find you when I have something," he told them. The door shut again, and this time stayed shut, leaving the four of them standing in the thickly carpeted corridor outside. Darick began to examine an interesting looking wood carving that stood to one side, but was interrupted by an embarrassed cough from the Storm, who was still clutching around him the tatty blanket Presto had retrieved from his carrier bag.

"Hey, dude, any chance of borrowing some threads?"

Blade blinked. "Oh yeah, sorry mate. Forgot about that."

A quick change of clothes for the Storm and an impressively long guided tour later, they found themselves in a basement room filled with large, stately sofas and expensive looking devices. The biggest crystal screen Darick had ever seen filled much of one wall while a long leather clad bar stretched the entire length of the other.

"Drinks?" Blade asked from behind the bar. He received a chorus of replies, so started grabbing glasses. Across the room, Dani had discovered some kind of full spectrum entertainment console of the sort normally found in bars or amusement arcades, and was busily engaged in dispatching a hoard of ghostly figures. The Storm simply sat fidgeting on a sofa, in a suit two sizes too big for him. Darick sat beside him. "How are you bearing up?"

"I'm fine, Father. Could just do with a couple of lines of…" He stopped speaking. "This is all a bit, like, weird."

"The destiny the SkyFather sets for us is not always apparent," Darick pointed out, hoping he wasn't sounding too preachy.

"Well, it certainly ain't too apparent to this string-picker. I mean, whatever joker set this up, why us? A rock star, a priest, an AdventureSport player, and, well, whatever it is Dani and Presto are."

Darick nodded. The initial shock might now be subsiding, but the situation was still making no sense whatsoever to him. He would have prayed for answers, but he wasn't sure which question to ask, and he wasn't sure he'd like any answers he might get. Personally, right now, he was quite happy to delegate the task of figuring out what was going on to Presto, and spend his time offering whatever level of spiritual comfort might be appropriate.

The Storm leaned in. "Speaking of Presto, I could swear I've seen the cat before."

It seemed Darick wasn't the only one trying to avoid direct consideration of their predicament. "Really?" he answered.

"Yeah. Can't put a finger on it, but there's something real familiar about him."

The rock star broke off suddenly as Blade approached with their drinks.

Another wooden carving sat on the coffee table. Darick picked it up and examined it. "Where did you get this from?" he asked Blade.

"It's Elven," Blade replied. "Picked it up when I went across the Western Ocean with a team from here to play a team from over there."

"Must have been quite an experience," the Storm said. "The Elven lands are the only place we've never played."

"Do they not like your music?" Darick asked.

The Storm smiled. "I don't figure they like any music made by us humans."

Blade came back from delivering Dani's drink and sat down. "Trust me, it isn't personal. They don't like anything of ours. I've never met as big a bunch of specieists in my entire life. Far as they're concerned they're superior to us in every way – and after telling you that to your face, they'll boast about how deeply spiritual and humble they are too. Best thing they ever did was piss off over the ocean in a monster sulk."

"You still bought this though," said the Storm, pointing at the carving.

"Well, they're pretty good at wood carving," said Blade, with a shrug. "Just a shame they're such complete gits in pretty much every other way."

One of Darick's many – he felt – misunderstood virtues, was a compulsive desire to defend those being attacked. He felt now the familiar urge to speak. "To be fair, they are an ancient and noble people."

"No, they're an old and decadent people," Blade insisted. "They'd quite happily watch you starve, drown, or die of the purple death while they sat around discussing the meaning of life. It's only them living such long lives that gives them a chance to love someone else long enough to get them pregnant, given how much of their time they spend loving themselves."

The Storm nodded in agreement.

"Now, look!" Darick said. "It's not as though we humans are perfect, is it?"

The Storm thought for a moment. "That's true brother. What some of those dudes down south do to their women is way out of order!"

Blade jabbed a finger at the coffee table's polished surface. "Yeah. I don't care if they did get the used end of the stick, being born in a desert and all that. It ain't right what they do!"

"That wasn't quite what I was thinking of," said Darick quickly. "I do think we've got to be very careful not to attack other people's faiths and beliefs, and the followers of the Church of the Sacred Box are very devout."

"Devout!" shouted Blade. "They keep their women locked up in small wooden boxes their entire lives!"

"It is a sacred box," muttered Darick, aware that he was on very shaky ground.

Silence settled, broken only by the sound of Dani dispatching further hoards of ghostly zombies. Darick felt his eyelids growing heavy, and as Blade and the Storm traded reminisces about their world travels, he fell into a restless sleep full of tangled dreams involving Archbishop Ulfred, Mrs Torden, and her skin-flick appearing daughter, all of whom appeared to have a strong desire to shout at him. He was just about to receive another dressing down from the archbishop, who – bizarrely – appeared to be moonlighting as a second-hand buggy salesman, when he was awakened by a loud crash from outside his dream.

It was Presto, standing beside a door that had presumably been recently opened with a reckless degree of enthusiasm. "Gentlemen and lady. I think I might just have it!"

Chapter Five

The image on the lab's crystal screen spun first this way then that, with each fresh viewing angle rendering the overall picture less rather than more comprehensible to the Storm's currently misfiring brain. He focused hard on the multi-coloured blobs and lines rotating around the screen. "So that's, like, the spell that kidnapped us?"

Presto paused for a moment before answering. "Yes and no."

"Can you be a bit more specific?" Dani asked, smiling.

Presto pulled a face. "I wouldn't want to blind you with a blizzard of magical terminology."

"Well, assume we know absolutely nothing about magic," said Darick.

"I was," said Presto. "That's the problem. It's like trying to explain property law to a cat."

"Thanks!" said Dani.

"No offence intended."

"None taken. Yet."

"How about you make a start," said Blade, interjecting himself into the discussion, "and we'll let you know if we're getting stuck."

Presto thought for a moment, and then nodded. "That seems reasonable. So firstly, yes, what I have displayed there on the screen is the signature left behind by the teleportation spell that transported us to the park of pillars."

"So that's the spell that kidnapped us!" the Storm blurted.

A pained expression appeared on Presto's face. "As I said, yes and no. Firstly, a signature is not so much a blueprint as a shadow. It suggests the structure of the spell, rather than describing it. But secondly, and more importantly, the answer to the question really depends on who you consider the agent of the kidnapping."

"You've lost me, dude," the Storm told him, noticing the others nodding in agreement.

Presto sat down. "Have you ever studied how modern magical devices are produced? Crystals, carpets, whispers, wagons, fridges, and well, pretty much every item that moves, heats, or communicates?"

"Some wizard designs them, and then casts a spell to enchant the physical item?" suggested Blade.

"No," Presto told him. "That is indeed how it once was, back when magical devices were rare, precious, and handmade. A weaver would weave a rug, a wizard would cast a flight enchantment spell on it, and ta-da, a flying carpet."

"But it's not like that now?" asked Darick.

"No. For a wizard to cast a spell he must first draw in mana from the surrounding environment to power the casting. It's tiring and time consuming and not too good on the nerves, literally as well as figuratively. But it's possible to cast spells that can themselves cast spells, repeatedly, again and again, drawing in their own supply of mana each time. The technical term is a meta-spell, but they're often termed living spells. To mass-produce a magical artefact, the wizard will design the device, and then create a meta-spell that can itself cast the spell that performs the enchantment. Once cast, such a meta-spell can repeatedly cast the enchantment spell twenty-four hours a day, seven days a week. So where once you had small scale artisans' workshops with a resident wizard, you now have production lines where the physical items are gradually assembled, with meta-spells enchanting them as they move down the line."

"Okay, that's super great and all, but what's it got to do with us?" asked the Storm.

Dani answered before Presto. "I'm guessing he's about to tell us that it's a living spell that's casting the teleportation spells."

"Exactly. There are certain tell-tale signs on the signature that reveal that this spell was spawned from another spell. Quite an old-fashioned one from the looks of it."

The Storm wasn't used to this degree of intensive thinking, and frankly he was finding it hard work. "So it wasn't that some geezer used a spell to kidnap us. It was a spell that was doing the kidnapping?"

"Yes."

"And there's no way to figure out who the cat was who originally cast that spell, and why it was us poor bastards he aimed it at?"

"No."

There followed several seconds of silence that stretched towards a minute. Finally, it was Blade who spoke. "If we've been kidnapped twice, does that mean this living spell's still out there, and could kidnap us again?"

"That's a distinct possibility. It's quite possibly following us around, monitoring us."

The Storm didn't like the sound of that. He looked at Blade, and

Blade looked at him, and then finally Blade asked the question that was currently bouncing around the Storm's brain. "Can you get rid of this living spell? You know, terminate it, shut it down."

Presto took a deep breath before he replied. "Possibly. But it's a split-second process. I'll need help."

Presto had given the Storm just one job to do, which was to operate something called the interface filter by sliding a slider on a crystal touch screen up and down. At least, he hoped to seven hells that sliding a slider up and down was all he had to do, because if there was more to it than that then he'd managed to miss it during the quick training session Presto had given him.

A steaming mug of black coffee appeared on the desk in front of him, courtesy of a hand that turned out to belong to Darick. He mouthed a quick thanks to the priest. It wasn't the three lines of neatly chopped herb he actually needed right now, but it was several ways better than nothing. He took a deep swig and burned his tongue, which sharpened him up, though not quite in the way he'd been hoping. Concentrate, he told himself. Do not screw this up.

At the desk beside his, Dani was operating something that he now knew to be an etherscope. It was a considerably more complex device than his interface filter, with an array of blobs of varying colours, shades, and textures drawn across its crystal screen. During the earlier briefing, Presto had explained that the etherscope displayed a scanned window onto the local ethereal plane. When the Storm had previously heard people talking about the ethereal plane, he'd thought they were speaking in metaphor, but it appeared he'd been wrong; the ethereal plane existed, and was where magic lived. And from the clutter on the screen, there was clearly a lot of magic about.

He'd mentioned that to Presto, and the wizard had merely laughed and said that people had no idea just how much magic went into making their modern lives work, until one of their many household devices broke and they were straight on the whisper demanding that someone come round and fix it.

As the Storm watched, Dani leaned forward, tapped on the screen, examined something or other, and then relaxed. They'd been waiting an hour and a half now with nothing spotted save a roving false alarm that – after five, rather tense minutes – had turned out to be Blade's cat Mr Bubbles, or more specifically, the cat-flap unlocking charm he wore attached to his collar.

Blade sat behind them, at another console, ready to play his part.

The thought of magic turned the Storm to thoughts of his lute, and its practice amp. He missed them, and hoped someone had retrieved them from the arena. A roadie perhaps. He harboured no naïve illusions that any of his bandmates might have bothered. He looked across at the etherscope's screen, and wondered if his lute and amp would appear on it if he were to turn them on.

He suspected they would. They were both magically powered, after all. But it was a strange thought.

"Heads up, people!" said Dani, sharply. "We've got something coming in!"

Presto walked across and peered over her shoulder. "Can you zoom in?"

Dani tapped and traced across the screen, causing the image to enlarge in the manner Presto had apparently desired, if his grunt of satisfaction was anything to go by. "That's it. Do you see the way the edges are fuzzy and oscillating slightly? That tells us that it's a free-floating spell, and not something bound to a physical object located on the material plane. What's the range?"

"About four miles and closing," she told him.

"Perfect. It's noticed we're together, and not moving, and it's coming in to see what we're up to."

"Three miles."

"Come to Papa."

"Two miles. Looks like it's slowing down."

"It's a cautious little thing. Doesn't want to get too near."

"One and a half miles. Almost stopped."

Presto put a hand on the Storm's shoulder. "Take the filter up to twenty percent."

The Storm reached out and gingerly slid the slider up, concentrating on the big number displayed beside it. One. Three. Seven. Fifteen. Eighteen. Nineteen. Twenty. He pulled back from the screen.

"Good," said Presto. "That will make it just that bit harder for the spell to see us. Let's see if that tempts it to come a little closer."

"Holding at one point two miles," said Dani. "Appears to be orbiting us."

"It can still see us well enough, eh?" Presto looked down at the Storm again. "Take it up to forty percent."

The Storm slid the slider up, a little more confidently this time. The number settled on forty. Presto had told them that the filter set up a local interference pattern in between the ethereal and physical planes that would impair the ability of observers in one plane to observe the other. Only Dani's etherscope, which was linked into the interface filter, and thus could compensate, would peer through unhindered.

"It's moving again," said Dani. "Passing through one mile."

"It can't quite see us, and it's wondering where we've gone."

"Do I need to go up again?" asked the Storm.

"Not yet. We want to make it curious enough to come nearer, not scared enough that it runs."

"Coming up to half a mile," announced Dani. "It's slowing again."

"Okay," said Presto. "Fifty percent."

The Storm slid the slider up.

"Accelerating again. Past two thousand feet."

Presto said nothing.

"Still moving. Passing through fifteen hundred feet."

The silence in the lab was so absolute that the Storm's heartbeat sounded like the base drum intro to a seriously heavy number. He took a deep breath. Perhaps he wouldn't ask for a second cup of coffee.

"Through a thousand."

Silence.

"Five hundred. Slowing."

"I need it within two hundred to be sure," said Presto. He looked down at the Storm. "Take it up to sixty percent."

The Storm slid the slider up.

"Still coming. Four hundred. Three hundred. Slowing slightly. Two hundred and fifty. Two hundred and thirty. Two hundred and twenty. Two hundred and ten. Two hundred and five. Two hundred."

The Storm looked round and saw that Presto was no longer standing behind them, but had instead retreated a few steps. The wizard's arms were raised and his face was alive.

And then he began to speak.

This was highly illegal, but Presto didn't care. Sure, they'd shamed him, taken his license away, taken his life away, told everyone that he was no longer a wizard and that the magic was no longer his. But he still knew how to punch a hole in the universe and make it scream, and no one could ever take that away. For ten years he'd cast nothing save minor cantrips too small to register on the Kellen-Rettner scale, and too trivial to raise an alert on a spell-cop's monitor. For ten years he'd denied himself the ecstasy that came from grabbing hold of reality and making it dance. For ten years he'd rotted like a fallen leaf.

No more.

Breaking through to the ethereal plane was a force five casting or more, but it was a cast he was damn well going to make. The words of magic erupted from him, power words, syllables that turned locks built into existence itself and threw open the doors of space and time. Power flowed through his body, his waving arms directing it like a conductor directs his orchestra. It built to a crescendo, paused, reality itself laid out before him, and then–

He was somewhere else.

The ethereal plane was spread before him, ablaze with a thousand colours, not one of which was red, blue, or green. And there was the spell, barely moving now, pulsing irregularly as though lost and confused. Presto was nothing more than consciousness and awareness and magic here, but with arms that were metaphor and lips that were thought he pointed and spoke. A jet of energy spat out from the point of awareness that was him, blasting over and around the spell like a fisherman's net. The spell struggled, but the net held. It pushed back, hauling Presto with it; but he anchored himself hard, took the strain, and began pulling, every fibre of his soul straining.

This was no longer about magic. It was about guts, determination, and pure will – his against the spell's, and whomever had cast it. With metaphorical teeth gritted, his ethereal presence pulled and tugged, guiding the still-struggling spell towards the gently glowing rectangle that marked the lab's containment device, currently protruding only slightly into the ethereal plane.

To those in the lab, he would be nothing more than a standing, frozen, statue-like figure. With his consciousness departed from the physical plane he had no way of speaking to them, no way of leading them. He could hope only that they did the jobs he'd briefed them to do, Dani on the etherscope monitoring the movement of the spell, and Blade on the containment device, triggering when Dani gave him the word.

Nearly there. One more mental pull, and... there.

The ghostly walls of the containment device slid up, right on cue, cutting through the now-redundant netting that had bound Presto to the spell and locking their quarry away. Presto relaxed. With the spell securely contained they could study it at their leisure and then destroy it. He moved slowly in, curious. The spell was still moving, rebounding around the walls of its prison, seeking an escape it would not find. It stopped, retreated to the centre of the space, and pulsed.

Then pulsed again.

And again.

Around Presto, for mana-mile after mana-mile, the ethereal plane was going dim. Multi-coloured blazes damped down to flicking lights. Across an entire neighbourhood, lights would be going out, kettles would be failing to boil, and carpets would be making emergency landings. Presto wasn't quite sure just what was building, but he sure as hell didn't fancy being around when it happened. He thought a quick command and dropped back into reality. Frightened faces greeted him.

"I got a whole bunch of errors coming up!" Blade shouted. "Energy readings off the scale and a load of warnings about possible containment failure."

"And I've lost everything except the spell!" shouted an equally rattled Dani.

Presto barked an order at the Storm. "One hundred percent! Now!"

And then the world exploded.

Chapter Six

Blade came to with a cough, a splutter, and a worried thought about the state of his house insurance, followed – with a tinge of guilt – by worried thoughts about Mr Bubbles, Magda, and Magda's husband Gruss, who served Blade as head gardener and general handyman. What the hell had just happened? He remembered a flash of light and a roaring, and then this: darkness, dust, and confusion. There was a muttering from somewhere, and then a light flared in the blackness. It was Presto, holding up a flame-tipped finger. "Everyone okay?" asked the wizard.

Blade looked around, seeing Dani, Darick, and the Storm in various forms of discomfort, but apparently largely unharmed. They appeared to be in a cramped and newly-formed chamber presumably located in the ruins of what had once been his house, a chamber featuring a brick and rubble floor and a low, concrete slab roof that was supported only by walls formed of loose debris. An unpleasant realisation occurred to him. "I don't want to spook anyone," he said, "but I ain't quite sure what's holding this slab up."

"I am," said Presto. "I cast a bubble spell to create a force wall around us."

"Thanks," said Dani.

"You're welcome."

"How long will it last?" asked Blade.

"A few hours. It's squashed down to about half the size it was when I cast it, but it's stable now."

"And there was me thinking I had the SkyFather to thank," said Darick, as he hauled himself out from beneath a scattering of dust and splinters.

"You do," said Presto, smiling. "He created me." The wizard reached around and touched a few protruding bits of brick and concrete with his flame-tipped finger. Each touched object flared into light before settling into a dim, but constant, glow. "That should let us see better." The wizard gave his outstretched finger a quick stare, and the small dancing flame at its tip went out.

"Thanks," said the Storm, in a slightly squeaky voice.

In the new light, Blade could see the rock star better, and frankly, he looked pretty scared. "You okay, mate?" he asked him.

"Not really," the Storm replied, uneasily. "I don't much like enclosed spaces. Never have done. And that's when we're talking about enclosed spaces designed by an architect and featuring a door."

"Well, if it's any consolation," said Darick, "I'm not too keen on them myself." He looked down. "My father was a miner, and he was killed in a cave-in. Whenever I'm in a small space, I think of him alone, trapped, and dying."

"You're not helping," the Storm told him.

"Sorry."

The Storm reached into the pockets of the trousers he'd borrowed from Blade, then muttered a curse. "Any of you guys tried calling for help?"

Dani held up her whisper and pointed at its tiny, glowing crystal screen. "Yep. No signal."

Presto waved his hands, mumbled a few words, said nothing for a while, and then spoke. "The explosion's left interference right across the ethereal plane. It's blocking everything."

"About that explosion," said Blade, trying to keep his voice steady. "You got any idea what in seven and a half hells happened? I mean don't get me wrong, I'm grateful to still be alive and all that, but I'm a bit pissed off about my house being blown to buggery."

The wizard shrugged. "It would appear that the spell had some self-defence measures written into it, which triggered when we attempted to capture it. For what it's worth, I'm sorry about your house."

Blade considered that for a moment, then reached down and pulled a useful-looking length of iron rod from the rubble. "Well, if it's all the same with you guys, I think I might try making us a door."

He selected a loose-looking bit of brick at the edge of the concrete slab and started to dig.

Two hours of vigorous exercise and five minutes of "You first... no, after you... no, I couldn't, really" later, the five of them emerged blinking into the early morning sunlight. Blade wasn't sure how the others had made use of those two hours and five minutes, but he'd spent them considering how he was going to explain the sudden transformation of a luxury mansion into a smoking pile of rubble. The City Guard. The insurance. Tenny. His ex-wife Toozie. The press. Oh gods, the press. They'd all want answers he frankly didn't have. But when he finally emerged, there was no one there.

No guards. No firefighters. No para-healers. No press. No Tenny.

No Magda. There was in fact just one observer: Mr Bubbles, who was sitting on a summit of rubble with a seriously pissed off expression on his stern little face. Blade picked the cat up and gave him a few strokes. Mr Bubbles looked up at him, unimpressed.

"You'd think someone might have noticed," said Dani.

Blade said nothing.

"It must have been an awfully big bang," said Darick.

"Probably blew half the magical devices in the neighbourhood," said Presto.

"That'll be nasty," said the Storm. "I had that once when I had a carpet explode in an underground garage. It was awful. I lost every crystal in the house, a couple of oracles, and half the lights."

Blade waved a slow and deliberate hand across the rubble that had once been his house and then spoke in a cold voice. "I just lost my entire house. Pardon me for not empathising with the plight of my now slightly less gadget-heavy neighbours."

The Storm looked at his feet, embarrassed. "Sorry dude," he muttered. "Point like, taken."

"So what should we do now?" asked Darick, interrupting the resulting silence.

"Don't know," said Blade. "But there's something I need to sort out first." He set off across the lawn with a still unhappy Mr Bubbles tucked against his chest

Magda and Gruss lived in a small bungalow in the grounds. Its curtains were open, which implied someone was home, but when he knocked no one answered, so he let himself in. He found the two of them in their living room, crouched in front of a dead crystal like identical twins with beards, jabbing furiously at the on switch. Blade had known several dwarves in his life and knew they were often single-minded to the point of obliviousness. So after spending several seconds waiting unsuccessfully for them to notice him, he gave them a discreet cough as a clue, following that with several progressively less-discreet coughs. Finally, at the point at which his throat was on the verge of starting to hurt, they turned around, giving him a pair of confused looks.

"Mr Blade!" growled Magda. "What's wrong? Why are you here? And why have you got dirt all over your clothes?"

Gruss said nothing. Blade waved a hand at the living room's window, which was now neatly framing a view of a pile of rubble, instead of the neatly framed view of the mansion it had previously been its mission to show.

The two dwarves stared hard through the window for several seconds, then turned, as one, to face him. "Why's the house blown up?" growled Magda. Gruss threw in a couple of emphatic nods. "What did you do?" she asked.

"I didn't do anything!" protested Blade. He thought for a moment. "Well, all right, I did, but that's not the point. What counts is I'm okay, you two are okay, and so's Mr Bubbles." He thrust the cat at her, and she accepted it, with just a slight hint of reluctance. She and the cat stared dubiously at each other.

"What are you going to do now?" she growled.

"I ain't quite figured that out yet," he told her. "But can you look after Mr Bubbles? I might need to get some things done."

She nodded, and he headed for the door.

"What should I tell Miss Toozanna if she calls?"

He turned back to face her and thought for a moment. "Tell her I blew the house up." He headed out the door and back to where he'd left the others, next to the pile of rubble he'd formally termed his home. He found them sat in a circle on makeshift seating salvaged from the wreckage. They weren't saying anything. "Any ideas?" he asked them.

They shrugged.

"We could perhaps call the guards?" suggested Darick.

"I'd get arrested for illegal spellcasting," said Presto. "And you'd all get arrested as accomplices."

"That's where I've seen you!" exclaimed the Storm. "There was some kind of shit storm a few years back at the Imperial University. You said something dodgy that got a load of ink in the press, and the University, like, sacked you."

Presto said nothing for several long seconds, then delivered a tight-lipped reply. "Yes."

A long, but expectant silence greeted that reply, a silence that eventually compelled him to elaborate. "I was teaching an archaic but still useful branch of magical theory relating to the discernment of inner nature and morality."

"Which means?" asked Dani.

"Spells that detect the presence of inherently evil people or things."

"And that got you sacked?"

"Strictly speaking, no. Saying that men exhibit a significantly higher tendency to possess such markers of inherent evil compared with women was what got me sacked."

"But isn't that a bit, well, sexist?" asked Darick.

Presto shrugged. "Well in my defence the statistics I quoted were correct, and I thought it raised some interesting philosophical questions. But with hindsight I could perhaps have raised the question in a different way."

"And that got your license taken away as well?" asked Dani.

"Let's just say that I didn't handle my sacking in as mature a fashion as I could have done."

"So you'd say that contacting the guards might be an unwise course of action for us to take, then?" asked Darick.

"Yes."

Dani leaned forward, clearly choosing the words she was about to say very carefully. "I'd probably rather avoid being in contact with the guards myself."

"You've had issues with them?" asked the Storm.

"No. Never had any contact with them. Would like to keep it that way."

It was at this point that Blade reached some kind of internal explosion level. "Well, what in the name of the seven kinds of hell are we going to do then? Some bloody something's just blown up my sodding house, and came damn close to killing us all in the process, and we're sitting around debating what we can't do! What I want to know is: what exactly can we do?"

Presto looked up at him. "We could go to Craagon's Reach."

"Where the hell's that?"

Presto was about to deliver an answer, but was forestalled by a whoop from Dani, who was waving her whisper at them. "I got a signal!"

She began tapping away on its tiny keyboard. "Okay, Craagon's Reach. Let's see what we have."

The five of them stared at the tiny device as they waited for it to deliver its answer. And waited.

"The transmissions are likely still being interfered with," said Presto. "That'll slow data delivery down."

Blade nodded. No point getting angry with those whose only crime was to share his predicament. Finally, Dani leaned forward, and started scrolling data across her whisper's tiny crystal screen. "Okay, there's an orc reservation out east called Craagon's Reach."

"Nice place to put it," muttered Presto. Blade gave him a questioning glance, but the wizard failed to elaborate, instead merely waving a hand at Dani, who was continuing to scroll through her whisper's displayed data.

"And about fifty miles north of that there's an abandoned research complex, also called Craagon's Reach."

Presto nodded. "That's the place I was thinking of. Around thirty years ago the team there were researching new techniques for capturing and storing mana."

"Were?" asked Blade.

"The complex went bang in a rather unpleasant way. The whole area's contaminated with raw, chaotic mana and will be for the next ten thousand years."

"Apparently, there's a thirty mile exclusion zone around it," said Dani, who'd continued reading while Presto was talking.

"I'd have made it sixty, myself," sniffed Presto.

"What about the Sleeping Dragon?" asked Darick.

Dani tapped away again, and then, after a slighter shorter pause, spoke. "It's a child's cuddly toy; a brand of male, erm, performance enhancer; and about thirty thousand other references."

"Any of you people get the feeling we're looking for a very small needle in a bloody big haystack?" asked the Storm.

"So that would leave Craagon's Reach then," said Darick. "Right?"

"Which one?" asked the Storm. "The orc reservation? Or the place that will cause our nuts to glow green and our future wives to give birth to minotaurs?"

"Might I suggest we should start with the former?" suggested Presto. "Unless any of you have any better ideas?"

Dani coughed. "It's about four thousand miles away in a place so far off the beaten track you could walk a thousand miles in any direction and not see anything other than trees. Any idea how we might get there?"

Blade smiled, and pulled his keys from his pocket. "Would it help to know that you're looking at a fully-licensed private carpet pilot with a fully licensed private carpet?"

Dani smiled back. "Why, yes. Yes, it would."

Chapter Seven

Blade's carpet was sleek as silk and dripping with power and it was eating up the distance between Empire City and Craagon's Reach at a rate of more than six hundred miles every hour. But still the Eastern Territories scrolled beneath them, burnt, dry, endless, on a scale so vast as to be utterly incomprehensible until one tried flying across them. Sure, one could study maps and globes, or steal a history book from a passing schoolchild, and read of the explorers and conquerors of four centuries ago who'd swarmed over the World's End Mountains and into the steppe beyond – and didn't stop until they reached the ocean a third of the way round the world. Or one could talk one's way through three hours of polite conversation, an hour of silence followed by an hour of arguing, a half hour of planning, and then seventeen and a half games of "I spy", and still find the same brown featureless grasslands scrolling beneath one. Only then could one truly understand just how big an area the Eastern Territories occupied.

Darick and Dani were sitting in the back of the carpet, on the plush leather bench seat, with the flight-phobic the Storm jammed uneasily between them. The top and the windows were down, allowing Darick to lean over the door's edge and take a good look down (making sure not to extend his head outside the carpet's air deflection field – he'd done that early on in the journey and his scalp was still feeling the chill). The landscape did have a certain magnificence to it. You could still see the SkyFather's brushwork, but if this part of the world were a painting, then it was one he'd painted with a subtle palette onto a canvas of epic scale. Several times now they'd soared over rivers so wide that in the western homelands they'd have been historic highways of civilisation. Here, they meandered, empty and unsettled.

In the driver's seat, Blade was talking into his headset. "Craagon Control, this is carpet Candle Dagger requesting vector approach."

The reply came back within seconds, blaring out of speakers set around the carpet's cabin.

Carpet Candle Dagger, this is Craagon Control. You are cleared for visual approach on vector fiver-niner.

Blade punched a few buttons on the crystal screen in front of him. "Craagon Control, this is carpet Candle Dagger beginning approach

on vector fiver-niner."
Happy landings carpet Candle Dagger.
The voice paused for a moment, and then continued, presumably talking to someone else now.
Skyship Sword Griffin, please descend to flight level two-three...
The carpet swung through a graceful turn and then began a slow descent.

In earlier times, the Eastern Territories had been wild and dangerous. There was a reason the World's End Mountains that marked the Territories' border were so named – because beyond their reach the world might as well have ended. Only fools and heroes ventured beyond the frontier; the fools rarely returned, and the heroes often shared that fate.

This had been a lawless realm of vile beasts and viler beastmen, and the vilest of them all were the chaotic and evil orcs. The creation myths told by the Church's priests said that orcs had been created at the dawn of creation by the SkyFather's evil half-brother Seqq, who broke open the clay jar into which the SkyFather had poured all the world's evil and from its contents conjured forth a species of pure wickedness. True or not, the civilised world feared and despised the East and all that dwelled in it.

Every few decades or so, during the occasional pauses that marked their otherwise ceaseless warring, the orc tribes would unite and pour across the mountain passes into the peaceful lands beyond. Much blood would be shed to stop them, and in the meantime they would take whatever they wanted – which basically amounted to anything that could be raped, looted, or pillaged. Many crusades were called for, and some were even attempted. But how can you defeat an enemy that has no cities to capture and an endless steppe to retreat into?

That was then, of course.

With the coming of mass-produced magical devices, several enterprising wizards had realised the martial (and commercial) possibilities of a portable lightning bolt firer easily used by anyone who understood the concept of a trigger. True, the early models suffered from the inherent drawbacks of using actual lightning – namely that said phenomenon had a tendency to ground itself on the nearest object, which may or may not have been what it was aimed at. But those were merely teething troubles, and soon a horde of eager adventurers were crossing over the World's End Mountains armed with devices that fired accurate and deadly bolts of pure mana.

The resulting geopolitical and economic changes were rapid, violent, and permanent. Innumerable ancient and abandoned dungeon complexes were looted, causing a price inflation so severe that paper money had to be rapidly invented as a more portable and convenient alternative to wheelbarrows full of gold. Dragons, be they gold, red, green, or fashionably mottled, were hunted to extinction, along with pretty much everything else bigger than a house cat. And the orc tribes were broken, their remaining peoples settled onto what were euphemistically named "reservations".

The sprawling collection of shacks that Blade's carpet was now flying over, and which humans called Craagon's Reach, was one of those reservations. A few miles beyond the reservation's central community was a small skyport, not much more than a square of tarmac marked with several landing circles. Blade dropped the carpet smoothly onto one of the circles and cut the drive. "I could've landed us somewhere in town," he said, "but I figured we're better off parking here and getting a ride in."

Presto nodded agreement. "A wise move. Land this thing somewhere in that hive of degenerates and within fifteen minutes you'd have nothing left save an empty shell being used as a public toilet."

"Isn't that a little harsh?" asked Blade.

Presto thought for a moment, then shrugged. "Probably." He looked across at Blade. "Nice landing, by the way."

"You sound surprised," Blade told him. "Did you think an AdventureSport warrior wouldn't have the brains to fly a carpet?"

"Honestly? Yes."

Blade considered that for a moment, then smiled. "Well, that's certainly honest. Anyhow, let's get going. I'll hire a buggy to take us into town."

An initial cruise down the main drag of Craagon's Reach established that it had one church, one general store, one hotel-cum-hostel, a guard station, five fast-food joints, and thirty-seven drinking establishments of some kind. Initial reconnaissance completed, they pulled into the parking lot of the optimistically named "Luxury Inn" and rented a set of rooms.

Dani was still packing her things away when there was a discreet knock at her door. She'd stayed in a variety of low-end sleeping establishments in her time, under a variety of anonymous names, and this one was no different. Although where these types of places typically had a suggestion of an unpleasant smell, here it was less a suggestion and more a strong implication. She gave a stuck drawer enough of a thud to send it sliding home, then answered the door.

It was Darick, wearing an uncertain expression on his face. "I don't know what the others have in mind, but I thought perhaps we could have a look-see? See what we can find?"

"May as well," Dani told him, grabbing her jacket from the broken chair she'd thrown it over. "Won't learn anything sitting around here."

The Storm had always prided himself on not judging people – or orcs, come to that – on their looks, but after thirty seconds of elliptical conversation with the Luxury Inn's front desk jockey he was rapidly coming to the conclusion that the poor bastard really was as stupid as he looked. He decided to try and approach his true intentions from a different tack. "Hey, man, you like a drink now and again, right?"

The orc looked confused. "Drink?"

"You know, alcohol?"

"Oh! Booze!"

The Storm breathed a silent sigh of relief. "Yeah, booze. You like some booze now and again, right?"

The orc shook his head, solemnly. "No. I like booze all the time."

"Okay. Right. Whatever. This is good. We're making progress. You like booze, but like, where do you go when you want some booze?"

"Home. That's where I keep my booze."

The Storm took a deep breath. "Okay. But where do you get that booze from?"

"From the Quicko-mart."

"But is there anyone who does special booze? Cheap booze? Cheaper than the Quicko-mart?"

"No. The Quicko-mart does really good offers."

"Right. But what if you couldn't get booze from the Quicko-mart? Is there any other guy you could get booze from? A guy you could make a deal with, for booze?"

"Yeah, Racko."

The Storm relaxed a couple of notches. It sounded like he was onto a man who might have what he needed. "Cool. So this Racko cat, he can like, get things, can he?"

"He's not a cat. He's an orc."

"Yeah, yeah. But he can get things, right? Things that people need?"

The orc thought hard. "Well, only booze. That's because he runs a bar."

"He runs a bar?"

"Yeah. Racko's bar. That's where I'd go to get booze if the Quicko-mart didn't have any."

"But what if Racko's bar wasn't there?"

"I'd go to Ped's bar."

The Storm fought down an urge to shout, deciding instead to spend a few moments attempting to stop his hands from shaking. "But what if booze wasn't allowed, man?" he asked. "What if it was like, illegal? Where would you get it from then?"

"What's illegal?"

Presto headed through the lobby and into the weak sunshine beyond, ignoring the Storm, who was apparently attempting to procure – without obvious success – some herb from the orc behind the lobby desk. The best Craagon's Reach had to offer sprawled before him. It wasn't much.

Back in the cold light of an Empire City morning, he'd been all fired up to dig hard into the mystery they were entangled in. But now, here, after several hours spent wedged into a carpet, breathing in clear, pure air that managed to be several degrees colder than that of Empire City, his earlier resolve had dribbled away. If pressed to describe his current state, he could have wrapped it in an obfuscating blanket of technical words, obscure synonyms, and indirect passive language, but the honest, brutal summary would be that having got to Craagon's Reach, he had no idea what to do next.

And from the way his four companions had disappeared to their rooms upon checking in at the hotel, he figured he wasn't the only one. Pulling his jacket tighter around him, he walked past a couple of bars and headed into what he'd have termed a greasy spoon café, if he'd been confident its inhabitants would have been capable of using cutlery. Inside was a motley collection of plastic chairs and tables, none of which matched, a dubious smell that could be charitably described as "spicy", and a lone customer busily engaged in eating what looked like roast dog deep fried to buggery and back. The orc customer paused, wiped some grease from his several chins, gave Presto a long hard stare, then went back to stripping the meat from the bone with his oversized fangs. The orc behind the counter gave Presto an equally stern stare. "Hu-man. We don't get many humans here. What'll it be, hu-man?"

This wasn't an establishment Presto would ever have considered had circumstances been anything like normal, but they weren't. He hadn't eaten since the day before yesterday, the excitement and adrenalin of the night's events had worn off, and his stomach had woken from its slumber and begun to complain rather loudly. He was very, very hungry, and thus prepared to overlook a whole load of ethical, philosophical, historical, cultural and – most relevantly – culinary objections he might otherwise have had.

The cafe's server waited expectantly, his fangs jutting from his mouth either side of his moustache. Presto looked at the menu and tried unsuccessfully to decipher the semi-literate scrawl that passed for the orc language.

"Tea and toast?" he ventured. "With marmalade, perhaps?"

The orc merely stared hard at him, then shook his head.

Presto took another look at the menu. Maybe he should just find a bar and have a drink. That usually worked when he was hungry.

Dani was a habitually cautious individual, especially when she found herself in a seriously scary-looking dump full of even scarier looking people (assuming you counted orcs as people, and either way, they were still bloody scary).

Darick appeared to have no such worries. "Hello," he said cheerily to a couple of passing orcs. "How are you chaps doing?"

The orcs were dressed in dirty canvas pants and stained smock-shirts that struggled to contain their bulging muscles and even more bulging bellies. Blinking in dull confusion, they paused, momentarily. Darick appeared to take their stopping as an invitation to a conversation, rather than what Dani took it for: a prelude to a beating. "Have you ever heard anything about a sleeping dragon?" Darick asked them.

The two orcs looked at each other, then turned their attention back to the priest. "Dragons gone," the first said. "You bastards killed them all," added the second. They looked at each other again, shrugged, then walked away down the street.

Dani let out a long breath, then laid a hand on Darick's shoulder. "Maybe it's best not to raise the subject quite so directly."

"You think?"

"Yeah. We want to get information, not give it away." She looked around, then pointed across the street at the first in a long line of bars. "Let's try in there. If you want to know anything, you're always best off asking a barman. Oh, and you might want to tuck your holy symbol into your shirt."

Dani couldn't say for sure that the establishment's original architect had been going for the breezeblock and corrugated steel look, but if the bloke had been shooting at a higher target then it was a target he'd well and truly missed.

From the outside, the bar had looked like a shit-hole. But the reality revealed by its thankfully dark interior turned out to be far, far worse. Lingering above a badly tiled floor covered in dirt and unswept cigarette butts, an indescribable smell wafted. On a far wall, an ancient looking crystal with a knackered screen was playing a silent image that was two parts music flick and three parts static. Public health posters, decorated with what looked to be dried spit, hung curling from the walls on either side. Add in a handful of orc patrons gathered around a semi-naked orc female wrapped around a pole, and you had a place that put the "d" into dive and let you off the cost for the "i", "v", and "e". Dani shuddered; tried not to think about what she might be stepping in; resolved not to breathe in, ever; and then headed off towards the bar's lone barman, who was using a dirty rag and his own spit to clean some glasses.

"It's erm, it's erm, it's… well…" said Darick from behind her, before breaking into a coughing fit that stopped just short of retching.

Dani whispered out of a nearly closed mouth, ventriloquist style. "I think the word you're looking for, and I'm being charitable here by not attaching any adjectives, is dump."

Darick pulled the facial equivalent of a shrug. "Well, we've got to take socio-economic and historical factors into account," he managed, before breaking off to cough again.

"It's still a dump."

A memory surfaced in Dani's mind; a distraction so old and blurred as to be almost a memory of a memory. A woman, blonde and beautiful, leaning over her and singing a nursery rhyme from

another age.
Their teeth are out, their tusks are up, they're setting us all a-shout.
Where are the brave knights to chase these teeth and tusks out?
"That's supposed to be about orcs, isn't it?" asked Darick.

Dani realised she must have been humming the tune aloud. She shook herself. "So they say. Sorry. Just remembering something." At Darick's questioning look she continued, "My mother used to sing it to me. It's my first memory of her." A small pain flared within her; a pain she'd thought gone. "It's pretty much my last memory of her too, actually."

A look of genuine sorrow appeared on Darick's face. "Is she not with us anymore?"

"No," Dani told him, in a flat tone that failed to reveal the pain behind the story. "She was a herb addict. Both my parents were. They OD'ed on a bad batch when I was three and my sister was one. The two of us were bought up in care."

Darick touched her on the arm. "I'm very sorry to hear that."

Dani shrugged. "It's okay. I've had a lifetime to get used to it." She looked around and noticed the stares they were getting from some of the patrons. "And I don't think this is really the place to be talking about it. Come on, let's get some drinks. They might help take away the smell." She nodded at the barman, who nodded back before spitting into another glass. "Preferably something we can drink straight out of the bottle."

Chapter Eight

The whisper's dialling tone rang and rang and finally clicked onto the answer daemon.

Hi, this is Tenny. I'm either not with my whisper at the moment or you're not important enough for me to bother with right now. If you think I'll care enough to call you back then leave a message after the tone. Beeeeep.

"Tenny, it's Blade," said Blade. "If you're getting this, call me back. I had a problem last night." He paused for a moment, couldn't think of anything to say, and eventually gave up, shoving his whisper back into his pants' pocket. It was bloody chilly at the top of the rickety iron fire escape, but it seemed to be the only place in this godforsaken hole where his whisper could actually get a connection through the ethereal plane to what was presumably a far distant receiving node.

He sat down on the ice-cold steps. He'd been the one who'd been gung ho for doing something, but now he was here he had absolutely no idea what to do. It was easier in the arena. The problems there were hard and challenging, but clearly defined. Destroy this construct. Defuse the trap. Climb that wall. Hard and challenging, but clearly defined, and therefore nothing like life. He pulled the whisper back out and dialled another number. There were only two numbers he'd so memorised that it was easier to dial them than hit the speed-dial. One was Tenny's.

This was the other.

The dialling tone rang and rang, and this time there was no answer daemon to take away the dilemma of when to give up. He let it go several rings more, then hung up, shoved the whisper back into his pocket, and headed on down the fire escape. There didn't seem much else to do.

Dani had ordered a couple of ruinously expensive beers for herself and Darick, which they proceeded to drink straight from the bottle. If the barman was offended, he didn't show it, but merely continued cleaning his glasses while he watched them drink. "Don't see many hu-mans here," the orc finally ventured, his voice hissing past his tusks.

Dani shrugged. In her experience, the best way to learn things was to listen and let other people talk.

"A few people from the reservations agency, they come now and again to poke their noses around. And the do-gooders at the health centre and all the other government people. But you don't look like them?"

"We're not government," said Dani. She took another swig of beer and left it at that.

"So why are you here?" The barman's friendly tone seemed a little less friendly now, and there was a suspicious edge to the way he was examining his current glass for marks.

"We're looking for something," said Dani.

"What?"

"A sleeping dragon."

"Ain't no dragons left. You hu-mans killed them all. Shot them out of the sky like you shot us down."

"It might not be an actual dragon. Have you heard anyone talking about a sleeping dragon?"

The barman thought for a moment. "No. And I hear more than most."

Darick leaned past Dani. "Is there anyone else here who might know about things that are happening?"

"You could ask the chief of the tribe," suggested the barman.

"That sounds good," said Dani. "Where can we find him?"

The barman pointed past them, at a vomit covered orc asleep in a chair.

"He's just over there."

Blade found the Storm slumped over the front lobby desk, observed by a somewhat bemused lobby clerk. "I think your friend wants some drink," the clerk told Blade. "But he don't want to pay for it." The clerk leaned in close to Blade and dropped his voice to a low whisper. "We get loads like him here. They blow their welfare cheque on the first day, then have to spend the rest of week begging for booze."

Blade gave the clerk a nod and a smile and grabbed the Storm. "C'mon mate, let's go take a walk." From the way the Storm's hands were shaking, Blade had a pretty good idea of what it was he actually wanted – but that wasn't a conversation he particularly wanted to have.

Craagon's Reach hadn't looked particularly salubrious that afternoon when they'd arrived. But now, as the afternoon sun slunk below the horizon, the settlement was managing to add an additional splash of threat to its previous cocktail of depressed unpleasantness. Blade was reminded by his rumbling stomach that he hadn't eaten for a while. He pointed at a sign hanging from a shack a few buildings down the main street. "Bite to eat?" he suggested.

The Storm peered dubiously at the rusted sheet of metal, whose peeling paint proclaimed that it belonged to, "Fry's Fry House".

"Sounds lovely," the rock star said, a wry smile on his face. "Do you think they do salad?"

"Wouldn't bet on it."

They headed in, and found Presto at a table inside, picking delicately at a slice of burned toast.

Blade slid into the seat opposite the wizard. "Anything you'd recommend?"

Presto showed him the toast. "Yes. Leaving." He resumed eating, a look of slight distaste on his face.

Blade twisted round and waved a hand at the orc behind the counter. "Hi, mate. Can we have two black coffees and four slices of toast please?"

The orc stared back at him.

Presto paused between mouthfuls. "I don't think they offer waiter service."

Blade got up and wandered over to the counter, the Storm following him with a noticeable lack of enthusiasm. Blade gave the orc behind the counter a friendly nod. He'd always taken people as he found them, and saw no reason to change that now. "What would you recommend?" he asked brightly.

The orc shrugged. "Most folks here 'bouts have the deep fry."

"Deep fried... what?"

The orc shrugged. "People don't ask and I wouldn't know. My boss puts it in the fridge and I deep fry it."

Blade looked back at the Storm and mouthed a questioning, "Toast?" at him. The Storm nodded. Blade turned back to the orc. "We'll stick with the toast and coffee, thanks."

The orc nodded, then said, "That'll be nine golds."

Blade pulled a ten gold piece note out of his wallet and tossed it onto the counter. "We'll be over there," he said, hooking his thumb at the table where Presto was sitting. "Will you bring it over when it's ready?"

"No."

"Right. Okay."

The orc looked hard at the Storm. "Why's he shaking?"

"He's excited. He's really looking forward to the toast."

They retreated back to Presto's table, the orc giving them an extremely sideways look as they did so. "I know it was my idea to come here," the wizard said to them between bites. "But now that we have, I find myself at something of a loss as to the course of action we should pursue. Have either of you two gentlemen got any ideas?"

Blade thought for a moment, then looked back over his shoulder at the orc. "Excuse me, mate. You ever heard anything about a sleeping dragon?"

Dani and Darick had gone through two beers each now and had achieved nothing save a mild alcoholic buzz that had Dani wondering quite what was in the juice they were drinking. Sadly, though, the buzz wasn't quite enough to make the bar feel at all warm, welcoming, happy, or clean.

Meanwhile, Darick had spent the last hour engaged in a simple plan that involved greeting everyone with a nod, a smile, and a cheery "hello!", and had somehow managed to avoid receiving the hard punch in the face that those he greeted generally looked to be considering. Instead, the orc in the faded work suit had told him to fuck off; the chief had vomited a second time, and then told him to fuck off; and the guy in the corner, who Dani hoped to the gods merely *looked* like he was playing with himself, had just snarled.

Darick leaned in towards her and whispered, "There is one person we haven't tried talking to."

"Who?"

Darick nodded to the orc girl currently wrapping her legs around the pole in the centre of the floor. "Her."

Dani hadn't much looked in that direction. "Is she the girl that was on when we first came in?"

"I don't know," said Darick, in a distinctly embarrassed tone. "I wasn't really looking."

"Good call."

"How is one supposed to talk to her? It seems rude to approach her while she is performing. Should we wait until she finishes?"

Dani coughed. "I think you should perhaps hold out some money, and then ask if you can have a private dance afterwards." She pointed at the screened off booth that lay to one side of the room.

"I'm a servant of the SkyFather. I'm not sure that would be

appropriate. Couldn't you go and have the dance?"

"I'm not exactly the target gender, in case you hadn't noticed."

"Perhaps we could both go?"

A sinking realisation settled upon Dani that it really wouldn't be fair to make him go in there by himself. She paused for a protesting second before giving him a resigned, sighing shrug of acceptance. "Okay. We'll both go."

The priest took out his wallet. "Would thirty golds be appropriate?"

Dani took a quick, squinting glance at the orc woman. If she wasn't six feet tall she was only an inch or so shorter and she had to be packing two hundred pounds of solid muscle. "I'd make it forty. I'd hate to piss her off."

Behind the curtain were a couple of comfy chairs, a tattered carpet, and a different, but equally unpleasant smell that Dani was trying hard not to think about. There are some experiences in life so horrific that the men and women who experience them are bonded for life as brothers and sisters in arms. Dani had a horrible feeling that she and Darick were about to undergo just such an experience.

The orc girl hoisted up her skirt, shoved one foot on the armrest of Dani's chair, and breathed hot meat-flavoured breath in her face. "What do you fancy, hu-man?" Then she paused, eyes blinking as she focussed. "You girl?"

Dani stifled a cough. "Erm, yeah."

The orc girl thought for a moment, then shrugged. "So what you do want, girl hu-man?"

Dani sent Darick a desperate look, and received a horrified look in return. "Perhaps we could just talk for now?" she suggested.

The orc girl's face crinkled in confusion, her thick uni-brow bouncing up and down. "Talk? Are you sickos? They say lots of you hu-mans are sickos."

"No, no, we're quite normal," spluttered Dani. She pointed at Darick. "He's a priest!"

"You're a priest?" the orc girl asked Darick, suspiciously.

"Well, yes," he answered uneasily, giving Dani a furious look.

"I heard you hu-man priests all sickos. I heard you do bad things to small boys."

"Well, now," said Darick, looking pained. "It's true that there have been some very unfortunate and high profile incidents, but the church has instituted a strict screening programme for applicants together with an integrated child protection policy to be followed at all levels."

The orc girl listened to that with a frown that showed increasing degrees of puzzlement with every three syllable word he used, then turned her attention back to Dani. "He's not a sicko then?" she asked, confused.

"No," said Dani. "He's not a sicko."

The girl thought about that for a moment, then nodded. Darick tried a smile on the girl. "What's your name?"

"My name?"

"Yes. What can we call you?"

The girl beamed a big tusky grin. "My name's Grunda." She looked wistfully off at nothing in particular. "No one ever asked me my name before."

"Well, hello, Grunda," said Dani, extending a hand.

The orc girl took her hand, crushed it in a grip that could have cracked walnuts, and then started to dance. "I give you a good dance, hu-mans," she told them. She started to pull the hem of her dress upwards.

"Whoa!" chorused Dani and Darick together.

The orc girl paused. "You not want a dance?"

"Does the phrase sleeping dragon mean anything to you?" asked Darick.

The girl smiled, her canines sliding up and down her cheeks. "No. But if you want I can try and wake it up."

She began to bend down towards Darick's crotch, only to find that crotch moving rapidly away from her propelled by its owner's desperately flailing feet. The rear legs of Darick's chair caught on the lip of the booth's carpet's encircling frame, and between the immovable lip and the considerable force being exerted on it by Darick's legs, the resulting tipping chair flipped Darick into a backward roll through the gap in the curtains and into the bar beyond.

The upturned chair, empty now, rocked on its back beside Dani. The orc girl looked at it with some confusion. "He gone? Why he gone?" She shook her head, shrugged, and then planted her meaty hands on Dani's shoulders. "Lucky you, hu-man wo-man. You got me all to yourself."

Darick backward-rolled across the dirty plastic flooring before cannoning to a stop against something that was less solid than wood, metal, or plastic, but far more solid than flesh had a right to be. It shifted, kicked, hiccupped, and then vomited a long stream of foul brown liquid onto the floor beside Darick. He rolled again, and then sprang to his feet, just in time for his face to enter into conversation with the orc chief's clenched fist.

The impact sent Darick sailing clear across the room and through a set of table and chairs, in total disregard of the fact that the table and chairs were currently occupied by three orcs and a few dozen glasses. Through greyed vision and a punch-addled mind, Darick watched the orc chief walk slowly over to him. "You want trouble, hu-man? You think you can walk into my town and into my bar and act like you own me?"

The chief leaned over Darick, who was still lying on the ground – not because he thought it was a good idea, but because the many and varied good ideas he was having were all dependent on his brain first re-establishing communications with his legs. A fist loomed large in Darick's face, touched his nose, and then withdrew, winding up for what looked to be a consciousness ending – and possibly life-ending – punch.

Darick whispered a quick prayer.

SkyFather, erm, now would be good?

A voice spoke in reply. Clear. Authoritative. A voice that made all who heard it stop, and listen. "He's with me. I'd think very carefully about what you do next."

Chapter Nine

The interior of the bar was dark, and it took Blade's eyes a few seconds to adjust. Which put them several minutes ahead of Blade's nose, which had spent its first few seconds in the bar attempting simply to comprehend the sheer awfulness of the aroma squatting in the cramped and fetid space. It was a truly terrible smell, the sort of smell that would send paint screaming off its wall and have the dead hammering on their coffins, pleading to be released.

Some smells are offensive; this was so far beyond that as to approach an incompatibility with continuing life. Blade gritted his teeth, motioned to the Storm and Presto to wait by the doors, and then strode forward to stand a little way in front of the orc. Just near enough to have presence, but far enough away to not be a threat. He hadn't been in an honest, old-fashioned fistfight for nearly twenty years now, not since his old man had gone for one last punch and found that his eighteen year-old son had decided that enough was enough.

He didn't aim to break that record now.

The orc stepped carelessly over Darick's prone form, and lumbered towards Blade on unsteady legs. The scent of alcohol and stale meat wafted across Blade's face. "This is my town, hu-man," roared the orc. "And you're surrounded by my people. You think you can just walk into my bar and tell me what to do?"

Blade held up a placatory hand. He'd had trouble over the years. Any high-profile AdventureSport warrior did. But presence, reputation, and a calm, clear head had always seen him through. "I ain't telling anyone what to do, mate. I'm just saying that the guy down there's my friend, and I ain't going to stand by and watch you attack him. Whatever insult you think he made to you, I'm sure he didn't mean it."

People didn't understand. The sight of him wielding a sword with the elegance that had bought him a name as well as fame made them assume combat was his joy in life. They were wrong. He loved the game, but it was the challenge that was his love, the thrill of setting himself against unfavourable odds and the exultation of then winning through. No one ever seemed to understand: not his father; not the various idiots in bars who over the years had challenged him to "go outside"; and not Toozie, who'd loved him then left when he chose the game over her.

He'd been an idiot for letting her go. What did it matter if she hadn't understood what the game meant to him? She'd understood that he'd let it mean more to him than she did, and at day's end that was pretty much all that counted. He could now have taken the anger this realisation always aroused and channelled it into a confrontation. But he slapped that thought down. He wasn't his father, and he never would be. This was just another idiot in a bar. Granted, he'd never faced an orc idiot before, nor one who appeared to be wearing a vomit sporran. But this was just a bar, and the orc was just a guy, even if he was the size of a two-seat brick outhouse with a smell to match.

The orc reached out and jabbed a finger in his chest. "You think you're a big man, hu-man? You think you can talk your talk and make me your friend?"

"I'm just telling you how it's going to be," said Blade. "It's up to you whether you want us to be friends."

"Maybe you be my dog," drawled the orc, turning round to wave for laughter among his audience. He turned back to Blade with a snarl on his face, having received only two weak cheers, a hiccup, and a semi-enthusiastic yap from some kind of mongrel wolf that had sneaked in while Blade wasn't looking.

The orc slowly drew back his fist, leaving himself so open that if he'd been a construct in the arena Blade could have got in three punches and a couple of kicks and ended it there and then. But this wasn't the arena and the orc wasn't a construct, so Blade calmly waited until the fist ended its backward journey and launched itself towards his face, then ducked beneath it and swept the orc's legs from under him.

The orc crashed roaring to the floor, raised his head for a moment, then fell into an alcoholic stupor. Blade swept a stern gaze across the watching few, trying to send a message to each one of them that this was over, and that any attempt by them to restart it would be a bad idea. For a worrying moment, he thought that the wolf-dog might be about to have a go, but after several seconds of locked eye-contact it let out a pathetic whine and wandered off to a tattered blanket set by the side of the bar, where it launched into an energetic bout of testicle licking.

Presto and the Storm appeared by his side as he was helping Darick to his feet. "Nice one dude," said the Storm. "It was looking a bit hairy there for a while."

Blade nodded acknowledgement, then looked around. "We probably ought to be leaving." He looked at Darick. "Was Dani with you?"

"Yeah," said the priest, looking a bit awkward. He nodded towards the curtains. "I think she might need rescuing."

After a quick retreat from the bar, they'd adjourned to Darick's hotel room for a brainstorming session, which had ground to a halt in a depressing short period of time. Blade looked around the now quiet room, seeing Dani sipping at a chipped mug full of instant coffee, Darick looking urgently puzzled, Presto apparently lost in thoughts, and the Storm nervously chain-smoking the last of Presto's cigarettes.

"So no one's got any ideas then?" Blade asked.

They all shrugged or shook their heads. Blade looked out the window, thinking. Outside, the sky was already dark – it wasn't actually that late, but when you were this far north at this time of year the days were short. He stood up. "Look, none of us got any sleep last night, so it's been a pretty long day that began yesterday morning. I figure we may as well knock it on the head, get a good night's sleep, and then see if we can figure out the next move tomorrow over breakfast. Sound good?"

They nodded. He grabbed his jacket and headed for the door. "See you tomorrow in the lobby about eight, then."

Sleep didn't come easily for Blade that night. In fact, it didn't come at all. He eventually gave up, and got up, pulling his clothes and jacket back on. The cheap dial in the corner was flashing "01:37" at him, but with the time difference it would only be late evening back in Empire City. He grabbed his whisper from the bedside unit and headed on out.

When he opened the door to the fire exit the chilly, icy blast took his breath away. If he'd thought it was cold before, that was nothing compared to now. He quickly clambered to the top of the metal steps, and then huddled into the lee formed by the wall and a ventilation unit. The wind's probing fingers weakened somewhat. He took a look at his whisper. It had a signal – weak, but enough. He dialled in the number, and this time she answered straight away.

"Blade?"

It was nice to know she still had his number in her whisper's address book.

"Yeah, it's me."

"What the hell's going on? It's all over the news crystals that your house has been destroyed in an explosion and every time I try to call you I just get a recording saying your whisper's turned off."

"I had a bit of an accident."

"Accident?" she screamed. "The whole fucking house has been blown up!"

"It was a big accident. Look, Toozie, it's good to speak to you."

"I wish I could say the same. What the hell am I supposed to tell the kids? I managed to put them to bed before they saw it on the crystal, but I'm going to have to tell them tomorrow. People will be talking."

"Tell them Daddy had a little accident and blew the house up, but that he's okay, and Mr Bubbles is okay, and Magda and Gruff are okay."

"Gods, it's moments like this that remind me why I divorced you."

"Toozie, I think I'm in some kind of trouble."

"Trouble?" she asked, an edge of concern in her voice.

"Yeah…" Something flickered at the corner of his eye. "Hang on a minute," he told her.

Down below, at the base of the fire escape, four shadowy shapes were moving, with a soundlessness that no legitimately moving thing had a right to possess. "Call you tomorrow," he whispered, hitting the off button before she had a chance to reply.

The shapes paused at the base of the fire escape, then began moving carefully up it, becoming less shadowy and more real as each upward step took them into the light cast by the lamp in the adjacent street. They were slim and supple – these were men, not orcs. And they were carrying bolts in their hands, two-handed auto-bolts that could spit so much mana at a man that there'd be nothing left of him save a tangle of burned flesh and a possibly awkward request for those still alive to attend an inquest.

Guards? They didn't look like it. Not in black jumpsuits and woollen, face-covering masks, with hardware you'd only usually expect the military to be carrying. Crooks then? But why the hell would a bunch of professional-looking thieves have come to a dump like Craagon's Reach just to break into a dive like the Luxury Inn? Which bought him back to guards. Reservation guards, perhaps? Someone had to police the reservation, and he couldn't believe it was the guy who'd been vomiting over himself at the bar. Maybe whichever government agency policed the orc reservation had heard about the confrontation in the bar and had come tooled up in accordance with the habitual caution that anyone policing orcs would presumably learn to use.

The men paused by the fire door to the second floor that Blade had left partially open. What looked like a whispered discussion ensued, accompanied by a variety of urgent military-style hand signals, and ending in a round of very un-military-style shrugs. The man who looked like the leader launched into some kind of countdown on his fingers.

Blade began to walk down the fire escape towards them. Whatever kind of misunderstanding was going on, it had to be best to nip it in the bud here and now. He cleared his throat and began to talk, getting as far as, "Hey mate, what's–" before one of the men whipped round, raised his auto-bolt to his shoulder, and pulled the trigger, sending a stream of raw mana straight at Blade. Most men would have died at this point, but luckily for him, his children, and his on-a-percentage-share agent, Blade wasn't most men. As the auto-bolt's barrel had risen to face him, his arena-trained instincts had already taken over, sending him vaulting over the railing at the side of the fire-escape's steps and into the void beyond.

As survival strategies go, it wasn't great, given that he was now three stories above a tarmacked alley, towards which he was about to start accelerating at thirty-two feet per second. But it did at least shift the time of his demise from "right now" to "some time during the next second or so" and thus give his brain a couple of hundred milliseconds to get its shit together.

The ventilation unit exploded loudly above him as he dropped past the fire escape's second floor landing. Blade reached out and caught hold of a passing strut, swung, and then released, turning his downward fall into an upwards swoop that deposited him onto the landing in front of the four men. All four of their bolts swung to face him, but he was already pushing into a low dive, his reactions operating ahead of theirs. He rolled into the first of the men, sending him crashing to the metal deck, then flicked a sharp kick at the crotch of the second – the man who'd shot at him.

The second man doubled up and staggered backwards, ruining the aim of the third, who'd had a bolt aimed straight at Blade and a trigger finger that was just about to tighten. The shots fired anyway –

loud, wide and screaming – and something across the alleyway exploded with a bang. The first man was scrabbling, trying to get a grip on his bolt, which was hanging loose from the strap around his neck. Blade punched him, grabbed the bolt, used it to pull the man's face hard into his outstretched elbow, then shot the third man in the shoulder.

A spear of mana punched through the third man's black jumpsuit and the fragile flesh beyond – exploding, tearing, burning. He tumbled backwards, colliding with the fourth man. Blade rammed the butt of the bolt into the first man's face, ripped the strap free from the man's neck, swung the stock of the bolt, club-like, down onto the back of the still-doubled up second man, and then pivoted a high kick into the chest of the fourth man, sending him crashing down to the landing's mesh floor.

Twenty seconds later, Presto popped out of the fire-exit and found Blade pointing the bolt at his four assailants, who were all in varying degrees of consciousness. The wizard sized up the situation in one quick glance, then cast a short spell. A gently glowing and foamy mould formed around the wounded shoulder of the third man. "That won't heal him," said Presto. "But it will stop him bleeding to death for long enough that the para-healers can get to him." He cast a second spell, one that bound the four men in an only partly visible net. The first man, the leader, was coming round now. He struggled against the net, but stopped when it began to visibly tighten.

Dani appeared silently in the doorway, a knife resting easily in her hand, followed by a sleepy and confused Darick. Blade noted the knife, but said nothing. Dani gave Blade a calm but quizzical look. "What happened? I heard shooting."

Blade shrugged helplessly, caught in the crash-down of a post-adrenaline rush. "No idea. I was up top on the whisper to Toozie, saw them sneaking in, started down to ask them what they were doing – and they started shooting. They tried to kill me!" The first man was looking up at him. Blade was very tempted to plant a well-aimed boot in his face, but settled instead for reaching down through the magical net and pulling the man's mask off. A harsh, angry face he'd never seen before glowered back at him. "Anyone recognise this guy?" he asked.

"Never seen him before," said Dani. Presto and Darick shrugged in agreement.

Presto motioned them to the other end of the fire escape's landing.

"Might I suggest we travel back to Empire City and report it there?" he whispered. "Whatever passes for guards round here, I'd be wary of trusting them." The wizard looked down at the four masked men. "You stay here and make sure they keep quiet while we grab your things. Then I suggest grabbing the buggy and making a run for the skyport. We can call the para-healers from there and then report the attack to the guards when we get back to civilisation. Oh, and someone had better wake up our musician friend."

"Sounds good to me," Blade told him. "Sooner I'm out of here the better I'll feel."

The flight back took more than seven hours, but to Dani it seemed to slip by in an instant. Presto, Darick, and the Storm spent the journey either dozing, or staring at the dark, shadowed landscape below. Meanwhile Blade, who was sitting beside Dani at the carpet's controls, seemed totally absorbed in the task of flying the craft, leaving Dani alone with her thoughts about what had just happened, and what the ramifications might be. It was still dark when they began their approach to Empire City, which confused Dani until she remembered that they'd been flying west, racing away from the rising sun. Beside her, Blade was flicking switches on the carpet's whispercast unit. "Empire City Control, this is carpet Candle Dagger requesting access to controlled airspace for transit to private landing location Griffin Wand two fiver."

There was a short pause before the voice of sky traffic control responded.

Carpet Candle Dagger, this is Empire City Control. Request that you switch to Central Skyport approach path four-seven for landing at Central on pad three-two-niner.

Blade looked at Dani, his thumb resting lightly on the unpressed transmit button. "Why do they want me to go straight to the skyport?"

"I guess someone back at Craagon's already whispered ahead about the trouble we had. Someone probably wants to get a statement from you." She wasn't actually sure it would be quite that simple, but she didn't think there was anything to gain by verbalising her fears.

The Storm meanwhile reached over from his position on the back seat and slapped Blade on the shoulder. "It'll be fine dude. You were attacked, right? If they try to make something out of it, there's nothing there a good lawyer wouldn't laugh out of court in his sleep."

Blade thought for a moment, shrugged, then hit the transmit button. "Empire City Control, this is carpet Candle Dagger. Understood. Heading for approach path four-seven for landing at Central on pad three-two-niner."

Welcome back, carpet Candle Dagger.

Blade dropped the carpet smoothly onto the centre of the pad and cut the power. The faint crackle of a discharging mana field disappeared, along with the lights on the dash's display and the shimmering air-deflection field that had enveloped them during the flight. Two men had been standing by the side of the pad. They were dressed in guard uniforms accessorised by identical, standard-issue spectacles, and as they approached the carpet they wore identical stern grimaces. The one who stood on the left pulled a sheet of paper from an inside pocket and consulted it for a moment. "Lothar Petros, known as Blade?"

For a moment Blade didn't answer. Dani wasn't sure if that was shock at the situation he appeared to be in, or perhaps just that it had been years since anyone called him by his real name. Eventually, he managed a numb nod.

"You're under arrest," the man told him. His gaze tracked across Dani, and the three others sitting behind them. "As are all your companions here."

Dani said nothing. She'd never actually been in this situation before, but she'd been taught by those who had. Say nothing. Her compatriots, however, had obviously received no such advice, because they immediately erupted into a chorus of protests, threats and general expressions of surprise.

The man held up a halting hand. "You have the right to remain silent, but anything you say will be noted down and may be used in evidence against you." He paused for a moment, and then spoke again. "And there's no point complaining to us, anyhow. We're just skyport guards sent here to pick you up."

"Who does want us then?" asked Blade.

The man gave him a pitying look. "The Serious Crimes Division. I don't know what it is you've done, but you're all in a hell of a lot of trouble."

Chapter Ten

The interrogation room was cold and damp and the paint was peeling from its walls. Inside, a single table stood, flanked by a set of cheap, plastic chairs. Two guards led the Storm to one of the chairs, sat him firmly down, handcuffed his arms to its arms, and then left, locking the door with a solid clunk behind them. The table-top was worn and dirty, as though it had stories to tell that were long on action but short on style. Hours must have passed since they were arrested, and taken to Empire City's central guard headquarters. Hours in which he'd been held alone in a cold cell, with no food, little information, and a singular absence of his legally entitled whisper call.

And no herb.

He looked up. Two figures in civilian clothes stood at the far wall, next to a battered looking coffee maker. A dwarf and a halfling. The halfling smiled at him, while the dwarf merely stared.

"I'm Detective Inspector Snagglepipe," said the halfling. "And this is Sergeant Ironhammer. Have you been treated well here?"

The toxic cocktail of fear, herb withdrawal, and lack of sleep that the Storm was currently running on was making thinking damn near impossible, let alone actual speech. He threw out a confused nod followed by an arthritic shrug, then managed to croak out: "Had it worse." He paused for a moment. "Like, why am I here?"

The halfling smiled again. "Because accusations of a quite serious nature have been made against you and your companions. We've already spoken to some of them, and now we're speaking to you." The halfling walked around the table, and stood beside the Storm, their eyes level. "You're nervous. I can see that. You've probably never been in this situation before, you're trying to work out how it's going to go, and all you have to go on are crap crystal flicks full of half-truths, laughable inaccuracies, and plain damn lies." Snagglepipe paused for a moment, as though smiling to himself, and then continued, "And you're probably thinking the same as everyone does when they see us. It's always the same. Halfling, good cop. Dwarf, bad cop. It's insulting, and it's wrong. You know why?"

His tiny fist slammed into the Storm's face. Blood splattered from the Storm's shattered nose; the unbelievably sharp pain drove all fatigue from his mind. The halfling took a step back, and pointed at his dwarven subordinate. "Because he's the good cop."

The dwarf slid a plastic cup of coffee across the table and smiled apologetically. The halfling meanwhile glared at the Storm with a face now so full of anger it would have made a granite obelisk want to take a step back. "Tell me what I want to know and I might let the Sergeant here free an arm so you can drink that coffee, instead of just look at it."

Darick had spent most of the time since his arrest praying, but he wasn't sure it was doing any good. He wasn't arrogant enough to expect the SkyFather to directly intercede on his behalf, but a slight stiffening of his resolve would have been good, and thus far his resolve felt distinctly lacking in any kind of external enhancement. But he'd read enough theology to know that faith didn't work that way. Faith came from within, and not without, no matter how much one might wish otherwise. The door opened, interrupting the dressing down his internal monologue was giving him, and a voice gruffly ordered: "You. Out. Boss wants to talk to you."

He followed the guard down a bare corridor, with another guard following. A door opened, out of which the Storm staggered. His nose looked to be broken, and his face was blood splattered. But that wasn't the worst of it; his eyes were vacant, like someone was at home but they weren't answering the door. He stared unfocused, at somewhere past Darick for a moment, before another guard led him away down the corridor.

Darick felt what little resolve he'd had dribble away. *SkyFather,* he thought. *I don't care how it's supposed to work. I'm not sure I've the strength to handle this.*

After the two guards had handcuffed him to the chair and then left, the halfling who'd been in the room when he entered simply stared hard at him for what felt like an eternity, and must have been at least two full minutes. Through all of this, the halfling's dwarven companion simply looked on, impassively. Finally, the halfling spoke. "Don't bother giving me the cover story, because I've already heard it from your companions. You never met each other prior to the day before yesterday, a spell kidnapped you—"

The dwarf tapped the halfling on the shoulder, and then held up two fingers.

"Sorry. A spell kidnapped you twice. You tried to dispel it, but it blew up your AdventureSporting friend's mansion in retaliation, and then you all decided to fly straight off to an orc reservation four thousand miles away."

Darick shook his head frantically. "That's it, exactly! Except that when we got there, a bunch of armed men attempted to break in and kill us. Blade had to fight them off."

The halfling detective leaned in close and snarled, "Really? And I suppose they were wearing black suits and full-face masks, were they?"

Darick felt a surge of relief. "Well, actually, yes, they were!"

"So why, when I contacted the Craagon's Reach office of the Orc Reservations Liaison Agency, did they report no incidents whatsoever save a dispute in a bar the previous evening?"

This made no sense to Darick. They'd called the para-healers. One of the men had been shot. How could that all just evaporate like dawn dew beneath a rising sun?

"I know you're all lying," screamed the halfling. "If someone doesn't start telling the truth pretty soon, I'm going to start getting very nasty. And since you're the one who's here right now, priest, you're the one I'll be getting nasty with!"

The dwarf shrugged apologetically from his standing position over by the wall.

The halfling grabbed a second chair, placed it across the table from Darick, then climbed onto it, sitting perched on top of the back with his feet upon its seat. He sighed, took a deep breath, and then spoke again. "How about we just start again, from the beginning?"

Darick nodded eagerly. If he could just tell the story, he was sure they would get things sorted out.

"With the children."

"Children?" Darick blurted out. "What children?" he added, even more befuddled than he'd been previously.

A mask of fury and hate appeared on the halfling's face. "The dead orc children whose bodies we found in the wreckage of your friend Blade's mansion. The dead orc children who you'd travelled to Craagon's Reach to replace." He leaned forward and spat his next words straight into Darick's face. "You and your kind are scum, priest, and I'm going' to make sure they lock you in a hole so deep you'll spend the rest of your life dreaming about sunlight."

After a further two hours of questioning, the guards had taken Darick back to his cell and patched up some of his more obvious wounds, before dressing him in a bright orange, loose-fitting jumpsuit. A few minutes later the door opened, to reveal a guard he hadn't seen before. "Get up. We're shipping you and the other scum to Stonehaven for the night."

The ancient and imposing stone structure of Stonehaven Tower was Empire City's central prison. Darick had visited it once as part of a deputation of prison visitors, but now it appeared he was about to see it from the other side of the bars. He followed the guard down the corridor and out into the station's rear yard. It was already falling dark, and a bitter wind was sweeping across the exposed space. An armoured wagon stood alone at the far side of the crumbling tarmac, its rear doors open to reveal a windowless interior of bare metal walls, ceiling, and floor.

Blade, the Storm, and Presto were already inside, dressed in the same fetching orange jumpsuit that Darick himself now wore. Blade and the Storm had their arms and legs secured by metal restraints built into the seats. But in the case of Presto, those restraints were augmented by additional bindings on his hands and fingers, and by a gag in his mouth, presumably to render him incapable of casting spells. A guard standing in the centre of the vehicle grabbed Darick by the neck of his jumpsuit, hauled him in, and shoved him roughly into an empty seat before snapping the restraints down, each one clicking shut with a very definitive double-clunk.

A few seconds later Dani appeared. Unlike Darick, her hands had been handcuffed behind her back, perhaps due to her having put up a stiffer resistance than Darick's pathetic compliance. As the guard supervising the loading tried to haul her into the van, the grifter's foot caught on the final step. She slipped out of the guard's loose grasp and fell face-first into the van's metal floor. Darick couldn't help but wince, first at the thud, and then her agonised cry.

"Try not to damage the prisoners any more than SCD have already done, sergeant," said a voice from outside the wagon. For a moment the guard merely glared in the direction of the voice, then he reached down to tug at the bleeding, semi-conscious Dani. "Stand up!" the guard screamed, following up with a sharp punch to the kidneys when she proved either unable or unwilling to comply. After a few seconds and a sigh, the guard hauled her to her feet, reached behind him to unlock the handcuffs, then dropped her limp form into one of the last two empty chairs. "Good riddance," the guard muttered, as he snapped the wrist restraints home before heading off out the back of the van, still cursing angrily under his breath.

The door slammed shut, leaving the interior lit only by the dim illumination of a single light set flush into the ceiling. For a moment there was silence and stillness. Then the magical motor set beneath the floor hummed into life, and Darick felt the wagon pulling away. A cold desolation descended upon him.

Dani looked up cautiously, still playing the role of the semi-conscious prisoner. It wasn't too hard an act. The trip might have been deliberate, but the resulting fall had been genuine; that and the following punch had hurt like hell.

There were no cameras set into the wagon's far wall that she could see. She slowly turned her gaze left and right. Nothing obvious there either. Didn't mean they weren't there, but she had no choice save to assume they weren't. Of course, if they'd put a guard here in the compartment with them, all thoughts of cameras would have been moot. But they hadn't, which was pretty typical: the more systems people had, the more they relied on those systems.

She looked across at Presto, who was sitting opposite. The wizard's eyes locked onto hers and something in them said "yes" to whatever she might be thinking. She looked around at the others. "I think we should get out of here," she whispered. If there were microphones, then whispering wouldn't help, but, assuming there weren't, there was no point speaking so loudly that the drivers in the adjacent cab might hear something.

"Wouldn't we get into even more trouble?" asked Darick. "Surely if we just sit tight the guards will work out that it's all a big mistake?" The priest looked on the edge. Beside him, the Storm nodded in agreement.

Blade was sat beside Dani, his frame tight as though every muscle in it was yearning to break free. "How much more trouble could we be in? Someone's trying to frame us. I think if we do nothing they'll destroy us." The warrior looked across at Presto.

The wizard nodded, as much as his head restraints allowed him. A few seconds later so did the Storm, followed, reluctantly, by Darick.

"Okay," said Blade, continuing. "We're agreed that we'd like to be out of here. But how?"

Dani looked across at Presto. "You're bound and gagged because they think that if you can't speak or move your hands you can't cast spells, right?"

The wizard nodded.

Blade broke in. "I know what you're thinking. But even a minor cantrip requires a whisper and a wave of a finger. The sound and movement is what unlocks the magic. You can't just cast a spell by force of will, however minor it is."

Dani ignored him, and looked straight at Presto. "Can you cast a telekinesis spell by will alone?"

The wizard shrugged, awkwardly.

"How heavy a thing do you want him to shift?" asked Blade.

Dani turned her hand and opened her fingers, revealing the cardkey she'd picked from the guard's trouser pocket when he'd hauled her to her feet.

"That."

Slowly, agonisingly, the card lifted clear of Dani's fingers, hanging in the air a few inches away. Opposite her, Presto's forehead was glistening with sweat and his knuckles were white from the effort of keeping the small rectangle of plastic under control. The wizard grunted, and the card slipped down a couple of inches before steadying. He took a few deep breaths, and then dropped the card down a couple more inches, bringing it tantalisingly close to its target – the card slot set into the left-side portion of Dani's chair.

The card swayed, then started to slide away, as though running down an invisible slope. A bead of sweat was now running down Presto's forehead and onto his nose. He closed his eyes, grimaced – and the card stabilised. Dani allowed herself just a half-sigh of relief. She had plenty of ideas she could work through once she was free of the chair, but as to getting free, this was it. There was no plan B.

Presto had to get the card in the slot.

The card held steady for a few seconds, and then began sliding back towards the slot. There was no sound at all inside the van's hold, save the humming of the motor and the muffled sounds of the outside city. But if hard, desperate stares were shouts then four people would have been shouting loudly and continuously. The card paused for a moment in front of the slot, moved forward to tap the chair's metal surface just above it, dropped down just a fraction, then slowly, agonisingly, slid in until only a half inch stub remained clear of the slot.

But the red light on the left armrest of Dani's chair stayed red.

"You need to click it home," Dani told Presto. The wizard nodded, paused for a few seconds, blinking and breathing deeply, and then screwed up his face. A muffled but agonised moan emerged from his gagged mouth as the card clicked into place – and the red light turned green. Dani pulled her right arm up hard, and felt the catches of the restraint release to let it pull free.

They were in business. Now they just had to get out of the van.

Chapter Eleven

"The thing about these security wagons," Dani told her freshly released companions, "is that while they look like a custom made item, they're actually just an armoured box built around a standard wagon chassis. A Danborn G500, in this case."

"And the significance of that is?" asked Blade, who was already stood by the wagon's locked rear door like a caged tiger ready to fight.

"All the various models in the G series have a design feature, well a flaw really, whereby the outward and inward mana control channels leading to the rear light assembly pass through a single conduit under the floor, just about – here!" Dani pointed at a spot on the metal floor. "The channels are shielded from each other, but not from above. It sometimes causes trouble when a wagon carries a highly magical cargo."

"What sort of trouble?" asked Blade.

"The cross-interference briefly blocks the flow of mana which causes the wagon's main control oracle to crash and restart."

"And that would that open the doors, would it?" asked Darick.

"No. At the moment the wagon is in lock-down mode, which means that it can't be opened from the inside."

"And that's why you can't just shove the card in that slot?" said Blade, pointing at the slot set beside the door.

"Exactly. But they also have a maintenance mode, for when people are in here cleaning out the interior and don't want to get locked in for the weekend if the wind blows the door shut. And when the main control oracle first starts up–"

"–it's in maintenance mode," said a smiling Blade.

"Exactly. Now if I had some equipment with me, I'd put a couple of mana storage units on the floor there and short-circuit them. But since I don't, I'm hoping that our handy dandy wizard friend here can discharge a bit of raw mana just where my foot's pointing."

"I can indeed," said Presto. "Should we wait until the wagon stops at some traffic lights?"

"That's probably best."

They waited, the tension increasing with each second of near-silence broken only by the humming of the motor. Then, finally, they felt the wagon slow to a halt. Dani took a step back from the critical spot and nodded at Presto. The wizard spoke a few words, wove a pattern in the air with his hands, and then pointed at the floor. A bolt of raw, cracking mana arced out to the metal surface. For a moment, nothing happened. Then absolute darkness and a muffled silence fell upon the wagon's interior, as the overhead light went out and the motor beneath the floor died.

"Wait for it," murmured Dani.

A second later, the light snapped back on, its cold white rays flooding the wagon's interior. Dani stepped over to the slot beside the door and rammed the card home. A click came from somewhere in the vicinity of the door's lock and the red light beside the card slot turned green. She grasped the door's handle, twisted it down, and pushed. The door swung open. Early evening light flooded in, a wan mixture of sunlight and streetlight.

"Okay," said Blade, pushing past her. "Let's go."

When Blade hit the ground, senses wired, muscles twitching, it felt bizarrely like the start of a match in the arena; except that in all the matches he'd played in, he didn't recall ever starting in a noisy, crowded street surrounded by finger-pointing shoppers, and facing two guards sitting a few dozen feet away in a buggy that was stopped only four cars behind the van he'd just jumped out of. And stretched beyond that was what looked to be a whole convoy of guard buggies following them, each containing at least two guards, who were now piling out into the street with some haste.

Dani appeared beside him and shouted in his ear. "We need to move!"

Blade spun around. He knew this street, had driven down it hundreds of times. Hell, he'd walked down it on several occasions when the traffic was so awful he'd been forced to dump his buggy and continue on foot. And looming above the row of shops on the right-hand side of the street was a huge, white edifice that was very, very familiar. Somewhere inside the lump of grey matter his ex-wife had refused to believe was a brain, a cluster of neurones engaged in conversation came up with something that qualified as a course of action, if not quite a plan.

A buggy was trying to sneak up the inside of the halted wagon. Blade stepped in front of it, causing it to brake, then grabbed Dani by the shoulders. "We need to head that way," he told the grifter, pointing down the intersection to their right. "Grab the others and get going!"

The driver of the halted buggy waited the requisite half second before leaning on his horn and mouthing something that looked like an accusation about Blade's mother and a particularly well-endowed unicorn. The wailing of the horn spread like a cough at a billiards match; by the time Blade had used an ancient hand gesture to suggest that the honking driver self-impregnate himself and then turned back to look at the wagon, an entire orchestra of horns was playing an improvised but intense symphony. The Storm and Darick were in the street, and a white-faced and shaking Presto was climbing awkwardly down from the van's rear door, helped by Dani. A whole bunch of cops meanwhile were already out of their buggies.

They needed more time.

The street was crowded, as you'd expect on a Lastday afternoon. He waved at a couple standing at the crossing that marked the intersection. "It's okay to cross," he shouted. They looked doubtfully at the illuminated red standing man on the box above the crossing, then – realising that the traffic was stalled in both directions – shrugged and began to cross, followed on both sides by the mass of people struggling to move along the crowded pavements. The converging human walls met just in time to cut off the first of the cops, but it would only take his pursuers a few seconds to fight their way through. He turned back to the buggy he'd forced to brake and aimed a deliberate kick at the driver-side headlight. It shattered. The driver stared, stunned for a second or so, then started to get out. But by then, Blade was already moving.

At the side of the street were a couple of teenage fashion victims who'd had themselves polymorphed into catmen. Blade stopped in front of them and hooked a thumb in the direction of the buggy whose headlight he'd just kicked in. "Jerk there called you beastmen. That's why I kicked his headlight in." The catboys lurched past him, snarling.

A triad of teenaged girls stumbled towards him, giggling. One held out a glossy, pink-coloured magazine and a pen. He scrawled a quick signature across the front, then bent down to whisper in the girl's ear. "I'm doing a reality crystal thing. See the guys dressed as guards? If you kiss them, they'll give you a ticket to a private match." The girl gasped, giggled, then ran towards the guards, shouting at her friends to follow. Blade signed another couple of autographs then turned to run, finding the catboys and the enraged driver in front of him.

"Call us beastmen, yeah?" shouted one of the catboys.

"Outta my way, you furry freaks!" shouted the driver.

Blade jinked past them just as a set of snarls, shouts, crunches, and slaps erupted. It sounded like a wrestling match, but with more violence and less script, and suggested the buggy driver wasn't faring too well against the two catboys. Blade might have felt bad if it hadn't been for the accusation about his mother. Moving quickly now, he rounded the intersection. The rest of the guys were up ahead, Dani in front, Darick struggling along behind with an arm around Presto, and the Storm stalled someway behind them by a crowd of autograph seekers. He ran up to the rock star, let him sign a final autograph, signed one himself, and then grabbed him, shouting: "Sorry, he's running late."

They headed off after Dani, Darick and Presto, pursued by the autograph seekers, however many cops had managed to disengage from the kissing girls, and a gaggle of laughing children who probably had no idea why they were running and probably didn't care. An old adage states that no matter how much it might seem that the world specifically revolves around you, it doesn't. Right now, the truth of this adage was being neatly demonstrated by the fact that while Blade was currently at the centre of a sprinting procession numbering in excess of twenty people, the street the procession was attempting to sprint down was currently full of several hundred other people who were trying to get their shopping done, thank you very much.

He ducked underneath one woman holding a shoe up for examination, ran across a rare five yard gap in the crowd, cannoned off a man who'd chosen that precise moment to exit a passing rug shop holding a rug, apologised, side-stepped, and found himself alongside Dani just as the sprinting grifter reached Gregorio's. Gregorio served the best coffee this side of the Middle Sea, but it wasn't his coffee that attracted Blade right now – it was the back entrance that he'd often used as a surreptitious escape route.

"This is the guards!" shouted a pursuing guard from some way down the street. "Stop them! They're dangerous criminals!"

His appeal to public spirit and civic responsibility had the exact effect one would expect it to have in the middle of a large urban conurbation in the Second Millennium of the Third Age, that effect being none whatsoever.

"This way!" Blade shouted at Dani, shoving the grifter through the doorway, then looking back to grab Darick, Presto, and finally the

Storm. "Keep going through the back!" he shouted.

"Mr Blade!" boomed Gregorio, from his place behind the counter when Blade followed the rock star in. "Your usual?"

"I'm a bit busy, Mr G!" Blade shouted as he ran through the shop and into the tiled corridor that led to the toilets and the back door. "Be back later." He vaulted past Dani down the flight of three steps that led to the door, hammered down on the bar that opened it, thanked both the gods and their worldly bureaucrats for fire exit regulations, and tumbled through into the dusty back access road beyond.

A carpet whined low over them, white with orange and yellow stripes and blue flashing lights, and the word "Guards" helpfully written on the underside in big blue letters. It turned, and swooped back. They didn't have long. Half the guardsmen in the city were probably converging on their location. But Blade knew exactly which way to go – left, towards the huge structure that rose beyond the surrounding urban sprawl. He grabbed Dani and pointed at it. "Head there! Down that alleyway on the right, follow it round, black door with limo parking area. Ask for Janno, tell him you're with me."

"You'll be following, right?" asked Dani, concern in her eyes.

"Right behind you," Blade told her. He looked back through the doorway, down the narrow passageway, and into the coffee shop beyond. The guards were already appearing. Four guys in uniforms, with the halfling and dwarf who'd interrogated him following up behind them, and no doubt more to come. They all spotted him at the same time, turning themselves into a shouting, tangled mass as each of them tried to be the first to charge through the coffee shop's narrow interior. Then they were coming, led by a tall blond guy with a grim look of determination set upon his harsh face. Blade waited until the blond guard had launched himself at the open doorway, then slammed the fire door shut with his shoulder, bracing it with all his weight. The door shook with an impact that sent pain across his shoulders and into his ribs, accompanied by a scream of agony from the other side of the wooden planking.

Blade gave it a second, then wrenched the door open. The blond cop was lying in a heap on the floor, but the wiry redhead who'd been following him was already sending a fist in Blade's direction. Blade ducked underneath it, chopped the redhead down with a sharp uppercut to the jaw, waited until a third guard had launched himself at the doorway, then slammed the door shut again.

Another wail of pain emerged through the door. Blade grabbed a handy bit of wood that had been lying next to the door, snapped it in half, then wedged the broken off end hard under the door.

A window popped open beside him, and Gregorio leaned out, a takeaway cup of coffee in his hand. "I made your usual, Mr Blade!" he said happily.

Blade took the cup and sipped through the hole in the lid. Sweet and strong but milky, just how he liked it. "Thanks," he told Gregorio. Beside him, the door thudded as someone hurled their weight against it, and at the far end of the alleyway he could see the nose of a guard buggy emerging cautiously. It was time to get going after the others. He nodded a goodbye to Gregorio and then began sprinting down the alleyway, towards his comrades, and towards the only place where life had ever made sense.

Chapter Twelve

The commentator shuffled his papers as the production assistant finger-counted down to zero and the little light beside the camera went red.

"And we're back. I'm Brod Rellend, with me is Kren Krennella, and you're watching Lastday Night AdventureSport on EBS1, bought to you in association with StayFresh toothpaste, the toothpaste that leaves your breath fresh all day, every day."

He took a quick glance at the slightly rumpled middle-aged man sitting next to him, received a quick nod in return, and then resumed speaking.

"We're just moments away from bone-crunching action, with Blade's Marauders scheduled to be making the first run of the evening in a little over two minutes. Now there have been a lot of rumours swirling around the ageing legend over the last few days, so what should we be looking out for, Kren?"

His middle-aged companion took a last sip from the something-on-ice that sat on the desk in front of him, and then spoke.

"Well Brod, firstly we'll be looking to see if he comes out at all. We know that after three heavy defeats in their last three outings the rest of his team are unhappy."

"I think unhappy's an understatement. Isn't Denbi Tallfellow suing the league for specieist discrimination?"

"That's what the rumour mill says, Brod, but I hope it's just the news-slates trying to sell copy. It would be a new low for the modern game and a sad, sad day."

"Not how it worked in your day, eh, Kren?"

"Certainly isn't. In my day you took your lumps in the arena and then went out and got drunk and perhaps picked up a girl or two. Now they get one scratch and they're off to see their psychological consultants. The whole game's gone soft, if you ask me!"

The first commentator chuckled.

"Well, you're here to be asked Kren, and you're certainly never scared to give us answers. Are there any other problems we should be looking out for in the Marauders?"

"Would that be in addition to the fact that their leader's the wrong side of thirty and looking to be on an inevitable slide to retirement, Brod?"

"Sugar-coating it as always, eh, Kren?"

"Just calling it how I see it, Brod."

The first commentator threw in another chuckle. "One minute," said the voice of the producer in his earpiece.

"So, in addition to that, what should we be looking out for, Kren?"

"Well, like I said Brod, it's not even certain that we'll be seeing them at all. Some highly placed sources have told me, off the record, that his sponsorship deal with Pete's Adventure Warehouse is up for renewal and that they're looking to end it."

"That would be a blow for him, right Kren? Pete's have sponsored him since pretty much the start of his career, haven't they?"

"Fifteen years, at record levels. Landmark deal. But like they say, Brod, everything comes to an end."

"Well, we've talked about the first team we'll see tonight. Let's talk a little more about the run they're going to get. The big news is that the course is designed by Konigshi Tenneka. He's built up quite a reputation in his native Sun Empire, but this is the first time he's ventured to our side of the continent. What are you expecting, Kren?"

On the crystal monitors in front of them, the image changed from head and shoulder shots of themselves to a long, slow pan across the arena. Beneath a majestic domed ceiling flecked with gold ornamentation, serried rows of banked seating surrounded an oval-shaped arena floor that measured something over a hundred yards in its longest diameter. But where that floor would usually be filled with the obstacles forming the evening's run, this floor was empty: an expanse of featureless black. A metal disc only six to eight feet across floated thirty or so feet above the floor, apparently unsupported. A mesh net with strands so fine as to be nearly invisible stretched from the disc's circumference to the arena's edge, the whole a shimmering cone with the disc at its top, like a giant translucent tent topped with silver.

"Well, as you can see Brod, Konigshi's started with a very minimalist design. Just a levitated metal disc surrounded by the inevitable safety netting, in an otherwise empty arena."

"Still not a fan of safety nets, eh Kren?"

"Certainly not, Brod. In my day we either didn't fall off or we took the fall."

"That you did, Kren. But how's this set-up going to work? We're used to starting with the whole arena in play and then shrinking it down. Konigshi's starting with an area in play of only, what, six or eight feet?"

"He is, and I think we're looking at a tight start. But expect that to change once the game gets going. Konigshi's got a reputation for using arena elements in imaginative ways."

"Do we have any idea how he's even going to start? There's no obvious way for the athletes to enter play."

"All my sources will tell me is that we should expect the unexpected, Brod."

The first commentator took a glance at the dial that sat on the desk before them, watching its numbers tick down. "Match start in five seconds," said the voice of the producer in his ear-whisper. The first commentator took a quick sip of water and then a deep breath, put his game face on, and spoke.

"Well, we're going to find out, because the match is starting right… now!"

Nothing happened that second, and it continued to not happen for several more long seconds.

"Maybe they're not coming out, Brod."

In the changing room, it was all chaos, which wasn't doing much for the headache that was currently attempting to explode through Presto's skull. Blade was shouting at a bloke called Janno, the bloke called Janno was shouting back, and the Storm was staring with some bewilderment at the piece of plastic in the shape of a lute that Blade had thrust into his hands just twenty seconds earlier. Meanwhile, a bunch of other hard looking men – the other AdventureSport teams, Presto surmised – sat around wearing smirks they made no attempt to hide.

"These guys aren't registered!" Janno was shouting. "You can't just take them into the arena. Their points won't be valid. It ain't my fault the rest of your team didn't turn up. And what about insurance?"

There was a commotion from outside, in the direction of the athlete's door through which they had just entered, and judging by the shouts of "This is the guards!" it didn't sound as though it was merely a group of over-enthusiastic fans trying to see their heroes. The doorman appeared to be putting up a good fight, telling the guards that no one but no one ever entered the athlete's complex unless they were with the athletes, but his resistance wasn't going to endure forever. Presto wasn't sure Blade actually had a plan, but staying put clearly wasn't an option. He tugged on the warrior's sleeve. "We need to get going."

As if to emphasise the point, an urgent voice erupted from the speakers set into the ceiling. "Blade's Marauders to enter the arena now! You are sixty seconds late and the crystal folks are climbing out of their prams!"

Blade grabbed Janno by the throat. "I don't care about insurance and I don't care about points. Now get these guys into their sensor sets and get us into that arena, now!"

The first commentator paused for a moment, and looked across at the production assistant. The young man – who, in the first commentator's not-so-private opinion, was far too young for anything beyond tea and biscuit procurement – simply shrugged, and launched into a frantic series of "keep talking" hand gestures. On the monitors, the same view of the empty arena sat, unchanged.

It was every crystal man's nightmare – dead air, terminally so. In the two minutes since Blade's Marauders had failed to emerge, they'd discussed the reasons why this might be, talked again about the near empty initial set-up of the arena, and reminded the viewers that this broadcast was brought to them courtesy of StayFresh toothpaste, the toothpaste that leaves your breath fresh all day, every day. "Say something," screamed the voice of the producer in his ear.

"So Kren, going anywhere nice on your holidays this year?"

"Well, Brod, I thought I might try the Empire of the Sun. I played a few matches there during my playing days, and let me tell you, the girls there do this thing—"

From across the arena, a loud amplified chime interrupted Kren's semi-senile, and no doubt obscene, anecdote. The two commentators looked up through the huge windows set in front of them, the voice of the producer in their ears screaming, "Camera three wide-angle!" The monitors changed to a zoomed out view showing the entire arena: platform, netting, floor, and crowd. On the far side of the building, on a section of wall above the crowd where the organ had been in the days when they still played live music, a panel slid smoothly upward to reveal five circular openings. The first commentator stuttered out a line.

"What do those openings look like to you, Kren?"

"They look like openings, Brod."

There was a loud, echoing, elongated boom. Five shapes shot out of the openings, arched over the crowd, over the arena, over the small disc-platform, and bounced down into the near portion of the safety netting. Five figures, tiny at this distance, dressed in plain, orange jumpsuits broken only by the tiny green lights of AdventureSport sensor harnesses. On the monitors before them, the view zoomed in, showing Blade Petros and four individuals the commentator had never seen before, scattered across the swaying and treacherous netting. The first commentator found himself momentarily lost for words.

"*Erm... Kren?*"

"*Well, Brod, it looks like Konigshi's already starting to weave his magic. That's not safety netting, that's part of the playing area. Genius.*"

"*And that was one heck of an entrance, up and over the crowd.*"

"*It certainly was, Brod, and I'm even more impressed that he got it past the health and safety dragons.*"

On the monitor before them, a kneeling Blade Petros had drawn his blunted arena-sword from the scabbard on his back. His four companions, meanwhile, simply sat or lay dazed upon the netting.

"*His team don't seem to be reacting fast though, Kren. Do you think they're dazed by the force of either the firing or the landing?*"

"*No, I think they're just inexperienced and possibly useless. The bard's still got his lute clipped to his back, I can't even tell which one's the wizard because no one's casting any preliminary spells, and what the seven heck's with those costumes?*"

"*Plain orange. I guess that means the sponsorship deal really has been pulled.*"

"*Pulled, buried, dug up again, and cremated, I'd say.*"

"*Interesting pause in action here from Konigshi. What do you think he's got—*"

From somewhere up near the arena's domed roof, another loud, echoing chime sounded. Eighty thousand spectators looked up at the ceiling, just in time to see a few dozen cuddly bears drop out of the darkness towards the arena below, each bear wearing a small float unit strapped to its back and a set of tiny knuckledusters strapped to its paws.

"*Cuddly bears... with knuckledusters?*"

"*They do have a strange sense of humour in the Empire of the Sun, Brod.*"

Between the beatings by the corrupt guards, the strain of a telekinesis spell cast whilst bound and gagged, the frantic run from the wagon to the arena, and then the shock of being fired out of a giant cannon into a frankly rough piece of plastic netting, Presto wasn't having a good day. And that was before a mechanical cuddly bear dropped onto his back just as he'd managed to get to his feet on this stupid, sodding net. He crashed back down, getting a nasty rope burn across the face, and then felt tiny paws starting to claw at his back. He pushed himself back upright, and reached over his shoulder: something fluffy wrapped around his hand and wouldn't let go.

A few feet away, the Storm was staggering across the netting with a bear clamped fully across his face; blind, he tripped and fell flat. Some of the lights on the harness he wore changed from green to orange. A still-seated Darick appeared to be trying to negotiate with three bears that had him cornered, Dani was hacking with a dagger at a bear clamped to her arm, and Blade was furiously swiping at bears with his sword.

Three inactive bears already lay at the warrior's feet. Blade looked across at him, and waved urgently. "Do something. Get rid of them!"

In front of Presto, four bears were picking their way across the netting towards him, with a bunch more of the little sods following behind them. He raised his one remaining free hand and shouted, screaming the language of magic louder than perhaps he'd ever screamed it. And the universe danced for him, as it always had.

A fireball erupted, visible both on the monitors before them, and through the windows behind which they sat. A huge, incandescent billowing fireball like nothing the first commentator had ever seen before. He screamed instinctively into his headset.

"And the wizard goes huge with a fireball! Kren?"

"Awesome, Brod, just awesome. We haven't seen raw spellcasting like that since the fifties!"

On the monitors, the wizard was throwing more spells: fireballs, bright beams of raw mana, and force walls, leaving behind a field of shattered, broken, and incinerated cuddly bears, even as more of them dropped from the ceiling.

"This is real old-school stuff, right Kren?"

"Certainly is Brod. Tight, restrained spellcasting's the curse of the modern game, but this guy just doesn't seem to care!"

"But they're losing points for every spell he casts! Surely they're going to be racking up one heck of a mana-use penalty?"

"They are, and I'm sorry to say that'll come back to haunt them when the scores are totted up, Brod."

Blade pointed his sword upward, towards the platform at the top of the netting. "Up there!" he shouted. "We need to get up there!"

Presto threw out a quick hammer-fist spell at a bear that was just a bit too close for his liking, and then clawed his way awkwardly over to Blade. The noise of the crowd was incredible, and he had to shout just to have a hope of Blade hearing him. "Why? What's up there?"

"The next step to the end of the run, which is where we'll find the exit!"

Presto had a horrible feeling that bad as this day was, it was yet to reach its nadir. "That's the plan, finish the run and then find the exit? Why in the world did we come in here if the plan was then to leave?"

The warrior shrugged helplessly. "I don't know. I'm making this up as I go along!"

"Clearly!" Presto hissed. He spun round and pointed the other way, towards the encircling crowd.

"Why not downhill and out through them?"

"The whole playing arena's surrounded by an industrial strength force-wall to keep the crowd safe. We wouldn't have a hope in seven hells of breaking through it."

Presto began counting to ten, but gave up on three and started to climb up the netting, cursing its designer each time one of his feet slipped and bought his crotch into violent contact with a section of the thin rope from which it was formed. After a few seconds he risked a look behind him. Darick and the Storm were a little way back, side by side and moving with some speed, if not skill. Dani and Blade meanwhile were conducting a fighting retreat, with Dani wielding her knife like she had some idea of how to use it.

Then the chime from above sounded again, followed shortly after by a boom from across the arena. Presto looked up, and saw five tiny figures soaring towards him. For a horrible instant he thought he and they were going to collide in a highly unpleasant way, but then they cleared him by several feet, crashing down on the netting just beyond Blade and Dani. Presto took a close look. Four men in guard uniforms and a halfling who looked awfully familiar.

Bugger.

The first commentator was screaming now and he frankly didn't care.

"Those... those look like people, right Kren?"

"Well, if they're constructs Brod, they're the best I've ever seen. I've never seen a mechanical construct look winded before. Hell, if those are constructs, I'm going to find out who made them and ask them to make me a gal I can take home with me."

The first commentator laughed nervously.

"I think you might have to ask Mrs Kren about that first!"

"Mrs Kren left me last year, Brod. I kind of figured you'd remember that. She got into Elvish practices and went off with a girl schoolteacher from the Northlands."

"You fucking imbecile!" screamed the producer down the ear-whisper. "It was in all the fucking news-slates. Just stop the senile old fart talking!"

"Anyway, back to the game. Konigshi's just thrown real, live actors into the mix. What does that mean, Kren?"

"Well, I'm not even sure it's legal, Brod. Nobody's used actors since the forties. Twelve different teams are supposed to be making this run. How can they ensure a constant level of difficulty when they're using actors?"

"I guess that's one for the after game analysis, and I think we're going to be talking about this one for a long time to come. But the Marauders are making their way up the netting, pursued by the four guard characters and the halfling, who are themselves having to fight their way through the bears."

"The halfling's just got himself a bear across the face, Brod. He looks pretty unhappy."

"This game is just getting better and better! Where do you think Konigshi's going with the guard characters, Kren? Guards and cuddly bears seems an odd story mix?"

"No idea, Brod. But it looks like the first of the Marauders are about to reach the top disc, so I guess we'll be finding out pretty soon."

By the time Presto reached the disc he was physically, mentally, and magically exhausted, and it was all he could do to haul himself onto its flat surface and then lay there, breathing heavily, and feeling the replenishing mana seeping back into his body. A little while later, Darick and the Storm arrived, looking almost as knackered as Presto felt, followed a few seconds later by Dani and Blade. Blade took a moment to kick a stray bear off the platform, and then looked around. "There's got to be something we can do here. Something to activate the next level."

"And what exactly would that be?" asked Presto, still not feeling any particular need to lift his head from the floor.

"How would I know? I was never the one who did the puzzles." Blade looked around them. "Okay, Darick and the Storm, keep the guards off. Dani and me will try to figure out what we need to do." He looked down at Presto. "Probably best you stay there and recharge."

"I'm not a battery," muttered Presto, but Blade was already turning to answer a query from the Storm.

"How the hell are we supposed to keep them off? Ask them nicely?"

Blade ripped the plastic lute from its harness on the musician's back and shoved it into his hands.

"You're the bard; play the lute."

The rock star looked at the thing he'd been given. It was a plain piece of solid white plastic in the shape of a lute with five multi-coloured buttons on its neck and some kind of sensor grid where the bridge should be. He looked back at Blade. "What the fuck's this?"

"It's a lute!"

"Where's the fucking strings?"

"Well, it's not an actual lute, but if you play it right it will weaken the bears."

"What about the guards?"

"It'll make their lights go orange."

"Will they care?"

"Erm, no. Look, just improvise." The warrior turned away from the conversation, just as the snarling face of the halfling detective appeared above the edge of the disc, conveniently framed in Presto's sideways eye-line.

"You're all under arrest!" the detective shouted. "Again!"

Chapter Thirteen

The first commentator was in full flow now.

"Well, we're still not sure what role the actors are playing, but I guess we're about to find out because the lead halfling's just reached the edge of the disk, and – oh! The bard's given him a brutal, brutal kick to the face that's sent him tumbling back down the netting."

"From the look on his face, I'd say the bard enjoyed that, Brod."

"He certainly did, Kren. Seems to be shouting something back at the halfling, who's getting up and seems to have blood all over his face!"

"Well, it was a hell of a kick, Brod, launched straight and true with both passion and venom. Sort of thing I like to see."

"Disclaimer, you twat!" shouted the voice in his ear-piece. "Disclaimer! The lawyers are going mad."

"Now of course, this is the arena, and these are—"

"Camera three, close-up – I want to see broken teeth!"

"—highly trained athletes who know what they're doing."

"You think, Brod?"

The face of the halfling loomed large on the monitors in front of them, angry and shouting.

"Well he's certainly getting into his role, Kren."

"Not hard to act angry when you've just been kicked that hard in the face, Brod."

"Very true. But it brings us back to a point you brought up earlier, Kren. How are they going to achieve consistency over the runs? Are they going to use fresh actors?"

"I think they'll certainly be needing a replacement halfling, Brod."

Words scrolled across the bottom of the monitors. The first commentator took them in as he spoke.

"And we're getting some whisper messages from some of you guys. You may recall the news stories of a couple of days ago about a bizarre stage incident involving the band, Northern Fire. Well Pella, of Coldman's Keep, thinks that the Marauder's bard is a double for their lead lutist. You want to weigh in with an opinion, Kren? I'm not sure how familiar you are with the works of the Fire?"

"It's all just noise to me, Brod. Not like the proper music we used to listen to in my day."

"Nothing's like it was in your day, eh, Kren?"

"No. Ask me, it's all turned to—"

"ANYWAY, you're watching Lastday Night AdventureSport on EBS1,

the home of AdventureSport, and we're watching Blade's Marauders attempting to solve the puzzle at the top of the conundrum that is Konigshi's floating disc. And meanwhile, they have magically animated cuddly bears coming at them up the netting, four guard characters, and a very, very angry halfling."

Blade didn't know who'd designed this scenario, but he was rapidly coming to the conclusion that he should find out just in case he ever met him at an after-match party, so he could give him several hard punches to the face interspersed with a few hard-learned pointers on game design. He hated enigmatic conundrums, and being stuck on top of a tiny, featureless disc was enigmatic to the point of infuriating. He kicked another bear off the edge and into the void, and then turned back to Dani. "Anything?"

The grifter was on her hands and knees, feeling across the bare metal surface. "No. Yes. Maybe." She stopped, and ran a hand back across the section in front of her. "This patch is warmer than the surrounding area."

Presto was looking thoughtful, lifting himself up on his elbows.

"What?" Blade asked him.

"Is it also more slippery?" the wizard asked.

Dani felt again.

"Yes."

"Then that's not metal. It's a metal coloured force-wall covering a hole in the disc." He got up onto his knees, shaking his head angrily. "I should have cast a detect spell, instead of just lying here!"

"Can you dispel it?" Blade asked.

Presto didn't reply, but instead spoke a few words of magic, waved his way through some incantations, and then pointed at the area of the disc Dani had found. A spark of power arced from his finger to the metal-looking surface, which promptly disappeared, leaving a small, square hole around six inches on the side and four inches deep. Inside was an abacus and an envelope. Dani lifted them out. "What the hell are we supposed to do with these?"

Blade looked out across the arena, seeing guards beginning to line up the other side of the force-wall surrounding the playing area. Then he sensed an almost imperceptible movement: the disc had begun to descend. As though on cue, the chime echoed around the arena, followed by another loud boom. Five more blue-clad figures arched across the arena to land on netting whose slope was decreasing with each passing second. "I'd start with opening the envelope!"

A guard had appeared at the edge of the disc in front of him. Blade ducked under the man's clumsy punch and hit him hard under the armpit with his sword. The lights on the guard's sensor harness went red. "You are dead!" said the harness's synthetic voice. "Please leave the arena!"

For a moment the guard blinked in confusion at the voice's message, before taking a step forward and throwing another slow and obvious punch. Blade ducked under that one, threw his clearly useless sword away, punched the guard hard on the jaw and then – as the man rocked on his heels – shoved him hard in the chest. The guard fell back in a low arc, beginning a balletic tumble down the netting. Blade turned back to Dani and Presto. "Whatever it tells you to do, do it fast!"

Dani quickly ripped open the envelope and pulled out the sheet of paper that lay inside. Four lines were written upon it.
Two
Three
Five
?

"It's a bloody logic test!" shouted Blade, when she read them out. "I hate bloody logic tests."

Dani took a look down the netting slope. Most of the guards were engaged in fights with the cuddly bears, which had the dual benefit of keeping both them and the bears off the disk and away from her and her comrades. But there were still plenty of both guards and bears heading up the netting towards them, including one familiar, and very pissed off looking, halfling. She looked down at Presto. "Any ideas?"

"I don't know," said the wizard. "May I have it?" He held out his hand for the paper. Dani handed it over. Presto stared hard at it for two or three seconds before looking back at her, nodding at the abacus that she still held in her other hand. "I think the answer is a number, and we're supposed to put the answer into that."

"Well, what's the number?"

"We've got two, three, five, and a question mark. It's a number sequence, but the question is which one." He thought for a moment more. "Thirteen. It's the prime numbers in the Febonecchi sequence."

Dani reached for the abacus, then paused. "Are you sure?"

"Yes!"

Blade dropped back to stand beside them. "If you get it wrong, it will probably lock you out for thirty seconds!"

"I'm bloody sure!" shouted Presto. "The sodding answer's thirteen!"

Dani nodded and lifted the abacus – and then realised she'd never actually used one. "How does this work?"

Presto swore, grabbed it from her, and started flicking at the beads. A rumbling vibration rippled through the disc. And then they started to lift.

The first commentator was scribbling on the printed notes in front of him, speaking as he did so.

"*That's a pretty impressive time on the first puzzle section, Kren. They'll pick up bonus points there.*"

"*Certainly will, Brod.*"

"*Apparently, the riddle listed the first three members of the… Feb-on-ecchi sequence of prime numbers. Did you get it, Kren?*"

"*I'm afraid I didn't, Brod. I always left that end of things to my wizard, Randell.*"

"*How is old Randell? You ever catch up with him lately, Kren?*"

"*Not since he died of unhealable stomach cancer, no.*"

The producer shouted something so loudly in the control room behind them that muffled echoes reached their commentary booth through the wooden partition. The first commentator couldn't quite make out the words, but it was fast and angry and it sounded a little like "loser" and "fired". He kept talking.

"*Anyway, the Marauders are now on their way to the next stage of the scenario. What should we be looking out for, Kren?*"

"*With a game like this, I have no idea, Brod.*"

As the disc rose higher up into the space beneath the huge domed ceiling, Dani managed to take her first proper look at their surroundings. What she could see was awe-inspiring, even under lighting that left the crowd in a shadowed gloom with only the playing area itself fully lit. Tiered seating rose steeply up from the arena's edge, broken only by the darkened openings of the access tunnels and several rings of private boxes, all of it draped in shiny gold trimmed with red velvet. She looked round at the others. Darick and the Storm looked nervous, bewildered even. Presto appeared plain, damn exhausted. And Blade? Blade just stood calm, and impassive.

Waiting.

The disc slowly rose, higher and higher. Dani looked over the edge. The bears below were motionless now, and the cops had reached the top of the netting, only to find more netting where the disc had been. The halfling detective took out a whisper, looked at its screen, and then angrily shouted something.

Blade was beside her. "The force-wall cuts out all transmissions. Stops cheating."

Dani pointed at the guards making their way down the aisles to the edge of the arena. "Doesn't really help us much. You got a plan?"

Blade shrugged. "Dunno. Get out of here. Think of something."

Somehow, Dani found herself smiling. "And there was me thinking you were just making this all up as you went along."

The disc eased smoothly to a halt, leaving them stranded some hundred and fifty feet above the arena floor. The noise of the crowd lowered to a dull, but expectant murmur. "Now what?" asked the Storm.

"I guess we're supposed to go somewhere," said Blade.

"Where?"

Presto spoke a few words, gestured, and, for an instant, sections of the space around them glowed green before disappearing. The wizard walked over to where a solid green slab a foot wide had briefly extended out from the disc, and pointed. "There's some kind of force-wall structure extending out just here."

Blade walked over to him. "That was a detect spell, right?"

"Yeah. But there's some sort of anti-detection effect hiding the rest of the structure."

The warrior turned to Dani, his hand extended. "There'll be a bag of sand in your belt-pack."

Dani quickly rummaged through the belt-pack that the changing room attendants had strapped onto her and found a clear plastic bag full of something that looked awfully like sand. She handed it over to Blade. The warrior opened the bag, pulled a handful of sand out, and threw it in a long, low fanned arc in the direction Presto had pointed. It hung, glittering, in the air before arcing into a fall. Most of it continued falling, but a line of it stopped, scattered grains hanging in the air in a narrow path extending from the disc. Blade took a step out, and then another, and then another, following the line of the hanging sand. He turned, standing apparently unsupported on thin air, and waved the others to follow him. "I figure the way out's this way."

Dani followed.

The first commentator felt now that just as the game was finding its rhythm and routine, so was he. He'd described the athletes' progress through the invisible maze of force-wall platforms, all twists, turns, and awkward backing-ups. He'd put in several intelligent asides as they made their way up and down the staircases that added a three-dimensional element to the maze. And in the three minutes that had elapsed since they'd figured out the trick with the sand, he'd even managed to pass the conversational baton to his co-commentator without producing a sound-bite that was likely to increase his chances of dismissal from "worryingly high" to "may as well place a bet on it to get something out of it". But now, finally, it looked like the Marauders were reaching the end of the run, and frankly it couldn't come too soon for him.

"So, Kren, what's your thoughts about the scenario design?"

"A bit too cerebral for me, Brod. I liked the start, but the middle period has been too much slow puzzle and not enough action. It's a good test of teamwork and efficiency, and maybe that's how they like it over in the Empire of the Sun, but I think the crowd here were hoping for a bit more."

"Fascinating as the invisible maze has been, I think I agree with you, Kren. I suppose the question is: has Konigshi got a last card up his sleeve?"

A movement on the monitors caught his attention; it was the disc slowly descending towards the guard characters waiting below. He carried on speaking, segueing into the new line as though he'd been planning it all along.

"And I guess that's the last card being played. The Marauders have got quite a head start, but the pursuing guards will have the route all marked out for them. Who's your money on, Kren?"

"With the distance they've got to go, I think the Marauders will make it. Unless Konigshi's still got tricks to spring."

The left hand monitor was zoomed in on the figures making their way across the void beneath the arena's high ceiling. The figures stopped now, apparently engaged in animated conversation.

"Seems to be a problem down in the Marauders ranks. What do you think it might be, Kren?"

"I think maybe they've run out of sand."

Chapter Fourteen

"What do you, like, mean, you've run out of sand?" asked the Storm. He'd never been too good with heights and being at the back of the line wasn't helping.

"I mean, I've run out of fucking sand!" Blade shouted back. "It's not a magic fucking bag and now it's fucking empty."

"Some escape attempt this has turned out to be," muttered Presto, just loud enough for the Storm to hear.

The crowd, quiet for the last few minutes, were starting to get back into things now. The Storm looked back, just in time to see the psycho halfling detective rising up atop the disc, accompanied by nine guards. He didn't look very happy. "Well, you'd better figure something out quick, dude," the Storm told Blade. "Because we've got company on the way."

"Can you cast something?" Blade asked, presumably at Presto. "Either to guide us, or to slow them down?"

The wizard spoke a few words of magic, then replied, "No. There's a displacement field covering this entire area. There isn't enough mana to cast anything bigger than a cigarette lighter cantrip."

The Storm took another look behind. "They're starting to get bloody close, guys!"

"I might have an idea," said Dani.

The first commentator waited for his colleague to take a sip of his drink, then asked him a question.

"So Kren, do you think this is a resource management issue or an intentional scenario challenge? Or to put it another way, did the Marauders use too much sand, or was the scenario built to need more sand than they've got?"

"I think they used too much sand, Brod. I'm baffled as to why Blade Petros was leading the way. He's a warrior and should leave scouting to his thief. I think he's finally starting to let his status go to his head."

In the monitor view, the Marauders' intense discussion paused for a moment as the unidentified thief player removed a plastic jar from her backpack and thrust it at Blade Petros. The argument resumed, with even more apparent intensity. Meanwhile, the pursuing guard characters were moving swiftly and efficiently through the maze, following the trail left by their quarry.

"It's certainly shaping up to a nail-biting end, Kren."

"It is, Brod. It is."
"Do you think they have a backup plan?"
"Well, they're certainly talking about something."

"Look, I'm not pissing in a jar in front of a hundred million viewers and that's that!"

From his position at the rear, the Storm wasn't able to see anything outside of Darick's back – and he wasn't about to lean out to peer around that at two hundred feet up on an invisible ledge, thank you very much. But he could tell from the edge in Blade's voice that the warrior wasn't in a yielding type of mood. "What's the problem?" he hissed into Darick's ear.

Darick twisted round. "Dani came up with the idea of replacing the sand with urine, but now they're arguing about who has to fill the jar."

The Storm risked a peek behind and immediately wished he hadn't. The guards were looking awfully close now, with an epically pissed-off halfling at the front. The Storm figured he was about thirty seconds away from an incident that would make this morning's encounter with Mr Fist look like a polite conversation over tea. "Tell them I'll bloody well do it, then!" The jar was swiftly passed back. The Storm paused for a moment, thought of what the halfling would do to him if he caught up, then swiftly unbuttoned his jumpsuit's flies.

For a single, horrifying, career-destroying moment, the left-hand monitor was filled with a zoomed-in shot of a heavily pierced, gold-clad penis pouring forth a yellow stream into a glass jar.

"Wide angle on camera four! Now!" screamed the producer, genuine panic in his voice.

The first commentator stifled a nervous chuckle.

"Well, that's not something you see every day, eh, Kren?"
"Depends on what kind of mens' rooms you hang around in, Brod."
"Er, yes."
"Interesting display of metal work."
"Yes, anyway, it's an interesting and perhaps radical tactic that might have the Marauders fined for ungentlemanly conduct."
"I believe it's called a Prinz Eugene."
"–And the jar is passed back to the front, and Marauders are on their way again, with Blade Petros spraying a thin stream in front of him to find the way."

But those pursuing guard characters are looking awfully close."

Blade stepped slowly forward, feet either side of the thin trail of piss that fell from a jar already more than two-thirds empty. How much more of this bloody maze could there be? Then he took just one step more, and the previously empty space beneath his feet turned a solid looking silver. He stood now on the edge of a floating slab that measured more than thirty feet square and led to a tubular slide that swooped down to and through an opening set into the base of the dome. They were here, finished. All they had to do was cross the slab and drop into the slide's welcoming maw.

Then a giant mechanical spider measuring some twenty feet across dropped out of the dark void above to land lightly just in front of him.

Not quite finished, then.

There had been some pretty dicey moments along the way, but the first commentator thought he was home free now.

"And just when the Marauders thought the run was done and dusted, just when the crowd thought the run was done and dusted, just when we thought the run was done and dusted, Konigshi surprises us again!"

"I didn't think it was done and dusted, Brod."

The first commentator could have hit his colleague, and quite possibly would have done were it not for the reactions camera mounted in their commentary cubicle and the impossibility of conducting a good old-fashioned and non-farcical fist-fight in a space that cramped. He consoled himself with a promise to do everything he could to get the senile old alcoholic sacked before the next show, took a deep breath, and resumed speaking through gritted teeth.

"Well, I guess that's why they pay you to sit alongside me, Kren."

"Guess it is, Brod."

The spider was a bastard: fast, agile, and with an AI of such viciousness and cunning that it seemed to Blade as though the devils themselves had programmed it. They'd tried going round it, but it had blocked them easily. They'd tried going under it, but it had responded with a flurry of "poison" tipped leg swipes that knocked them back and had their sensor harnesses flashing orange, red, and – in the Storm's case – black. They'd tried sending Dani scrambling over it, but that had achieved nothing save nearly losing her over the edge. If this had been a game, they'd have been on their way to a big, big loss, but this wasn't a game and points and penalties didn't matter a damn. All that mattered was getting past this sodding spider, and that was looking to be easier said than done.

This was going to end in utter humiliation and a public one at that.

He'd had games they'd screwed up so badly his team had needed a guard escort to protect them from angry punters waving now useless betting slips. But he'd never had the guards escort him out under arrest. A cough from behind roused him from his thoughts. He spun round and found the halfling cop and his nine minions all smirking and clearly spoiling for a fight.

"Are you going to come easily, or are you going to let us have some fun first?"

Quite frankly, the first commentator wasn't quite sure what was going on, but the first thing a broadcaster learns is that the red light is your god. It doesn't matter if you're about to wet yourself, or the studio is on fire, or you've just been told that your mother has only a few minutes to live – as long as that red light stays lit then you stay talking. The red light was still lit so the first commentator was still talking.

"Fascinating combat, eh, Kren?"
"Fascinating, Brod."
"What's your take on the situation?"
"I think the Marauders are in deep trouble. They're fighting both the spider and the guard characters, they look all out of ideas, and they're two people down."
"Yes. Both the cleric and the bard are flashing black, and risking a disqualification for not leaving the game immediately. I'm a little confused why they're hanging around, literally so in the case of the bard."
"Perhaps he just doesn't want to let go?"

It's amazing how much power one can find in one's fingers when one's hanging off the edge of a platform with said fingers being the only thing separating one from a very long drop to a very hard looking surface. No matter how many times the Storm's brain told his fingers that there was a net between him and the floor, and no matter how many times the cop who'd knocked him over the edge stamped sadistically on those fingers, they insisted on pursuing their own agenda, that agenda being a simple and straight-forward one of not letting go.

Ever.

The Storm was looking up, not down – he'd tried down once and it really hadn't agreed with him – and so was getting a good look at the cruel smirk plastered upon the stamping cop's face. Then the face's expression changed, from smirk to surprise, accompanied by a forward movement of his body. Ever so gracefully, like a high-diver easing into a competition dive, the cop fell forward, the elegant effect broken only by the furious backward windmilling of his arms. Then he disappeared past the Storm with a blood-curdling scream that turned, after a few seconds, into a surprised grunt, when he presumably hit the net. A second face appeared over the edge of the platform – Darick.

"Sorry!" the priest called down after the cop. Then he reached down to the Storm. "Do you want a hand?"

The first commentator decided that with the game seemingly deadlocked, it was time to begin the final preliminaries.

"So, Kren. Your player of the run?"
"It would have to be the bard, Brod."
"The bard?"
"Yeah, the bard. He's put in a pretty useless performance, but two things are standing out for me: his refusal to exit the game even after being killed, and the sheer joy with which he kicked that halfling in the face. Wonderful moment."

The first commentator could already see the complaints coming in, and tried to steer the conversation onto safer, non-racial territory.

"That would be the character of the guard leader?"
"Yeah, yeah, the halfling."
"Well, I don't think we should attach any significance to the fact that a halfling actor was playing the role."
"Rubbish. It being a halfling he kicked in the face was what made it so funny! Like stamping on a puppy!"

The red light went out. And stayed out. "What's going on?" asked the first commentator.

It took a few seconds for the producer's reply to arrive at his headset. "No idea. Someone at network just pulled the plug."

The first commentator took a hard look at his colleague, who merely shrugged, and took an even larger than usual swig of his something-and-ice.

One of the floating cameras that had been following them all game swooped down to follow Presto as he ducked and wove through the chaos of the battle upon the platform. Here he was, his pictographic memory packed full of more spells than a superstore branch of Pete's Adventure Warehouse, and he was rendered helpless because of a total absence of free mana. It would have been enough to make him cry had he not been on camera before a few hundred million people. He skipped over an unconscious guard whom Blade had punched out thirty seconds ago, ducked under a punch, punched his assailant back, and then was stopped nearly in his tracks by a flash of memory so vivid it was practically painful. Stupid party trick it might be, but right now it could be a lifesaver.

He skipped back over the unconscious guard and reached down to grab the man's torch. With one fluid movement he unscrewed the end, then flipped it up, allowing the mana-battery inside to drop out into his waiting hand. He dropped to one knee, placed the battery against the floor with one hand, and then paused for a moment to deliver a big beaming smile into the camera, which had edged right up to him.

"And remember children, don't try this at home unless you're a fully trained wizard." He raised the now battery-less torch high. "And only then when you're drunk at a party." Then he smashed the torch down onto the battery. The battery's thin metal case buckled, allowing the resin honeycomb inside to first deform, then crack, releasing all its stored energy in one insane, nerve-burning release. Presto screamed in both agony and ecstasy, a scream that started as pain but segued neatly into the words of magic. He caught the released mana, shaped it, and then cast it back out. For just an instant, a roughly circular area of the force-slab blinked out of existence, allowing the mechanical spider to fall through the resulting hole. Presto still had dregs of mana remaining, just enough for him to spin round and cast the same partial dispelling spell on those areas of the force slab where the halfling cop and the seven remaining active guards were standing. They too fell, dreamlike, some stunned, some screaming, through their individual holes just as the surface blinked back into grey-silver and apparent solidity.

Blade caught him just as he was about to collapse. "I ain't quite sure what you just did, but it was bloody good."

Presto waved a weak hand in reply, then pointed to the slide.

"Good thinking," said Blade. He dragged Presto over to the slide, loaded him on feet-first, and then gave him a good shove on his way.

The wizard accelerated through one swoop and round a long sweeping bend, then found himself hurtling through a dark opening. He felt the G-force of a very steep and sharp drop, followed by an upward rise that slowed him somewhat – and then he was out of the blackness and sliding to an awkward crumpled stop on a shiny wooden floor. Light flooded the room from the windows set along the far wall. A nervous looking attendant dragged him clear a second or so before Darick popped out of the chute. The Storm, Dani, and Blade followed in quick order.

A stern looking man approached with a clipboard. "Not too good a run, I'm afraid," he said. "You were disqualified for twice continuing play after death status was reached." He pointed at the Storm and then Darick. "Mind you, with the amount of deviations from the script, I'm not sure it's even worth scoring it." He sniffed.

Blade walked straight past Presto and the scorer, to look out of the windows. "Sorry guys," he said, shaking his head. "There's a shit load of city guards out there. Looks like I led you off the frying grill and straight onto the coals."

Presto forced himself upright, staggered over to where Blade stood, and looked out at the plaza far below. There were indeed a lot of guards out there. Scores of buggies and hundreds of blue uniforms, ringing the arena in multiple lines. They were trapped, like crabs in a pot waiting to be thrown into boiling water. He looked over at the Storm. "Perhaps kicking our halfling friend in the face wasn't the cleverest move. I have a horrible feeling we might be meeting him soon."

Chapter Fifteen

Blade felt a surge of anger. This was his fault. He'd led them here. He needed to lead them out. "Bollocks to this!" he shouted. "I'm not just going to walk back to them so they can frame us for something we never did when I don't even know why they're framing us."

Dani caught his eye. "You got any suggestions?"

Blade looked at the sniffy scorer with the clipboard, who was still staring haughtily at them. "Take a hostage?"

The scorer ignored him and continued speaking in a tone that was somewhere between patronising and sarcastic. "If you could please vacate the area, you'll find the post-run changing rooms where they usually are, down the far staircase. And as always, your clothes and personal possessions will have been brought there from the pre-run changing rooms."

Nobody moved.

Blade noticed Presto staring at something on the far wall. "How many people are there in this arena?" the wizard asked.

It was the scorer who answered him. "I believe that today is a full attendance of eighty thousand, four hundred."

The wizard stepped over to the thing on the wall that had attracted his attention. It was a fire alarm, a bright red button under shiny glass. "Well, I think it's time for them to be leaving." He muttered a few words and waved a finger at a paper-towel filled bin, which promptly burst into flames, then smashed the glass and pressed the button. A chorus of whooping alarms erupted throughout the building, and from the arena beyond came the muffled sound of eighty thousand and four hundred people groaning with the realisation that their evening had just been ruined. Presto looked back at Blade and the others, smiling, and then nodded at the door. "Didn't your mothers ever tell you that you're supposed to leave a building when the fire alarm goes off?"

By the time they got two floors down, they were being joined by cleaners, maintenance men, and other various worker types. After another two floors, they were being joined by the crowd who'd been sitting in the cheap seats at the highest, farthest reaches of the arena, where the players were generally no more than multi-coloured ants somewhere in the distance. And by the time they reached the ground floor they were part of a swell of humanity so great that exiting the arena was destiny rather than choice. The crowd poured out through doors and barriers that had been thrown wide open, and scattered into the streets beyond like ants leaving the nest. Blade led them into a narrow side street and then a couple of even narrower alleys, where they paused for a moment, hidden behind a giant dumpster. He checked behind them. No one seemed to be following them. "Okay, now what?"

"We need to lose these orange outfits," said Dani. "We stand out a mile."

"No shit! Any ideas?"

"Yeah. Wait here."

She disappeared around the far corner of the alley. A minute went by, then another, and then a couple more, long enough now for tension to start mounting.

"Do you think she's all right?" asked Darick.

"You think maybe she's, like, ditched us?" asked the Storm.

"No," Blade told them. Blade was a man who assigned trust on the basis of intuition, and as ironic a thought as it was to have about someone who he strongly suspected made a living as a professional criminal of some kind, everything told him that Dani was someone he could trust.

Thirty seconds later, she confirmed his intuitive trust by reappearing around the corner, dressed now in a stylish smock that neatly complemented her cropped, blonde hair, her arms laden with plastic-wrapped business suits and shirts. She handed them out one by one. "I had to judge the sizes by eye," she explained, "so they might be a little off."

"Where in the planes of hell did you get these from?" Blade asked.

"Sorry, mate," she replied. "Grifter's code. Can't reveal secrets."

Blade gave her a hard look.

She shrugged. "I noticed a dry cleaners' when we came down the street and figured there'd be a back entrance down the alleyway. And there was."

"So you broke in and stole some other people's clothes?" asked Darick, shocked.

"Yeah. It's a bit less subtle than I'd normally pride myself on, but I figured it was an emergency."

"But that's theft!"

The Storm, who was already pulling on his illicitly-acquired trousers, paused. "I'm sure the SkyFather will understand given the circumstances, Father."

"I'm not sure about that."

The Storm thought for a moment as he zipped up his flies. "Didn't the god-prophet Muna once steal a loaf of bread from a tax collector?"

"Well, I think you're drastically simplifying the theology behind—"

"Muna's the patron-god of grifters," interrupted Dani.

"Yeah?" replied the Storm. "Never knew that."

Darick looked as if he was about to continue the argument, but then gave up and began removing his suit from its plastic wrapping. "I'm not happy about this," he muttered.

"Objection noted," said Blade, who'd already put his suit on. "And the next question is, where now? I figure we need somewhere to hole up, but they might be watching all our places."

Dani looked awkwardly away.

"You know somewhere?" Blade asked her.

"I might know someone."

"Someone who you can trust?"

"Yeah." The grifter thought for a moment. "I need to find a whisper box I can call her from. Make sure she's in. And that she's okay with me dropping you guys on her."

"You sure you can trust her?"

Dani looked Blade straight in the eye. "Always. Only one I ever could."

After making a whisper call from a badly vandalised call-box outside a foul smelling fast food joint, Dani led them across the city by worm, obtaining five tickets by a method that appeared to involve a piece of chewing gum paper inserted into a strategic spot.

"Old design flaw they've never bothered to fix," she explained to Darick when he asked. "The peppermint in the gum's faintly magical, and the residue of that in the paper breaks the circuit."

After a change from the Red line to the Green line, and a long winding walk through a part of town that Darick found frankly scary, they arrived at a badly painted wooden door set at the top of an iron fire escape that wound up the back of a downmarket general store. Dani rapped lightly on the door.

"Would you like us to wait outside?" Darick asked.

Dani shook her head. "Don't want people noticing."

The door opened, to reveal a redheaded vision of a girl who Darick would probably have thought stunningly beautiful if he hadn't taken a vow of celibacy, and if she hadn't been so clearly upset.

"You'd better come in," the girl said, sighing, before turning on her heel and walking away down the hallway and into the room beyond. The five of them followed her into what turned out to be a small, but tastefully decorated room with a kitchen off one corner and a sofa along the far wall. Darick settled himself on the sofa along with Presto and the Storm and tried not to feel like a voyeuristic intruder at a private family row.

"There's just been a news-flash on the crystal," the girl said, shaking her head. "You're wanted for... Actually, I don't think I want to say what you're wanted for."

"They mentioned me?" Dani asked.

"No," the girl said, then pointed first at Blade and then the Storm. "They mentioned him and him a lot. They mentioned your other two friends briefly. Then they referred to you as an unidentified woman. But how long's that going to last?"

Dani shrugged helplessly.

"What in the skies above have you got yourself involved in?" the redheaded girl asked. "Look, I've never talked about what you do. Figured I was best off not knowing. But now, this..."

"Would you two perhaps like some privacy?" asked Darick.

"Where?" the girl asked him, a bitter smile on her face. "This is a one room apartment, unless you're including the bathroom!"

Darick looked round at the others. "Bathroom's good, right chaps?"

If there was one person Dani had never wanted to hurt, it was Laliana. Dani was the big sister. It was supposed to be her looking after Laliana, not Laliana looking after her. Dani gulped, and thought, and tried to figure out just where to begin, but then Laliana took her hand, squeezed it, and smiled an almost-smile. "How about you just start at the beginning?"

Her sister was angry, but for her, not at her, and right now that was good to know. So she did as Laliana suggested, and told the story, starting with the initial kidnapping by the spell and moving through the attempts to dispel it, the journey to Craagon's Reach, and the arrests upon their return. After she'd finished talking, Laliana spent several moments in thought before finally speaking. "So you've got no idea why someone decided to frame you?"

"No. Look we just need somewhere to crash for a few hours, the night maybe, while we figure out what to do next. I know this is a big ask but—"

"You can stay as long as you need; them too."

"You're not involved in this. You don't have to be. I'm not even sure you should be."

"Don't be stupid. If you're in trouble, I'm in trouble. Us against the world, right?"

Dani shook her head. "I'm not sure."

"Dani." Laliana took her hand and squeezed it. "You're my big sister. You were always looking out for me, and now it's my turn to look out for you."

For the first time in a while, Dani felt like maybe things were going to be okay. "Thanks, sis."

Laliana smiled. "Anytime. And I think maybe we ought to get your friends out of my bathroom before they use up all the oxygen."

They'd been in the flat for three days and had achieved nothing save avoiding capture. According to the crystal, which they'd spent most of those three days watching, said capture was "inevitable", "imminent", and "necessary for the maintenance of public confidence in the guards and the justice system".

Blade was pacing like a caged tiger Darick had once seen in a zoo – and frankly, the flat wasn't big enough for pacing. The rest of them were still hunched around the crystal, save for Laliana who was insisting on cooking them breakfast each morning before heading off to work.

The man whose face currently occupied the crystal's screen smiled a big toothy smile, the sort of smile that extreme wealth brings, both in the reassuring financial security it affords, and in the elaborate dental work that it allows one to install. "And now," the man declared, "we enter the bonus jackpot round, where all answers score double. Your starter for twenty: what was the last battle of the Orcan Wars?"

"Dantonville," said Presto.

On the crystal, a buzzer buzzed, and the view zoomed in on a nervous young man standing behind a garishly coloured plinth. "Dantonville," said the man.

"That's correct, Darv! And now your bonus question. In what year was the battle of Dantonville?"

"Nine fifty-seven," said Presto.

"Erm... Nine seventy-two?"

"Idiot."

"I'm sorry, Darv, the correct answer is nine fifty-seven. Now onto another open question, fingers on buzzers... Which second age painter—"

The crystal clicked off. They all looked around and found Blade holding the control wand. "Are we going to actually do anything?" he asked, a barely controlled edge in his voice.

"We're lying low," said Dani. "Waiting for things to die down."

"Fine. We've laid low. Things have died down. They're not going to die down much more, and the longer we wait the colder the trail gets."

"Yeah, maybe," replied the grifter, not quite conceding.

Blade looked around for support, but got only vague shrugs and a few longing looks at the now blank crystal screen. Silence settled.

Back in the seminary, when he was training to be a priest, Darick had attended a course in conflict resolution. It was part of a new package of training for what the church described as "the challenges of the modern age", and which also included public relations, relationship counselling, and a whole bunch of psychological screening tests that had a fancy name but basically amounted to "Dear gods, we can't afford any more scandals with small boys." He thought perhaps he should put that conflict resolution training into practice. "Let's just say that we were to decide to do something," he said.

"We haven't agreed that," said Dani.

"No, but let's just say for the sake of argument that we did."

"Okay."

"If we did decide that, what would we do?" He looked at Blade.

The sportsman thought for a moment, then shrugged helplessly. "I don't know. I just figure we need to do something."

Presto leaned forward, his face set in a concentrated frown. "The key is still the spell. It always was."

"I thought the key was finding out who the bastards who framed us are," said the Storm. He'd been very twitchy for the first two days, but was now starting to settle down, though his eyes were still slightly saucer-like.

"No. That's our goal. But it was the spell that triggered these events and the answers will likely lie there."

"Yeah," said Dani. "That makes sense. But how can we study the spell? The last time didn't go so good, and that was when we had access to a full lab."

"The trouble is that we never had the actual living spell to analyse. All we had was the secondary spell created when it was cast. What we really need is the original spell's source text."

"Its source text?" asked Blade.

"The text that would be written in the spell book of the wizard who cast it; the instructions that would tell him how to cast the spell. Not that anyone uses big leather tomes anymore, of course. It's all on interactive readers."

"But how are we supposed to find its caster's spell book when the whole problem is that we have no idea who cast it?" asked Dani.

Presto smiled. "Remember I said it seemed like an old spell?"

"Yeah?"

"A really old spell?"

"And?"

"What do you think wizards do with their spell books and their notes and all that stuff when they die?"

"Leave it to a university or something?"

"Bingo!"

Blade was enthusiastically stabbing the air now with his finger. "Okay, so Presto needs to go to a university with a good library, and see if he can find the spell's whatever text."

"Source text."

"Whatever. Where's the best library for this sort of thing?"

"The Imperial University, here in Empire City. My alma mater."

"Your alma what?"

"It's where I studied, and where I then worked as a lecturer and researcher, until the incident that I seem to recall us discussing a few days ago."

"So you were probably fairly well known there, right?"

A rueful smile played across the wizard's face. "Fairly. And my reaction to my dismissal was perhaps a tad extreme."

"How extreme?" asked Blade.

"Well, first I told the vice-chancellor what I thought of him, both professionally and personally. Then I repeated the process with the head of Magical Studies, taking particular care to mention his affair with the vice-chancellor's wife. Then things escalated a little."

"Things got worse?" asked the Storm. "Than that?"

"There was some dispute about who cast the first spell, but in the cold light of day I suppose I really ought to admit that it was in fact me. Aura-shock, right across the chest. Bastard never saw it coming." The wizard shook his head. "Anyway, the university guards were called, it all got a bit unpleasant, and I ended up being carried out bound and gagged and told never to return. Oh, and then they took my license away."

Dani coughed. It seemed to Darick that she was trying to frame her words carefully. "So it could be said that you're probably quite well known at Imperial U. Bit of a legendary figure, and not necessarily in a good way?"

"Yes."

"Isn't the Imperial University the one with big stone walls around it?" asked Blade.

Presto nodded. "And there's a whole load of modern technology added on top of all that. Lots of valuable stuff there, and they don't like mixing with the proles."

"So," said Dani. "All we've got to do is figure out a way not only to get you past the walls, but also to get you all the way into the library, without anyone recognising you?"

Presto smiled. "That's about it." He thought for a moment. "Would be nice to see the old place again."

Chapter Sixteen

Sergeant Tormac had been serving in the Imperial University Guard Force for more than thirty years now, and in that time had soaked up the ancient institution's many and various traditions like a sponge plunged into water. And chief among those traditions was that when a university guardsman stood at his gate that guardsman was god. No one – student, professor, vice-chancellor, or the Emperor himself – could pass through those gates without submitting to the searching gaze of the guardsman on the gate. That's how it had always been, and that's how it always would be.

Tormac had served on the gate so long that that he sensed its rhythms like a salmon senses the river. And something in those rhythms caused him to look up now, an hour into his morning shift, just as some new arrivals arrived at his realm. There were two of them, carefully shepherding a wooden box that floated between them. The box was of impressive dimensions – about six feet long by three feet wide by four feet high – and looked to be expertly constructed from some expensive and highly lacquered wood. Brass fittings capped its various corners and small, but ornate, carvings decorated its outer surface.

There was a door on the side of the box facing Tormac, about two feet high and eighteen inches wide, locked shut with a shiny brass padlock. The man leading the box was short and dark and vaguely effeminate and wore long flowing robes of the style worn in the burning lands that lay far to the south of the Empire. Tormac – who always claimed that he was "not prejudiced, but" – made sure his pain-stick was hanging from his belt, and strode out to challenge the man. "Good day, sir, how can I help you?"

The man gave him a confused look, and pointed through the open gateway. "We wish to enter the university," he said, in tones that to Tormac's ears sounded strange and foreign and just a tad too high-pitched. "We are studying here."

"Certainly. If you could just show me your student identification card." He held out his hand.

The man looked confused. "No, it is not I who is the student. It is my wife who is visiting the university. I am merely going in as her guest. She will sign me in."

Tormac looked at the other figure. It was swaddled in various robes and wore some kind of turban, but he could see enough to know that if that was the man's wife, then she was the ugliest looking woman he'd ever seen.

The first man caught Tormac's gaze and reacted angrily, his voice growing shrill. "That is not my wife! That is her eunuch!"

Tormac took a longer look at the second figure. The bloke certainly didn't look very happy, but that probably wasn't surprising if the poor bastard was missing a couple of key bolts from his undercarriage. The guardsman took a quick glance around the area to check he hadn't missed anything, and then returned his attention to the man. "But your wife isn't here?" he asked carefully.

"Of course she is here!"

The bloke was looking seriously angry now. Tormac considered giving him the pain-stick, but the thought of the hours he'd have to spend filling in the paperwork for pain-sticking a non-student dissuaded him. He decided to just play it polite but dumb for now. He looked first left, then right. "I can't see your wife here."

The man looked at Tormac as though he were an imbecile, then pointed at the box. "She is in the box!"

"In the box?"

"Yes! My wife and I are members of the Church of the Sacred Box and she is in the sacred box!"

Oh gods, thought Tormac. It's one of them magic box nutters. "Well, does your wife have ID?" he asked.

The man banged on the side of the box. "Woman! He wants to see your ID!"

A small flap set into the door hinged upwards, and a couple of manicured fingers emerged holding a student ID card. The man grabbed it and shoved it into Tormac's hands. Tormac ran it through his reader. The screen filled with data read from the University's oracle, indicating that Mrs Amida Bacshar was indeed a post-graduate student at the university. "Okay sir, the card is valid, but I need to run an aura scan to verify that your wife is indeed the person who this card is registered to. If she could perhaps leave the box for a moment?"

"What?" the man spat.

"If she could get out of the box?"

The man gave a snort so long it would not have disgraced a stallion who'd just had its member trodden on, and when he resumed speaking his words were spat out with undisguised venom. "My wife was placed in that very box when she was just twenty minutes old and has not left it in the twenty-seven years since. She has lived, learned, suffered illness, and given birth to three children in that box. And, heavens above forbid, when she dies, she will be buried in that box. It is her haven, her protector, her sanctuary. It shields her from the weapons of those who might harm her and from the cruel eyes of those who might judge her. When people address the box they are forced to address the mind within and not the body that contains the mind!"

"Well, yes, but—"

The man reached into his robes and pulled out a brass key that hung from a gold chain around his neck. He looked lovingly for a moment at the padlock that secured the box's narrow door, then returned his withering gaze to Tormac. "When my beloved wife's father entrusted me with the key to her box, it was the proudest day of my life."

Tormac noticed that there were two other keys hanging from the chain. "But you have two other keys?"

The man shrugged. "I have two other wives."

Tormac lifted the reader, awkwardly. "Well, you know, I can't scan her through the box."

The man fixed him with a very fierce glance. "You would ask her to leave a sacred sanctuary that has protected her for her entire life merely because you think she is a liar?"

"I didn't say she was a liar," protested Tormac.

"And yet you do not believe her when she says that the card is hers? What is that, but an accusation of lying?"

"But she hasn't said anything to me at all!" exploded Tormac. "I haven't even seen her! All I've seen is a couple of fingers and a bloody box!"

The man staggered back, displaying such shock and horror that it was as though Tormac had rammed the pain-stick up his arse and dialled it to max. "You insult the sacred box? You speak of it as covered in blood?"

Oh shit, thought Tormac. He tried a placatory smile. "Look, I wasn't meaning anything—"

The man cut him off with a sharp wave of his hand. "This behaviour is unacceptable. You have humiliated my wife, and discriminated against her on the basis of her religion. She will not stand for this. I will not stand for this. My community will not stand for this." The man reached into his robes and pulled out a whisper. "I shall call my friends and my brothers and the priests at my temple. You, sergeant, will soon find yourself facing the righteous fury of my people. Here. Within the hour. We will force you to allow my wife to enter with her religious faith respected."

A chill was running up and down Tormac's back, like the touch of death on a man's last day. He could see it now: the screaming mob; the flaming effigies; the placards declaring, "Burn those who insult the sacred box of peace!"; the crystal news teams, lapping it all up. The vice-chancellor would be there, with the chief commissioner of the university guards and the head of public relations alongside him, and they'd all know exactly who they could pin the blame on. Him. Sergeant Tormac, 4823, nice chap, shame we had to sack him. Even deeper shame about those chaps who broke into his house and killed him. Still, let's hope that's the end of it.

This situation had the potential to be very, very bad, terminally so.

Tormac stepped forward and put on the sincerest face he could summon. "Sir. I'm very sorry for any offence that I might have inadvertently caused. I can promise you that it wasn't intentional, but I think in this case I can use my discretion and allow your wife to enter without being aura-scanned." He offered the identity card back to the man.

The man considered this for a moment, then took the card, smiling a very tight-lipped smile as he did so. "Well, I suppose that will be acceptable. But if I ever have a repeat of this behaviour I will accept no apology." He nodded to the eunuch, then strode through the gate, the box gliding smoothly behind him.

Tormac let out a breath he hadn't known he'd been holding. That had been the sort of encounter that could ruin a man's entire day. He sat back in his cubby-hole and tried to focus on his news-slate. Maybe the next person attempting to pass through his gate would be a late-running student who'd missed the overnight curfew; someone he could pain-stick.

That would put his day back on track.

With six people in it, the flat had been claustrophobic; with only three it now seemed empty. Blade understood why he and the Storm, celebrities both, had been left behind. But it didn't make it any easier. He needed to get out. And he missed his kids. How were they doing right now? What might they have heard?

The Storm arrived back from the kitchen alcove clutching a couple of steaming mugs. He handed one to Blade and one to Laliana, who wasn't due on shift until that evening, then headed back into the tiny kitchen to get his own drink. Blade took a sip of the coffee, finding it to be hot, strong and sweet, just as he liked it. And just what he used to jokingly tell Toozie she was like. He wondered how she was doing.

The Storm sat down in the chair opposite him. "You okay, dude?" he asked.

Blade shook his head. "Just thinking about things. Family. You know."

The Storm nodded. "Family's the thing you miss, once you haven't got it anymore."

Blade gave him a "go on" type of nod. The musician paused for a moment, and then continued.

"I never really knew my dad. It was my mum who bought me up. She scrimped and saved to get me lute lessons because she was convinced I had some sort of talent."

"Well, she was right!" said Laliana, who was sitting on the sofa next to Blade with her feet curled up beneath her. "Look at what you achieved with Northern Fire."

The Storm gave her a wan smile. "I don't think Northern Fire was what she had in mind. Anyhow, she never lived long enough to see it, so I guess it doesn't matter."

She leaned over and gave his knee a quick pat and him a quick smile. "At least you got to know her. I don't remember either of my parents."

"Yeah. Dani told us. Sorry."

She shrugged. "It's okay. Never miss what you never had and all that." She paused for a moment. "What about you, Blade?"

This wasn't something Blade normally dwelled upon. Serious A-Sport fans generally knew his family history anyway, and made sure not to ask. "My dad was in the game," he told them. "Pretty good, but not great. So he decided that what he couldn't do, I would. Drills, practice, and games from when I was four years old."

"Is that so bad?" the Storm asked. "Look where he got you."

"Yeah, but I wasn't a son to him, I was a project. And my mum just left him to it. Only real family I ever had was Toozie and the kids, and I sure screwed that up."

Laliana gave him a reassuring smile. "Maybe when this is all over, you might get a chance to try and make that better?"

"You think this is going to get better?"

Laliana fixed Blade with a stern look. "Well, if this Toozie was so great, why'd you screw it up?"

It was a question Blade had asked himself a thousand times, but one he'd never had the guts to actually answer. He looked at the Storm for support, but only got a not-so-helpful shrug in return. "I was eighteen when we got together, she was seventeen. Things were different then."

"How so?"

The Storm answered while Blade was still thinking. "That was before you were famous, right?"

"Yeah. I was just an apprentice; a trainee on a youth feeder team trying to prove that I was more than just my father's son. I think most people figured I was only there because he'd pulled strings. No one thought I'd amount to much, including him. Then I met Toozie, and she didn't care who my dad was, or what I could do in an A-Sport arena."

"So what went wrong?"

What had gone wrong? They'd been an item within a day, soul mates within a week, and living together in a one-room hovel within two months. By his nineteenth birthday Blade had graduated to the junior warrior's slot on a senior team and they'd moved into their first proper home, a two bedroomed apartment on the edge of the canal district. Blade had once heard it said that life was wasted on the young, and he now knew that to be true. Those years in that apartment had been the best years of his life, but he'd let them slip through his fingers like sand in the surf. Too young to appreciate what he'd had; too stupid to realise that he'd never have it again.

"So what went wrong?" Laliana asked again.

"What he said," Blade told her. "I got famous."

Chapter Seventeen

Dani waited until they rounded the corner into the main university square before she let out her breath. "Gods, for a moment there I thought he wasn't going to go for it."

Darick came round the box and planted himself in front of Dani, a finger scratching an itch under his turban. The box stopped moving. "I'm not happy about this!"

"I know."

"It's an abuse of a religion!"

"It's an abusive religion that deserves to be abused."

There was a knocking from the box, and the small flap set in the door opened. Presto's voice emerged. "What's the hold up?"

"We're debating the ethics of our actions."

"Why?"

Darick bent down to the flap. "I thought we were merely going to use the box to get you through unobserved, but we manipulated that man on the gate and sowed fear and distrust of a religion in the process."

Presto didn't immediately answer, taking, presumably, a moment to think, although with the box you couldn't really tell. He could have been scratching his nuts for all Dani knew. Eventually a reply came back. "Didn't a famous archbishop once say that the achievements justify the methods?"

Darick shrugged awkwardly. "Yes, Idenn the First."

"Shortly before he led a crusade against a particularly stubborn orc tribe," added Dani.

"Well, yes."

"Which resulted in the deaths of over two thousand orc younglings?"

Darick looked pained. "It wasn't a particularly good time for the church, and I personally feel that his interpretation of scripture wasn't totally sound." The priest looked down for a moment, and then sighed. "Perhaps we should leave this discussion for a later date."

"Agreed."

An upward pointing thumb emerged from the box.

Dani pulled a folded piece of paper from a pocket somewhere inside her robes and opened it up, revealing the sketch-map that

Presto had drawn the previous evening. She took a moment to orient herself and then pointed across the square. "Back entrance to the library's over there. Let's go."

She set off, the box floating loyally in her wake.

The back entrance to the library turned out to be up a not particularly spacious spiral staircase constructed of stone so aged that several millennia of treading feet had worn depressions in it. Built in an era when issues of access basically boiled down to "Those who can walk can enter, those who can't walk are cursed by the gods and are lucky we're not burning them at the stake", it had clearly not been designed to allow the passage of a wooden box measuring some six feet by four feet by three feet. This fact was neatly demonstrated by it taking a mere twenty-five seconds for Dani and Darick to get the box stuck to a degree that could easily be described as "fast" and possibly approached "permanent".

"Try pushing the back section in a bit," Dani told Darick.

The priest grabbed hold of a protruding handle and pulled hard, producing a sharp grunt from his gut but zero movement from the box. He shook his head.

Dani thought for a moment. "Maybe it's the lift field that's holding it in place. I'll try turning it off." She fished the box's controller from inside her robes and flicked the switch. From inside the now sharply inclined box came a muffled scream and then a dull thud, at which point she remembered that the lift field also generated a localised gravitation field that kept the interior of the box at its own local level, no matter what the box's actual attitude might be. Or at least it did until some idiot turned the field off.

Muffled cursing emerged from the box's interior.

Dani crawled up over the box's near edge and dangled down over the side to where she could reach the flap. She lifted it up. "Sorry 'bout that. We were trying to get the box unstuck."

"I didn't realise it was stuck!" said Presto.

"Yeah. We thought turning off the field might unstick it."

"Did it?"

"Don't know. Hang on a minute." She hauled himself back over the box's edge, braced her shoulder up against the polished surface, and gave a hard shove. The box entirely failed to move. She gave up, and crawled back over the top to hang down beside the flap.

"No."

The wizard's reply was strained and a little nervous. "Then I'll just have to get out here."

"What if someone sees you?"

"Do you have an alternative plan?"

"No."

"Then open the sodding box. I'm getting seriously claustrophobic in here."

Dani lifted the key chain from around her neck, selected the appropriate key – which wasn't the one she'd shown to the gate-sergeant – and opened the padlock. She carefully twisted it free of the door's latch and pulled the door open. Presto's pale and strained face appeared. The wizard awkwardly levered himself out of the small opening, and into the equally small void between the box and the staircase wall. "You may as well lock it back up. It might delay anyone who finds it."

Dani nodded. "Good idea." She quickly threaded the padlock's shackle through the latch and snapped the lock shut, then headed off after Presto, who was already climbing the stairs. The wizard stopped two landings up, opened the door a crack and peered through, then paused for a moment to allow Dani and Darick to catch up.

Above the door was the caption: "Department of Magical Studies Library".

Presto bent down to whisper in Dani's ear. "There's a librarian at the desk at the far end of the room, but she's busy with some paperwork, so if we go in and turn straight left, I think we'll be okay. I can't see anyone else around."

"Okay, let's go," Dani told him.

Dani eased through the door, and turned left, Presto and Darick following her, into a room so huge their footsteps echoed as they made their way along its edge.

The cavernous space was four storeys high, its four walls each divided into upper and lower portions by a solid stone balcony that encircled the room. The entire surface of those four walls, both upper and lower portions, was covered by oak bookcases; bookcases that were themselves so tall that extended shelves set halfway up their expanses served as additional balconies, accessed by steep sets of ladder-like stairs. Equally tall freestanding bookcases filled the room's interior, with additional spidery wooden catwalks threading across the room and along the bookcases to allow access to their upper levels.

Halfway along the back aisle they found a small table with an oracle sitting upon it. Presto sat down before it and flicked the keyboard. The previously darkened crystal screen came to life. "Okay," the wizard said. "They've been spending ten million golds a year for the last twenty years supposedly indexing all this stuff. Let's see if they've actually achieved anything." He began to tap away on the keyboard.

"Anything we can do to help?" asked Darick.

"Yes," Presto replied, not breaking from his tapping. "You can stop interrupting."

Idly, Dani began to examine the books nearest her. The text on the leather spines was handwritten, archaic, and so faded as to be barely legible. She leaned forward for a closer look, running her finger along the spines.

"I wouldn't," said Presto, still tapping away.

Dani turned back to face him. "Why not?" she asked.

The wizard continued speaking, never once looking away from the screen. "This is the black magic section. Demonology, necromancy, and various practises so dodgy they never gave them a name."

Dani quickly jerked her finger away.

Presto looked up now. "Pretty much every book there reeks of evil and was spawned in blood, and I'm not necessarily talking metaphorically. There are tomes in here so steeped in dark and terrible magic that they possess a degree of self-awareness, a degree that so sufficiently approaches sentience that activities performed on them require the permission of the university's ethics committee. Oh, and I'm pretty sure some of those volumes are bound in human skin."

Presto turned his attention back to the keyboard, but continued speaking. "I certainly wouldn't recommend those books to anyone with a vested interest in preserving his own sanity."

"Have you read any of them?" asked Darick.

"Yes."

"What was it like?"

The tapping stopped, as Presto sat back and considered the question. "You know that moment when you wake up from a really bad dream, during that awful, choking, confused second before your conscious sanity snaps back into place? That, but worse, and continuing through each turn of a page."

"So not particularly good then," said Dani.

"No. And that's precisely why I headed for this section. It's always quiet here, and this oracle's nearly always free."

Silence settled, broken only by the sound of Presto tapping away on the keyboard, and the almost imperceptible hum of a faraway and whispered conversation. Dani sat down on a spare chair and tried not to think about the books that lay behind her.

Several minutes of tapping later, the wizard let out a relieved sigh. "I think I've got something. Aisle D, Case 57, Shelf 5. General Archives of the Eighth Century."

Dani reached into an inside pocket for the pen and notepad she'd put there, intending to give them to Presto so that he could note down the details, but, having sniffed once in satisfaction, the wizard pushed back his chair and headed for the library's interior. Dani put the pen and notepad back, then nodded to Darick. The two of them set off after the wizard, following him through a maze of tangled bookcases, up a rickety looking wooden staircase so steep as to be more of a ladder with ambition, and along a narrow wooden balcony that was not much more than a moderately wide shelf with a railing. Presto stopped in front of a particular section and began to run his finger along the spines, searching.

After a few seconds he found something. "Here it is." He pulled out a small but fat leather bound notebook. There was no marking on the cover save for a yellowing sticker on the spine bearing a long string of numbers.

"What is it?" Dani asked.

"A spell journal and notebook of one Magninninto Kellen."

"Kellen, as in a three hundred Kellen kettle or a ten MegaKellen mana storage unit?"

"That's the one."

"And he's got something to do with our spell?"

Presto tapped the book. "Don't know. I'll have to read through this. The index didn't give any kind of page number."

There was the sound of footsteps from the polished wooden floor below, and a clearing of the throat. "Excuse me," said a voice from the direction of the footsteps. "Readers are required to sign in at the reception desk before using the library."

Dani motioned to Presto to look away, and then leaned over the railing to face the source of the interruption. It was a middle-aged woman, with a set of glasses hanging from a chain around her neck that neatly framed a distinctly sour expression. Dani gave the woman her best reassuring smile, hoping it still worked when she was pretending to be a male desert nomad. "Sorry, we forgot. We'll just finish what we're doing here and then come over to you."

"I'm sorry, I must insist that your friend puts that book back and that you immediately come to the reception desk. And I'm afraid that I'll have to take down your details and report you to the university authorities. Now come down here, right now!" The woman walked to the base of the staircase they'd climbed a few minutes earlier, and planted herself, arms folded.

"We'd better get going before she makes a scene," Dani whispered. The other two nodded. She moved in front of Presto, shielding the wizard while he slipped the journal into his jacket. Then they walked along the catwalk balcony and down the stairs, Presto looking everywhere except at the librarian.

The woman was waiting for them, foot tapping. "This is most irregular, and certainly not—"

She stopped speaking and took a very hard look at Presto. "I remember you! You used to work here! You're the one who…" She took a step back and began to scream for help.

Presto spoke a few words and waved his hands and then shot a bolt of energy at her. The sound of her screaming stopped; her mouth was still opening and closing, but no sound was coming out. "Mute spell," he explained. "We'd better get going." Abruptly, an alarm began to sound, a harsh honking sound that echoed around the building. "Dammit!" said the wizard. "I'm an idiot. The entire library's wired up with mana sensors. Any use of magic sets off the alarm."

"Come on," Dani told him, setting off towards the back exit through which they'd entered. They headed down the stairs, vaulted, slid and tumbled over the stuck box, and bashed through the doors into the square beyond. A gaggle of five guards were heading straight towards them. The one in front had three stripes on his arm. A look of amazed recognition appeared on his face, and he lifted his arm to point straight at Presto. "That's, that's… Tannarton! Grab him!"

Presto turned his back on the guards and shoved the journal into a pocket in Dani's robes. "Get that out of here. I'll never make it, but I can buy you time." Then he spun back round and began spitting a stream of spells at the oncoming guards. More alarms sounded, and further figures began spilling from doorways. "Go!" the wizard shouted.

Dani grabbed Darick by the arm and pulled him back through the doorway. She took a last glance back at Presto, and saw the wizard engulfed in a storm of spellfire. The two of them hustled away into the building's gloom-filled corridors, leaving Presto behind.

Back at the flat, the crystal was still tuned to the rolling twenty-four hour news channel the Storm had fired up when the conversation about Blade's ex-wife had ground to an awkward halt. The Storm came back from making himself a cup of tea just in time to see the picture change to a library image of him playing on stage. That image then faded, to be replaced with a montage of Blade in the arena. He grabbed the control wand from the coffee table and turned the volume up, giving the lost–in-his-thoughts Blade a poke as he did so, followed by an explanatory wave at the screen.

"*...and the guards are still searching for Blade Petros and Northern Fire's lead lutist, the Storm, together with their three accomplices. We go now to a press conference at which the commander of the investigation will report on progress.*"

The picture changed again, swinging across a crowd of journalists, pausing for a moment on the still-empty table at the head of the room, and then sweeping down the side, where a string of suit-clad men with the unmistakable aura of guards lounged against the white-painted wall looking bored and vaguely contemptuous. For an instant the camera halted on a man the Storm had never seen before but who Blade apparently had, given his immediate shout of, "That's him!"

"Who?" asked the Storm.

"Him, that bloke." Blade pointed at the crystal, but the view had returned to a wide-shot of the room. "It's gone now, but the guy who was just on…"

"What about the dude?"

"He was the leader of the guys who tried to ambush us at Craagon's Reach. That was him, there in that room."

"Well what the fuck does that mean?"

"I have no idea."

Chapter Eighteen

Presto awoke to a last memory of going down fighting in the main university square under a scrum of university guards, random members of the magic facility, students, and his old foe, the Head of Magical Studies. He had managed to get one particularly good zinger off at the Head before going under, which was something at least. Now, though, an unknown period of time later, he found himself lying on an uncomfortably hard and awkwardly narrow bed in a room constructed entirely from grey metal, save for the harsh light set into the ceiling.

In the corner of the room stood a bare metal toilet. Presto's bladder was full, painfully so, so he padded over to it and let fly. Relieved, in bladder if not in mind, he padded back to the bed, sensing as he did so a low, constant vibration coming up through the floor and into his feet. He found his ankles flexing, and he realised the floor had tilted slightly, his inner ear detecting it a second or so ahead of his conscious mind.

I'm on a skyship, he realised. Why? And more to the point, where am I going?

He tried a quick cantrip, but as he spoke the words and made the movements he knew his answer already; where he should have felt the warm surge of mana, there was nothing. There was clearly a pretty heavy-duty mana damping field covering the cell, which explained why he was neither bound nor gagged. He tried banging on the door, but nobody came, so he gave up and lay back down on the bed. Someone would want to speak to him eventually, and then maybe he'd get some answers.

The mood back at the flat was grim. Darick and Dani had managed to make it back, just, but Presto was gone, and the journal might as well have been written in Elvish for all the good it was doing them. They'd all tried reading it, and had all failed to find anything understandable that looked even vaguely significant.

Darick was sitting across from the Storm, watching him make a final attempt to get something out of the leather-bound volume. After several minutes during which his facial frown worked its way from determined concentration through bemused confusion to exasperated defeat, the rock star put the book down with a sigh and leaned back in his chair. "Don't ask me what the hell any of it means. I understood the bit at the start where it said that it was the fourteenth journal of Magninninto Kellen, but then he pretty much lost me. Half of it seemed to be using a completely different alphabet and most of the rest seemed to be in a different language."

"Sorcerac," said Dani. "It's the language of magic – what spells are cast in. And the other stuff, I think that's the notation they use to describe the really low level nuts and bolts of magic use."

"You know anyone who speaks this Sorcerac?"

"Yeah, but the last time I saw him, he was getting jumped by a bunch of guards at the university."

A depressed silence settled. Darick had always thought that a priest's primary duty was to help those in need. Admittedly, he'd never quite planned on being one of those in need, but he figured the principle still applied. The four of them – five he guessed, now Laliana was with them – needed to determine just how to solve this problem, and it was his job to guide them to the solution. Now was as good a time as any to start on that job. He looked around the room, catching each person's eye. "The question is, what are we going to do now?"

"We need to get Presto back," said Blade. "And we need to figure out what's going on."

"Okay," said Darick, in the calm and moderated voice he'd been taught at theological collage. "Do we have any ideas about how we could do that?"

Blade thought for a moment. "I know a bloke who knows people. If anyone knows, he will."

"Okay," said Darick brightly. "Good. Anyone else?"

Dani shrugged. "There's a guy I know. He's in touch with certain… unorthodox channels of communication."

"Excellent." He looked across at the Storm.

The rock star pushed himself out of his chair, and looked carefully around the room at his comrades. "Sounds groovy to me. Cup of tea, anyone?"

Time still existed in the cell in which Presto now found himself imprisoned, but intangibly so, not so much a symbiotic partner as a parasitic guest. There were no dials to tell the time, or windows to show the passage of the sun, and the sole light set into the ceiling burned with a constant and unnatural glare. If time passed for the cell and its inhabitant, it passed on its own, unobserved and unrecorded. Minutes that could be hours. Hours that could be days. To a man raised in a world of timetables and time-pieces, to lose track of time was to risk losing track of reality.

Which was clearly the point. Why torture a man when you can disturb and disorient him merely by locking him inside a featureless box? It helped to understand this, and it helped to have a brain full of knowledge and memories to which one could retreat. Presto had spent the hours that must surely now have passed replaying the events of the last few days, searching for clues to the understanding he sought. When that had failed he'd retreated further, to his days at the university, good days mostly.

Then – hours later, days? – the door opened, and a man in a featureless grey uniform appeared in the doorway. "Sit up," he ordered. He waited until Presto swung his legs down off the bed and then entered the room, followed by three other men. They cuffed his hands behind him and pushed a gag hard into his mouth, then led him roughly from the room, directing him with hard shoves in the small of his back. The skyship's corridors were as featureless as the cell, all bare metal and strip lighting. They passed a window, and for an instant Presto got a glimpse of a green landscape far below, only half visible through a veil of low cloud.

Then he was shoved again and the outside world was gone. Where the hell was this thing taking him?

The journey through the skyship ended in front of a small metal door. The lead guard thumbed a code into the keypad set beside the frame, making sure to cover the number with his body, and then pushed the door open. A small bare room lay beyond, into which Presto was unceremoniously pushed. The room was empty save for a narrow metal table with two metal chairs set around it. The guards released Presto's handcuffs, pushed him down into the chair, and then re-handcuffed him to the chair's solid metal armrests, before removing the gag so roughly that it damn near took his jaw with it. Then they left, saying nothing.

Presto tried a quick, whispered cantrip, but felt nothing. Another mana dampening field. It seemed there was nothing to do but wait.

He waited.

An hour had surely passed, perhaps two, before Presto was joined in the interrogation room by a powerfully built man who exuded an air of menace – and whose chiselled face was somehow familiar. The man sat down in the chair opposite Presto and smiled as he presumably waited for Presto to recognise him. Tired and disoriented as he was, it took a moment for that recognition to arrive. It was the man who'd led the attack on them at the hotel in Craagon's Reach, Presto realised.

The man's smile broadened, and then he spoke. "I was wondering how long it would take you to place me."

"Who are you?" Presto asked.

The man shook his head. "I'm afraid it doesn't work like that. I ask the questions, and you answer them."

"Just like that?"

The man pulled a face. "Well, if you want strict accuracy then the sequence is usually that I ask the questions, you refuse to answer them, I torture you with a savagery and enthusiasm that even I sometimes find disturbing, and then you answer my questions. I was just hoping that we could perhaps find some middle ground that saves you some pain and the cleaners some work."

"Torture's illegal!" Presto shouted, trying to keep a quiver out of his voice. "I'm an Imperial citizen. I have rights!"

The man shook his head. "Not here. Not now. You're not in a guard station in the middle of Empire City. You're on a skyship at an altitude of thirty thousand feet. If you scream, no one will hear you. If you try to complain, you'll find no one to complain to. This is my domain, and everything and everyone in it belongs to me. Including you. I can do whatever I want to you and there's no one here to stop me. Do you understand?"

Presto nodded, slowly.

"Good. Now I'm going to ask you one simple question, and I want a full and complete answer. Give me that and we might avoid further unpleasantness."

The man got out of his chair and leaned across the table to spit his next words straight into Presto's face.

"What do you know about sleeping dragon?"

Chapter Nineteen

Whoever had surrounded Blade's target with a ten foot high stone wall doubtless thought it an adequate defence against any and all who might attempt to penetrate it. But Blade was neither any nor all and the wall was no barrier; he was perhaps the greatest AdventureSport warrior of all time, and it took more than ten feet of crumbling block-work to stop him. At the wall's end, it made a neat right-angle with the back wall of an adjacent building. Blade hit that angle at a run, bouncing off first one wall, and then the other, until his upward momentum carried him to within grasping distance of the wall's top. He grabbed, gripped, paused, and then pulled himself upward into a smooth arc that took him over the wall and into the space beyond. He landed like a cat, bounced into a roll, and came up in an alert, kneeling position.

This was his objective: the small but elegant rear garden of the Last and First Club. A number of expensively dressed men sat at tables set around the garden, studiously ignoring him as they ate their expensive food, drank their exceedingly expensive drinks, and smoked what were no doubt stratospherically expensive cigars. A man in a waiter's uniform approached him, showing no apparent surprise at either Blade's presence, or his unorthodox manner of arrival. "Is sir a member, or is sir here to see a member?"

"Sir's here to see a member," Blade told him, brushing bits of grass and soil from his hooded jacket. "Tennod Whitewillow."

"Very good, sir. I believe he's in the smoking room. If you'll just follow me."

There was of course no smoke in the smoking room and hadn't been for more than ten years. Most of the older members and a good few of the younger ones had grumbled profusely when the ban on smoking in public places had been brought in. But when promised push came to actual shove, they submitted, grumbling, heading to the garden if the weather was good, and huddling around the rear doorway if it wasn't. Personally, Blade considered it a great improvement, given that he could now both breathe and see with neither difficulty nor discomfort. He spotted Tenny reading a news-slate at the far end of the room, sat beside a fireplace built to such a size that only the scale of its setting prevented its cavernous interior from qualifying as a room in its own right.

Blade made his way over, conscious of how out of place his hooded top and sunglasses would make him look, but equally conscious of how out of place he'd look were people to recognise him. He sat down in the chair opposite Tenny. The agent didn't look up from his news-slate, so Blade gave a discreet cough. The agent still didn't look up, but this time he did at least speak. "Wondered when you might be turning up."

"Look, Tenny–"

"You clients of mine, you're all the same. All of you. Doesn't matter if you're an ASporter, or a rock star, or an actor, or a writer. Whatever situation one of you people have got yourself into, however much trouble you've caused, you always figure I can just wave my hand and make it all okay. I've got a bunch of clients Blade, not just you, and there's not one of you where the twelve and a half percent you give me is worth the grief that ends up coming with it."

"I'm not expecting–"

"Bullshit. You've got a problem, and you're thinking that somehow, maybe, I can sort it out for you. You're nothing special Blade. Sooner or later, everyone I have the misfortune to represent screws up and expects me to wave my apparently magic hand. My whisper will go, at like three AM, and fool that I am, I answer it. 'Tenny, I've got a bit of a problem,' the guy on the other end of the line says. No problem, I tell him. What is it? 'I crashed my car,' he says. Fine, I tell him, I'll call the insurance company. 'It went into a lake,' he says. Okay, I tell him, I'll arrange a crane. 'I was a bit drunk,' he says. Well, then you're going to lose your license, I tell him, but it's okay. I'll hire you a chauffeur. 'Thing is, he says, there was a hooker in the car when I crashed it.' That's bad, I tell him. But we can sort it. I'll tell the papers you're suffering from a sex addiction and buy your wife some flowers and a diamond ring. 'But the hooker didn't make it out of the car before it sank,' he says." Tenny stared hard at Blade. "And then he sits there on the other end of the whisper, waiting patiently for me to explain how I'm going to make his dead hooker go away. And you know what I tell him, Blade?"

Blade shook his head, wishing Tenny would speak a little less loudly. Annoyed faces were already starting to turn in their direction.

"I tell him that there are some things that even I can't do, and making dead hookers go away is one of them. And let's face it Blade, you're in much deeper shit than a single dead hooker. Do you get what I'm saying?"

When Dani was just a fifteen year-old runaway from an unhappy foster home, Griff had been there for her. The old halfling had taken her under his wing and taught her the knowledge needed to survive on the City's harsh but bountiful streets. He hadn't needed to, but he did it anyway, because Griff was that kind of guy. Dani generally worked alone now, and Griff was pretty much retired. But they kept in touch from time to time and Griff had always said to holler if she ever needed him.

Griff was a hard man to search for but an easy man to find – if he wanted you to find him. It took Dani only half an hour and a couple of well-placed questions to get herself across a table from the old halfling, in the back room of an otherwise unremarkable inn. It was reassuring; she was ten-foot dungeon pole toxic right now and yet her old mentor was not only still willing to see her but to have that fact known.

Griff took a slow sip of his ale, the fifth such sip he had taken since Dani had finished explaining her predicament. Griff liked to consider things from all angles, and Dani knew better than to hurry him. Finally, the old halfling spoke. "You're in a lot of trouble."

"Yeah."

"There's talk."

"What's it saying?"

Griff took another sip. "There's some powerful people looking for you and the other four guys. They don't know who you are Dani, not yet. But they've got your picture and they're asking hard and pretty soon they'll know."

"Powerful people?" asked Dani. "Government?"

The old halfling shrugged. "Don't know. Maybe."

"So what do I do?"

Silence settled as Griff took another long sip, and thought. A frown settled upon the old halfling's face. "It's a tricky one."

Griff had finished his first ale and was halfway through his second before he spoke again. "Trouble is like the wind. A reed hit by the wind bends and survives. But a mighty oak that stands proud before the wind risks being ripped from the soil. Sometimes you must bend before trouble. Be like water, not rock."

Griff could be maddeningly cryptic sometimes. Dani was still pondering over the meaning of his statement when there was a crash from downstairs, and a cry of, "Guards!"

A look of distress flickered across the old halfling's face. "Someone's grassed you up. If they're mine, I'll make them pay."

Dani was already out of her seat. "I need to be gone. Do you have a back way out?"

"Out the window there, along the wall, over the garage and into the alleyway beyond."

Dani opened the window, then turned back for a moment to face her old mentor. "Sorry for bringing this down on you, Griff."

The halfling smiled. "I'll be fine. Now go, girl. Go!"

A small coal fire was burning in the huge fireplace. Blade got out of his seat, grabbed the brass poker that hung from a hook on the wall, and gave the coals a vigorous series of stabs, more for something to do than a desire for extra warmth.

"It's magical, you arsehole," said Tenny, the first words he'd spoken in more than thirty seconds. "It's been burning since last autumn."

Blade muttered an apology and sat back down. "I just thought that perhaps you might have some advice for me."

"Advice? On what subject exactly would you be wanting advice? On how to avoid capture whilst on the run? Or on how to rebuild your reputation after being arrested for kiddie fiddling? With bloody orclings!"

"Advice on why this is happening? Who's doing it?"

"What do you mean, who's doing it? The guards are doing it, obviously."

Blade tried to keep his voice down to a whisper. "Yeah, but who's telling them to do it? That's what I need to know."

"Oh, I see," said Tenny, slapping his thigh and laughing. "It's a conspiracy. Of course. How stupid of me." He stopped laughing and leaned forward to look Blade straight in the eye. His voice was harsh now. "You've got more imagination than I credited you for, Blade. You ought to take up novel writing. Under a pseudonym, of course."

The waiter who'd earlier led Blade here appeared now next to them. He bent down into the space between them, turned his face towards Blade, and then spoke in a low but calm voice. "I'm afraid we have some gentlemen from the City Guard in the front lobby asking questions about sir. Perhaps it would be better for all concerned if sir left via the rear entrance."

Blade hesitated.

"If sir would follow me, we have a discreet route through the kitchens."

Blade stood up, confused. "Sorry, the guards are asking for me out front, and you're going to help me escape out back?"

The waiter straightened up, affronted. "This is the Last and First Club, sir. No one is allowed to harass our members or their guests, be they angry wives, aggrieved husbands, or the forces of municipal law enforcement." He grabbed Blade by the arm. "Now sir really does need to be leaving."

Presto's interrogator was a clearly a pro. As he probed, he ducked and wove both verbally and physically; switching from subject to subject and from a friend's tone to a foe's; prowling around behind Presto, only to suddenly appear beside his ear to snarl a question. But underneath the variations of approach and tone, always the same question. "What do you know about sleeping dragon?"

The more Presto told him though, the angrier he became, his professional mask breaking down after some hours to reveal the clearly frightened man who dwelt behind it. Three times now he'd punched Presto hard in the face when he disbelieved an answer; twice he'd slapped him when an answer had not been forthcoming. "Okay," he said, visibly seeking calm. "Let's recap. There was a spell, and it contacted you all, and told you to go to Craagon's Reach?"

"Yes," said Presto through lips dried by thirst and split by the punches.

The man appeared again in front of him, close enough for the spittle launched by his angry words to reach Presto's face. "I don't believe you. I don't believe this spell exists. I don't believe you only met your four associates five days ago. This is a final warning. No more lies. You're going to start telling me the truth, starting with all the things you've refused to divulge so far." He began to count off on his fingers. "One. You're going to tell me the name of your fourth companion we've not yet been able to identify. And don't bother repeating the false identity she gave the wooden-tops at the guard station. Two. You're going to tell me where she and your three other companions are currently hiding out. And three," he said, unfolding a third finger. "You're going to tell me how the five of you met, who recruited you, and why."

Presto resisted the urge to point out that he was currently two fingers short of the five pieces of information he'd actually asked for, and instead said nothing.

"And finally," his interrogator continued. "And most importantly, I want you to tell me everything you know about sleeping dragon."

The man took a step away, and then made a nod so imperceptible that Presto would have missed it were his interrogator not the most important person in his life right now. The door opened, and two goons in the now familiar, featureless grey uniforms entered, each slapping a pain-stick into an open palm.

"There you go, boys," said the interrogator, heading towards the still open doorway. "He's all yours." The door closed behind him.

The two guards advanced, smiling.

After a further three interrogation sessions – or was it four? – spread over a day and a night – or was it two full days? – Presto's sense of both time and reality had begun to blur. Events that logic told him had been distinct and consecutive were, in his memory, smeared, jumbled, and fused. Shorn of the foundations normally granted by a knowledge of what and an awareness of when, he found himself gripped by a feeling of disorientation and dislocation unlike anything he'd ever yet experienced. Under no illusions that he was any kind of hero, he'd revealed everything he knew save for two things: the current location of his four comrades; and Dani's name.

His torturers had started with pain-sticks: tools of the devils that produced pain in its purest form, unsullied by injury, exertion, or blood. When that had failed they'd resorted to more traditional means. Beatings. Water, both dripped, and as a fluid to be submerged into. And in between interrogations, when he was taken by the two guards back to his bare metal cell, he had to endure constant, loud deafening music played through an overhead speaker – a Northern Fire greatest hits sphere on constant rotation, which was a nice touch, Presto thought.

And still the questions and the beatings continued.

He wasn't sure he could take much more of this.

He needed food.

He needed water.

He needed sleep.

He needed to get out of here.

Chapter Twenty

Some time later the guards again came to his cell for him. They were joking as they cuffed his hands behind him and pushed him roughly ahead of them into the corridor, laughing as he bounced off the far wall. It was just as it had been on each previous time they'd come for him except for one detail, which that this time they'd forgotten – or perhaps just not bothered – to gag him. With his hands cuffed behind him, and his throat parched and his lips so swollen that he could barely speak, not bothering to gag him was a reasonable move to make. A typical wizard in his state could reasonably be expected to be helpless. But the guards had overlooked two things: Presto wasn't a typical wizard, and he wasn't in the mood to be reasonable.

He shouted, his lips nearly splitting with the exertion; just a handful of words of Sorcerac so simple that an apprentice wizard would learn them in his first week of an applied magic course. It wasn't much, but half-dead and bound it was all he could do, and the exertion of just this had him rocking on his feet. A glowing sphere appeared in the corridor in front of him and the guards.

"Don't make a move," Presto croaked. "Or I'll set it off. It'll make a big enough bang to snap this ship's backbone in two."

The two guards hesitated. It was actually just a simple glow-globe cantrip, the sort of thing that students learn as their first spell. But Presto was gambling that they might not realise that. He turned to face them. "Uncuff me."

They hesitated once more, trading scared and confused looks with each other.

"Do it, or I'll set it off. So help me I will. I'll send you, me, and everyone else on this ship plummeting to the ground. I'm not scared to die." He paused for a moment, and then delivered what he hoped would be a verbal coup de grace. "I found peace in the box. The sacred box."

The scared but confused looks morphed into looks of distinct panic as the two guards practically fell over themselves to get him uncuffed. He backed away from them. "Don't attempt to follow me."

He took a step backwards, and then another, and then – the globe went out. *Bugger*, he thought, remembering a fact he'd learned in his first year of magical theory which he really should have remembered: the world's mana field falls away with altitude, and from the glimpses he'd got out of the window they were at least thirty thousand feet up. He turned and ran down the corridor, feeling heavy footsteps behind him. He smashed through a door, vaulted over some boxes that some damn fool had left on the floor and rolled, tumbled, and fell down a flight of stairs so steep that had this been a building it would have been banned at least three times over under health and safety codes. A loud klaxon sounded from speakers set every few metres down the corridor. The guards were right behind him now; it was not so much that he heard them with his ears as he sensed them with the hairs on the back of his neck. He skidded round a corner and saw a sign.

Carpet deck.

He didn't know how to fly a carpet, but figuring this would be a good time to learn, he followed the sign's left-pointing arrow, slid down another steep flight of stairs, continued down a corridor and through yet another door, and found himself in an empty carpet deck.

Damn.

The two guards crashed through the door behind him. He held out warning hands as he stepped slowly backwards.

"Give it up," the first guard warned him.

"You've got nowhere to go," the second added.

They were right. There were only two ways out of the carpet deck: the door he'd come through, which now had two very angry guards between him and it, with more surely following; and the wide maw at the other end of the carpet deck through which carpets could be launched. He snatched a quick glance over his shoulder. The air beyond looked thin and cold, and he knew it was only the shimmering force wall stretched across the opening that was keeping the three of them upright and breathing. He looked back at the guards, and shook his head.

"Sorry."

Then he was turning, and sprinting, and throwing himself into the force wall. For a moment he thought it was going to hold, and bounce him back into captivity. But then its treacle-like texture yielded, and he found himself spearing through it, tumbling into the cold, thin air of more than six miles up. He breathed in, but felt only an agonising burning in his lungs. He spun once, twice, the skyship careering across his vision as the world rotated around him, then finally settled into a face–down attitude. Far below him, white fluffy clouds stretched from horizon to horizon, a blurred background of green and brown visible through the wisp-like tears in their forms. An increasingly biting wind whipped at him as he began to fall. His eyes stung with tears.

He had to fall. Here, in this high altitude region never meant for human beings, survival would be measured in minutes, if not seconds. Only gravity could save him now, pulling him to safety with a speed that increased by thirty-two feet for every additional second he survived. His eyes were closed tightly now, his mouth clamped shut; he put his hands against his sides and tried to aim down headfirst like an arrow, orientating himself through only the confused signals from his inner ear.

Seventy seconds after he exited the skyship he plunged through the clouds, sensing rather than seeing, experiencing a dim memory of damp clammy fog on a cold winter's day. His lungs were screaming for air, his heart thumped, and what remained of his awareness was shrinking to an inner core barely aware of the outside world. He was conscious, and therefore continuing to exist, but that was the extent of his universe right now. A voice somewhere told him that he was about to black out, but he ignored it, blocked it, shut it away. His eyes might have been open now. He wasn't sure. But if they were, they were seeing only grey. His mouth opened, and he breathed – cold air, thin air, but air, breathable air. He felt a fragment of awareness return.

More awareness, returning.

He was falling, he remembered that. A rote-learned instinct fired, his hands moving through long-ago-learned but never forgotten patterns, his lips speaking words that were torn away by the wind. The first attempt failed, the spell's ignition point failing to trigger the mana release. He tried again, shouting the words this time, daring the wind to steal them away from him, and this time it worked. He felt an invisible hand tugging at him, fighting the gravity and momentum that kept him hurtling towards the world below. One jerk, and another, slowing him. But still he fell. Another longer pull, his body sensing the struggle between spell and reality. And then he was crashing into something hard but yielding, needles scratching at his face. He tore through a score of thinner branches, the spell still fighting to slow him, bounced off a larger branch, and then crashed hard into a horizontal surface.

Awareness retreated, leaving only the dark.

The Storm was deeply absorbed in a daily soap opera he and Darick had started watching three mornings ago when he became aware that the desk whisper was ringing. He'd been at the apartment five days now and it had never rung before. He grabbed the crystal's control wand and muted the sound. The desk whisper's chime echoed around the now silent apartment, its only competition the noise from the bathroom, where Dani was having a shower. The Storm and Darick looked first at each other, and then at the whisper. Blade's head popped round the arched opening that led to the apartment's tiny kitchen. "Is that the whisper?"

"Yes," said the Storm.

"Are you going to answer it?"

"You think I should?"

"Don't know."

The whisper continued to ring. The door from the bathroom crashed open, revealing a wet and dripping Dani with a towel loosely wrapped around her frame. "Is anyone going to answer that?"

Blade shrugged. "We don't know who it is."

Dani acknowledged the point with a pained nod."

"I think we ought to answer it," said Darick. He looked up at Dani. "You could answer it. You're her sister. You can just say you're visiting."

Dani shrugged awkwardly. "I don't think she tells people she's got a sister."

"Why?"

"Long story."

Still the whisper rang.

Three times. Four. It occurred to the Storm that there really was no sound louder or more annoying than an unanswered whisper set against an otherwise unbroken silence. Five times. Six. "Oh for the gods' sakes, I'll answer it!" he snapped. He reached over, grabbed the handset, and lifted it clear of its cradle. "Yes!" he growled into the speaking end.

A croaky, but recognisable voice sounded in his ear. "You took your damn time answering."

"Presto?"

"Well, who else knows you're there?"

"Good point, man! It's real good to hear from you." He held the whisper away from his face for a moment so he could talk to the others. "It's Presto!" he told them.

"Where is he?" asked Dani.

"I don't know." He put the handset back to his face. "Hey, er, where are you hanging, man?"

"In a forest, under a tree."

"He's in a forest, under a tree."

"What's he doing there?"

"What are you doing there?"

"Lying down."

"Lying down?"

"I fell out of a skyship."

The Storm nodded, then looked up at the others. "Says he fell out of a skyship."

"Like you do," muttered Blade.

The Storm realised that sound was coming out of the whisper's handset. He put back to his face. "Sorry, what was that?"

"I said, can someone please come and pick me up?"

"Okay. He wants to be picked up."

"Where is he?" asked Blade. "If we could get hold of a carpet, I could fly it."

Dani broke in. "I can steal you a carpet."

Blade held out his hand, smiling. "Deal."

"We can fly out and pick you up," said the Storm. "Where are you?"

The fall might not have killed Presto, but its partner-in-crime, the impact, had certainly given it a good go. As someone on the crystal had once pointed out, "Flying without a carpet's easy, it's the landing that's tricky."

Summoning up the energy to perform the whisper spell had so pushed him to his limits that he'd nearly blacked out with the exertion of then seeking out a connection with the nearest basestation. Now they wanted to know where he was, and he suspected they were looking for something more definitive than under a tree, in a forest. He looked around for landmarks, but saw only trees, flamewoods in fact, planted in neat rows. A plantation. But since, after several centuries of enthusiastic logging, that was the case for a good half of the forests in the Empire, it was no help in locating him at all.

A carpet whined by above, low. His erstwhile captors were out looking for him, probably assuming he was dead, but just wanting to make sure. Before long they might have boots on the ground, and he needed to be gone by then. Casting another spell would increase the risk of mana-detectors finding him, and if they had a half-decent wizard up there he was sunk – but it was clearly a risk he was going to have to take. He searched through the dark recesses of his mind for a spell he'd learned more than fifteen years before and hadn't used since then. Other, lesser, spellcasters needed the assistance of written spells. But one of the benefits of a pictographic memory is the ability to visualise the source of every spell you've ever cast. And at times like this that could be pretty useful.

He saw the spell now, as though it were written on a sheet of vellum floating inside his eyeballs. He read the words off his memory page, speaking them softly, his arms weaving the accompanying patterns. The mana flared within him; somewhere in the ethereal plane a tendril was sneaking upwards, joining the existing tendril he'd created for the whisper spell. The whisper's connection was along the ground and hopefully lost in the ground clutter – flamewoods, being faintly magical, create a lot of interference. But this new tendril was heading straight upward, reaching for a spot more than twenty-three thousand miles away, at a point so high that an object placed there would remain stationary above the world.

A little over five seconds after he'd created it, the tendril made contact with the satellite's receiving field; a second or so later, data began to flow into Presto's mind. He cast a second spell, which sorted, filtered, and processed that data to gave him the answer he needed. 32.357 degrees east. 55.298 degrees north.

He shut down both spells and switched back to the whisper spell. "Thirty-two point three five seven degrees east. Fifty-five point two nine eight degrees north."

There was a pause, broken only by the sound of a pencil scratching across paper. "You hold tight, man. We'll be there before you know it."

Chapter Twenty-One

A little over four hours after the Storm had made that promise, Blade and Dani picked Presto up from the forest in a carpet they claimed to have "borrowed". There was no sign of the skyship in the sky, but in the east a couple of carpets were patrolling back and forth. Blade took the carpet low and fast along a wide river valley for several miles before popping out of the valley's cover and setting a course to the west.

"It'll be about three hours' flight time," he told Presto, who was sat in the back seat fighting to keep his eyes open. "I'll take us in low and we can dump the carpet by the docks and then scoot."

"Where did you find it?" Presto asked.

"Former neighbour of mine," Blade replied. "Never liked him."

Presto felt his eyelids dropping as the sound of Blade and Dani quietly talking faded to a mere background hum. When awareness returned to him, it was an awareness that was back on the skyship. The interrogator was shouting at him. "What do you know about sleeping dragon?" And then a punch. Shout. Punch. Shout. Punch. Shout. Punch, punch, punch. Childhood music played in the background, and now his interrogator was a clown, clad in the same scary face that had terrified him at his fifth birthday party. The laughter of his uncaring parents echoed around the metal room, distorted, as though replayed from an old and scratched sphere.

A voice boomed from somewhere far away. "This is the guards. Begin immediate descent to landing pad eight niner three. We repeat, this is the guards. Begin immediate descent to landing pad eight niner three."

"What do you… what do you… what do you…"

Presto's eyes opened, almost of their own volition, as he found himself emerging into the confused disorientation of an abruptly forced awakening. He was in the carpet, sitting behind Blade and Dani. Below them, the endless spires of Empire City stretched across rolling hills to every horizon. Some miles ahead was the endless blue-green white-flecked expanse of the Middle Sea, separated from the city by the twisting ribbon of the coastal highway and its accompanying stretches of beach and docks. And all around them, set high in the sky above those reaching spires, were the thousands of floating multi-coloured illusionary gateways that guided the city's fleet of carpets across its three-dimensional airspace.

Up front, Dani and Blade were speaking in tones that indicated that whatever discussion they were having had already reached the recriminatory stage.

"I thought you said your neighbour wouldn't notice his carpet was gone until the evening!"

"I guess today was the day he finished work early!"

Still blinking sleep away, Presto twisted round towards the source of the voice and found, travelling a little way behind them, a blue, white, and fluorescent yellow carpet with a mirror-imaged "Guards" written across its nose in large, neat, white lettering. He turned back to his two companions. "Sorry, can someone tell me what's happening?"

"We tried to come in on a standard flight-path using the neighbour's ID," said Dani. "But the guards appeared straight away. He must have reported it stolen."

The voice boomed out again. "This is the guards. Begin immediate descent to landing pad eight niner three."

"Well, what are we going to do?" Presto asked.

Blade looked momentarily back at him. "I have no idea."

The carpet soared onwards, passing through a blue floating rectangular gateway the size of a rackets court. A similar blue rectangle floated a few hundred feet in front of them, the next link in a chain of such gates that stretched as far as Presto could see, arcing over the docks and the bay beyond, marking out a virtual highway through the sky. A few hundred feet to the right, at the same level, a chain of red gates paralleled the blue; as Presto watched, a carpet zipped past them, heading east to their west. Above and below, other gates sketched out similar routes, linked together by curved connecting lanes, the whole forming a complex three-dimensional net sitting above the city.

They soared through another gate and over a route whose paired north-south gates were coloured green and yellow. A second white / blue / fluorescent yellow carpet with white writing exited that route and started arching up towards them.

"We need to get off here," said Dani.

"Where to?" asked Blade.

"Anywhere!"

"Right!"

Blade drove the carpet through the latest gate, and then wrenched the stick to the right, sending them into a hard turn that pulled their lungs down into their stomachs and their stomachs down into their bowels. Then the carpet lurched again as he pulled it into an equally savage turn back to the left. It levelled, straightened, and shot through a red gate, narrowly missing a carpet that was hurtling in the other direction.

"This wasn't what I had in mind," said Dani.

Behind them, a siren began to wail.

Another carpet headed towards them, two equally panic-stricken faces visible for an instant through the windscreen before it flashed by, terrifyingly close.

"Perhaps we should go down?" suggested Dani.

"Fine!" snapped Blade, immediately pushing the stick hard forward and launching the carpet into a dive so abrupt that Presto felt his seat belt digging hard into his shoulder as it fought the negative G-forces currently attempting to eject him out of the vehicle.

He was glad he didn't have a lunch to hurl, because had he had one he'd certainly have hurled it.

After a couple of seconds the negative G-forces eased off, but when Presto opened his eyes he discovered that this was only because the carpet was now falling towards the ground at pretty much the same speed as a brick would. Before they'd begun their dive, the city below had possessed the "model village" look that the world always does when viewed from a height. But as the carpet corkscrewed crazily down, the model village look was rapidly ceding ground to a terrifyingly real vision with the words "crash site" written all over it.

It occurred to Presto that he perhaps ought to be leaving, but some instinct made him stay. He would have liked to ascribe it to loyalty, but in truth it was more likely down to terrified indecision.

A few seconds later, at the point at which the big blobs below had become wagons and the small blobs were in danger of looking like people, Dani's voice emerged from the front seat, broadly calm but with a clear undercurrent of fear. "Shouldn't you think about pulling up?"

Blade shrugged. "Yeah, probably." He paused for a moment, and then pulled back hard on the stick.

Presto managed to get one hard stare in at the back of the warrior's head before the G-forces forced his chin down onto his chest and turned his vision grey.

After a couple of seconds of grunting strain the carpet levelled out, and his aching bowels returned to their customary home a couple of inches north of his anus. They were now flashing along one of Empire City's wide boulevards at a highly illegal altitude of about two hundred feet, and attracting quite a bit of attention while they were at it. Blade gradually drifted the carpet even lower, until they were below the level of the street's flanking buildings.

The noise of the siren resumed above and slightly behind. Presto twisted round and spotted a guard carpet tracking them, but was beaten to the verbal punch by Dani.

"We've still got company."

"Any suggestions?" asked Blade.

"Take the third exit at Victory Square. It's just coming up."

A few seconds later, the carpet flashed over Victory Square, which, name notwithstanding, was actually circular. Eight wide boulevards met here, driven through medieval slums back in the days when such large-scale urban renewal required only a megalomaniacal emperor with dictatorial powers, and when such megalomaniacal emperors had been in generous supply.

Traffic blocked the road circle that now circumscribed the square, which was probably a blessing, since if there was one thing scarier than a traffic-blocked Victory Square it was a Victory Square where the traffic was actually moving. Men who took their wagons through "the Square" counted themselves lucky if they emerged at the other end missing only a wing mirror or two and with only a few extra scratches to match those their paintwork already had. Presto had taken his wagon through the square some twenty years ago upon first gaining his driving license; that had been the first and last time.

If there was anything that could make you feel good about travelling in a stolen carpet at an illegally low altitude while being pursued by the guards, it was zipping across Victory Square in a matter of seconds and arcing straight over a set of red lights into the Gustov V Boulevard.

"Why the third exit?" asked Blade, as they flashed down Gustov.

"Sorry, I meant the fourth. I always get confused."

"Why didn't you just tell me you wanted Federick?"

"I wasn't sure you knew which one that was."

"I did! Unlike you as it turned out."

They zipped past the near-stationary traffic below at a terrifyingly fast rate. On a good day, you could usually make it from one end of Gustov to another in about an hour, assuming – of course – that you'd abandoned your wagon by the roadside and proceeded on foot. Blade managed to do it in thirty seconds. They flashed over the Bay Pier complex and past the harbour. A couple of guard carpets hovered over the water.

"Now we're completely out in the open!" shouted Dani.

"Fine! I'll go back!"

The nose of the carpet pitched up so sharply that Presto's brain felt like it had relocated to his ribcage and was now apartment-sharing with his lungs. For a crazy moment up was down, down was up, sea was sky, and sky was, well, not sky. Then the carpet dived over the Bay Pier complex, flashed past a pursuing guard carpet, and headed back down Gustov.

"Was your neighbour rich?" asked Dani, a few seconds later. Presto looked up, and saw that the grifter was rummaging through the glove compartment.

"What?" said Blade, confused, the carpet lurching alarmingly as he took his eyes off the street for a second. "He did okay, I think. I mean, he had a private carpet."

"Let me put it this way," said Dani, as they flashed over Victory Square for the second time. "Was he the sort of guy to keep several hundred thousands' worth of high denomination golds in his glove compartment?"

"What?"

Dani held out a thick wad of notes, secured by an elastic band. "They're all five hundreds."

Presto leaned forward. "I don't want to seem rude or ungrateful, but could we perhaps postpone this discussion until later? Assuming there is a later, which right now appears doubtful."

Dani nodded, then slapped Blade on the arm. "I think we should fly back to the Square."

"Why?"

"I've got an idea."

Chapter Twenty-Two

The pictures playing across the crystal's screen were sobering, the accompanying voiceover sombre, and the mood of the Storm and his watching companions, positively funereal.

"And we can see the riot guardsmen sweeping across a darkened Victory Square, pushing the rioters away from the Statue of Deliverance, apart from a hard core section on the top of the statue's plinth, who are raining missiles down on the guards. These are truly shocking scenes."

The camera took a slow pan across the square, taking in all the standard players traditionally seen in the kind of impromptu urban renewal programme that is a full-scale riot: the anarchist, face hidden by a black scarf to enable him to deal out violence with little chance of identification; the riot-guardsman, face also hidden by a black scarf to allow him to similarly deal out anonymous violence; the adrenaline-junkie rubber-necker, there to see a little history in the making, or unmaking; and the totally innocent bystander, the only participant who didn't choose to be there, and therefore by far the one most likely to end up getting his or her head bashed in.

"Unbelievable, man," said the Storm, shaking his head. "Just, totally... unbelievable."

"It's now nearly four hours since the disturbances started," intoned the crystal's commentary. *"Let's go to our reporter in the square, Frod Danberry. Frod, what can you see?"*

The image changed to a head-and-shoulders shot of a reporter, then slowly zoomed out to reveal the guard-lines behind him, quarterstaffs methodically falling and rising.

"Well, Petr, as you can see the guards are slowly pushing the rioters across the square, and away from the Gustov shopping district."

"Do you have any more information about what triggered the riot?"

"No, not really anything more than we already have. A group of individuals flew over Victory Square in a carpet, threw several hundred thousand golds' worth of high-denomination notes into the sky across the square, and then landed. As you can imagine, complete chaos erupted, which turned into a riot when the guards attempted to gather the money, and confiscate what had already been collected. I have heard reports that the individuals had previously overflown the square several times and that they were already being pursued by guard carpets, but that's unconfirmed."

"I can't believe you threw all those yellowbacks out of the carpet," said the Storm, looking at Dani, who was perched on a chair opposite him.

"Do the guards have any information about who the occupants of the carpet were?"

Dani shrugged. "Well, strictly speaking, I didn't throw it all out."

"No. They escaped in the confusion caused by the fall of the money. It's thought they made it to the worm station and took a worm out. As you know, five lines converge at Victory Square so they could have made it anywhere."

Darick sat bolt upright. "Sorry, what?"

"Do the guards have any thoughts about the source of this money?"

Dani held up a thick wad of notes. "I kept fifty thou' for expenses."

"As you can imagine, they're not saying anything on the record at the moment..."

"We can't just keep that money, it's not ours!" spluttered Darick, getting a nod of agreement from Laliana who'd arrived back from work a half hour ago.

"...and my sources are understandably having to be discreet. But I have talked to a number of them..."

Dani pointed at the rioters on the screen. "Well, it's not theirs either!"

"...and they believe it likely originates from a criminal source."

Darick folded his arms. "I'm not sure that's quite the point."

"Screw that," said the Storm, cutting across Darick. "Did you cats not hear what they just said about the money, about it being dirty?"

"What?" said Darick.

Laliana was giving Blade a very hard look. "Just whose carpet did you guys steal? Who exactly is your neighbour, and what does he do?"

Blade shrugged, confused. "I dunno! I thought he did something in advertising! Look, whoever he is, he's the least of our worries right now."

Silence settled, broken only by the continuing commentary on the crystal, recycling the same facts, opinion, speculation and rumour, and by the occasional awed curse from one of the flat's appalled, but still watching, occupants.

And then Presto, who'd dived into Kellen's journal as soon as they'd arrived back at the flat and hadn't surfaced since, cleared his throat. "Ladies and gentlemen, I think I might just have something."

Something? It was a measure of just how deep in the shit they were that this one word, "something", travelled straight from the Storm's cochlea to his knees and had him rising to his feet while his brain was still processing the statement. "What, like you've found a clue?" he stuttered out.

Presto took a moment to reply. "Well, this is all based on a chance remark and some cryptic notations, but I think I might have found a back door into the program that will bring up a control panel."

Now it was Blade's turn to butt into the discussion. "So, that means what? That you can instruct the spell to come on over, tell it you're the boss, and then control it?"

"I should be able to, yes, assuming of course that it's still out there monitoring us, which I somehow suspect it is."

Blade got the question in before the Storm could wrap his tongue around what he felt was the appropriate blend of politeness and urgency. "Could you do it now?"

"Yes." Presto put the journal down. "We'll need a clear area. Perhaps you could put the coffee table in the bathroom and move the ornaments off the shelf over there?"

Simply to hold such an object in his hands was a privilege beyond measure to Presto; to actually turn its pages was to feel the presence of greatness upon your shoulder. Presto might have considered himself to be the greatest wizard currently alive, but Kellen... Kellen was something else beyond even he. Only a fool would have denied that, and while Presto would happily admit to a strong streak of arrogance, he prided himself on being no kind of fool. That such an object had been lying around on a dusty shelf all this time, indexed but otherwise forgotten, seemed almost a crime. Tearing his attention away from it, even momentarily, was an effort, but Presto forced himself to do so.

He pushed and prodded his five companions into a circle. There was no particular reason for this. But he couldn't help feeling that the momentous nature of what they were about to do deserved a certain degree of ceremony. Then he waved through the appropriate motions and spoke the appropriate words and conjured up a link spell. This was simple stuff, schoolboy almost, but the weight of what he was doing pressed so heavily upon him that he only just managed the cast. The link spell reached out, searching for other spells or devices, carrying with it parameters encoded by the casting: the spell identity, user name, and password that he'd found scribbled in a margin in the journal. He could feel its progress, searching, probing, finding, communicating – and then it had found its target, and he was in.

A ghostly set of illusionary images appeared, floating hazily before him in the centre of the circle. A control panel, simple and primitive in nature, but world-shatteringly advanced when set in its historical context. "Ladies and gentlemen," he said, his voice quivering. "This is quite possibly the first touch-sensitive, active spell control panel ever designed."

He left that utterance hanging in the air for just a moment, to allow the significance of the event to settle in. Then all order and control dissolved, as his companions crowded into the spaces either side of him, practically fighting in the rush, shouting away simultaneously, jabbing fingers at the control panel all the while.

"Hey, shouldn't there be, like, an about button?"

"Scroll down!"

"What's the icon in the corner do?"

"Could you possibly increase the font size a tad?"

"Shut up!" Presto shouted.

They shut up.

He held up a hand to ensure that they stayed shut up, and then began to study the control panel. It was cluttered, designed in haste and without care, for use by its creator and not by other users. But it was still magnificent. Towards the bottom was a small button with what looked like a picture of a scroll upon it. Presto reached out a shaking finger and pressed it into the ghostly image of the button. For an instant nothing happened, and then the set of ghostly images dissolved and were replaced with a new, different and simpler set. There were only three buttons now, captioned, with a fourth icon that might have been a back button. The buttons said: Play, Record, Clear.

Presto reached forward and pressed play.

The control panel faded, a three dimensional image appearing in the centre of the room to replace it. Five tiny human figures, ghostly, shimmering, and yet wonderfully real, standing together, floating incongruously a couple of feet above Laliana's rug. Dani leaned forward. "Isn't the bloke on the left Sir Ethelded? As in the statue?"

Yes it is, thought Presto. *It is. And standing beside him... Dear God. That's Kellen.*

In the middle of the image was a figure clad in priest's robes. He began now to move and speak. *"Sorry, are we recording?"*

The image of Kellen gave the image of the priest a hard stare, before adding in a clear if slightly tinny voice, *"Yes."*

Darick leaned forward. "I think that's Archbishop Idenn IV."

In the image, the priest nodded, looked back towards Presto, cleared his throat, and began to speak. *"Hello. Erm... I'm Archbishop Idenn, and these are my colleagues in arms."*

The other four miniature figures waved, awkwardly. Presto found himself suppressing a strong urge to wave back.

"Now then," said the image of Idenn, *"we are the greatest heroes of our age."*

"Modest, isn't he?" observed the Storm.

A hissed *"Get on with it!"* emerged from somewhere in the vicinity of the projected image. The tiny Idenn turned and sent a long stare in the direction of the equally tiny, leather-clad scout who stood to his right.

"And...?" asked Blade, making winding motions with his hand, just as the priest resumed speaking.

"Yes. Quite. I expect you're all wondering why you've been brought to this place?"

The image paused again, as though expecting an answer.

"They really should have scripted this," said Dani.

"Ah, yes. Anyway, by time you hear the words I am speaking, five hundred years will have passed and we will all no doubt be forgotten."

The fifth figure in the image, a man of beauty so ethereal it risked compromising his manhood, stepped forward, played a chord on the harp cradled in his arms, and then spoke in a clear and pure voice. *"You may be forgotten, Idenn, but some of us have left our music to eternity."*

"Who's that?" asked Darick.

"Search me," said the Storm.

The miniature Idenn ignored the interruption and continued.

"The five of you who are listening to this message are the five greatest heroes of your age—"

"Say what?" exclaimed the Storm. "Us? Heroes? Greatest?"

"—have created a spell that will seek you out, transport you to this place, and then play this recorded message to you."

"Why?" asked the Storm, Blade, and Dani simultaneously.

"They might want to know why," said the miniature image of Kellen.

"I was just about to get to that!" spat the miniature image of Idenn, pausing just long enough to get a conciliatory nod from the wizard.

"*You probably want to know why we have created a spell to recruit you.*" He paused again, long enough to get a jab in the ribs from the leather-clad thief, then resumed speaking, his voice dropping half an octave as though to emphasise the importance of what he was about to say. "*We have dedicated our lives to the protection of this world, and one of the tools we use to alert us of threats is prophecy. Thus far, we have always prevailed over those threats, but now we face a threat that we cannot defeat – because when it arrives we will be long dead.*"

"I'm getting a really bad feeling about this," said Dani.

"*We have learned this: in five hundred years from our time – in your time, that is – the sleeping dragon will arise and destroy your world.*"

"But what the bloody hell is the sleeping dragon?" shouted Blade.

"*We do not know what the sleeping dragon is.*"

"Well, that's just sodding great."

"*But we know that it will bring about the fall of all civilisation across the whole of the world, from pole to pole and ocean to ocean, along with everything that implies. Plague. War. Famine. Destruction.*"

The image of Archbishop Idenn paused, sombre, creating a silence that no one watching him felt compelled to break. Finally, he resumed, speaking brightly now.

"*Which is where you come in!*"

The Storm banged his head into the arm of the sofa a couple of times, and then left it there. "I knew he was going to say that. I knew it. I knew it."

"*–designed the spell to find the five greatest heroes of the age. And it has found you. Each one of us has entered the parameters that will define who amongst your era is best set to be his successor. He who is the greatest warrior.*"

The image of Sir Ethelded nodded.

"*He who is the greatest bard.*"

The image of the beautiful–to–the–point–of–implausibility bard stepped forward and played a long tinkling chord on his harp, receiving in return a grimace from Sir Ethelded and what looked like a muttered curse from the thief.

"*He who is the greatest wizard.*"

The image of Kellen nodded, almost imperceptibly.

"*The greatest, ahem, scout.*"

The image of the leather clad thief nodded.

"*And, well.*" The image of Idenn smiled a smile that was presumably intended to be self-depreciating and which with a touch more sincerity might have achieved that goal. "*He who is the greatest priest."*

He smiled and nodded, and then resumed speaking.

"Our master mage, Kellen, has created the spell so that upon finding you five heroes, it will bring you to this location and play you this message, to inform you of this task. After that, it will continue to monitor the world for information that might be relevant to your quest, and will – if it finds any – transmit that information to you telepathically."

Idenn smiled again, then paused as though remembering something and went into a furious huddle with Kellen.

"Well isn't this all just sodding brilliant?" said the Storm from the other end of the sofa.

"There's one thing I ain't getting," said Blade. "It never played us the message, which means we ain't the five selected. So why did it kidnap us in the first place?"

This was a question Presto's brain had been crunching over in the seconds since learning of the message's existence, and he had a horrible feeling he knew the answer. "I suspect that none of us passes the criteria that our illustrious predecessors programmed into the spell, but are instead merely the five best candidates it has thus far found."

"So that's why it never played us the message? Because it's still searching?"

"Yes." He shrugged. "It may be that no-one in this modern world of ours fully fulfils their requirements."

"Why kidnap us then?"

"Syntax error, I suppose, triggered when it found some information to pass on to us."

"Syntax error?"

"A design fault. I don't think the possibility of the spell being unable to find five old-style heroes occurred to Kellen. The spell found something, presumably about Craagon's Reach, so it called up the five people whose profiles were currently sitting at the top of its memory banks."

That reply was still hanging in the silence when the image of Archbishop Idenn emerged from the huddle.

"Ah, yes. Kellen wanted me to remind you of one thing. Just in case you were thinking about trying to manipulate the spell, it does have a number of defensive routines coded into it."

"Defensive routines?" muttered Blade. "Bastard thing blew my fucking house up!"

152

Idenn's voice cut across Blade's response.

"Well, that's about it. Good luck! Now, how do we turn this thing off?"

Then the image vanished, leaving only an empty space, and a stunned silence.

"That's it?" said Dani, eventually. "Good luck?"

Another silence ensued, this one broken eventually by the Storm. "This is insane. I can't handle this." He got up and headed for the door, pausing only to peel some notes from the wad of cash Dani had earlier revealed.

"But what about saving the world?" shouted Darick at his retreating back.

The rock star turned to face them. "If the world needs us to save it, then it's well and truly buggered. Me? If there's no tomorrow, then I'm going to start partying like hell today."

Chapter Twenty-Three

The night sky was clear, but the neither the high moon nor the low moon were anywhere near full, which left deep pools of shadow between each streetlight. Blade was lurking in one of those shadows, smoking. He'd given up the cancer sticks in his early twenties for the sake of his future health, but upon hearing the news that the only thing standing between the world and its imminent destruction was him and four other misfits he'd decided that giving up had clearly been a hasty and unnecessary decision.

He sucked the smoke into his lungs. It felt good, which was more than he could say about pretty much anything else connected with his life, the universe, or any other aspect of objectively observed reality. He hadn't stayed long at the flat after the Storm's departure, but it had been long enough to witness the complete collapse of whatever cohesion the group might once have had. They'd all left: Darick to pray, Presto to drink, and Dani to do whatever the hell it was Dani did. Blade had made his apologies to Laliana and headed off too, first stop a corner-shop convenience store and a request for twenty Danburg Lights.

And then here.

A light was on in Toozie's house. The living room. The kids would be asleep, but it looked like Toozie was still up. He took a last drag on the cigarette, threw it to one side, then walked quickly through the shadows to her front gate and down the path to the door. He pressed the bell once, lightly; he didn't want to wake the kids up. He was about to try it again when he saw the hallway's light come on through the door's frosted glass and heard footsteps. The door opened, to reveal an unsmiling Toozie. "Had a weird feeling it might be you." She nodded towards the interior of the house. "You'd better come in."

He followed her down the hallway and into the lounge and sat himself down on the comfy chair by the fire. She sat down on the sofa opposite, her legs curled underneath her in a way that sparked a thousand memories. Behind her, the crystal silently played images of the rioting at Victory Square. Blade had no idea what to say. With a thing like this, where did you begin?

"You look like crap," she said.

"That's how I feel."

"You want to tell me about it?"

He shrugged, realising as he did so that the shrug was a lie. He'd come here to tell her about it. He'd always been coming here to tell her about it. "The stuff they're saying I've done; you know it ain't true, right?"

Toozie sighed. "Of course I know it isn't true. You might have many flaws, and the gods know that after spending nine years married to you I probably know them better than anyone else, but you're not that." She gave him a look that sat somewhere between sympathy and pity. "What in the world have you got yourself mixed up in?"

"It's a long story."

She smiled. "I'll get some coffee."

Blade paused and went to take a sip of his coffee but found he was down to the last bitter dregs. He put the mug down and continued. "So anyhow, Presto then managed to get into the spell's control panel, and played a message that the people who cast it recorded into it."

"A message?"

"Yeah. A 3D message with visuals and sound."

"And what did it say?"

Blade paused before he spoke. "That the world's going to end."

"The world's going to end?"

"Yeah. Pretty much. Plague, famine, war, and destruction was the general gist of it."

"Why?"

"Something to do with a sleeping dragon."

"The one you went to Craagon's Reach to look for?"

"Yeah."

Toozie shook her head in confusion before launching into an angry reply. "So what are these people who cast the spell going to do about it?"

"Nothing."

"Nothing?"

"Well, nothing more. They did do something about it. They cast the spell."

"What? You've lost me."

"They lived five hundred years ago. They found out about this through some kind of prophesying. They cast the spell to find us, so

155

we could save the world when the time came."

"You're supposed to save the world?"

"Apparently."

"You and the rock star and those other misfit friends of yours?"

"Yeah."

She fixed him with a very hard look. "I can see why you're so depressed."

The tatty sign above the gate proclaimed the price, twenty golds, and a date, which was today. The Storm joined the queue streaming in. It was years since he'd come here regularly, and even then he'd done it wrong: high on herb with people who acted like they were on a trip to the zoo to see the monkeys flinging poo at each other. It wasn't those days he was reaching for now, like a fat man reaching for comfort food. It was further back he was recalling, from before those days, from before everything. To when life was genuine, and real, and safe.

Finally, he reached the turnstile. He handed a crisp twenty gold note to the operator and the turnstile clicked him through. The press of the crowd carried him along; the sights and sounds inside settled upon him like a comfort blanket.

After a fruitless walk of the streets, Dani had returned to the flat to find it empty save for Laliana. Over warm mugs of hot chocolate, cupped in both hands, they talked through their options. Should they run, hide? And if so, where to, and what from? The message seemed pretty clear: the whole world was toast. Even when they'd been in the orphanage, or in the succession of short-lived foster homes, things had never been so bleak. They'd always had each other, and the future.

Now it was just each other.

Darick prayed.

Presto drank.

Toozie came back with a cafetière of fresh coffee. "Times like this I wish I still smoked," she remarked. Blade reached into his jacket pocket, pulled out the packet of Danburg Lights, flipped open the top, and held it out to her. She looked first at it, and then at him. "When did you start smoking again?"

"About an hour ago."

"There's only thirteen left."

"I've been very depressed."

She shrugged, then reached for the pack. He fished out the cheap disposable lighter he'd bought from the convenience store and lit the cigarette for her. She sucked deeply, thought for a moment, exhaled, and then spoke. "So what are you going to do, love?"

"What can I do?" Blade said, feeling lower than he'd felt for a long time – since the day when Toozie had told him she was leaving him, in fact.

But her next words jolted him back upright. "Save the world?"

"What?"

"Save the world," she smiled. "I'm serious. The spell chose you, right?"

"Well, we think there might have been a bit of a malfunction."

"But it still chose you."

"Yeah, I guess."

"And your friends."

"Yeah."

"So save the world. Do it. Do what the spell tasked you to do. Save the world. Save the kids. Save me. And save yourself."

"I'm just a has-been player in a stupid sport. How in any of the planes of hell am I supposed to save the world?"

"You're the greatest AdventureSport warrior the world's ever seen. I've seen you do things in the arena that took my breath away. And despite whatever I might have said about you…" She shook her head and smiled now. "You're a good, good man."

Blade thought for a moment, doubt, fear, and confusion pushing away the pride he might otherwise have felt at her words. "The arena's the arena. This is reality we're talking about now. How am I supposed to save the world when I don't even know what I'm supposed to be saving it from?"

"Isn't that wizard friend of yours some kind of genius?"

Blade shrugged. "Brain the size of a planet according to some archived net articles the Storm dug up."

"Then he'll figure out how to save the world. All you have to do is stand by his side and protect him from anyone who might try to stop him."

"You really think we can do it, Toozie?"

She smiled. "Wouldn't choose anyone else. Now maybe you'd

better go round up your friends from wherever they've got themselves."

Chapter Twenty-Four

It had been a while since the Storm had experienced being himself, and not "the Storm". Safely hidden as he was behind a deep-hooded top and a pair of wraparound shades, he was no longer a rock star to be disdained or admired or both. None of those around him were asking him for autographs or pictures on their whispers or for some of the hundreds of millions they were sure he had salted away.

(Which he didn't quite have salted away – herb, hangers on, and all the other accoutrements of a rock star lifestyle didn't come cheap).

No, to the people now milling happily around him he was just an anonymous Josf, albeit an anonymous Josf who was enough of a dickhead to wear a teen vandal's hooded robe-top and a pair of shades at night. He didn't care. Tonight, he didn't want to be the Storm, and if the price of that was looking like a dickhead instead, it was a price he was happy to pay. He approached one of the various stands set along the edge of the track and held out a pair of fifty gold notes. "A hundred golds on number seven."

The bookie pocketed the notes with an ease that spoke of decades of practice and then wrote out the betting slip. "There you go, mate. Hundred golds on number seven."

The Storm grabbed the slip and headed back into the stand. Those one hundred golds had been the last of the cash he had on him, but he didn't particularly give a damn. Not when the clock was ticking on reality and the big hand was about to reach twelve.

It was years since Blade had been to the chorgs, but he'd come here now, and his hunch had turned out to be right. He snuck up behind the Storm while the rock star was looking at the starting tape and tapped him on the shoulder.

The Storm jumped, then relaxed when he turned and found Blade looking back at him. "Whaa? What? Blade! How come you knew I was here?"

"I guessed," Blade told him, keeping his voice at a whisper. "I remembered you talking about going to the chorgs whenever you were feeling down, on account of how your dad used to take you when you were a kid, before he split."

"Oh yeah, right." The Storm thought for a moment, then bent his head in close to Blade. "But how'd you spot me in the crowd when

I'm wearing a disguise?"

"That's how I spotted you. It's nearly ten pm in early spring and out of the five thousand people here you and me are the only ones wearing sunglasses." Blade glanced across at the track and nodded at the white, fluffy chorgs currently munching grass behind the starting tape. "Who's your cash on?"

"Number seven. Figured he looked pretty nervous."

Given that chorgs as a species had a reputation for nerves and cowardice – not to mention a good spoonful of stupidity – that wasn't necessarily saying much. But while the other nine chorgs were busily engaged in vacuuming up the cut grass that had been scattered across the sandy track, number seven – dressed in a red coat with yellow stripes – was occasionally pausing for a quick look-see.

The Storm nudged Blade. "They're about to start."

The voice of the announcer burst out of the cheap and scratching speakers dotted around the stadium.

"And race number five is about to start. It's a two lap sprint, the wolf is running, and we're ready for the bell… now."

Just behind the grazing chorgs, a bell sounded for just a second or so. As one, the jumpy herbivores lifted their heads from the grass, turned, and looked behind them, just in time to witness a stuffed toy vaguely resembling a wolf come round the bend towards them, propelled along a rail attached to the inside of the track. The ten chorgs screamed in terror, and immediately set off in the opposite direction, hooves scrabbling on the loose sand, along the straight, and into the first turn.

"And it's number six into an early lead," screamed the announcer, breaking through the roaring of the crowd. "With number seven hard on his hooves."

"Come on number seven!" shouted Blade, forgetting for a moment where he was, who he was, and just how many serious crimes he was currently on the run from. A woman nearby gave him a "you really, really look like someone I know" look, and he gave her a smile and a "hi, there" nod in return, which would no doubt confuse the hell out of her.

"And it's number six still in the lead," said the announcer as the chorgs tore along the back straight and into the second turn. "But number seven's dropping back through the pack."

"Dammit!" muttered the Storm.

The chorgs scrabbled around the turn and into the home straight.

Motoring now, they tore across the finish line in front of Blade and the Storm and into the first corner for the second and last time, a relaxed looking number seven now trailing. The chorg looked left, then right, appeared to realise that he was now at the back with only sand and air between him and the wolf, and let out a long wail. Hooves scrabbling, he started to barge his way back through the rest of the pack.

"And it's number six still in the lead, but number seven's now moving back through the pack – but has he left it too late?"

"Come on number seven," Blade found himself muttering.

The chorgs shot along the back straight, the roar of the crowd now so loud that the speakers were having difficulty punching the voice of the announcer through it. "Number seven... moving... five from... six. Number seven... Number seven..."

The pack came round the final bend and into the main straight, the red-with-yellow striped coat of number seven somewhere in the mix. The terrified chorg jinked left, butted his way between four and five, and then put in a final sprint that took him past number six's blue coat just as they crossed the line. Around twenty percent of the crowd went wild. Somewhere over their roar Blade heard the announcer giving the official result. Number seven by a head from number six. He nudged the Storm. "Come on, mate. Let's go get your winnings."

"What's the point?" asked the Storm. "World's ending, mate. Didn't you get the newsflash?"

"World ain't ending, mate," Blade told him with a smile. "It's going to get saved."

"Who by?"

"Us, of course! Who else?"

The Storm wasn't quite sure about the whole saving the world thing. It was all right for Blade to casually declare that they were going to save the world; he was a warrior, able to kill, maim, or generally ruin the day of a man in at least fifteen different ways. The only way the Storm had ever ruined a man's day was by vomiting on his carpet, or by enticing his girlfriend away backstage and then giving her a damn good seeing to. He could see where the spell had been going with Blade; but it had clearly seriously malfunctioned when it decided he might have a role to play. What was he supposed to do? Play tunes to keep up everyone's spirits? And he couldn't even do that seeing as he'd left his lute the other side of the world.

He missed his lute. Blade was asking him something he hadn't caught. He shook his head. "Sorry, what was that mate?"

Blade repeated the question. "You got any idea where we might find Presto?"

They were sitting in a cheap, all-night cafe, eating an all-day breakfast that was long on grease and fat and short on anything resembling nutrition. The Storm sliced off a bit of sausage, speared it with his fork, smeared a wodge of beans and scrambled egg on top of that, and then shoved it in his mouth.

He always thought better when he was eating. "He did mention a pub he used to drink in," he told Blade, once he'd finished chewing. "The laughing something. Sounded like a right dump. Wasn't too far from here."

"How about Darick?"

"He'll be in that church just round the corner from Laliana's place. Praying."

"You reckon?"

"It's what I'd be doing if I was religious."

The laughing something turned out to be the Laughing Pikeman, and was indeed a dump. They found Presto slumped over a cluster of glasses in the far corner, alone, and drunk nearly to the point of unconsciousness. "Well, at least he's not in a position to argue," said Blade, scooping the wizard up and throwing him over one shoulder.

"Hey mate!" said the barman, as they walked past him towards the door.

Blade raised a questioning eyebrow.

"Anyone ever tell you you're the spitting image of Blade Petros?"

Blade laughed. "All the time, mate. I keep on thinking I'm going to get arrested at any moment."

There was a worm station just a few doors down from the pub. They descended into its dank and cramped tunnels and eventually found themselves on a worm heading back towards Laliana's place. A particularly loud clack as the worm sped between two stations woke Presto up. "Nother whisky, no water, no ice, no umbrella, no crap." He blinked, made something of an effort to focus on the Storm, then looked around the carriage. "We going somewhere?"

"Yeah," Blade told him. "We are. We're getting Darick."

"Why?"

"So he can help us save the world."

Presto thought for a moment, then shrugged. "Makes sense. Can we stop by a grog shop on the way?"

Darick had been praying now for several hours, but still the answer he sought had not come. No answers had come, in fact, and while it was not for him to question the ways in which the SkyFather might move, to have no answer at all was having a worryingly corrosive effect on his already shaky faith. *SkyFather*, he thought. *What would you have me do? What is your purpose in subjecting me to these trials? If you can give me no answers, then at least give me a sign!*

The door crashed open, propelled on its way by a tripping Presto. Behind the now fallen wizard were Blade and the Storm. "Sorry about that," slurred Presto from the floor. "I was trying to open the door. Might have slipped."

"We came to pick you up," said Blade. "We're going to save the world."

"Do you think that's the SkyFather's will?" asked Darick.

The Storm smiled. "Isn't everything?"

The next morning, back at the flat with Dani and Laliana, fuelled by copious quantities of strong coffee and a good supply of toast, they sat down for a brainstorming session. When Blade had arrived back at the flat the previous night, with the Storm, Darick, and an epically plastered Presto in tow, announcing that they were going to save the world, Dani had assumed that the sportsman had some kind of plan. This was an assumption that very quickly died as the brainstorming session settled into an awkward silence, broken only by the metaphorical whirring of brain cells firing random signals in the hope that somewhere along the line, a couple might collide and bring forth a new thought. Dani decided she'd better try to get a grip on things. "Okay. Let's start again from the top. What do we know?"

"We're looking for a sleeping dragon beneath Craagon's Reach," said Darick.

"But when we tried, like, going there, some cat tried to ambush us," added the Storm.

Presto leaned forward. "The same individual who was questioning me on the skyship, and–" He stopped speaking, his face blank, as though a memory had surfaced and triggered a sudden realisation. "It's not a sleeping dragon. He kept on asking me what I knew about sleeping dragon. Not the sleeping dragon, or a sleeping dragon, but just sleeping dragon. It's not a thing, it's a name."

"What, like the code name of a project, say?" asked the Storm.

"Exactly."

"Does that help us?" asked Darick.

"No," said Dani, realising the implications. "If it's just a code name then it's no help at all."

"What about the skyship?" asked Blade. "Can you remember anything about that?"

Presto lapsed into thought. "All I saw were blank corridors and grey-suited guards. Save for one glimpse of countryside below and the people interrogating me, I never saw anything or talked to anyone."

"That's a shame—"

"No, wait. When I fell out, I spun round, once, twice." The wizard screwed up his eyes. "I saw the ship spinning around me. It was dirty white, no markings, except for a number near the tail. GH dash... something. Sorry, that's all I managed to see."

Dani was already grabbing Laliana's portable oracle. "That's all we need."

"You can identify it from that?"

"I can do more than identify it. There're skyspotters out there logging everything that moves from the Western Ocean to the World's End mountains. And those logbooks will all have been uploaded to the net. We might not be able to find out where it was going, but we'll sure as hell be able to find out where it's been."

Presto sipped his coffee as Dani's fingers danced across the oracle's keyboard at a speed that strongly suggested that this was a task to which they were accustomed. After a few minutes of tapping and pausing, the grifter looked up, smiling. "Got it. GH-78. Plain, white. Left Empire City West skyport a couple of hours after Presto was captured, departed on an easterly heading."

"Which tells us nothing!" said Blade.

"Yeah, but if I look at the history…" She tapped away again, and then let out an interested, "Ah!"

"What?"

"It's got a whole bunch of locations, but with weird gaps between them, like it'd been heading off to private strips where you don't get spotters. But there's one place that it's visited three times in the last four months, and the last time was only a few days before it picked Presto up."

Presto put his coffee down. "And that place was?"

"Upabove."

Chapter Twenty-Five

Upabove was an obsolete relic that shone with the light of ages past; a name that conjured up images of wealth, intrigue, and decadence. It had been founded a little over three hundred years ago by a group of refugees fleeing the carnage brought by the Empire's Great Succession War. Desperate, they'd set out by carpet across the Middle Sea towards the independent lands beyond; a destination far beyond the range of that era's early and crude flying vehicles. Reaching safety would require them to ditch in the sea while their vehicles' mana stores recharged, in carpets not designed for ditching.

Many refugees undertook those sorts of desperate journeys, and many were never seen again. But fate, chance, and geography smiled upon this particular group, for at the halfway point of their journey they encountered a unique and hitherto unsuspected anomaly: an area a mile or so across, around five thousand feet above the surface of the sea, in which the background level of mana was more than five times the standard. The downward progress of the charge needles in their carpets, which had been moving relentlessly towards zero, halted, and then reversed. The needles began to rise, and within hours were sitting at the top, fully charged. The refugees realised they were sitting atop some kind of flaw in the world's mana field that leaked mana like a volcano leaks magma.

People with lesser ambition, or who were less blessed in imagination, would have waited until their carpets were fully charged, and then resumed their journey, thanking the gods and fate for the good fortune that had spared them a risky and possibly terminal ditching. But these were not such people. Instead, they took the older and slower carpets and lashed them together, building a temporary shelter for the children, the old, and the sick. Then a group sped back to the Empire, returning with supplies, building materials, and people. From those ramshackle beginnings they built a floating city that they called Upabove.

Upabove grew fabulously wealthy in its first two centuries. Its skilled magical artisans were able to use its high background mana level to create items that were both better and cheaper than those produced elsewhere; its position at the centre of the Middle Sea allowed skyships and carpets to travel directly across the sea rather than around its periphery, stopping at Upabove to recharge.

Upabove was never technically an independent state; in fact it was never a state at all, consisting legally of nothing more than a collection of skyships, tethered together. But its inhabitants used their wealth and power to gain a de facto independence, registering their floating palaces under a succession of flags of convenience with border principalities on the fringes of the Empire. They called their state a republic, and themselves merchant princes. But then, some hundred or so years ago, a series of advances in magical technology rendered Upabove obsolete. Improvements in mana storage and more efficient motors meant that skyships and carpets could now fly not hundreds of miles on a single charge, but thousands. And new techniques for magical item production allowed finer items to be crafted using far less mana.

On Upabove, little appeared to change. The merchant princes continued to party as decadently as before, but now the money was flowing outward, not inward. It was said by some that it had taken the inhabitants of Upabove two centuries to earn their fortunes but less than one century to squander them. Others joked that while Upabove was now bankrupt, its inhabitants would notice this only when the drinks tab ran out. Like a neglected gemstone, Upabove started to tarnish. The magnificent palaces, now old and their maintenance neglected, showed signs of rust under layers of peeling paint. Meanwhile, Upabove's hard-earned quasi-independence grew fragile, maintained only by the inability of surrounding governments to agree on what its new status should be. People whispered of mortgage defaults and hostile takeovers, and talked of an invasion by stealth.

But through all of this, the merchant princes partied on. Upabove might have been a relic, and a bankrupt one at that, but it was still Upabove.

And it was still magnificent.

When Dani walked out of the docking tube's open maw she found the arrivals hall quiet, its customs and security men bored. This was good. She was the last of the team to arrive, and if anything had happened when the guys had arrived on their earlier flights the place would have had that buzz of recent excitement. She approached the customs desk with a smile and handed over the fake passport she'd bought the previous day from an old contact who specialised in magically encoded documentation.

The customs man took a cursory look at the document, then ran it under some sort of scanner that – after a moment's pause – produced the right kind of beep. "Purpose of visit?" the man asked in a bored monotone.

"Bit of business, bit of shopping maybe," Dani told him, throwing in a simpering smile when she got to the shopping bit.

The customs man considered that for a moment, then pushed the passport back across the desk. "Enjoy your stay."

Ten minutes later, her recently purchased suitcase collected from the baggage belt, Dani was crowding into one of the array of lifts that connected the skyport to Upabove proper. Most of her fellow passengers got out at the main pedestrian level, but Dani exited the lift a stop later, at the level marked "cabs". A cab would get her to her hotel room quicker, but her choice of cab over foot was driven not by speed but by a simple universal truth: that there's no individual on earth more talkative than a cab driver.

Upabove was built like a spinning top, albeit one made from hundreds of separate pieces that merely floated in formation, connected by a spider's web of walkways. The "disc" consisted of a ring nearly half a mile in diameter, with a rounded outer surface sculpted to deflect the strong winds that blew at this altitude; and an inner surface terraced into gardens, balconies, and public walkways. Floating inside the ring were hundreds of separate buildings, some squat, others shaped like long, thin cigars set on end with their tops and bottoms extending far above and below the ring's protected inner space.

At the centre of the "disc" was a long, thin needle that extended both further above the ring and further below than every other part of Upabove. At its bottom were clusters of docking ports, connected to which were more than a dozen large skyships, including the one that Dani had just arrived on. At the needle's top, a forest of communication dishes and antennas sprouted. And somewhere in between was the long narrow platform of the cab rank, upon which Dani now found herself.

A line of carpets painted in yellow and black checkers floated next to the platform. Dani stepped carefully into the first of the waiting vehicles, which was piloted by a slightly chubby man just this side of unkempt. "Far Clouds Hotel, please," she told the cabbie. "But could you take the long way? This is my first visit here and I'd like to see a bit of the place."

"No problem love," the cabbie told her. "I'll take a loop around the hoop." The man smiled, clearly pleased with the rhyme.

The carpet glided away, passing over the floating buildings that made up Upabove's "disc". The cab pilot started pointing out various features. "That building there, the one that looks like it's covered in gold – that's the casino. And see that group over there that form a square? That's Founders' Place, where the Opera House is."

Dani looked further down, at the docking platforms below. "A friend of mine said her skyship was docking at Platform Twenty-Seven. Do you know which one of them that is?"

"Ain't any of them, love. Twenty-seven's over there." The cab pilot hooked his thumb back at somewhere the other side of the central needle. "It's not down there on the hub. It's a private platform attached to one of the buildings on the eastern side. Think your friend must have got her numbers mixed up."

"Really? I was pretty sure she said twenty-seven."

"Yeah? Tell you what, I'll show it to you."

"There it is," said the cabbie. "Palace Gennaro, home of the Gennaro family." He was pointing at a tall building, shaped like a squat cucumber standing on end, and clad in what looked to be real marble, incongruously so given it was floating five thousand feet up. Reflections played across its smooth, rounded surface.

The cabbie brought the carpet down to a slow, drifting crawl and began to point out various features. "It measures more than three hundred and fifty feet from top to bottom and it's more than a hundred feet wide at its widest point. At the bottom, there's your docking platform twenty-seven." Before Dani had a chance to do much more than glance down the cabbie was pointing out more things. "And see all the gargoyles around the middle?"

Dani followed his outstretched finger. At a dozen or so evenly spaced points around the building's equator, jets of water sprayed out, turning to mist as they fell towards the sea five thousand feet below. And at each originating point was a tiny protuberance, visible at this distance only as a marring of the otherwise smooth perfection of the outer surface. "Are those the things spraying water?"

"Yeah," the cabbie smiled. "They're supposed to be caricatures of certain members of other families."

"Where do they get the water from?"

"Some kind of continuous spell teleporting it up from the sea below, apparently."

"Isn't that burning through a lot of mana?"

"This is Upabove. We've got mama to burn. And there's no one who could tell them any different if there wasn't. Each palace is its own sovereign territory, independently registered." The cabbie pushed at the controls, and the carpet sped up, curving in a loop around and down. "The original structure's more than two hundred years old. Makes it one of the oldest buildings here."

Dani let out a tourist style exclamation: "Wow! That's pretty old. Are they an old family, then?"

The cabbie laughed. "Very. Lord Gennaro's great-great-great and then some grandfather was one of the first settlers, on one of the nine carpets that found this place. On Upabove, that's as old as it gets."

"Who's Lord Gennaro?"

"Lord Georgu Gennaro. Current head of the family and member of the Council of Five."

Dani tried to look the right kind of interested. She'd read up a bit on Upabove before they set out, but she knew from past experience that what was written down was too often an official lie rather than an actual truth. Playing a dumb tourist now might tell her something the Overnet hadn't. "The Council of Five. Is that sort of like your parliament?"

"No. That's the Grand Council, except that all it does is meet every six months to waffle and then elect the Council of Five. It's the Five that actually does stuff."

"And Lord Gennaro's a member of the Five?"

"Yep. Pretty big man round here, although rumour has it not as big as he'd like to be. People say he figures he should be the Chairman of the Five, but the Pederton family have had that job sown up for the last hundred and fifty years and it doesn't look like it's going to change anytime soon."

Dani thought for a moment. What she'd read on the net had strongly suggested that Upabove was a republic in name only, given that only members of the founding families got to vote for the Grand Council, and that all actual power appeared to be vested in the Council of Five – which, just to confuse things, actually had seven members, including its chairman. And now, in this mystery within which she and her companions were both pursuer and pursued, a new character had appeared, one who was powerful and yet disaffected, and who had access to a personal landing pad that Dani strongly suspected bypassed whatever customs and security Upabove might possess. A landing pad that had been visited three times in the last two months by the ship that had taken Presto away.

The cabbie shrugged. "Oh well, better get you to your hotel, love. Far Clouds, wasn't it?"

"Yeah. Thanks for the tour. I appreciate it."

"No problem. I'll probably be back here quite a few times tonight."

"Really? Why would that be?"

"Tonight's Lord Gennaro's annual masquerade ball. Practically anyone and everyone with a vote for Grand Council gets an invite. Come eight tonight this place will be so thick with carpets you could practically walk across them."

The Far Clouds turned out to be a modest, utilitarian establishment built high in the western portion of the encircling ring, with a lobby that offered a spectacular view of the floating palaces scattered across the "lagoon".

Dani's room, alas, didn't offer a view of anything, and having failed miserably in the view department, it entirely failed to make up for that in the size department, consisting as it did of only a tiny shower and a bedroom barely large enough for a single bed and a built-in wardrobe. Nonetheless, Blade, Darick, the Storm, Presto, and Laliana had somehow managed to join Dani in its small interior, allowing her to brief the others.

Having outlined what she'd found about docking platform twenty-seven and its aristocratic owner, she moved onto the subject of the evening's event, but was interrupted by Blade before she got three words in.

From the look on his face, it seemed he wasn't quite sure he'd heard her right. "A masquerade ball?"

"It's a party," Dani told him. "Where people wear masks, and costumes too, according to the cabbie I talked to."

"I know what a masquerade ball is. I'm not quite sure why we're going to one." The Warrior looked around the tiny hotel room and got a series of nods from Darick and the Storm on the bed, Presto in the room's only chair, and Laliana sitting cross-legged on the floor.

"Like I said, the skyship was visiting this bloke's palace. That means he must be involved somehow in whatever it is that's going on. And if he's holding a masked party that's too good an opportunity for poking around around to ignore."

Blade shook his head. "Seems like a risk. Heading in without checking out what's going on first."

Dani could see where he was going, but frankly didn't want him to get there. Bitter experience had taught her the cost of failing to seize passing opportunities. Normally, she worked alone, and decisions on when to duck and when to dive had always been her call to make. Having to justify her plans to others was a new experience for her, and one that thus far she wasn't particularly enjoying.

She took a deep breath and made a conscious effort to look patient, but firm. "When you've only got one lead it's a bigger risk not following it."

Darick raised a hand. "But surely it will be by invitation only? And if it's a masquerade ball they'd have to have some kind of actual invite."

"I'll get us invites."

"How?"

"Don't know yet. But I've got until eight tonight to figure it out."

It was the Storm who raised the next objection. "And what are we supposed to be doing when we're there?"

"Look. Listen. Poke around if possible."

She turned her attention back to Blade, figuring that if she could get him on side, the others would follow. He considered things for a moment, then nodded. "Okay. I'm not sure you've actually got a plan but I sure as seven hells ain't, so I figure we may as well go with this." The warrior looked around at the others and got a series of vaguely affirmative nods. "What do we do?"

Dani snapped back into action. "Laliana? You go with Darick and find some kind of costume shop. We want masks and costumes, nothing too cheap. We need to look like we belong. Presto? Go to the library and get reading. Anything and everything about Upabove. Get that pictographic memory of yours working. Blade, Storm?"

The two of them looked eagerly at her.

"Stay here. Don't get captured."

Chapter Twenty-Six

Dani was discovering that Lord Gennaro was not a man for half measures when it came to party invitations. His invites for the party had, it transpired, been hand delivered to more than four hundred invitees by messenger boys dressed in a uniform of traditional sky blue Gennaro colours, who handed over to their designated recipients a honeywood box inlaid with unicorn horn and lined inside with preserved dragonskin. Nestling inside the box was a smooth, egg-shaped piece of pure firestone which, when held by a human hand, turned a milky-transparent to reveal inside a three dimensional image of a pulsing, rainbow-coloured snow-eagle. Meanwhile, the "egg" would telepathically transmit a message from Lord Gennaro himself straight to the invitee's brain, inviting them and their companions to the party, and giving them the relevant details.

Dani was no expert on the construction of custom magical artefacts, but the raw materials alone in each invite would easily have cost in excess of five thousand golds. Not that Dani had an invite to examine, of course. The above had come straight from the pages of a glossy magazine article that described in breathless tones the party that Gennaro was planning.

She muttered a silent curse, and took another sip of coffee.

This might just be harder than faking a paper ticket. She remembered what Griff had always said in these situations: think the problem through. As invitations went, these were pretty much unforgeable. And given that the location in question was floating more than five thousand feet up and had only a couple of ways in, all of which would be guarded, getting in without an invitation was not an option worth pursuing. Which by process of elimination left only one option.

Getting hold of an actual invite.

Dani had long ago learned that the more apparent security you have, the more everyone involved relaxes, lowering their guard and putting aside their suspicions. In this case, with a party that would be pretty much impossible to gain entry to without an invitation, the corresponding and equal effect would be that possession of an invite would pretty much guarantee entry to the party, no questions asked. But these weren't just trivial bits of paper that people would be happy to trade, nor worthless items that they might leave lying around, unguarded. This was a prized event to which everyone would want to go, and even if someone didn't plan on going, a limited edition artefact worth in excess of five thousand golds was something you tended to hang on to.

You could still purchase one, of course. There would always be someone willing to sell if the price was right, but in order to buy something you typically have to find someone who wants to sell, and that would involve putting themselves out into the open, especially given they'd only had a few hours to set it up. No. They needed a more elegant approach, one that wouldn't blow their cover before they'd even begun.

She tossed a twenty gold note onto the coffee shop's counter, shoved the magazine into her shoulder bag, and left, heading over to the library, still thinking. A way to get hold of an invite that didn't require someone who was looking to dispose of it. A way that let that person dispose of it without even knowing they'd disposed of it. She found Presto in the reference section, his head now home to an encyclopaedic knowledge of Upabove's geography, politics, and culture. As Dani ran various ideas and questions past him, a thought began to form in her brain. Of course. A masquerade party. Everyone masked. She headed out of the library, leaving Presto to continue his reading, then pulled the cheap pay-as-you-go whisper she'd bought the previous day in Empire City out of her pocket and dialled Laliana's number. Her sister answered on the third ring.

"Yeah?"

"It's me. Are you still at the costume place?"

"Yeah. How would you feel about something skimpy for yourself?"

"Badly. Listen, I need you to get a few extra outfits."

"No problem. What do you need?"

"Basic security guard outfits for Darick and me. The sort of things door staff wear. Padded jacket, smart shoes, that sort of thing. But see if you can have them trimmed with something sky blue, a sash maybe."

"Okay."

"And a chauffeur's outfit, jacket, cap, that sort of thing, for Blade."

"Right. Why do we need all of this?"

"You'll see." She hung up and began scanning through the small ads attached to a community noticeboard mounted in the library's entrance. Three rows down, two columns in she found exactly what

she needed. She dialled the number in. "Mr Henraan?"
"Speaking."
"Excellent. I've just seen the ad you put up. Would you have a free slot tonight? Eight o'clock onwards?"

Lord Kormac Quentiara had packed a lot of living into his twenty-two years, if you define "living" as consisting exclusively of drinking, taking herb, attending parties, and having sex with lots of fabulously good looking women. Of course, if you define living as having anything to do with working, responsibility, or care for others, then Lord Kormac had managed to experience very little in the way of living in the twenty-two years since he'd popped out of the surrogate. (His mother being too posh to be pregnant, let alone push.)

Tonight was going to be fabulous. Mega. Because tonight was Lord Gennaro's ball, the must-see, must-be-seen social event of the year, and he had an invite! But of course he would. Was he not Upabove's most famous socialite, playboy, and gossip-column staple? The man every girl wanted to date, just so that they could bask in the reflected glory of being his latest dumpee? It was all too much. He tapped out a couple of lines of herb from the gold-clad, pearl-lined box his mother had given him for his sixteenth birthday ("Only herb-whores snort herb straight out of the wrap, darling!"), sniffed it up, and then made a last couple of adjustments to his outfit: a mask of silver set with dozens of sparkling diamonds, a costume of gold thread, and not much else.

Perfect.

He snapped the herb box closed and shoved it into his small shoulder bag alongside the smooth, firestone invitation egg. There was a knock at the door. A servant clad in the Quentiara colours of green and orange entered cautiously. "A limousine has arrived, my lord, and the driver has given the code word specified in the message."

As a general rule, Lord Kormac never hurried for anything. People who live their life in the belief that the Universe rotates around them rarely do. But on this occasion he made an exception, because something very exciting was happening, even more exciting than he'd been anticipating. Lord Gennaro had sent a personal message to his whisper that afternoon, explaining that this year he was doing something even more different, even more special – and Lord Kormac couldn't wait. This was one merchant prince who was going to party hard tonight.

He hurried out to the carpet platform on the palace's fifteenth floor and found the limousine waiting, floating next to the platform with the door to the rear cabin already open. He hopped in and settled into the luxurious leather seat. The door closed with a clunk, the magnetic grapples holding the vehicle to the platform released with a second clunk, and then the limousine glided smoothly away.

"Be just a few minutes, m'lord," said the limousine's pilot, from his seat at the front. Kormac couldn't see much of the driver, his view blocked as it was by his seat. But there was a gravel in that voice, and muscles beneath the arms of that uniform, and when he caught sight of those eyes in the rear-view mirror there was a piercing quality to them that cut right through him.

He made a mental note to ask Lord Gennaro to book this driver for his return journey home. Ordering him to stop on the way so whichever female companions Kormac had picked up could shag the man senseless would be the perfect way to chill-out and wind-down after the party. A few minutes later the limousine glided to a halt beside a frankly nondescript looking bar located in the unfashionable western side of the lagoon. Lord Kormac looked out of the window at it. It was plain, and crude, and...

The chauffeur caught his eye. "Everything okay, m'lord?"

...and it was perfect. Lord Gennaro was a genius. It was just as he'd said on the message. All his previous parties had been held at Gennaro Palace, but the message had explained that this year he was doing something different, something to mess up the plans of the news-slate pictographers who on previous years had crowded the walkways opposite his palace, taking pictures of the guests as they arrived. This year they wouldn't be able to. Because this year he was holding the party at a different, secret location, to which guests would be taken by the limousines Lord Gennaro would dispatch for them, whose drivers would give code-words to establish that they were Lord Gennaro's men. And this was that location.

He looked back at the chauffeur. "Everything's perfect."

The man nodded and reached down for a control. The door beside Kormac opened smoothly, to reveal a couple of doormen – one male, one female – clad in security-guard type uniforms trimmed with Lord Gennaro's sky-blue. A handwritten sign behind them stated that the bar had been hired for a private function. Handwritten. How delightfully quaint.

The doorwoman extended an arm to help him climb out of the limousine, no doubt copping an eyeful as she did so. She was cute, if a little boyish. Lord Kormac brushed invisible lint off what little there was of his costume, then headed towards the open doorway, from whose darkened interior was emerging a thumping soundtrack, set over a background hum of excited chatter. The doorwoman stopped him politely, hesitantly, with an arm. "M'lord? The invitation?"

Oh yes. He reached down into his shoulder bag and pulled out the egg. The doorwoman examined it for a moment, then nodded, satisfied. "We'll look after it here for you. You can collect it when you leave."

Lord Kormac didn't answer her. Flunkies were for talking at, not to, and to offer a reply would have been to talk to her, not at her. Besides, he was already heading through the doorway, into a space that was full of people, all masked, all costumed, already dancing, already partying.

This was going to be the best night ever.

Blade didn't realise he'd been holding his breath until Dani and Darick had piled into the back of the limousine and he'd accelerated smoothly away. "Everything go okay?"

Dani nodded. "Yeah. I had a bunch of lines rehearsed in case he wanted to hang onto the egg, but he went straight in."

"So how long do you think it will take him to realise he's not at the actual party?"

Blade was watching Dani in the rear-view mirror as she considered the question for a moment before speaking. "Hard to say. Sooner or later, one of the people there's going to blab that they're actually an actor or actress hired for some kind of PR gig. But he looked like he was already pretty herbed up, so I'd guess somewhere between a fair while later and never. Long enough for us to pick up the rest of the guys and use his egg to get in anyhow."

"Sounds good," Blade told her. He guided the limousine past a floating restaurant and over a couple of walkways. Three familiar looking figures were waiting for them at a cab rank. "And there they are."

Chapter Twenty-Seven

Within ten seconds of entering the Grand Ballroom, Darick had come to the conclusion that all those present were quite likely destined to spend their afterlives in one of the less pleasant, lower planes of eternity. Within twenty seconds, that conclusion had been upgraded from "quite likely" to "highly probable", and within thirty seconds it was homing in on "nearly certain".

Debauched, depraved, and degenerate didn't even begin to cover it.

The several dozen trays of canapés alone probably qualified as a collective sin of shame, given that they appeared to contain enough food to feed a hungry village for a month and – if the sneering waiter who'd glided over to Darick was to be believed – had apparently been created at a cost sufficient to purchase enough regular food to feed said village for decades. Fabulous pastries topped with unicorn's milk cheese, the waiter had declared. Three hundred year old hard-boiled dragon eggs, decorated with truffle shards and topped with iced-caviar from the northern lakes. Deep fried sea serpent, flavoured with shavings of its own skin. Roast basilisk, carved from a creature that had been raised by blindfolded stockmen with a life expectancy lower than a sacred box suicide bomber, and then killed by slaughtermen bearing mirrors. Every piece of fruit was carved into a flower. Each vegetable, no matter how small, had been stuffed.

And that was just the start of it, the appetiser to the party's full spectrum of awfulness.

Beyond the many and varied sins of condemnation too numerous to count, most of which involved various combinations of masked-nudity and uninhibited sex, there existed an array of full-blown sins of damnation, carried out without any apparent shame or embarrassment or even awkwardness. In one corner of the room, three individuals with the dirty clothes and drawn faces of homeless men stood in a cage, watching as party goers pulled fifty gold notes from a stack set before the cage and gleefully lit them, using a cigarette lighter supplied by one of many ubiquitous, sky-blue uniformed staff.

In the centre of the room, an enthusiastically screaming woman was mounted upon an anatomically correct model of the SkyFather, an activity deeply blasphemous, in addition to being stratospherically obscene. On gold-rimmed crystals mounted around the room, skin-flicks played on an endless loop. Levitating, herb-laden trays bobbed through the gathering at just below nostril height.

Above the guests' heads, magically animated flying gold penises flew around the room in a swarm, silver wings flapping, ejaculating pearls in choreographed displays. A five piece chamber ensemble, naked save for their instruments, played music of a quality rendered incongruous by the degree to which it was wonderful while all around it was not. And over everything, flavouring everything, came the superior tones and harsh laughter of people raised without empathy into a life without compassion or thought.

Dani appeared at Darick's elbow, clad now in the costume of a witch-adjudicator of the Second Age. "You know, there's apparently at least one noble house around here with a very dysfunctional family tree on account of someone accidentally shagging his own mother at one of these type of events," she muttered, before moving smoothly away.

It was a scene beyond any horror Darick could ever have imagined. He would have closed his eyes were it not for the certainty that the scenes would continue to play on the insides of his eyelids. There was nothing good in a place like this. Nothing of worth. Nothing that any decent person could possibly hold dear. He took another look at the plate held by one of the sneering waiters as it glided past him. Gluttonous sins aside, the food did look awfully good, and he was quite hungry.

He reached out to grab a canapé, muttering a silent prayer of forgiveness to the SkyFather as he did so.

After dropping the guys off at the main entrance platform, Blade parked the carpet at a long pier, ten floors down and round the back, in amongst those carpets that had already arrived. Still clad in his chauffeur's uniform, wearing coloured contacts, with his hair dyed, and holding out the entrance ticket he'd been handed ten floors above, he strode into the Palace Gennaro servants' quarters projecting a nonchalance he sure as hell didn't feel.

A sky-blue clad security man swiped the ticket through a scanner then waved a vague hand at the entrance behind him. "Down there, second door on the left. There's coffee, snacks, and the Lastday Night ASport game on the crystal."

The second door on the left led to a plain, but functional canteen style room, with booths down one side, a table on the other laden with sandwiches and urns of tea and coffee, and a sixty-inch crystal mounted on the far wall upon which a thankfully muted Brod Rellend and Kren Krennella were silently mouthing a stream of what would almost certainly be bollocks. A handful of other chauffeurs were already in the room, some of them watching the pre-game build up, others engaged in a group discussion that apparently involved much passionate gesticulation.

Blade poured himself a coffee, piled a couple of sandwiches onto a paper plate, and slid into an empty booth as far away from the crystal screen and the other chauffeurs as he could manage. Three bites into the sandwich and two sips into the coffee, a figure in a gold trimmed black uniform slid onto the bench opposite.

"Mind if I join you? I'm not one for the game, and the politics they're arguing over bore me rigid."

Blade nodded as noncommittally as he could manage.

"You're new here, right? Haven't seen you around. What brings you to Upabove?"

It wasn't until he'd decamped to the gents' toilets that the Storm realised that his First Millennium era Gladiator outfit lacked a certain flexibility in the bathroom department. Eventually, however, having figured out how to detach his armoured codpiece, he settled in for a long, relaxing, and much needed pit stop at the nearest urinal.

He felt good.

Well, strictly speaking, he felt nicely herbed up and a little drunk, but that was close enough to good for government work, right? His long stream eventually diminished to a dribble, and after the requisite several shakes and one for good luck, he grabbed his cod-piece from the marble shelf upon which he'd deposited it. He was still engaged in figuring out just how the codpiece might be reattached when he was roused from his thoughts by a feminine sounding cough from behind him.

"I hate to break it to you dear, but this isn't the gents. And that—" her hand reached past him to point at the urinal "—isn't a urinal."

The Storm looked closely at the urinal, blinked, focused, and then made a second attempt at observation. Upon closer examination, it did appear to have taps, of the sort more usually associated with washbasins than urinals.

Ah. Bugger.

He spun round, his codpiece in his hand, his mail leggings still around his thighs. A middle-aged, but still strikingly attractive woman stood before him, her jewel-encrusted mask pushed up onto her forehead. She smiled. "Having a little costume trouble, dear? Let's take a look, shall we?"

She grabbed the codpiece and bent down, examining the various straps and clips that surrounded his penis.

"Ah, yes. I think I can see–" She stopped speaking abruptly, rocking back on her heels for a moment, before leaning back in to examine his penis in great detail. She looked at first one side, and then the other, then stood up to look the Storm straight in his masked face. "I know you!"

A masked ball is a great social leveller, the anonymity of the participants effectively neutralising the pre-existing social hierarchy. For Dani, who made her living from the manipulation of social situations, this was both good and bad. Masked anonymity eased her infiltration of the party's social hierarchy, but in turn hid that hierarchy from her. Being effectively invisible isn't so useful when everyone else is similarly invisible.

Her plan, such as there was one, had been to get herself close to Lord Gennaro. She'd hoped that even masked it would be obvious who the host of the party was. She still hoped that that might be the case later, but right now it appeared that Lord Gennaro was either being fashionably late to his own party, or was taking the opportunity to spy on his guests. At something of a loss, she'd instead resorted to circling the room, scanning for clues, hooks, and angles, while simultaneously keeping tabs on her companions. So far – fingers crossed – they were all good. Laliana was staying reassuringly close to her. Darick had spent twenty minutes grazing the canapés, before retreating to the balcony outside, presumably in search of an environment that was just a touch less offensive. Presto had spent the last ten minutes engaged in conversation with the back half of a costume horse, apparently oblivious to the fact that the front half of the horse was snogging the face off a man who wore a mask, a silk sock – which wasn't on his foot – and not much else.

The Storm, finally, had eschewed the food in favour of copious quantities of foaming fire-wine and sufficient lines of herb for Dani to be frankly relieved when he'd staggered through one of the doors leading to the Grand Ballroom's toilets, even if he had missed the gents and landed instead in the ladies.

Her relief turned out to be premature, though, as some minutes after entering the ladies the Storm came stumbling out, minus his codpiece and with his leggings still around his knees, followed by a statuesque brunette who appeared to be in something of a mood.

"I'd recognise that sorry excuse for a penis anywhere!" the brunette screamed at the Storm's awkwardly departing back.

She grabbed one of the levitating herb trays, grappled with it until its levitation spell gave up the fight, then flung it, Burning-Lands-war-discus style, at the Storm's head. The tray arched across the space between them, narrowly missing the rock star and instead slamming hard into the face of an attendee whose elaborate mask and spectacular dress failed to disguise her advanced age. She went down, pole-axed, blood pouring from her nose.

The Storm's leggings chose that moment to finally give up their battle with gravity, falling to his still shuffling ankles, an action that sent their owner crashing into, onto, and ultimately through, a table around which six people had been attempting to sit. One of them had been in the process of snorting a line of herb from a mirror when the Storm's tumbling body entered her life. The table gave way beneath her and she fell; and when as a result she hit the floor, the rolled hundred gold note that she'd inserted into her nose was rammed up her nostril and halfway to her brain.

She screamed.

Angry cries began to echo around the ballroom.

Luckily, Blade's unwanted companion had turned out to be of the talkative type, happy to drive the conversation as long as Blade threw him the occasional, vague reply.

"Me, I've always been into carpets and skyships," the other chauffer was saying. "There aren't many places where you can get work as a pilot, but still have a wild blue yonder out there where you can just surf the clouds, you know?"

Blade did know. When he'd started the path that led to a carpet pilot's license – the night classes, the distance study, the lessons – his motivation had been the challenge of mastering a discipline most had assumed would be beyond him. But he'd soon fallen hook, line, and sinker for the pure, simple joy of flight, of soaring through the empty blue skies freed of the prisons of an earth-bound life.

He nodded, an action that was apparently enough for his

companion to resume talking.

"And if you're into skyships, there aren't many places where you can get so close to the action, you know? Most places the skyport's way out of the city, but here, the skyport is the city. We see all sorts here."

Blade found himself sitting up just a little bit straighter. "Really?"

"Oh, yeah. And not just at the main docks down at the bottom of the Pillar. A lot of the palaces have their own skyport docking points. You know, part of that whole each-merchant-palace-being-its-own-sovereign-state, thing."

Blade pushed his coffee to one side, and leaned in, trying to let just a controlled fraction of his excitement leak through. "Yeah, someone was telling me that there was a skyship docked at this place just a few days ago, and it's made quite a few visits. White, no markings?"

His companion smiled, clearly happy to have found someone he could share his enthusiasm with. "Oh yeah, I know that one. Kind of nice sometimes to see a ship that isn't plastered with crappy logos, you know?" Suddenly, the man snapped his fingers. "I had a fare a couple of months ago who was catching a ride out on that very ship. He'd finished his business early and cadged himself a lift on it, and needed me to drop him off here."

"Really?"

"Yeah, gods' truth. He was a bit weird, actually. Not in a bad way. Professor type, you know? Academic, like."

"Some sort of university guy?"

"Yeah, except it wasn't a university. He paid on his corporate card, and I remember the name of his organisation was on my accounts summary at the end of that day. Now, what was it? It wasn't a university, but it was something like a university..." He trailed off, thinking hard.

Blade meanwhile sat rigid, only the violently shaking knee beneath the table revealing the amount of hidden adrenaline currently surging through him.

The other pilot clicked his fingers again. "That was it. The Institute for Advanced Magical Research. I remember thinking that it sounded like a pretty prestigious type of thing."

Just then, the door from the corridor outside crashed open, and one of the House Gennaro servants tumbled in. "Guys! You'd better grab your carpets! There's trouble up top!"

Chapter Twenty-Eight

Presto hadn't had this much fun in years.

He ducked under a punch, aura-blasted the fist's owner, slinked past a pair of women busy trying to rip each other's hair out, and grabbed a canapé from a passing waiter who was still attempting to serve food to the minority of guests who weren't involved in the mass brawl the Storm had sparked.

The canapé was exquisite; a streak of something savoury that practically melted on the tongue wrapped around a core of spiced sweetness. Still munching, Presto crawled under a table and found himself face to face with a cowering Darick.

"This is appalling!" the priest cried.

"Really? I'm finding it an interesting diversion, personally."

"I was outside on the balcony. I heard a noise, and came back in, and found... this!"

Presto grinned at him. "Great, isn't it?" He nodded a cheerful farewell, munched down the last of the canapé, and then crawled out the other side of the table. The fight appeared to be finding its feet now, with different zones for different styles. In one area, men clearly born into the wrong era were duelling with rather sharp looking swords; in another men were battering each other with an enthusiastic incompetence that wouldn't have been out of place in one of Empire City's dodgier dives. Others, meanwhile, were ripping tapestries from the walls whose total worth probably ran into the millions, and setting fire to them.

A flying, pearl ejaculating penis flew by Presto's head, and an idea began to form.

He started to chant the language of magic and the Universe began to answer.

This was turning into the mother of all fuck ups.

A person of indeterminate gender who must have been near twice her weight had Dani in a grapple tighter than a python's embrace. Dani wasn't sure if he or she was trying to shag her or kill her, but either way, it wasn't a situation she was happy with. She jabbed a finger into a spot under the armpit and felt the grapple give way – only for a moment, but that moment was long enough for her to wriggle free and hop and step away. She found Laliana with a gaggle of other guests sheltering beneath the anatomically correct model of the SkyFather. "We need to get everyone out of here!"

"Yeah." Laliana looked around. "But where are they?"

The ballroom wasn't huge; but comprising as it did an entire floor within which a few hundred people were currently attempting to batter the living crap out of each other, spotting individual persons within its chaotic interior was a task for which the phrase "non-trivial" might have been invented. Several long, sweeping glances later, Dani spotted Darick hiding beneath a table. She pointed him out to Laliana, and they sprinted and scrambled their way across to him.

"This is appalling!" the priest cried.

Dani shrugged. She'd long since ceased to be shocked at the depravity of the rich. "You seen Presto?"

Darick pointed out of the other side of the table. "He's over there. I think he's casting a spell."

Dani followed the outstretched finger, and spotted Presto in his own private clearing in the maelstrom, punching both fists skyward as he completed his spell. As he did so, every flying penis in the room stopped dead. Presto, meanwhile, was now pointing at a group of particularly obnoxious attendees who were throwing burning fifty gold notes into the faces and bodies of the caged homeless men, braying and laughing all the while. As one, the flying penises swivelled, and lowered, to point at the braying socialites.

"What's he doing?" Laliana asked, shouting to be heard over the surrounding noise.

Dani had a fair idea, but she wasn't sure she had the words to explain.

Presto held his pointing arm for a moment, then clenched his fist, and as he did so every flying penis began to ejaculate. Not at the previous rate of once every thirty seconds, but faster, much faster, perhaps three or four times a second. And not at a speed sufficient to generate a gentle arc, but hard and fast enough to send the pearls flying straight and true.

It was the sort of weapon the world might have invented had it not invented aura-bolts.

The note-burners went down screaming, each one hit by dozens of tiny flying pearls that must have stung like buggery. The wizard gave them a few seconds of that, his pointed fist tracking a group of them as they attempted to escape, before he unclenched his hand. The penises stopped ejaculating, but still tracked the wizard's pointing arm.

Dani grabbed Darick and Laliana. "Come on!" They set off in a weaving sprint and skidded to a halt beside Presto, who was apparently searching for new targets, his bloodlust clearly up.

"What are you doing?" Dani shouted at him.

"Dispensing a bit of applied karma on behalf of the dispossessed!" the wizard shouted back, grinning. "Why? What are you doing?"

"Trying to get out of here! Have you seen the Storm?"

"He went outside to the balcony. I think that mad cow who started this whole thing was still looking to geld him."

"We need to get him."

Presto sighed sadly. "And I was having so much fun. But I suppose we ought to rescue him."

The four of them set off through the obstacle course that the party – with its upturned tables, fighting guests, and underfoot pearls – now comprised. They made it most of the way to the wide double doors that led to the balcony before they were halted by a group of young bucks who appeared to be greatly enjoying the turn the party had taken.

"I say, chaps," one of them said. "Look what we have here." He smiled a smile utterly absent of any warmth, then tutted. "Cheap costumes. Utterly unacceptable." The young buck took a step towards them.

Dani held up a placatory hand. "We don't want any trouble. We just want to get to the balcony to see if our friend's okay."

"Really? Well, if you want us to move, I'm afraid you're going to have to make us."

Presto stepped past Dani, already lifting his arm to point at the young buck, his fingers flexing, prepared to fist. "I was so hoping you were going to say that."

The Storm's penis was so cold he could no longer feel it. Under normal circumstances, this would have been of considerable concern to him. But the degree to which these were not normal circumstances could be gauged by the degree to which the Storm was worrying about things other than his potentially frostbitten member.

The reason why his penis was currently chilled to some way below the ninety-seven degrees it habitually kept itself at was because it was currently located outside the air deflection field that surrounded

Palace Gennaro. And the reason it was currently located outside the air deflection field that surrounded Palace Gennaro was because the Storm himself was no longer located on the balcony outside the ballroom, but was instead hanging off it – a situation that he was most unhappy with given that the only thing between him and the sea some five thousand feet below was a potential thirty seconds of very unhappy free fall.

The mad woman from the toilet was still stamping on his fingers. He'd been hoping that pushing him over the balcony's surrounding rail and through the treacle-like deflection field might have sated her fury somewhat, but it appeared that his resulting refusal to fall to his death had only further wound her up.

"Look, I'm really sorry about whatever it was I did," he pleaded. "Maybe we can, like, talk about it?"

That at least got her to stop stamping, her elegant jewelled slipper pausing a couple of inches above his fingers. "Whatever it was you did? You mean, you can't even remember?"

A guilty thought smashed through the Storm's soul with enough force to temporarily banish all thoughts of his current predicament. He hadn't done anything awful, had he? He'd not led a good life, he knew that. He'd spent half the last twenty years herbed up to the eyeballs, and a good chunk of the rest drunk, and he knew that while others might celebrate his exploits with the ladies, there was nothing in his history to feel proud of. Groupies, one-night stands, brief relationships smashed by his infidelity – it wasn't good. But he'd always assumed there were lines he'd never crossed, wrongs he'd never committed. But so much was cloudy, so much forgotten, so many events lost to the herb or the booze. What if he was wrong? What if he had crossed those lines? He didn't want to know, couldn't bear to know. But he had to know. "I did something to you, right? We had sex, right? But something was wrong?"

The look of fury morphed into something that might almost have been amazement. "You really can't remember, can you?"

"No!" the Storm screamed. What had he done? In the name of the Gods, what wrong had he done to this woman. "I'm sorry. I'm so, so sorry. But I can't remember! I must have been herbed up!"

The fury was back now. "Oh, you were herbed up all right. And yes we went to bed. I took you to my private bedchamber! Men spend years courting me for the chance of one night. But you! The famous rock star – for you, I let you into my private and sacred sanctum an hour after meeting you. We went to bed, but I went to my bathroom to prepare, and when I came back, I found, I found…"

She trailed to a halt, too overwrought to spit the words out.

"What? What did you find?"

She took a deep breath, and then leaned over the balcony's rail, moving her face a few inches closer to him as she spat her words out one by one, each one laden with a hatred that the intervening years had clearly not diminished. "You'd shat the bed."

They hadn't found the Storm on the balcony, but they had found the still insanely angry brunette and a set of ten fingers clutching the bottom rail of the balcony's railings that she was busily stamping on. Dani usually prided herself on achieving her aims through subtle manipulation and indirect action, but the situation here was clearly in desperate need of very direct action, so she grabbed the brunette and dragged her away, getting several punches in the face for her trouble.

From the size of her pupils, the brunette looked to be pretty herbed up, and Dani suspected she'd had a pretty major case of privileged person's entitlement complex before she'd started snorting lines, so rather than try to reason with her, she instead just sat on her until she stopped throwing punches, by which time Darick, Presto, and Laliana had managed to haul a clearly shaken the Storm over the railing and back onto a solid, if not earth-bound, surface.

"Okay," Dani said, climbing to her feet, sending every warning body language signal she knew at the brunette as she did so. "Let's get out of here."

"How?" asked Darick, pointing past her towards the doorway through which they'd just exited the Grand Ballroom.

Dani turned and found herself facing an angry looking mix of young merchant princes and princesses, mixed in with a scattering of what looked to be bravos, paid muscle of the professional kind. Most of the bravos and a good few of the aristocrats had bolts of various sizes clutched in their hands. She backed over to the railing and looked down. The Grand Ballroom was towards the top of Palace Gennaro, high above the dense network of floating buildings and walkways that occupied the lagoon formed by the Ring's sheltering embrace. There were some platforms and walkways down there, but they were quite a way down.

The aristocratic mob took a slow, collective step forward. Young men and women, whose faces wore the sneering smile of a cat about to slowly dismember a rat. A few let out whoops and whistles, and a muttered "Time to die" emerged from somewhere.

"You got anything?" Dani asked Presto.

"I've got a lot of stuff," the wizard replied. "But in a close fight, outnumbered, against a bunch of tooled up people, I don't fancy my chances much. Best I could do is throw up a shield, but I figure as soon as I start waving my arms around they'll just shoot me."

The mob took another step forward. They were only a few feet away now, close enough that Dani could see the twitching creases at the corners of mouths. There was something hateful in the cold, slow way in which they were doing this. Then she glimpsed something in the corner of her eye and turned. A frightened collective cry emerged from the mob as they too saw what she had seen: a carpet, heading straight towards them insanely fast, smashing into the balcony's faintly shimmering air deflection field, which for an instant flashed every colour of existence before vanishing.

A cold, bitter wind swept across the balcony and its inhabitants, practically all of whom were wearing costumes utterly unsuited for the climate they now found themselves in. The merchant princes and princesses began a screaming, panicky retreat to the doors, guarded by their clearly unimpressed hirelings. The carpet, meanwhile, having flashed overhead at an altitude of mere feet, dropped out of view beyond the far end of the balcony, tumbling end over end.

Dani let out a breath she hadn't realised she'd been holding. "That was handy."

"Exceedingly," said Presto. "Now if you gentlemen and ladies will just link hands, I can float us out of here to one of the walkways below."

A thought occurred to Dani. "I wonder where Blade is?"

Presto somehow managed to speak while midway through shaping the spell. "I'm sure he can look after himself."

Getting the guys out of their predicament by deliberately crashing the carpet into the Palace's air deflection field had seemed like a good idea when he'd first had it. But it was now clear to Blade that he hadn't really thought his plan through, in that while he'd considered what the effect of his carpet upon the deflection field would be, he'd very much failed to consider the effect the deflection field might have on his carpet.

That effect had turned out to be a vicious loss of control that was sending him both spinning end over end and rolling, two, maybe three times a second. The view through the carpet's windshield was flickering sea-sky-sea-sky, fast enough for him to feel his thoughts starting to blur, and his vision start to grey. Much more of this and he'd black out; were he not a highly trained athlete he probably already would have.

Saving himself wasn't simply a matter of regaining control. When he'd hit the field, every display had blanked out. They were coming back one by one, presumably due to the various systems automatically restarting, but all this had achieved was to create a sea of flashing red and amber across the cockpit. The system restarts should have cured the problem, and the underlying automatic pilot should have been correcting the spin.

They weren't.

It wasn't.

Something was very wrong, terminally so.

Through all of this, the words of his instructor spoke in his mind. "Work the problem. Think about anything else, and you'll panic, and if you panic you're dead."

Blade was already manipulating the stick, but it was having no effect – was dead in his hands. Moving by instinct now, he reached across to the centre console and switched the main control systems over to the backup. He felt the stick bite, felt its effect on the roll, but something was fighting his inputs, countermanding them, preserving the insane tumbling that threatened to kill him. Still moving by a trained instinct that was racing ahead of his conscious thoughts, he reached down to a further set of gate-guarded switches; third one down, automatic-stabilisation controls, flip the gate, and off.

Again the stick bit, and this time it held. The carpet was still tumbling like a bitch, but now it was a bitch he was the pilot of. He fed manual inputs into the stick, one after another, correcting first the end over end spin, and then the roll, before finally pulling out of the dive to transition into a straight and level flight.

The water below him was terrifyingly close. A few seconds more, and a fatal impact with the sea would have rendered his fear of blacking out redundant. With the malfunctioning automatic-stabilisation controls turned off, the carpet was twitchy as hell, but as long as he kept his hand on the stick, she was flyable. He pulled her into a careful turn and began a climb back to Upabove.

Chapter Twenty-Nine

In his twenty-something years with the band, the Storm had stayed in a lot of hotel rooms. Some of them had been good, or at least as good as a hotel room can be when you arrived last night and are leaving this morning and you haven't slept in the same bed more than three nights in a row since Fathermas last. Sometimes they'd been bad, especially in those long hard years they'd spent working towards one day being acclaimed as an overnight success. And sometimes they'd been really, really bad, so shockingly, appallingly bad that only the fact that your so-called manager was sleeping in the same rat-infested, shit-encrusted hovel prevented you from beating him to death with the nearest available blunt object.

The Empire City hotel they'd booked into upon their return from Upabove was really, really bad.

The six of them were currently crowded into Blade and the Storm's twin room. A harsh, acrid smell was coming in through the open window, drifting across from one of the several chemical plants that sprawled along Empire City's Portside district. The Storm didn't mind the smell. It was why he'd opened the window; the underlying stench the room was generating was bad enough that he would have snuggled up to the arse of the most flatulent demon in the bowels of the pits in the Planes of Damnation if it meant not having to expose his nose to the room's odour.

Bit of herb would have helped too.

He dispelled that thought, and tried to concentrate on what Presto was saying.

"So," said the mage. "We have a lead. We know the white skyship is in some way connected to our adversaries, given that the man who led the ambush on us at Craagon's Reach and then turned up at the Empire City Guards' press conference was also the man who interrogated me on that very skyship."

The Storm couldn't help but notice the particular stress the wizard had put on the word "interrogated", and the not-quite-suppressed shudder that had rippled through his frame as he said it.

The wizard gave the corner of the room a thousand yard stare for a moment, and then resumed. "And that skyship has been making regular visits to a private docking station in Upabove, which given Upabove's various reputations could have been for a whole range of purposes, from money laundering to the procurement of specialised magical devices. At this point, we can only speculate as to the purpose behind its visits. But what we do know is that a couple of months ago, a visiting academic hitched a lift on that skyship, during one of its mysterious visits, which would seem to imply that he, and presumably the organisation he works for, is in some way connected to the people who appear so keen to keep this Sleeping Dragon project secret that they framed us for crimes we didn't commit."

"Crimes that no one committed!" broke in Darick. "Crimes that never existed."

"Quite. Which brings us to this Institute for Advanced Magical Research. If these people are connected to whatever it is that's going on, then our best avenue of investigation right now would seem to be to examine this organisation."

The wizard looked around the room, presumably to get confirmation that his colleagues were on the same song sheet, and then resumed.

"So I've been doing a certain amount of poking around. Nothing obvious. Public sites on the Overnet, forums where wizards congregate, that sort of thing."

"Learn anything?" asked Blade.

Presto shrugged. "Not about magic. But that's not surprising. The only thing one can learn from the Overnet is that most people are fools, and the bigger the fool the bigger the mouth. And after the ten years I've spent not looking at this stuff, it's still the same people doing the shouting." He smiled. "It's almost reassuring. I thought I had no life, but these chaps..."

"And the Institute?"

The wizard chuckled. "Ah yes, the Institute. A curious organisation. Established seven years ago as an independent, but non-profit making body, apparently funded by a number of unnamed wealthy individuals with a desire to extend the boundaries of human knowledge and prepared to donate reasonably large amounts of money to achieve it."

Dani leaned forward. "In my experience, not many people donate large amounts of money for purely altruistic reasons."

Darick snorted in protest. "I think that's a bit unfair! What about Kadien Konzalo? He's given away nearly his entire fortune."

"That would be Sir Kadien Konzalo, knighted for services to charity?" asked Dani.

"Well, yes—"

"The man who funded the Church's Konzalo Houses at children's hospices?"

"Yes, yes—"

"The man who last year was inducted as a lay member of the Overbishop's Inner Council, such position of which is popularly regarded as a pre-booked, pre-approved admission pass to the topmost planes of the afterlife?"

"Well now, I do think you're somewhat simplifying the theology involved—"

"The life president of the Konzalo Museum for the Modern Arts?"

"Yes, all right. Point taken in his case. But there are some people, poorer people, who do the most wonderful things out of pure altruism, people who have almost nothing, and yet still give that away!"

Dani nodded, conceding that point, before holding up a finger to add a clarification. "Yeah. But that's the poor people. Someone with the drive and ambition and ruthlessness to build up a fortune is not generally the sort of person who will then give that fortune away for nothing. They give away the money to regain the approval and respect they lost in accumulating it. They'll have reasons for funding this. I'd like to know what those reasons are."

"That's if these people actually exist," said Presto.

Dani raised a questioning eyebrow, and motioned the wizard to continue.

"This is largely intuition and guesswork, based on the public profile the institute chooses to present to the outside world. But I'm getting the feeling it's like an iceberg, with what we can see being merely the one-tenth poking above the surface of the water. Nothing about this setup makes sense. They clearly have quite a lot of funds available, and when they started up they headhunted the best – leading figures from across a host of magical research disciplines, plus a pretty large support staff. Then they went and bought a big, plush, fancy headquarters for them in the centre of town, just off Empire Square, which is a tad curious."

"How's that curious?" asked Blade. "Wouldn't giving people a nice place to work motivate them?"

"Yes, but research doesn't work like that. One doesn't work in isolation. You discuss things. You talk. You build upon other people's discoveries and they build upon yours. As the quote says, if we can see beyond the far horizon it's because we stand on the shoulders of our fathers. So personally, I'd have expected them to get somewhere in the University Quarter. Do you see what I'm saying?"

Blade nodded, then waved Presto to continue.

"But this is merely the mystery's beginning," said the wizard, resuming. "This is a research institute, employing the most brilliant magical researchers in the Empire, yes?"

"Yeah," replied Dani. "So?"

"Would you not expect them to actually be conducting research?"

"You're saying they aren't?"

Presto waved a dismissive hand. "Oh, they're doing some notional research. Do a quick search and you'll find a list of papers published, supposed advances made. And if you didn't know any better, you might even think it quite impressive."

"But you do know better?"

"Yes. I do. They've collected a team of such brilliance that I'm frankly jealous not to be involved and provided them with a source of constant, reliable funding. They don't have to teach. They don't have to spend months crafting research proposals and requests for funding. They just have to think, to be brilliant, to look into the darkness and uncover the light. And they're not doing that. Where we should have had brilliant leaps that shake the world we've had only competent, evolutionary steps."

Both Dani and Blade were nodding now, thinking. The Storm waited a few moments for someone to weigh in with an explanation, then when no one did spoke up himself. "Sorry, what does all this, like, mean?"

It was Dani who answered him. "Someone's spent a load of money to hire a dream team of magical researchers to do something. These people were already well known within their various fields, so they couldn't all just disappear. So they created some sort of research institute that they could notionally belong to. And they do just enough publishable research to not make it obvious that something's going on. But they're actually spending their time doing something else, something secret, something they're not talking about."

After a period where it had felt that he and the discussion had so parted company that they were living separate lives, the Storm felt meaning starting to reappear, as the dots the others had clearly already joined began, hazily, to join for him, too. "And that something would be Sleeping Dragon, right?"

Dani shrugged. "Seems like our best guess right now."

Presto broke in. "And whatever it is they're doing, they're doing it somewhere else. I know a good twenty or so of the people on their permanent fellowship list, but when I spent three hours sitting in the coffee shop opposite their headquarters at clocking-on time I only saw two of them go in." The wizard looked at Dani. "Did you check out the name I gave you?"

She nodded. "I did. Professor Rikard Jendon, Chief Executive of the Institute, and formally Junasian Professor of Applied Magical Theory and Practise at the Imperial University. Which you could have told me, seeing as how he used to be your boss."

"Didn't want to prejudice your thought processes."

"Thanks. Anyhow, unlike many of his staff, he is currently in Empire City. I've spent the last two days following him around..."

Sixty or so minutes later, by the room's cheap bedside dial – which kept track of time just as effectively as the Storm's now lost twenty thousand gold wrist-dial despite costing a faction of that price (money being able to buy you many things, but a more sophisticated form of time not being one of them) – Dani seemed to be coming to the end of her observations on Presto's erstwhile boss. "Now luckily for us, the Professor's bin collection is pretty early in the morning and he puts his rubbish out last thing at night."

"So you grabbed it?" asked Blade.

"Yeah."

"But surely that's illegal?" spluttered Darick.

"Technically, yes."

"Oh."

"Anyhow, once I sorted through all the standard crap, I did find a few discarded printouts. Seems our professor's a bit of a luddite when it comes to Oracles and still likes to print things out, including the guest list of a social gathering he's throwing at his apartment tomorrow night. There was also a draft of the invite that said something along the lines of it being a thank you for all the hard work so far and a last chance to get together and relax before proceeding with the big event."

"Big event?" asked Blade. "That's it?"

"Yeah." Dani looked across at Presto. "The guest list includes a number of the people publicly identified as working at the Institute, including one Jaquenta Quen, the Institute's Director of Research, and someone who, again, I believe you ought to know?"

"Given that I was for a period married to her, yes."

Blade sat up straight, blinking. "Your ex-wife works for the Institute? When did you find this out? And when did you plan on telling us?"

"To answer your questions in order: yes, two days ago when I looked at their Overnet site, and when or if it happened to come up in conversation."

It was Laliana who raised the question that was foremost in the Storm's mind. "How come you and her broke up? Was there a reason?"

"Let's just say that she liked being married to a brilliant wizard with a glittering academic future ahead of him rather more than she liked being married to a disgraced ex-academic with a permanently suspended magical license and a future not so much bleak as non-existent."

"So basically, she pissed off when you lost your job?" said Blade.

Presto shrugged a resigned shrug. "That's a blunt summation, but an essentially accurate one. One of the reasons that I've no knowledge of the magical community's last ten years is that I really, really didn't want to know what she was up to."

Dani broke into the resulting silence. "So anyway, tomorrow night the professor's having a party at his home. A good chunk of the Institute's top brass are scheduled to be there. I figure we want to know what they're talking about, but the obvious question is: how?"

Blade jabbed an enthusiastic finger into the conversation. "Presto. Isn't there some sort of spell you could cast, that would let us listen in on what they're talking about?"

"Yes," the wizard told him. "There are in fact several ways in which I could use magic to eavesdrop upon a dozen or so crack practitioners of the magical arts who are meeting to discuss a secret, and presumably magical, project, in one of said crack practitioners' own personal residences."

"You're thinking they might detect your spell?"

"I'm thinking they might, yes."

"Right."

The wizard returned Blade's gaze for a few moments, then steepled his hands, his eyes gazing sightlessly past the Storm as the brain behind them crunched facts and calculated. After several seconds, the wizard waved a hand and spoke, his gaze never moving, his eyes still focused somewhere else. "Wind back a bit, Dani. You said that he has a dog, which he takes for a walk every morning at the same place and the same time?"

"Yeah, a park just round the corner from his house. I got chatting with a woman walking her dog. She said she sees him there every morning, seven-thirty sharp. He stays exactly thirty minutes and then leaves. Creature of habit, the professor, it seems."

"And what does he do at this park while he's walking his dog?"

"Well, this morning he just wondered aimlessly around. Looked lost in thought."

"And the dog?"

"Is this going anywhere?"

"Yes. The dog?"

"It just sort of followed along behind him, sniffing. Why?"

"Did you get a good look at this dog? Do you know what it looked like?"

The grifter shrugged, and reached into her jacket pocket. "I got a pictograph as it happens."

Blade chose that moment to explode. "SkyFather's testicles – sorry Darick – why the hell are we talking about a bloody dog?"

The wizard ignored the warrior's outburst, instead taking the pictograph from Dani's outstretched hand. "Perfect. Absolutely perfect. Okay, here's what I need you to do…"

Chapter Thirty

When it comes to smiling, there's a fine line between smiley-happy and smiley-simple, and after five minutes of continuous beaming, the woman in the dog shelter seemed to Dani to be in danger of crossing it. "And this," she said, her tone as bright and cheery as her smile, "is where we keep the dogs." She waved a hand across a backyard filled with wire-fenced enclosures, filled with dogs whose moods appeared to range from sleepily-depressed to frantic, desperate, wide-awake excitement.

As scenes went, this was grim. If somewhere in the afterlife there was a doggy Plain of Damnation, this looked to be its waiting room. The woman's fixed smile was suddenly transformed from annoying to heart-breaking. As a child, Dani had craved a dog more than anything in the world, but when you live in constant transit from children's home to foster family to foster family to children's home, a dog could only ever be a dream, and an unattainable one at that. She hardened her heart as the woman resumed speaking. "Now I know they're all terribly cute, but we do need to consider which dog will be the best match for the two of you. Now we've got—"

Dani waved a hand to interrupt her. "I'm afraid we really have set our hearts on a Bogussian Snufflehound. When we phoned, you did say you had one?"

The smile dropped a barely perceptible notch. "Let's not get too hung up on specific breeds."

Dani set her face in an expression she calculated would indicate firmness backed by a genuine wish. "It's just that ever since I was a little girl I've dreamed of having a Bogussian Snufflehound."

"Are you sure you wouldn't be happier with an Eastern Orckiller? We have a lovely example just over there!" She pointed at the cage towards their left, which was occupied by a single, evil-looking dog that sported fangs thicker than Dani's thumbs. "We have to keep him on his own because he's plays a little too boisterously for some of the other dogs, but he really is a lovely dog who'd make a wonderful companion."

"Aren't Orckillers a little violent?"

The woman shook her head, just a little too quickly. "No, no, that's a myth. They can be a bit excitable, and it's best to keep them on the lead when other dogs are present. Or other people. And they're probably best not left alone with children. Or old people. Or people they don't know. But properly brought up they can make wonderful pets!"

"Has this one been properly brought up?"

The woman paused for a long moment. "Bogussian Snufflehound, was it?"

"Please."

Blade gave the dog a good stare, and got an equally good stare in return. It was a little on the short side of medium, with a mottled-brown coat still tufted in spite of Laliana's attempts to brush it smooth, a blunt snout, and floppy ears. "So how much did it cost you?" he asked Dani.

Laliana leaned forward. "It's not an it, he's a he. And his name is Rej!" She gave the dog a stroke. It gazed at her, then nuzzled the top of its head into her chin.

"Sorry," Blade told her. "I stand corrected. How much did Rej cost you?"

"A thousand golds," said Dani.

"A thousand? Has he got gold plated paws or something?"

"They don't just give dogs out," said Laliana. "They're supposed to take details. Do home checks. Make sure you're the right sort of person. You can't just walk in, hand over some cash, and walk out with a dog."

"At least you can't," added Dani, "unless you combine a reasonably convincing story with the offer of an extremely large donation."

Blade let his stare linger on the dog for a few moments more, thinking that perhaps some previously unseen point to it might spontaneously emerge, then turned his attention to Presto. The wizard was sitting at the room's small bedside table, upon which were scattered a dozen or so items. He appeared to be checking things off a mental list, muttering to himself as he did so. "Akbazian tree bark. Scale of a Slodonian tree lizard. Dried goblin finger–"

"Is that a real goblin finger?" asked Darick, appalled.

The wizard thought for a moment. "Would it help if I told you that this is merely an archaic term, and that while mages once used real goblin fingers, we long ago switched to a synthetic substitute, keeping the old name purely for tradition and continuity?"

"Well, it would help a bit, yes."

"Okay. While mages once used real goblin fingers, we long ago switched to a synthetic substitute, keeping the old name purely for tradition and continuity."

"So those are synthetic, then?"

"No, it's a real goblin finger. Some things can't be synthesised and goblin fingers are one of them."

"But you said—"

"No, I didn't. I just asked if you'd feel better if I told you it was artificial, you said you would, so I told you it was artificial."

Blade's irritation level was rising rapidly and heading for lift off. "Mother's tits, will somebody stop talking bollocks and start explaining what's going on?" He pointed at the items on the bedside table. "Starting with what's that shit?"

"This shit," replied Presto, with clearly unconcealed irritation, "which I might add cost us more than two thousand golds, is the components of a spell."

"Which spell?"

"The spell I'm about to cast, if everyone will just shut up long enough."

Blade paused for several seconds, then settled back into his seat with a sigh. "Sorry."

The wizard looked around, giving each inhabitant of the room a stern look in turn, including the dog. "I'm about to cast a spell that besides being about as illegal as a spell can be that doesn't actually kill or maim someone, is actually rather difficult, even for me. So unless you want to find yourself being the target of the spell, don't talk, don't move, and if you really want to be safe, don't even think. Understood?" He waited until he got a chorus of answering nods. "Then I'll begin."

Blade had seen magic cast before, not only in the arena, but during training, healing, and of course as a novelty act in parties and at clubs. But what he'd just witnessed was something else, something different, something clearly on another level. For fully ten minutes Presto had chanted, his hands weaving intricate patterns in the air around him, the items before him disappearing one by one, the power in the room growing, shaping; a primeval presence that made Blade's hairs stand on end and set his lizard brain screaming in terror. Now, finally, the wizard finished chanting, his arms dropping to his sides. "And that gentleman," he said, in a voice whose tone betrayed his utter exhaustion, "is that." He paused a moment more. "Those chemical factories this neighbourhood's infested with should have shielded us. They're probably running at a constant background level of five MegaKellens or more. But we'd still better shift within half an hour, just in case what I did got picked up on a detector somewhere."

Blade looked at him, confused. Nothing had changed. The room was exactly as it was before. "But what did you actually do?"

The wizard smiled the thin smile of an exhausted but satisfied man. "Can't you tell?"

"No." Blade looked around, at the room, at Presto, at Dani and Laliana, at the Storm, at Darick, and finally at the dog. It looked back at him, a confusion in its eyes where before there had been only incomprehension. It looked around, as though taking in the room for the first time. Then it turned its attention to Laliana. "Rrhat?" it said. "Rrere?"

Presto leaned towards it. "What is your name?"

"Rrej."

"Good. My name is Presto. Do you understand what I'm saying?"

"Rres."

Blade shook his head, trying to reboot his brain, and then looked hard at first the dog, and then Presto. "Is that dog trying to talk?"

"Yes. I've cast an uplift spell on it. It now has a level of intelligence and knowledge that approximates to that of a three to four year-old child."

Blade looked back at the dog. "Do you know where you are?"

The dog shook its head. "Rro."

"What?"

Laliana broke in. "I think maybe that's a no?"

Presto continued speaking after her. "Its ability to actually speak is constrained by the biological limitations of its voice box. There's nothing a sentience spell can do about that."

"So three thousand golds later we've got a dog with a speech impediment?"

"It is a bit hard to understand, dude," the Storm added.

Presto sighed. "Gods, what is it with you people? I've taken a brain the size of a walnut and raised it to sentience. I've transformed this thing from unthinking beast to thinking, feeling sentient being. I've bestowed upon it that which the very gods themselves failed to bestow upon it–"

"Well," said Darick. "Now you come to mention it, I fear this is all a bit blasphemous."

"Point duly noted and ignored," Presto told him. "I've cast one of the hardest spells ever devised, a spell I've never before cast on account of how illegal it is, under conditions about as far from a properly equipped magical laboratory as it's possible to get, a spell that requires the caster to build level upon level upon level, with absolute and perfect control, and after all of that, after a miracle such as this, all you lot can do is complain that when it speaks, it sounds like a sodding dog!"

Blade held up a placatory hand. "Okay, okay, fair point, Presto. Thank you. That was pretty impressive. Rej?"

"Rres?"

"Glad to have you with us."

"Rrank rru!"

"Can I just ask one thing?"

"Ask away," Presto told him.

"Why have we uplifted a dog?"

Chapter Thirty-One

Behind Darick's church had been a park. It wasn't much, just a scrappy patch of the land with a few rusting pieces of play equipment. The park in which he now found himself was much classier, with smoothly rolling lawns decorated by scattered clumps of bushes, behind one of which they were currently ensconced. But it wasn't his park, just as the church presumably wasn't his anymore either, if the statements the Bishop had given to the press were anything to go by. He shook himself back to the moment, aided in that task by the chill early morning air. Dani and Presto were talking to the dog, alternating and interrupting in a manner that struck Darick as neither helpful nor efficient.

"Okay," said Dani. "You get what we want you to do?"

"He understands the task. He just needs an awareness of the consequences he will suffer should he fail to complete it."

"When the man comes along Rej, we're going to grab his dog, and you're going to run out and replace him."

"You absolutely must not tell him who you are."

"You're going to pretend to be his dog."

"If you do anything to make him think you might not be his dog, you're for it."

Laliana physically interposed herself between Presto and the dog. "He knows what he's got to do. You're just scaring him now."

"Good. He needs to be scared." The wizard moved around her and grabbed the dog by the muzzle. "Are you listening to me, Rej?"

A muffled "Rres" emerged from the dog's closed mouth.

"Good. Here's the deal. You are illegal. The spell that created you is illegal. Everything about you is illegal. Do you know what illegal means, Rej? It means bad. It means naughty. It means that if anyone realises you can talk you'll be dog meat before you get a chance to speak. If we get caught I'll go down to the big house, but you'll go to the little doggy hunting ground in the sky. Bad men will do bad things to you. So you are going to follow the man and pretend to be his dog. You're going to listen very carefully to everything he or anyone else says, but you say nothing. Nothing at all. And then tomorrow we're going to grab you back and find out what you've heard. Do right by us and we'll do right by you. But so help me, if you try anything I will make whatever whisper calls are necessary to make sure that the rest of your uplifted life is short and unpleasant. Do you understand?"

The dog took a step back, his tail drooping, his snout dipped towards the ground. "Rres."

Laliana shot Presto a truly filthy look, then grabbed the dog in a warm and strong hug. "Don't listen to the nasty man, Rej. You just go in there, listen to what you can, and then we'll get you back and we will look after you. Promise. You're with us now. You're ours, and we're never, ever going to let anything hurt you."

"Which is pretty much what I just told him!" said the wizard, in a protesting whisper.

There was a rustle in the surrounding bushes, and Blade pushed himself through, a pissed off and protesting Bogussian Snufflehound clamped under his arm. "Okay. I've got him. Send Rej out."

Laliana kissed Rej on the snout. "Okay Rej, good luck. Just do your best."

The dog looked at her for a moment, then trotted off in the direction Blade had come from. The warrior handed the professor's dog over to Laliana, then headed back through the bushes after Rej.

A thought occurred to Darick. "Do you really think the professor won't notice that it's a different dog?"

Presto shrugged. "I'm gambling not. When I knew him he had a reputation for extreme absent-mindedness. They used to say that when his wife died in her sleep it took him two weeks to notice. I don't figure ageing ten years will have helped any."

"But what if they have some kind of magical detection stuff going?" asked Darick.

"What if they do? The process that enhanced and uplifted the dog's brain was a magical one, but now that it's done the resulting brain is just a brain, no more magical than yours or mine. Only way to notice would be to put him through a full medical scan." Presto gave Darick a disappointed stare, and sighed. "That was the clever bit about my plan."

"Oh. Right."

A few minutes later, Blade returned. "He's headed off back towards his house, with the dog on a lead following him." He shrugged. "Guess there's nothing we can do except come back here tomorrow."

The professor was late. Blade checked his dial for the umpteenth time, even while realising the pointlessness of the action: if the professor had already been late five minutes ago, another five minutes wasn't going to make him any less late. The gently glowing figures on the dial showed 7:41. The man was supposed to be a creature of habit. 7:20 leave the house. 7:30 arrive at the park. 8:00 leave the park. 8:10 arrive back at the house. 8:30 leave for work.

Obviously, today was one of those days where habit had been interrupted by circumstances. Question was, what were those circumstances? And just how badly were they going to ruin Blade's day? There was a rustling behind him. Blade glanced over his shoulder, and saw Dani's lithe form moving carefully through the bushes. The grifter dropped to the ground beside him. "What's the hold up?"

Blade motioned towards the park gates just a little distant from them. "They haven't turned up, that's what the hold up is."

The grifter nodded acknowledgement, but said nothing, eyes distant while her brain presumably calculated the odds, worked out the angles.

"Do you think the little furball's dropped us in it?" Blade asked.

"Don't think so. At least not intentionally. I'd like to think I'm a pretty good, and quick, judge of a person's character, and from what I saw of him I think he'll stick with us – for Laliana, if for no other reason."

"He's not exactly a person."

"True. But then he's not exactly a dog, either. I was talking to Presto earlier. He said that his psychology will be a mixture of dog and human, with an underlying dog's viewpoint of the world overlain with a human's analytical understanding."

"Which means?"

"I have no idea. But I don't think he'll shaft us."

"Right." Blade checked his dial. 7:43.

Two minutes later, the shambling figure of the professor and the slightly sprightlier figure of Rej appeared through the park gates. Dani let out the breath she'd been half holding for the last five minutes and stopped giving herself a mental kicking for not putting someone outside the professor's house. She nudged Blade, but the warrior had already spotted them. "Yeah, I see them. Looks pretty normal."

The professor took an agonisingly long period of time to cover the couple of hundred feet from the gates to the place where they were waiting, ambling along the concrete path clearly lost in thought. Finally though, he wandered past them. Dani waved at Rej and the dog quickly trotted over, diving past them and into the bushes. Dani followed him, Blade close behind. Presto, Darick, the Storm and Laliana were waiting in the cramped clearing at the centre of the clump of bushes with the professor's unhappy dog held back by a taut lead. Dani reached down and released the lead's catch; the dog sprinted off past Blade and through the gap they'd just squeezed through. Rej, meanwhile, was already on Laliana's lap, nuzzling his head into her chest and whining happily.

Dani patted the dog on the back. "Good boy, Rej. Well done."

The dog's tail wagged. "Rrank rru!"

Presto was eager to begin questioning the dog, but that desire was frustrated by Laliana's insistence that Rej had to be given his breakfast first, so he was forced to sit and watch the dog chase his bowl around the slippery floor in pursuit of the rather expensive chopped steak that lay within. Finally though, the dog had licked the last stain clean of the bowl and taken a long slurp of water, and sat back satisfied, licking his lips and stretching.

"Can we begin now?" asked Presto. A thought occurred to him. "Did the professor feed you before he took you for a walk?"

The dog looked guiltily away, and slunk over to Laliana, who was sitting on the room's only bed. She waved at him. "C'mon Rej, sit up here with me." The dog jumped onto the bed and lay down with his head on her lap, his eyes fixed nervously on Presto, who was leaning forward in what he genuinely intended to be a friendly pose.

"Two breakfasts, fine, whatever. Just don't come crying to me when you get bellyache. Okay, firstly, do you know why you were late this morning?"

"Rrate?"

Dani broke in. "Does he really understand the concept of time?"

"No," Presto conceded. "Probably not. Good point. Okay, Rej. What happened this morning?"

"Rruffink. Rran rrot rret rrup. Rrad rru rrake rrim!"

Presto looked pleadingly around the room. "Did anyone get that?"

"I think," said Laliana. "He's saying that the professor, the man, didn't get up and he had to wake him."

"Maybe he had a late night," suggested Dani. "Good party and all that."

That seemed pretty reasonable to Presto, so he moved onto the next question. "Okay. Did the professor have a party last night?"

"Rres!"

"Were you there?"

"Rres! Rrid rricks. Rrot rreats."

Presto looked quizzically at Laliana.

"Did tricks and got treats, I think," she replied.

"Well, that's just brilliant!" said Presto, not bothering to conceal his irritation. "So as soon as someone offers you a bit of food you forget everything about acting like the professor's dog and quietly listening in, and start doing the full street-performer, busking act instead. Nice."

The dog's muzzle dropped. "Rrey rrad rrood," he whined pathetically.

Laliana pulled the dog into a hug. "Ignore him, Rej. We understand. They had food." She looked back up at Presto. "When all's said and done, he's still a dog, and you can't blame him for acting like a dog."

"And besides," Dani added, "we don't know that the professor's dog doesn't do tricks, do we? And at the end of the day, the professor can't have rumbled that Rej wasn't his dog or he wouldn't have been taking him for a walk, would he?"

Presto realised the grifter was right. "Fair point." He turned his attention back to the dog. "Okay, Rej. Did you listen to what the people at the party were talking about?"

"Rres!"

"Good. Can you remember what they said?"

"Rres!"

Presto tried to be patient, reminding himself that he was talking to something with an intellect not much more than that of a toddler, combined with a psychology that was highly alien. "And what was it they were talking about?"

"Rroing rrumrare?"

"Going somewhere?" suggested Laliana. The dog nodded enthusiastically.

"Where were they going?"

The dog screwed up his muzzle, his whiskers twitching and his ears stiffening and his eyes rocking from side to side as he sought to recall what had been said. Finally he looked up at Presto.

"Rragans rreach?"

This time, Presto didn't need Laliana. "Craagon's Reach?"

The dog nodded. "Rres!"

Blade stirred from his vantage point beside the room's only window. "So they're going to Craagon's Reach? Is anyone else feeling like the puzzle pieces are finally starting to click together?"

"When were they going?" Presto asked the dog.

"Rrumorro?" The dog paused, then shook his head. "Rro. Rroday!"

"So they're going to Craagon's Reach today," Presto mused, thinking aloud. "Curiouser and curiouser." He turned his attention back to Rej. "Why were they going?"

The dog thought for a long while. "Rrowtoripe?" he said, clearly uncertain.

"Rowtoripe?" Presto asked helplessly. He looked at Laliana, but she was clearly as uncomprehending as he. Presto looked back at the dog, but received in return something that could only be the dog equivalent of a helpless shrug. Finally, Dani clicked her fingers.

"Prototype?"

"Rres! Rres!" The dog sat up and pointed his front paw at Dani, nodding excitedly all the while.

Presto thought. A magical institute taking a prototype of something to Craagon's Reach. It could only be some sort of magical device for testing. But what? He looked back at the dog. "What was it a prototype of? Did they mention that at any point?" The dog was looking a bit confused, so he tried again, simpler this time. "What was it they were talking about? It was some kind of thing, but what kind of thing?"

The dog lay back down with his head on Laliana's lap and thought some more, his muzzle moving from side to side. Seconds ticked by, the silence in the room overwhelming. Then, just as Presto had nearly given up hope of getting anything else, the dog sat bolt upright and barked out an excited reply. "Rrara rromb!"

Rara romb? Rara romb? The words of the recorded prophecy meandered across his thoughts. Plague, war, famine, destruction. Rara romb. Plague, war, famine, destruction. And then those two thoughts collided and in an instant he knew. The fools. The mad, stupid, arrogant fools. Pitiful, blind children playing at being gods, pulling at the levers that controlled the universe. Fragile mortal men more out of their depth than they could ever have dreamed in their

worst nightmares.
Plague, war, famine, destruction.
He put his head in his hands and moaned.

Chapter Thirty-Two

For long seconds there was no sound save the incoherent moans coming from the hunched-over wizard. Blade looked around the room but saw only confused and shocked faces. Rej jumped off the bed, trotted over to Presto, and pawed gently at his arm, his ears set at a puzzled angle. The wizard looked up, caught Blade's eye, and smiled a tight smile of such sadness that the sight of it nearly took Blade's breath away. He had tears in his eyes, Blade saw, and what looked like a nervous tick fighting to emerge from the corner of his mouth. "Care to let us in on the secret?" Blade asked him, gently.

"Perhaps starting with what a rara romb is?"

"Not a rara romb. A mana bomb."

The dog sat back and pointed urgently at the wizard, his head frantically nodding. "Rreh! Rrara rromb!"

The wizard continued. "That's what Sleeping Dragon is. A mana bomb. Or more accurately: a project to develop a mana bomb."

"I get that," said Blade through gritted teeth. "The question I'd like answered is what exactly a mana bomb is?"

"It's a bomb. Powered by mana. Except that it isn't, at least not in the way those morons at the institute think."

"Hang on a minute," interrupted Dani. "Morons? I thought they were supposed to be the most brilliant minds in the magical community?"

"They are."

"So how exactly are they morons?"

"Because if they're really doing what we've just figured out that they're doing, then they're morons."

Blade caught the wizard's eye. "Hey! Back up! What's the deal with the mana bomb? Is it like a very big bomb?"

"That's would be its intended function, yes. Some years back, a programme of research was conducted into the fundamental nature of mana generation and transformation. Looking into what mana actually is and where it comes from. Pretty low-level stuff, but from it came a theory that if enough mana was pulled out of a particular spot at once, by creating a chain of self-replicating spells, each one casting hundreds of copies of itself, a self-propagating feedback reaction would be set up that would start drawing power from the fabric of space-time, releasing a massive burst of magical energy several orders of magnitude higher than anything ever yet witnessed."

"That sounds rather bad," said Darick.

The wizard laughed bitterly. "Oh, it's considerably worse than that. If all we were talking about was a bloody big bomb designed to scare the shit out of the Elves – which I suspect is exactly what its creators are intending it to be – I wouldn't be particularly bothered. The problem lies with what you find if you probe deeper, and consider the resulting effects triggered by the feedback loop's establishment." The wizard paused for a moment before continuing. "It's quite a fascinating area. You're talking about a region of the universe that's regressed to the conditions that existed in the first seconds of creation, where the distinction between magical and mundane has dissolved and the very boundaries of the planes are disintegrating. The crucial thing is, what these idiots have obviously failed to see, is that it won't stop. It won't just detonate with a blast sufficient to destroy a city and incinerate a few hundred thousand people."

"It won't go bang?" Dani asked.

"Oh, it will go bang. And if you're standing within a few miles of it you'll probably be vaporised on the spot. But the chain reaction consuming the mana won't stop. It will continue, bouncing all round the world for days like ripples bouncing back and forth across a pond after you've chucked a damn great rock in. And by the time it's finished there won't be any mana left in the world, and won't be for a long time. It will take centuries for the background mana field to regenerate to the levels it is now."

"No mana?" asked Dani.

"Yes. No mana. Zilch. Gone."

"You're talking carpets falling out of the sky?" asked Blade.

"Yes."

"No crystals? No whispers? No heating? No fridges? No oracles? Buggies and wagons that won't move?"

"Not unless you're pushing them, no."

"But that would pretty much destroy civilisation!" exclaimed Darick. "It would take us back to, well, the dark ages, if not the stone age!"

The wizard smiled. "I believe the phrase was: Plague, war, famine and destruction."

"But how come you know so much about it?" asked Dani. "What makes you such an expert on this research?"

"It was my research."

"Nice," said the Storm. "So all of this is down to you?"

The wizard shrugged. "Hey, if they'd bothered to ask me to explain my research I'd gladly have done so. And besides, don't blame me: all this started when Kellen created the technology to allow spells to cast spells. Civilisation had been largely unchanged for thousands of years until then. He pretty much invented the modern world."

"Wow," Dani muttered. "Wonder if he foresaw the changes he was going to trigger?"

"Well, the curious thing is that the historians are confused as to quite why he did pursue that research. It was something he did relatively late in his life for no apparent reason that anyone can discern. One moment he's happily pottering along as a semi-retired adventurer, and then–"

The wizard stopped speaking.

"What?" Blade urged. "What is it?"

"–and then for no apparent reason, he invented the technology to create a spell with an ongoing persistence that could then start casting spells itself. It would be funny if it wasn't so tragic."

Dani leaned slowly forward. "Are you talking about the spell?"

"Yes."

"*The* spell? The one that kidnapped us? The one that started this all off?"

"Yes."

"So let me get this straight. Kellen and the others did some prophesising and found out that the world was going to end. To stop that happening, Kellen invented an entirely new and more powerful type of magic. But the reason the world is going to end is completely and entirely and solely because of his invention of that new type of magic?"

"Yes. This is why prophecy is generally regarded as a bad idea. Because the future event you're foreseeing is as likely as not to have been caused by your reaction to learning about it. As I said, it would be funny if it wasn't so tragic."

All those present settled into a moment's silence, to allow the horrifying realisation to settle in.

Blade was the first to pull himself back to the now. "So what can we do?" he asked. "Tell the authorities?"

"I doubt they'd believe us," said Dani. "And besides, isn't this them doing it?"

"I suspect the answer to that is yes, and no," said Presto. "My strong suspicion is that the top levels of the government are unaware of these events. If this project was official, albeit secret, those running it wouldn't have to funnel funds or technology through Upabove. But equally, this is too big an operation to be done without the resources of the state, and we know that it involves people who are part of the state. My gut instinct tells me that this is some sort of conspiracy within the military and the security services, high-ranking people bypassing the chain of command for what they no doubt would claim are higher purposes."

"So we could tell the authorities?" said Darick. "Have them shut it down."

The wizard shook his head. "No. We've got no proof, and we're wanted criminals on the run from the law. Even if they did start some sort of investigation, which I doubt, it would be slow and ineffectual, doubly so given the degree to which this conspiracy will have infiltrated the institutions of the state. These people are on the verge of a test detonation whose success they no doubt believe will be an unstoppable fait accompli. No investigation's going to stop that."

A long silence settled. Words flowed gently through Blade's mind, calm, yet insistent. Toozie. "Save the world. Save the kids. Save me. And save yourself." He stood up and took a pace forward. Five noses and one snout turned to face him. "How this happened doesn't matter. Why it happened doesn't matter. All that matters is that it is happening. And if we want it stopped we're the ones who need to stop it."

"Are you suggesting something?" asked Dani.

"Yeah. We go to Craagon's Reach, steal the bomb, and bring it back here to Empire City. Blow the whole, damn conspiracy apart."

"Just like that?" asked the Storm.

"Yeah, just like that." Blade looked around the room. "Who's with me?" For a long, stretched out heartbeat he got no response. Then Presto raised a hand. "I'm in."

Dani nodded. "Me too."

Laliana raised her hand, the dog raising a paw to match. "I'm in."

"Rrand rre!"

Dani shook her head. "You don't have to, sis. This isn't your fight. You weren't selected by the spell."

"Maybe. But this is my world too. When we were kids it was all about the two of us, us against the world, and that's how it should be now. If you're going up against fate and destiny you'll have me standing alongside you."

That left two: the Storm and Darick.

The priest shifted awkwardly. "But what can we do? I'm just a priest."

"And I'm just a rock star!" added the Storm.

Blade looked hard at them. "None of us is what we should be. When the adventurers of old went into the east to face beastmen and the wilderness they always used to take a bard and a priest with them. Now Darick, maybe you ain't an Archbishop Idenn, but then I'm no Sir Ethelded and he's no–" He went to point at Presto, but then stopped. "Actually, he might be another Kellen. But that's not my point. None of us is who the spell was looking for, but we're the people it selected."

The priest looked miserable, his faith appearing to be near breaking point. "I just don't see what we can do."

Blade laid one hand upon Darick's shoulder, and another upon the Storm's. "When the time comes, when we need you, you'll both be there, and you'll both play your part. Trust me."

The rock star nodded, then sighed. "Why not? We've all got to kick it sometime, right? Better this than choking to death on my own vomit."

Blade looked down at Darick. "Father?"

Darick nodded slowly. "I don't know why the SkyFather has set me this task, but set it he has. Wherever you go, you'll have me by your side."

Chapter Thirty-Three

Somewhere in the distance, a freeway sung with the background whine of commuter buggies heading home through the still evening air, their lights strung out like evening raindrops on sunset-lit grass. But the retail park was quiet, only the multi-screen picture house in its far corner still open. A figure emerged from the dusky shadows that flanked the huge slab-like building they were approaching. Blade walked forward and shook the figure's hand.

"Blade," the man said.

"Appreciate this, Pete. More than I can say."

"How long's it been, Blade? Fifteen years? I know you're not perfect. But this stuff they're saying you've done, I know there's no way you've done that. And there's another thing." Pete stopped, his feet shuffling for a couple of moments. "I was out of order, dropping you like that. I was doing what the suits with the charts told me. Putting profit over friendship."

Blade held up a hand to stop him. "Pete. It's okay. You had a business to run. I might have been going down, but I couldn't expect you to share the ride."

"Maybe. But I should have told you myself. Telling it to Tenny was gutless, and I'm sorry."

Blade smiled. "No apology's needed. But I appreciate it, and I appreciate this."

"Just trying to make us even."

"We can take what we like, right?"

Pete nodded towards the door. "I dismissed all the night staff. Told them I wanted some private time. Whole place is yours. Whatever you want."

"Well, what are we waiting for then?" Blade turned back to the others. "Come on guys, let's make like adventurers. Let's go shopping."

The Storm was finding the guided tour a little surreal. He'd never visited a Pete's Adventure Warehouse before, what with adventuring never having been his thing. Others might see an attraction in spending a weekend camping in the wilderness, hunting, exploring caves, and generally pretending to be back in the Second Age, but whatever the appeal was it had entirely passed the Storm by. And now here he was, not only in a Pete's, but being shown around by wiry, grey-haired Pete himself – the man from the adverts made real before him.

"Okay," said Pete. "Over there, potions." He pointed at a display upon which were racked hundreds of small jars, each with a brightly coloured top. "Red, physical enhancements. Blue, mental enhancements. Green, healing."

Dani grabbed a backpack from an adjacent display and started dropping potions into its open maw.

Pete pointed in the opposite direction. "Down there, swords." He smiled at Blade. "Half of which have got your name written on them. Literally." He moved on. "Over there, bolts. I'm supposed to do a background check with a waiting period for those, but grab what you want and I'll have them lost in the stock-control system." They continued on down the centre aisle. "That whole section over there's ropes, camping equipment, tents, general survival stuff. On the far wall we've got rations. Canned, dried, the works." He glanced at Presto. "Spell components over yonder, plus top-range spell tablets and combat-wands. What type do you favour?"

The wizard smiled. "I've always been partial to braided strands of unicorn tail hair wrapped in aged starwood with a dragon's tooth tip."

Pete nodded. "We've got just such a thing. It's locked in a case, what with it being worth twenty thousand golds, but I've got the keys and it's yours. Be nice to have it go to someone worthy of wielding it."

He looked over at the Storm. "Guess you'll be wanting a lute, then?"

The Storm was still mentally coughing over the twenty thousand golds – for a stick! He blinked. "Erm, yeah, I guess. Why?"

"I figure you're a bard, and bards are generally lute or flute and I seem to recall an axe being your weapon of choice." Pete set off down a side aisle, giving the Storm little choice other than to follow him. The older man stopped in front of a display case full of lutes above and amps below. "Standard field lutes, together with portable amps. I'd go for the Thunderstar XL7 paired with a Peyer-Tuan amp. Gives you good charge time, strong volume, and a reverb that'll make your teeth rattle."

"But what I am supposed to do with it?"

Pete fixed him with a friendly smile. "You play it, son. When the time comes, you play it."

The Storm always flew with a demon of fear churning his gut, but right now he was harbouring a monster. They'd lifted off a little after sunset in a stolen carpet under cover of darkness and rain and headed off east-north-east, on a path that Blade had promised would take them on a smooth arc passing just to the west of the thirty-mile radius that was the Craagon's Reach exclusion zone.

Except that while the carpet and its arc would be passing, they would not. When they'd decided to fly to Craagon's Reach, the Storm had assumed that the journey being discussed was one that would end with a landing. A subsequent conversation swiftly revealed this to be a naive assumption, failing as it did to consider the possibility that a carpet flying that close to the exclusion zone would be tracked, and any landing quickly investigated. No, all save the Storm quickly agreed that the best way for them to escape detection would be for the carpet to continue flying its smooth, high-altitude, cruising arc, straight past the zone, continuing north to end its journey only when it ran out of charge somewhere over the frozen reaches of the Northern Ocean.

Unfortunately that decision led inexorably to another, second decision, which was why the Storm's usual whimpering demon of fear was threatening to turn into a screaming monster. Voices spoke around him, calm, measured tones overlaid with the alien, incomprehensible syllables Presto was chanting. A hand touched him – Presto – and a magical shiver surged down his spine. Then Blade spoke.

"Thirty seconds. Get ready, people."

Shit, shit, shit. Bugger, bugger, bugger. Fuckity, fuckity, fuck. Somewhere deep inside him a child was screaming in terror. He put his head down between his knees and tried to breathe, but was brought back to the awful now by Blade's next words. "Okay. Go!"

He looked up, seeing a world rendered dreamlike by terror and adrenaline. Dani was standing, belts thrown aside, the sleek black survival suit she now wore further removing the scene from any kind of familiar reality. She stepped up onto the top lip of the front, passenger side door, smiled, pulled her breather mask up and onto her face, and was gone.

A few moments later, Laliana threw herself out of the seat to the Storm's left, the dog strapped to her chest, followed within a second or so by Darick from his seat to the Storm's right. Presto's voice called out from somewhere behind.

"Okay. Luggage... gone. See you down belo–" The last word was swiftly cut off as the wizard presumably exited the carpet.

And then there was just the Storm's whimpering self and Blade. The warrior unbuckled his own belt, flipped a series of switches on the console in front of him, and then eased himself through the gap between the two front seats, his hand outstretched. "Time to get off, mate," he said.

The Storm forced words through a dry, terror-constructed throat. "I. I. Can't."

Blade reached forward for the breather mask that hung from the Storm's neck. "Sure you can." He pulled the mask up and let it pop back over the Storm's mouth. The warrior made a questioning, thumbs up gesture, but the Storm could only shake his head in barely controlled terror.

Blade shrugged. "Tell you what, how about we finish this discussion down on the ground?" Without waiting for an answer, the warrior lunged forward, moving with a rapidity that was inhumanly fast even in the frame-by-frame slow motion the Storm's racing brain was currently operating in. The Storm went from sitting to flying without experiencing any identifiable, intervening stages. He didn't pass start and he didn't collect his four hundred golds. He tumbled lazily over the side of the carpet and across the invisible boundary that marked the edge of its bubble-shaped protective field. Cold air smashed into him with the force of a knuckle-dusted fist. He spun, head over feet and right hand over left. Sky turned to ground turned to sky. For an instant he glimpsed Blade diving out of the carpet with a grace that even in his current terrified state he couldn't help but admire.

And then he was falling. Faster and faster, even more so after he somehow managed to stop spinning. The world below was a mottled kaleidoscope of green and brown, but the brown was rapidly becoming scrub and the green was rapidly becoming trees. A single, repeating thought forced its way through the terror.

It hasn't worked.

It hasn't worked.

It hasn't–

And then he felt something tugging, gently at first, but then sharper, pulling at his back, and his heels, and his shoulders. Slowing.

Slowing. But still the ground was growing in size and detail, as still he hurtled towards it. He tried to twist, to get his legs beneath him, but there was nothing to push against, no lever he could work. He felt his body rotating, slowly, so slowly; the tugs on his shoulders slightly more vigorous than those on his heels. He had a last glimpse of green, and then he was smashing through a scratching world of green and brown that tore at his exposed hands and head. He banged off one branch and then another, and then crashed down onto the dry earth.

Alive.

Just.

Forty-five minutes after Presto made a hard but safe landing on a narrow stretch of scrub-filled clearing just a few hundred yards from the netted up mass of equipment, a very angry looking the Storm emerged from the trees, closely followed by Blade. The warrior tapped a warning finger against his temple, nodding as he did so at the Storm.

"You said that spell would make me float like a fucking feather!" screamed the enraged rock star, rapidly advancing to where Presto was setting up the portable chart. Twigs extended from various bits of his webbing and there was a long smear of mud across his face.

Dani, Darick, and Laliana, who'd arrived from the opposite direction some time previously, looked up from where they were repacking their backpacks, but stayed silent. Presto reached into the side pouch of his black utility belt, pulled out one of Pete's own-brand, ready-smoke, combat cigars ("…a special blend delivering a smooth taste and a boost to concentration"), lit it with a simple Finger Flame cantrip, took a few experimental puffs, and then delivered his response. "No. I think that if you cast your mind back you'll recall that I said I'd be casting a modified version of the Feather Float spell."

"Modified!" the Storm screamed. "Modified to do what? Modified to not float like a fucking feather?"

Presto took another couple of lip-smacking puffs. "Yes, I think that's a pretty fair description."

"I thought I was going to fucking die!"

"If I'd cast a standard Feather Float we would have taken an extremely long time to float down to the ground. Not only would that have massively increased the chances of our being detected, we would have been at the mercy of winds that might have scattered us halfway to the World's End Mountains. So I modified it to let us freefall to a pre-determined altitude and then slow us just enough to enable a survivable landing." He looked down at his cigar, then back up at the Storm. "Where did you land?"

The rock star waved a hand across the various bits of foliage to which he was still attached. "Take a wild fucking stab in the dark."

Blade stepped in beside the Storm. "Hey, we're all down and safe, right? Now maybe we could have been better briefed or maybe we were best off not knowing. Point is, we're down. Let's figure out where we are, yeah?" He nodded at the chart that lay on the ground in front of Presto. "Is that working?"

"It is," Presto told him. "But it's in passive mode, so it needs three sources to get a full fix. It's picked up two satellites. We just need a third." As he said the words, the status display at the chart's bottom-right corner changed from amber to green. "Looks like we just got it." The chart's display panned and then zoomed in, its map now showing scattered forest, with a pulsing blue dot at the chart's centre and a red line arcing from its bottom edge to its right top corner. "Okay, we're here, where the dot is. That red line's the thirty mile exclusion zone, with the complex itself–" he moved his finger to point at a specific spot in the chart's bottom right corner "–being located here."

"What about the aurascope?" said Dani, who'd apparently finished repacking her backpack. "Anything on that?"

Presto pulled a small, flat black box from one of his webbing pouches and held it out towards the south-east. Within seconds, its near side transformed from a plain, blank slab to a mottled and writhing expanse of green. "There's quite a bit of magical activity showing, most of it around the complex, but some of it spread across the exclusion zone."

Blade had been looking over his shoulder. Now he pointed at some of the brighter blobs at the screen. "What about those hotspots? Are they some kind of device?"

Presto shook his head. "Not necessarily. The disaster created a permanent wild node ten miles down, and many of those patterns are most likely areas where mana generated by the node is escaping to the surface."

"What mana level are we reading here?" Blade asked.

"We've got a background level of a little over fifty MilliKellens an hour," replied Presto. It had been the first thing he'd checked upon landing.

"Is that bad?" asked Laliana.

"It's about double the standard background level, but that's not the problem. There's nothing wrong with a strong mana field. We were in a much stronger field on Upabove. The problem is that this is all wild mana. Raw, twisted, chaotic, primeval stuff, the stuff that existed when the universe began and the stuff that will be left at its end. Clean mana is inert. It has the power to transform but will only do so when manipulated by a casting. But wild mana..." Presto shook his head. "It's constantly active, reacting, transforming."

Laliana shivered. "It's just horrible to think that it's out there. You can't smell it. You can't taste it. You can't sense it. But it's out there."

Presto tapped the small device attached to his belt. "Just keep an eye on your dosemeters. As long as they still show green you're okay."

"And what do we do if they turn amber?" asked Darick.

Presto shrugged. "Don't know. Re-calibrate your personal definition of okay, I guess."

Blade stood up and swung his backpack onto his back. "Well, the sooner we set out, the sooner we get there. And the less nights we spend out here the better, far as I'm concerned."

"Why?" asked Darick. "Are you scared of wolves or something?"

"Something. This far east, wolves aren't at the top of the food chain."

"I'm sorry?"

Dani touched the priest on the arm. "There are things that eat wolves."

"Right," replied the priest. "Okay. Going might be good then." He looked up. "Should I say a little prayer?"

"If you like," Blade told him.

The priest got down on one knee and paused. After a few seconds, Blade joined him, followed by Dani, Laliana, and the Storm. Rej looked up from the tree stump he'd been sniffing, wrinkled his snout in confusion, then dropped into a sit. Darick looked at Presto. Presto sighed inwardly, and then slid to one knee. The priest nodded, closed his eyes and began speaking. "Holy SkyFather, we beseech you to aid us in our quest. Grant that we may show wisdom and courage..."

Chapter Thirty-Four

Back in Empire City before they'd left, when this whole expedition was nothing more than maps, plans, and talking, this part of the endeavour had seemed to Blade to be one of the simpler parts of the scheme. Just a ten mile hike through a forest. How hard could that be? Except now, with boots on the ground and paranoia pushing his senses to their limits, it wasn't a hike and it sure wasn't simple. After half an hour of edging through the dense woodland, navigating a course, checking for threats, and making sure that everyone was still behind him, Blade found himself already nearing mental exhaustion.

He shook his head. This wasn't right.

He put his hand up to signal a halt, checked for anything that might be watching them, and then turned back. "I need someone to go out in front and scout, leaving me to navigate and look out for more general threats." He gave Dani a pointed glance.

The grifter smiled ruefully. "And you're looking at me because?"

"Well, I believe back in the days when people actually did this for a living, it was traditional for the thief-type person to serve as scout."

"Thief-type person?"

Blade stuttered out an embarrassed, "Well, you know, sort of–"

"It's okay. But that was what, five hundred years ago? I'm a city girl. You want someone's bank account emptied or a carpet lifted then I'm your woman. But here?" She shrugged, helplessly.

Blade swore inwardly as he realised the truth of what she was saying. What the hell was he doing, thinking he could break into a top secret base with a bunch of people even less well-qualified than he was? He closed his eyes for a moment, then looked around him, hoping for inspiration. The dog, bored, was sniffing at the base of a tree.

Dog.

He put on a friendly smile. "Rej?"

"Rres?"

"Let's have a chat."

They'd been climbing steadily for some twenty minutes, edging through the thick woodland as they traversed from the valley below to the ridgeline above. This was virgin territory, with none of the foot-worn trails you'd have expected of a forest back in the western heartlands. Blade took a look back. Darick was close behind him, followed by Presto, Laliana, the Storm, and finally Dani — with the grifter alone seeming to be looking beyond her next footstep, thinking of more than simply climbing the ridge.

Several feet ahead, Rej was sniffing his way carefully past a huge oak. The dog paused, stiffened, then sat down, his left front paw making "down" motions in the manner Blade had taught him. Blade turned, repeating the signal to those behind him, waiting until each of his companions had nodded and crouched down. Then he dropped into a crouch himself, and moved slowly up to Rej, travelling the last few feet in a cautious commando-crawl. They were now at the crest of the ridge, with another wooded valley laid out before them. "What is it?" he whispered.

The dog dropped to a lying position beside him and then pointed with his paw.

"Rrumbring rrare," the dog said in a low growl. "Rrin rrhees."

Blade's eyes followed the outstretched paw. The view was obscured with leaves and branches but through the gaps he could just make out a white pole topped by a sign. He got out his mono-scope, searched for a moment to find it in the zoomed-in view, and then found himself looking at a sign containing the universal symbol for dangerous magic, a gorgon's waving hair, with words written underneath: "CRAAGON'S REACH EXCLUSION ZONE ALL ENTRY PROHIBITED".

He gave the dog a friendly pat. "Good boy Rej, well spotted. Stay here and keep watch."

"Rrokay," the dog replied happily, his tail wagging.

Blade began easing his way back from the ridgeline and down the slope. Getting them to the Zone's perimeter might have been his job. But getting through it sure as hell wasn't.

Dani watched as Blade made his way back down the slope in a careful crouch. The warrior took a long, slow look around them, and then motioned them to gather to him. "Okay, we've reached the ridgeline. The exclusion zone boundary's a little way down the far slope, pretty much where we figured it would be."

"Anything visible?" asked Dani.

"Just a pole and sign that I can see. But that don't mean there ain't anything else."

Dani swung her pack off her shoulders and pulled a flat object out of one of its side pockets. It was a small, but highly powerful, portable oracle she'd got from Pete's loaded up with a whole load of cutting edge software that she most definitely hadn't got at Pete's. She reached back into the pocket and pulled out an even smaller device that also hadn't arrived on her person via any legitimate retail sales channel, plugged it into a port on the back of the oracle, then nodded at Blade.

"I'll need to take a look at it."

The warrior nodded, and motioned her to follow him up the slope. They worked their way carefully upward, and then eased in alongside Rej, who acknowledged their presence with a quick tail wag. Dani opened the oracle and ran up a general-purpose security-monitoring program available only to certified professionals in the security industry, and people like her. The screen, blank initially, gradually filled with a variety of icons of varied colours and shapes, each representing a particular device installed somewhere in the landscape before them.

"I'm guessing that means there's stuff down there," Blade whispered, nodding at the screen.

"Yeah." Dani jabbed a finger from icon to icon, listing each type as she did so. "We've got line sensors here, forward looking motion detectors over there, a belt of general proximity stuff, and then some general comms gear. All pretty standard. Good quality. But standard."

"Can you get us through it?"

Dani gave him a smile, then flexed her fingers. "Watch me."

A couple of hours after they'd ghosted through the Exclusion Zone's boundary, protected only by a bunch of hacks and gizmos that Dani had sworn would work and that Blade could only hope to the gods had, they crested yet another low ridgeline and paused to survey the valley that lay beyond. Blade lay down beside Rej and slowly scanned his mono-scope across the landscape. It was empty, as far as he could see, which didn't necessarily mean anything. Behind him, in the west, the sun was setting, casting long shadows, indistinct in the gloom. He told Rej to stay, then moved back down the slope to where the others were waiting. "Looks clear," he told them. "But we'd better have Dani check it out."

The grifter nodded, pulled out her oracle, and then set off up the slope.

Blade turned back to his four remaining comrades. "And it's getting late, so we'd better find somewhere to hole up for the night. Who's for first watch?"

Through a series of miscalculations and hesitations, Presto had ended up stiffed with the turd-end-of-the-stick second watch, which meant he'd spent most of Darick's first watch wide awake and worrying, eventually falling asleep just in time for the priest to wake him up with a cheery, "Your watch!"

He cracked open an alertness potion and glugged it down, then crawled out of the three man tent he was sharing with Blade and the Storm. This far north, and in the middle of the night, the air had quite an edge to it, late spring or no late spring. He gave himself a few slaps to try to get warm, then pulled on his owl-eyes goggles, grabbed his combat-wand, and set to walking around the perimeter of monitoring devices Dani had set up.

Around him, the forest murmured in the gentle breeze. Branches creaked. Unseen woodland creatures chatted, challenged, fought, and no doubt fornicated. Somewhere, a bear may or may not have been defecating. Presto stopped and performed a three-sixty degree scan, slowly turning on the spot. In the harsh green light of the owl-eyes, he couldn't help but feel that the clearing looked smaller than it had been when they'd first arrived and set up the tents. He checked Dani's motion sensors, each one glowing red in his artificially enhanced vision, visible through the trees.

Visible through the trees.

When they'd arrived, Dani had set the motion sensors up on the edge of the clearing, in front of the trees. Now they were in the trees.

Somewhere a tree creaked. And then another.

He stepped carefully backward to his tent, muttering the words of a general protective incantation as he did so. "Blade?" he hissed through the open doorway.

The warrior awoke, blinking. "Trouble?"

"Either that or I'm going mad."

Blade crawled out of the doorway, his sword clutched in his hand. He pulled his set of owl-eyes up and over his face and looked around. "Are you thinking that some of those trees have moved?"

"Yes."

Somewhere across from them a tree extended a root, then slid slowly forward, followed by another tree, and then another. From somewhere above, a long bough with a dozen twiggy branches reached across and down, its leaves whipping as it reached for Presto. The wizard felt the words rising almost unbidden within him, arms moving of their own accord, ears hearing a distant screaming which his too-slow brain vaguely recognised as his. He lifted his combat-wand.

And the magic flowed.

Chapter Thirty-Five

Dani woke, regaining consciousness to the sound of Presto's inhuman screams in an alien language, overlain by Blade's shouts of alarm. She grabbed the bolt that lay beside her sleep-sack, pulled the owl-eyes over her head, and crawled out of the tent and into chaos. Presto was firing jet after jet of fire from his combat-wand, at burning trees that screamed as though alive and moved as though sentient. Blade, meanwhile, was fighting off a trio of oaks, his sword moving inhumanly fast as he fended off the multiple branches snatching at him. Dani appraised the situation and came up with an impossible answer.

Walking trees.

Something moved, so peripheral in her vision that she felt it more than saw it. She dived down, just in time for a branch as thick as her waist to swing hard through the space she'd occupied a moment before. She rolled, brought up the bolt, squeezed the trigger, and sent a beam of pure green mana into the base of the branch, where the thick bough met even thicker trunk. The tree screamed, the cry coming from both nowhere and everywhere, but then took a remorseless step forward, swinging its bulk into another attack.

She continued shooting, once, twice, three times, until finally something in the tree died. It rocked back, tottering, and then fell slowly forward towards her. She threw herself sideways, clearing the falling trunk but not the mass of branches surrounding it. For long seconds she tore her way through the tree's dying death-throes, eventually emerging to find her tent crushed by the toppled tree. An icy fear wound tentacles around her spine, but then there were more trees coming at her, conifers, smaller than the oaks, but faster with it. She shot at them, numb, not thinking, aiming and firing, again and again, track, shoot, kill – until she felt her trigger click on nothing.

Out of charge.

Then Laliana was by her side, with Darick, Rej and the Storm close behind. Laliana tossed Dani the weapons belt she'd left in the tent. Dani caught it, buckled it on, thumbed her bolt's eject stud to send the empty mana cartridge falling to the ground, pulled a fresh cartridge out of the belt, and rammed it home, just in time to finish off the last of the conifers and then snap a couple of quick shots at a young elm that was sneaking in behind Darick. Across from her,

Presto was still spraying fire and death, keeping that side of the clearing at bay, but everywhere else they were being overwhelmed. Blade's sword was moving too fast for the owl-eyes to see, showing only as a blurred smear before him, but still there were more trees, with more branches.

They were losing.

Then a faint whine split the night air, rising above the sounds of maimed trees and an angry, out of control wizard. A spotlight flickered across her, followed by a second, both lights scanning this way and that across the clearing. Carpets, she realised. Two of them; big ones, coming in from above. She looked up and saw them, dim shadows under-lit by the fires burning beneath them. The pair of side-mounted heavy bolts each carpet sported opened up, spitting a rain of green energy that ripped great chunks of charred timber from the screaming trees surrounding Dani and her companions. The green-brown tide made one last surge, faltered, and then fell away. Stillness returned to a clearing now twice its former size and littered with the fallen trunks of dead and dying trees. A voice came echoing down from above, harsh with amplification. "Okay, we're coming in. Hands up and nobody move, unless you want to burn like those trees."

The first carpet dropped in on a quick, military style approach, covered from above by the second carpet. It bounced down onto the ground and disgorged two sets of troops, the green clad figures jumping out before it had even stopped rocking on its skids. One of the soldiers approached Dani, the man's two-handed bolt never leaving his shoulder and its dangerous end never pointing anywhere other than straight at her. The trooper had a blond moustache and blue eyes and was the only one of the eight troops who'd exited the carpet who wore an open helmet. Dani, noting him for the leader, nodded warily at him. The bloke might have just rescued her from death by tree, but she'd seen enough people shot to know that shootings too often come at the fag-end of a confrontation, when the furious certainty of violent conflict is collapsing into a chaotic and uncertain aftermath.

The bloke nodded back in unspoken acknowledgement, looked around, and then spoke into the whisper-mic attached to his helmet. "Alpha Leader. Position secure. All arboreal entities inert. Six unknowns in custody."

Dani took a very slow and intentionally obvious look around her, seeing Blade and Presto similarly paired up with bolt-wielding troopers, with Laliana, Darick, the Storm, and Rej in a group a little way off, the humans with their hands raised, the dog sitting, confused. One day, she thought, one of our plans might actually come together. This clearly wasn't that day.

The two carpets flew low across the night-shrouded forest, their pilots hugging the landscape with clear professional skill. Blade stayed in his seat, sharing the occasional glance with Dani and Presto, but making no attempt to move. Right now he figured they were out of options save that of allowing the sacred box to come to Mekkmet, the previous plan of having Mekkmet go to the box having failed at an embarrassingly early stage. Trees. Attacked by fucking trees. He'd never heard of anything so stupid – except perhaps for that time when an ex-team mate of his had got so herbed up that he'd tried to have sex with an exotic, semi-sentient pot plant, not realising that said pot plant was in fact carnivorous. Right now though, he'd take a highly embarrassing conversation with the doctor at the clap clinic over what was no doubt awaiting him and the guys.

Somewhere to their left was a green glow that was managing to be beautiful, alien, and very, very wrong, all at the same time. Blade nodded at the blond-moustached officer, who was sat opposite him, just behind the pilot. "Is that the old mana-generation complex?"

The man smiled. "Yeah. Don't worry, we're staying well clear of that. Go too close for too long and, well, let's just say that you might not be you anymore."

The carpets continued on their course for a few minutes, then banked sharply, cresting a low ridge to reveal a dimly lit expanse of concrete and hangars that sure as hell hadn't been on the aeronautical charts Blade had earlier consulted. A little way away, set between a cluster of hangars and a control tower, a skyship was docked to a mast. It was sleek and white, its exterior marked only by rows of portholes and the expanse of windows across its nose that marked its bridge. As the carpets slid past, Blade caught a glimpse of the number marked in foot high black letters across its tail.

GH-78.

Then the carpet was lifting its nose and slowing. The pilot held it there for an instant before dropping them into a smooth landing, markedly less abrupt than the one he'd made earlier in the clearing. The faint background whine of the repulsion field died. For a moment there was silence, and then the troops aboard the carpet began to bounce out of their seats in a manner that looked both well drilled and practised. The blond-moustached officer nodded at Blade. "Okay, we're here. Got some people who'd like to talk to you."

Having disembarked from the carpet, they'd been marched – or, in the case of Rej and the bound and gagged Presto, carried – to a waiting passenger-wagon, which had driven off as soon as they'd boarded. The moustached officer hadn't needed to give any instructions to the driver; arrangements were clearly in hand. The wagon had shot across the dark skyport, passing through some islands of illumination and skirting others before plunging, with no obvious halt, into the dark maw of a tunnel mouth. A line of reflective studs marked the twin edges of the tunnel, glowing bright in the wagon's headlight beams, endlessly curving away and down as they followed the tube. Down and down the wagon continued, heading deeper and deeper underground. Finally, the road levelled out and straightened, the reflective studs now stretching out before them, pointing to a far-distant vanishing point lost in the gloom.

Blade didn't try to engage the moustached-officer in conversation, figuring that the man was done talking. He took a look around the wagon's interior: Presto, bound and gagged; Dani, her usual unreadable self; Darick and the Storm, scared; Laliana, wary; Rej, excited, his tail wagging, his snout pressed against the side window. Despite it all, Blade found himself smiling at the dog's joy.

Then the wagon was slowing, and turning into a side tunnel that soon opened up into a huge, apparently natural cavern, whose floor had been filled with rough concrete, upon which sat a group of cheap-looking, prefabricated buildings. Harsh lighting shone from the ceiling above. The wagon pulled up alongside one of the structures.

"Okay, guys, here we are," said the moustached officer in a calm, but flat tone. He motioned Blade towards the wagon's side door, apparently confident that Blade wouldn't do anything stupid. The officer and his squad of soldiers guided them through a set of double doors and down a corridor whose floor, walls and ceiling consisted of unpainted plasterboard, broken only by the occasional motivational poster. The officer halted in front of a door, opened it, and pointed at the room that presumably lay beyond. "Through there."

For just an instant, Blade considered his options. He was unarmed and surrounded by armed men, and while the walls looked flimsy enough that given a few seconds he could probably punch his way through one of them, those few seconds would be easily long enough for the troops to punch or shoot their way through him. He allowed himself the luxury of a shrug so subtle it was probably imperceptible to those observing him, and walked through the doorway into the room beyond.

There, he found a man and a woman sitting behind a plain-looking table, a shimmering force-wall in front of them cutting clean through the table's shiny surface. A scattering of plastic chairs stood in a pair of untidy rows in front of the table. Blade grabbed a chair and sat down in it, not waiting to be asked. He didn't particularly look in the man's direction, because he didn't need to, not even with a semi-opaque force-wall between them – he'd clocked the guy as the bloke who'd tried to kill him at Craagon's Reach as soon as he'd entered the room.

He waited while his companions similarly took their places, or, in the case of Presto, were inserted into them, and then gestured at the force-wall. "You don't need that," he told the man, making sure to stare right into his eyes. "It just makes you look weak. Much as I'd enjoy ripping your stomach out via your bowels, I ain't stupid enough to try something with a shackload of infantry outside." This wasn't quite true. If the opportunity presented itself, Blade was quite tempted to try the option of grabbing himself a hostage–cum–body-shield and improvising from there, and he figured it was worth seeing if they fell for it. "So I'd drop the spell, assuming it was you that cast it." Blade took an exaggerated look around the room as though searching for hidden magic eyes or ears. "Or maybe the bloke who cast it's somewhere else, listening in on us?"

The man held his gaze for a moment, but then turned and tipped an ironic head at his female companion. She leaned forward, until her nose was barely an inch away from the force-wall, and smiled. "I think you're missing something, Mr Petros."

Thus far Blade's attention, the part of it that wasn't still casing the joint and checking out options, had been mostly focused on the guy. He belatedly examined the woman. She was good-looking, in a slightly stern sort of way, with the first flushes of middle age sitting easily upon classical features. Slim lips, marked out in scarlet, were framed by flowing chestnut hair that fell past her shoulders, with the look completed by a tight, fitted black jumpsuit unmarked by any patch or insignia.

Blade waited until she'd leaned back in her seat, and then returned the smile. "And this thing I'm missing is?"

"This is the Second Millennium of the Third Age. You don't have to be in possession of a penis to cast spells."

"I'm sorry?" Blade replied, genuinely confused.

"I'm the one who cast the spell. If you want it dropped, I'm the one you need to be asking."

"Oh, right."

"You've got two children, haven't you? A son and a daughter?"

"Yeah. Why?"

"I do hope you're teaching your daughter that she can be anything she wants to be. Or do you leave that for your son? Are you raising your daughter to be a good little girl whose ambitions will stretch only to grabbing herself a nice husband?"

"Course I ain't!"

Her smile turned quizzical. "Are you sure, Mr Petros? Sexism is a pernicious thing. It lives in the cracks of a man's thoughts, nudging his decisions, and clouding his perception. You modern men are so proud of how progressive you are, but deep down, you all still view the world through a deeply sexist lens."

"That's bollocks!"

"You saw a man, a woman, and a spell, and came to an immediate and absolute assumption that it was the man who had cast the spell, even though there was no evidence whatsoever to suggest that. And then, when you questioned that assumption, you concluded that if it had not been he who had cast the spell, it must have been another man somewhere else."

"Yeah, all right, maybe it's not bollocks, but still—"

"You're sexist, Mr Petros. That's fine. It doesn't mean you're not a good man."

They were only sixty seconds in, and already this interrogation was going far worse than Blade had hoped, and his hopes, frankly, hadn't been that great. "Yeah, well, whatever. What do you want, an apology? You want me to say I'm sorry I thought you were just some kind of personal assistant, when you're actually a fully paid-up member of the evil conspiracy?"

She shrugged, amused. "I suppose it would be a start. But no apologies are necessary. After all these days, these weeks even, of having you and your companions sniffing around us, it's nice to finally meet you. Although you aren't all strangers." She paused, then looked hard at the still bound and gagged Presto. "We've met before, haven't we, Presto?"

Chapter Thirty-Six

Presto had always looked down on the field of psionics, seeing it as very much a poor man's magic, powered not by logic and reason, but by instinct and emotion. Right now though, bound and gagged as he was and with several bucketloads of painfully raw emotion going to spare, he would have hugely appreciated the ability to telepathically psyche-blast the woman who sat in front of him or, failing that, telekinetically hurl something hard-edged and painful at her head. Because yes, they had in fact met before.

For a few seconds his eyes locked on hers, and for a moment, despite himself, despite everything that had gone before, he felt himself being drawn in, felt the layers of hatred and betrayal and hurt and anger starting to fracture beneath the pressure of emotions so buried he'd long thought them dead. Then she nodded at someone behind him, and spoke. "Remove his gag. There's not much he can do with his hands tied and if he does try anything I'll have no problem counter-spelling it." Her smile returned, that impish-smile-bordering–on-cruelty that he remembered so well. "You won't be stupid will you, darling?"

As the unseen person behind reached forward to remove the gag, Presto saw both Blade and his erstwhile torturer react to that final word; the torturer with a tight, tiny grimace of annoyance, Blade with a more apparent start of surprise.

The warrior leaned in to Presto. "Sorry. Do you know her?"

Presto took the deep breath the gag had been denying him before replying. "I used to."

"Oh yes, Mr Petros. Presto and I do indeed know each other. Intimately, in fact. Did he never tell you that he'd once been married?"

Blade stared hard at her for several seconds, and then turned his attention back to Presto, a confused finger pointing at nothing in particular. "Are you telling me that she's the ex-wife you mentioned?"

Presto shrugged, a shrug rendered doubly awkward by both the situation and his bonds. "Well, I don't believe I was telling you anything, but yes, she is the ex-wife I mentioned, the Jaquenta who very swiftly terminated our marriage when my academic career came to a halt."

"Darling. Would you have expected anything else of me?"

"Given what a cow you are, no. I'd say that it gives me pleasure to see that your own academic career has apparently flourished, but it doesn't."

She smiled.

Blade meanwhile appeared to be traversing through a range of emotions, confusion, anger, and distaste playing across his face in sequence, his gaze all the while switching between Presto and his former wife before eventually settling on amazed and slightly surprised admiration.

"You and her?" the warrior said, indicating Jaquenta with a tip of the head.

"Yes."

The warrior leaned forward to speak in a conspiratorial whisper. "Punching above your weight a bit there, mate."

Quite frankly, Presto wasn't sure if that should be taken as an insult or a compliment, but equally frankly, he didn't much care.

Jaquenta smiled. "Well, it's nice to see you haven't forgotten me."

"Trust me. I tried."

"Now there's no need to be so mean, darling. Why don't we have a catch up meal? For old times' sake. You must be terribly hungry. I'll have to keep you bound, but I could spoon feed you, like I used– Or perhaps that's more information than your friends need to know?"

Back when they'd been married, Jaquenta had possessed a taste in interior decoration that in Presto's personal opinion ill-suited her, being warm, eclectic, and homely; something that utterly failed to reflect every single other aspect of her personality, her lifestyle, and the way she conducted her affairs. If the quarters to which he'd been carried were indeed hers, then it appeared that she was still in possession of the same incongruous tastes, being decorated as they were by simple-but-charming halfling rugs, pictures of cats, and an excessive quantity of cushions.

The soldiers who'd carried him withdrew, swiftly followed by the two grey-clad individuals who'd delivered a couple of trays of sandwiches and other nibbles, and what looked to be a moderately expensive bottle of something sparkling. Only Presto's torturer now remained. He stepped back, but then paused in the doorway and looked hard at Jaquenta. "You going to be okay with him?"

She gave him a pursed-lipped reply. "Please don't try and play the old-fashioned white knight, Davan, it doesn't suit you." The security man – assuming that was what he was – went to speak, then bit back a reply with a snort and left, leaving Presto alone with a women who he'd desired, loved, and hated, not necessarily always in that order. Jaquenta waited a few seconds, then reached out for one of the nibbles, speaking as she did so. "Presto, darling, do you have any idea of the trouble that you're in right now?"

"I think I've got a pretty good idea, Jaq. You might have accused me of many things, but I don't recall a lack of intelligence being one of them."

"No. Common sense, perhaps, but the size and scope of your intellect was what drew me towards you. Sandwich?"

"No, thank you."

She accepted the refusal with a tip of the head. "I'm not talking about the faked crimes we trumped up to get you wanted."

"So you're admitting it?"

"Of course I'm admitting it, you idiot." She sighed, clearly exasperated. It was almost like old times. "You don't get it, do you? This isn't about laws, and this isn't about justice. The only reason we faked those crimes was to get the City Guard looking for you without us having to tell them the real reason. You were never going to go on trial for those crimes, not once we had you. The lies would have collapsed, the truth would have come out. You knew too much then, and you certainly know too much now."

"You don't know how much we know."

"You know about Sleeping Dragon. You know that it's here. If that's all you know, and frankly if it is I'd be disappointed, that's still too much." She looked at him in a way he knew of old, a look that he knew was about as close to actual sincerity and compassion as Jaquenta Buran was capable of. "The carpet that you stole ran out of charge and crashed in the northern wilderness some hours after you bailed out. The guards have already identified you as the people who stole it. Tomorrow your bodies will be discovered in the wreckage."

"So why am I here then? A final conversation for old times' sake? A last meal for the condemned man? Or were you hoping to turn me? Convince me that you could still save me if only I realised the glory and the truth of what you people here are doing and agreed to throw my abilities in with you? Are you going to dangle the prospect of a return to the light, of leaving the darkness I've been in for the last ten years?"

"It's been eleven years, darling."

"I wasn't counting, but to save you the time of saying all that and me the time of listening, the answer's no."

"And there was me thinking we could have a nice chat."

Presto shrugged. "We can still have a chat."

"Really?" An amused smile played upon her lips. "What about, exactly?"

"How about I try to turn you?"

Darick had been praying to the SkyFather for deliverance for just over twenty minutes when the door to the storeroom into which they'd been locked had popped open and Presto had walked in, the glamorous redhead whom they now knew to be his ex-wife following in his wake. The wizard gave them an ironic grin just this side of cheesy. "I believe, gentlemen, that this is what the crystal flicks refer to as a jail break."

Blade, who'd spent the last three hours prowling, was already past Presto and into the doorway. They'd been blindfolded when taken here; now the warrior's head was scanning to and fro, no doubt seeking out threats and evaluating their options. Dani, who'd appeared to spend the last three hours thinking, was up behind him, backing him up, with Laliana and Rej close behind. Only the Storm and Darick himself remained seated.

The rock star raised a pair of querying hands. "Erm, like, say what? How?"

"Is she with us?" Darick added, pointing at the redhead.

Presto waved a hand in front of his ex-wife's face, a face that Darick now realised was almost lifeless. Her eyes stared sightlessly ahead, even as the hand passed in front of them just an inch away. Her mouth was neutral, straight. And in some indefinable, but indisputable way, the spark that marks a human soul was gone.

"Zombie spell," the wizard explained. "She's operating under remote control now, and I'm the man holding the metaphorical controller."

"Like, how did you get to do that?" asked the Storm.

"Don't ask." The wizard pointed at the corner of the room. "And given that there's a seeing eye just over there, I think we ought to be leaving. Very quickly."

Presto ushered his companions out of the storeroom. Getting into this part of the complex had been one thing, but he was bitterly aware that getting out was likely to be very much another. After retrieving their equipment from the adjacent room in which it had been carelessly, but fortuitously, dumped, he led the group carefully down the connecting tunnel that led to the guard post that controlled all access to the area.

When he'd come through the post just a few minutes earlier it had been unmanned, and its barred gate had been open. But now the gate was closed, with a stony-faced guard standing a few feet behind it.

A security alert, he wondered?

Or just a general, scheduled elevation of security status ahead of the detonation?

In the end, it didn't matter either way. He motioned to the others to stay hidden around the corner, then headed on towards the gate, mentally guiding Jaquenta's controlled form to walk alongside him, as though it were she in control of him.

He stopped the two of them just before the gate, saying nothing, and hoping that Jaquenta's mute, haughty form might serve as its own, implied command.

It didn't. The guard took a step forward and barked a one word, interrogatory question. "Yes?"

Pro that he presumably was, the guard was making sure to stay just a bit more than an arm's length from the bars. This wasn't a surprise. When you've made sure to have a set of bars between you and the person you want to keep guarded, keeping far enough away that they can't touch you is pretty much security 101. Of course, that doesn't protect you from everything. When it came to counting his ranged options, Presto could have used all his fingers and all his toes, and still have had options uncounted. But all of those ranged options shared one thing in common – that being a degree of violence sufficient to trigger alarms and put the whole complex into emergency mode.

What Presto needed was something more subtle, and the subtle options all shared a requirement that he touch his target. And whoever had trained this guard knew that, which is why they'd trained him to stand well clear of the gate. Luckily though, Presto was packing an ace that the guard's trainers had perhaps overlooked.

The combat-wand he'd got from Pete's.

A wand enables a wizard to cast ranged and directed spells with greater precision and power, with the degree to which it can do that depending on the quality of the materials from which it has been constructed, and the skill with which those materials have been assembled. In the case of the wand that Presto now wielded, with its braided strands of unicorn tail hair wrapped in a sheath of aged starwood and tipped with a dragon's tooth, even a skilled caster such as himself would gain considerable extra precision at a greatly reduced mana casting cost. But a wand has another useful property: that of acting as an extension of the wizard's arm and thus extending his reach. Which is especially handy if you need to touch someone who is deliberately standing beyond the range of your fingertips.

Of course, wand or no, Presto still needed a spell, but in the spirit of "here's one we prepared earlier" crystal cookery shows he had just the spell he needed sitting ready in his mind, already partially-cast several minutes before and requiring only a final mental command to activate. Such pre-casting was never easy, and when you added in the fact that this was a spell he hadn't cast for more than twenty years – not since he was an undergraduate needing to get back in through the university gates after an unauthorised night out – you had a task that was decidedly non-trivial.

But there were some spells you never forget, especially when the last occasion in which you cast them involved a bullying guardsman with a pain-stick at his belt and a strong desire to use it.

Presto hadn't forgotten this one.

The wand was stuffed up the sleeve of the wizard's loose fitting over-smock. In one fluid movement he let it drop into his hand, flipped it into the correct hold, and reached through the bars to touch its tip against the guard's side.

Persuade, he thought.

The guard jerked alert at the touch of the wand, and began to reach for the whisper at his belt, but was stopped by Presto's firm command. "No."

The movement of the man's hand stopped.

"You don't want to do that."

"I don't want to do that."

"I am not a threat."

"You are not a threat."

"You are going to open the gate, let myself and my comrades go through, then close the gate and forget everything about this."

"I am going to open the gate, let you and your comrades go through, then close the gate and forget everything about this."

The man paused for a moment before walking forward to first tap a number into a keypad mounted beside the gate, and then press his hand against the aura-reader mounted beside it. The gate slid open.

Presto turned and waved the others to come forward, which they did, warily, casting suspicious looks at the now glassy-faced guard, but sensibly saying nothing. He waited until they had all passed through then followed, keeping Jaquenta alongside him.

Behind him, the guard triggered the gate closed, then retreated to his standing position before it.

Presto let out the breath he'd been half holding for the last few minutes. They weren't quite out of the woods, but they at least could see the trees.

Following someone else's instructions was an action that Dani was still finding unfamiliar, but right now Presto seemed to have a pretty good idea of where they needed to be going, which was a damn sight more than she had, so she let him take the lead and instead settled on keeping her eyes and ears open. After getting them through the guard post, the wizard had led them down a maze of tunnels, some apparently hewn from the rock, others natural passageways to which rails, steps, lighting, and walkways had been added, before eventually calling a halt in a small chamber lined along one wall by a bank of lockers.

"Okay, I think we'll be safe here for now. Touch wood, and SkyFather and his friends willing, we should be clear."

Dani tossed out the question she'd been wanting to ask for a while now: "And how exactly did you know the way to go?"

Presto didn't reply, but instead merely touched his ex-wife's forehead with an outstretched finger and spoke a few words of Sorcerac. The transformation managed to be both absolute and almost imperceptible at the same time. The sparkle returned to her eyes, the cynical turn returned to her lips, and the haughty tightness returned to her pose. She turned to face Presto.

"Did it work, darling?"

The wizard nodded a casual nod. "Well, I had to use the Persuade I had stored to get back out of the cell complex, but other than that, yes, it worked like a charm."

Blade had been facing away from them in a kneeling pose, peering back behind them to check for pursuers; now he pivoted sharply around to glare at Presto. "Hang on a minute, are you saying she's actually with us?"

Jaquenta gave him a look that mixed amusement and contempt in equal measure. "She, as you put it, has got a name, and she can be addressed directly rather than via her ex-husband."

"Look, love, don't start giving me the sexism shit."

"You were being a bit sexist," Laliana pointed out. "And referring to her as 'love' is disrespectful."

The warrior's previously controlled disposition began to evaporate, the calm readiness for action now shifting into clear anger. "Gods and goddesses, do we need to have this discussion now?"

Darick leaned in. "It is something that people feel very strongly about. We are talking about a legacy of clear and damaging historical injustice."

"Do your lot have women priests?"

"Well now," the priest began. "It's a very difficult theological question that, as you know, the church has spent much time debating, touching as it does on both the role of women in contemporary society and the manner in which we can best honour the SkyFather and gain his blessings."

"That would be a no, then?"

"Erm. Yes. That would be a no. For what it's worth, I cast my vote in favour when the matter was last voted upon at the Church's General Assembly."

A cough from Presto brought the conversation to a halt. "Gentlemen, fascinating as this subject is, could I perhaps suggest that we table it for later discussion and in the meantime return to the matter at hand?" He received in reply five nods of varying degrees of enthusiasm, an ironically raised eyebrow, and a floor-thumping tail wag. "Excellent. Perhaps I could just make a few points? After a discussion of the threat posed by the mana bomb, Jaquenta has agreed to join us. She allowed me to cast the zombie spell upon her so as to conceal that fact from her former colleagues. There's no advantage in breaking her cover now when we are likely to have need of it."

Presto paused for a moment before continuing.

"That said, I should point out to you all that Jaquenta is still in possession of all her previous character flaws, chief of which is a mischievous delight in fomenting discord and disharmony, as the discussion immediately preceding this one bears witness to."

"Darling, you say the kindest things." The mocking smile remained on her face for a few seconds, before disappearing as she raised a hand. "Look, I never claimed to be the nicest human being around, and I understand that you might all have difficulty trusting me. But I'm not a monster, and more importantly I'm not an idiot. Presto wrote the theories our research is based on. He knows them better than anyone else alive, and it's not just that I trust him when he says our theoretical model is flawed, it's that in less than an hour of discussion he poked half a dozen holes in it."

She looked around them one by one before resuming speaking.

"I deeply regret my role in all of this, and I've no doubt that at some point I'll have to answer for what I've done. But at least I'll be able to partially salve my conscience with the knowledge that in the end, I did the right thing."

It was Blade who broke the resulting silence. "Fair enough. Glad to have you on board."

"So what now?" asked Dani.

Presto nodded as he switched back to business. "The countdown is currently at T minus four and a bit hours. It's Jaquenta's belief, and this is something I'm in agreement with, that her former colleagues will continue with the test, believing that while we may have escaped, the core security around the bomb will keep us out. They've been working on this thing for several years. They're not in a mood to postpone."

Dani looked the wizard in the eye. "So we've got four hours to get to the bomb, disarm it, and steal it?"

"Yes. Now this place is an emergency refuge. The lockers over there should contain various supplies, including, hopefully, overalls – or failing that, helmets and reflective bibs. The Storm, Darick? See what you can find and grab us all some food. Dani? I need you and Jaquenta to go over the security systems around the bomb. Figure out how we can get in, and just as importantly how we can get out. Blade, Laliana? Your job's going to be to get us and the bomb out of here. And Rej?"

"Res?"

"Keep watch."

Chapter Thirty-Seven

From somewhere up high in the cavern's roof, the sound of a shouter-horn cut through the surrounding activity. "T minus three hours and counting. All nonessential personnel to detonation stations. Repeat, all nonessential personnel to detonation stations."

Presto and Dani were hidden behind a cargo crate, positioned so that they could observe Jaquenta as she headed across the open area, clad in utilitarian coveralls and a cap that would hopefully disguise her identity. Presto watched her for several seconds and then looked across at Dani. "How confident are you that this will work?" he whispered.

The grifter shrugged. "Depends on whether they've thought to shut down her system account. If they haven't and if she's got the privilege levels she claims she has – and frankly if she has then whoever set the system up deserves to be shot – then I should be able to get in, do everything we need to do, then clean it all up so when they do think to disable her account there will be no sign of it having been used."

"And if they have shut it down, or she hasn't got the privilege she claimed?"

"Then we're fucked."

Across the cavern, Jaquenta reached a metal door guarded by the ubiquitous side-mounted keypad and aura-reader, beyond which lay one of several security monitoring stations scattered across the complex. The two of them watched as she tapped a number into the keypad then held her palm against the aura-reader. For a frozen instant, which felt like Destiny's tick followed by Fate's tock, Presto held his breath. Then the door slid open and Jaquenta stepped through, the door closing behind her.

Beside him, Dani let out a sigh. "Guess her account's still working. Unless they're cleverer than we think, perhaps, and this is all a trap." Now it was the grifter's turn to give Presto a searching look. "How confident are you that's she going to do what she's supposed to do?"

Presto thought on that for a moment before replying. "Reasonably so. I'd like to think that after the amount of time I spent married to her I learned something about how to read her."

"Fair enough."

Seconds ticked by. Then Jaquenta appeared in the doorway, looked around, and rubbed her eyes: the prearranged signal that the monitoring station was currently unoccupied.

Dani rose into a crouch. "Okay. Let's go."

A little over two hours later, Dani, Presto, Darick, the Storm, and Jaquenta were sat in a small personnel wagon, parked in a deserted side-tunnel, with Presto giving a final briefing. "Right. The bomb is two miles down, in a shaft that lies three miles to the north-east of us. At T minus twenty minutes the security systems should go down. Anything to add, Dani?"

From somewhere down the tunnel, a distant shouter-horn interrupted Dani's answer. "T minus twenty seven minutes and counting. All personnel to detonation stations. Repeat: all personnel to detonation stations."

Dani waited for it to finish before replying. "I also disabled the monitoring systems and kicked in a bunch of concealment routines. They won't know the systems are down. Their specific monitoring systems will be replaying them the control readings they were comparing the real readings with, and their seeing eye screens will be showing them continuous loops of the previous sixty seconds."

The Storm broke in. "And they won't notice that because those are pictures of empty tunnels with like, nothing moving?"

"Exactly. This is one big demonstration of why giving a single account unlimited access is a hugely terrible idea."

Jaquenta laughed. "Blame typical academic narcissism. The security men and the techies wanted to lock the system down, but you know what wizards are like. Everyone convinced he's the greatest caster since Kellen, everyone insistent that he needs full access to the systems to get his research done."

Presto resumed speaking. "Once the system security goes down, we'll take the wagon along the main access tunnel to the head of the shaft, aiming to arrive there at T minus fourteen. Jaquenta, you'll then stay at the top with Darick and the Storm. Dani and I will descend the shaft using the built-in cargo lift, aiming to arrive at the bomb by T minus nine minutes."

He paused for a moment, then resumed.

"The shaft's lined with conventional explosives set to detonate at T minus thirty seconds, thus sealing the bomb in ahead of detonation. Which essentially defines our deadlines in rather absolute terms. By T minus thirty seconds we need to have disabled those conventional explosives. By T minus nought seconds we need to have disabled the bomb, obviously. Any questions?"

The Storm raised a hesitant hand. "Isn't this, like, all seriously tight? You haven't got much in the way of contingency if anything refuses to play nicely."

"Blame me," Dani told him. "I was afraid that if we took the security system down any earlier, there'd be too big a risk of them discovering it."

"And then they might cancel the test and come and arrest us all?" Darick suggested.

"Maybe. Or just decide to detonate the bomb a few minutes early."

"Ah."

Jaquenta put a hand on the priest's arm. "It'll be fine."

Another announcement came echoing along the tunnel. "T minus twenty-five minutes and counting. All personnel to detonation stations. Repeat: all personnel to detonation stations."

Dani slapped the side of the wagon with a confidence that hid the icy knot of fear in her stomach. "Okay, people. Five minutes before the security systems go down. Let's mount up and get ready."

The Storm paused partway into the wagon. "I wonder how Blade and Laliana are doing getting us our ride out of here?"

Dani gave him a hopeful shrug in reply. It was a question that was rarely far from her mind, but with no way of knowing, she figured it best to just assume that the other half of the scheme was going to plan, and instead focus her concerns on the outcome of her half.

Morning came late this far north, but it was finally, belatedly arriving, accompanied by a bitter northerly wind sweeping down from the frozen tundra and across the exposed skyport. Blade suppressed a shiver, then looked back to Laliana and Rej. "You good, guys?"

They nodded.

Blade edged sideways to peer around the crate behind which they were hiding. The complex looked still, with just the occasional flatbed moving across its huge expanse. He checked his wrist-dial. Almost time.

The vertical shaft's dim lights scrolled hypnotically by as the open platform plunged downward, its velocity rendered slow by the distance it had to traverse. Looking up to where Darick, the Storm, and Jaquenta were waiting with the wagon, the lights stretched to a vanishing point impossibly far away. Below, through the platform's mesh floor, the lights similarly stretched away to a dim infinity. Dani was roused from her thoughts by Presto's alerting cough.

"Have you looked at your dosimeter by any chance?"

"No. Why?" She looked down at the dosimeter that hung from her belt. A minute previously it had been coloured green. Now it was amber. She looked across and saw that the wizard's dosimeter was a similar shade. "Shit! The security system?"

"That would be my best guess. We know there's a wild mana node ten miles down. I suspect the security system had a force-wall diverting it away from the complex."

"Which we just turned off."

"Yes. Thus, providing several years' worth of trapped energy with a nice direct route to the surface."

"Anything we can do about it?"

The wizard shrugged. "The protection potions we all took will help a little for a while. Other than that, defuse the bomb and get the seven hells out of here. And if we fail to do that, then the colour of our dosimeters is pretty academic."

Dani let the dosimeter fall back to her belt. The shaft's lights continued to scroll slowly by.

The skyport was huge, its expanse so vast that after several minutes of leapfrogging runs, the cluster of skyships to which they were heading was still some distance away. Blade skidded in behind the wall of a carpet hangar, edged his way along it to peer round the edge, and then – when he saw the way was clear – waved Laliana and Rej to follow him. A few seconds later they slid in behind him. Blade took another peek around the building's corner, and was about to break into a dash when he was halted by Rej's warning growl. "What is it?" he asked.

The dog shook his muzzle in clear confusion. "Rown't row. Rumring rot rite."

And then Blade felt it too: a sensation creeping up his spine, setting the hairs on his neck straight. As Rej had just pointed out, something wasn't right, but what? He looked around, and saw the skyport apparently unchanged; but its early morning stillness was unnatural now, in a way that was no less real for being utterly indescribable.

"What is it?" asked Laliana.

She was not attuned to magic, Blade realised. Had not felt its effects week after week in the arena. Had not been the recipient of more healing spells than a person would care to remember. "Magic," he replied. "But strange. Wrong."

"The bomb?"

He looked at his wrist-dial. "Well, if it is, it's early, and from what Presto said I figure we'd have felt at least some kind of earthquake." Then a thought occurred to him: the security system. Followed by a memory of a game long ago, which featured a very unpleasant trap built around a force-wall with a shitload of mana trapped behind it. "Remember that underground mana node Presto mentioned? I'm thinking that maybe when your sister turned off the security system she might have released it."

"What does that mean?"

"It means that things might be about to get seriously unpleasant." He held up his dosimeter to her: it was flashing green-amber. Then, as though on cue, a bolt of lightning flashed down from a previously clear sky, followed by another, and then another. A cold draft of air blew across them, and then a breeze, which was followed within seconds by a gust hard enough to press them against the side of the hangar. Screams and cries began to echo across the skyport, muffled by the magical storm's fury. As Blade watched, a twister appearing out of nowhere picked up a wagon and threw it a score or so metres into the air, tiny figures tumbling out of it to fall, limbs waving, to the concrete below.

"'Steal a skyship,' he said," Blade muttered to himself. "'That's all I need you to do.' Bloody wizards." He turned back to the apocalyptic scene before him, trying to deduce the patterns of the dozen or so twisters currently weaving across the skyport in an attempt to compute a safe course between them. Then he reached back to scoop Rej up with one hand, and take Laliana's hand in the other. "Come on. Let's stick together."

Dani's AdventureTuff KZ2000 wrist-dial was set not to the time, but to the countdown. T-10:34. T-10:33. T-10:32. The platform stopped, abruptly enough to tip her into a staggering step forward. They were now stationary, the shaft's lights no longer scrolling past. The countdown on her wrist meanwhile continued. T-10:29. T-10:28. T-10:27.

"Why've we stopped?" Presto asked, an undertone of fear showing through his otherwise impressively calm demeanour.

Dani shrugged. "Don't know." She checked the control panel beside her. The direction lever was still on down, but a light beside it was blinking orange. She cycled the lever, pushing it up to neutral and then back down, but the orange light continued to blink. "Think the emergency brakes might have cut in."

"Triggered by an overload of background mana, perhaps?"

"Could be. Might be that nothing that isn't shielded will work right now." She ripped open the access panel below the controls and hunted for some kind of reset button. After several seconds of searching she found something that might have been it, and pressed it, but still the orange light blinked, and the platform stayed resolutely stationary.

T-9:52. T-9:51. T-9:50.

She felt Presto easing her aside. "It's probably all fried. We need something more direct."

The sorcerer spoke a few words of Sorcerac, and a thin tendril of energy shot out from his outstretched finger to connect to the components inside the control box. For several moments, Presto remained motionless, his eyes closed, as his consciousness presumably rummaged through the platform's innards in search of a solution. "Yes. The emergency brakes have cut in because of the failure of the main circuits. If I can bypass the main circuits, that should release the brakes." He concentrated for a few seconds more, and then, with a click from the brakes and a whine from the motor, they began to descend once more.

T-9:12. T-9:11. T-9:10.

Dani gave the wizard a smile she hoped was the right side of casual. "Nice one."

Chapter Thirty-Eight

The last fifty metres of the shaft were lined with long strips of explosive packs, all wired to a control panel some ten metres from the shaft's bottom. At Dani's nod, Presto bought the platform to a halt beside the control panel.

T-8:01. T-8:00. T-7:59.

Dani checked the panel for any obvious booby traps, then – finding none – gingerly opened it. Inside was what looked like a pretty standard setup of the sort used in construction and mining: mana battery, timer, detonation charm. She looked back at Presto. "Looks pretty normal. No booby traps or tricks that I can see."

The wizard shrugged. "Makes sense. Wasn't like they expected anyone like us to be doing this."

Dani nodded agreement. The small toolkit that had been in the chest pocket of her coveralls was already on the platform's floor and open. She reached into it for a set of wire-cutters, then carefully snipped the main detonation wire, knowing as she did so that if she'd missed something, it might be the last thing she ever did. A second or so later, still alive, she opened the eyes she hadn't realised she'd closed. "Okay. Let's get down."

The wizard set the platform in motion once more, taking it down the final ten metres of the shaft to reveal a short side tunnel, at the end of which was parked a flatbed wagon, upon which sat a metal egg perhaps three metres long and a metre or so fat.

"And that would be the bomb," said Dani.

They stepped cautiously over to the device, Dani letting the wizard lead, Presto already speaking words of Sorcerac, casting, analysing. The bomb stood alone. No wires, no cables. A single red light set in its side pulsed rhythmically.

The wizard completed his spell-casting and fell silent, saying nothing.

"Can you get in?" Dani asked.

Presto paused for a moment, and when he replied it was in a voice slightly less confident than she would have liked. "Well, there's no obvious interface, nothing for a control spell to latch onto. And the thing about bombs is that you generally make it so that once you turn them on, they're not terribly easy for the people you're dropping them on to turn off."

"So can you turn it off?"

The wizard gave her a grim smile. "I'll have a go."

Dani checked her wrist-dial. "Well, no pressure, but you've got five minutes and... forty-five seconds to find out."

A twister roared by, close enough for Blade to feel it tugging at his coveralls. The three of them dashed across the gap between two hangars, wove past an upturned carpet, and set off across another gap. Another twister appeared a hundred or so metres ahead of them; it was huge, twenty, maybe thirty metres across, and heading straight at them. They set off sideways, trying to sprint out of its path, but it turned, tracking towards them as if it were being guided by a vengeful weather god.

And then it was on them, ripping them from the ground with a fury that reduced gravity to an irrelevance: pulling, spinning, tumbling. Blade locked his grip around Laliana's wrist and from somewhere found the strength to pull her into him, wrapping his arms around both her and Rej, operating on intuition now, certain only that to lose his hold on either of them would be to lose them forever.

Something hard thudded into him: a wagon tumbling by, its strapped-in driver still numbly turning its steering wheel. From somewhere he heard the sound of screaming, and realised it was his cry, of fear, defiance, and anger – and then he saw something.

As a younger man, Blade had once been active in the sport of feather-falling, an activity that involves throwing oneself out of a perfectly good carpet or skyship, trusting in your feather-fall pack to magically float you to the ground. As he'd progressed in the sport, he'd jumped from higher and higher, freefalling for ever greater periods before activating the pack. Freefall wasn't flying, but it wasn't quite falling either; a waved leg here, and a waved arm there, could send you first this way, and then that.

Some way below them, and a few metres further out, a pilot-less carpet was orbiting the twister's central pillar. Acting now on near-forgotten instincts, Blade found his encircling arms changing the orientation of Rej and Laliana, his legs too making adjustments.

Slowly, gradually, the carpet moved towards them. Closer. Closer. There.

Blade reached out a leg, hooked it somehow underneath the pilot's console, and pulled. The carpet twisted underneath them, away, and then towards for just an instant, the dash floating past Blade, and in that instant he reached out and hit the power button. Calmness cut in for just a moment as the air-deflection field powered up, only to depart when the carpet rolled once more; the field might be keeping the fury of the twister out, but momentum and gravity both were still smashing at them. Blade kept his foot hooked under the console, knowing that the field would not hold them in were he to lose his hold. Then Laliana was reaching and pulling herself into the front passenger seat, grabbing the belt and clicking it home to secure herself. She reached out for Rej and Blade handed the dog over, his protesting foot sliding free as he did so. He twisted, making a desperate grab at the pilot seat's headrest even as his feet sliced through the air-deflection field and into the fury beyond. One boot was ripped away, and then another. Within seconds his exposed feet were chilled to the bone, but then he was pulling himself back into the field, hand over hand, fighting the carpet's chaotic end-over-end tumbling and hauling himself into the pilot's seat through sheer force of will.

For an instant the carpet paused, as a counter-clockwise tumble transitioned into a clockwise tumble, and in that instant Blade snapped the belt around himself and grabbed hold of the controls. Beside him, Laliana looked close to blacking out, her face as white as the knuckles with which she was grasping Rej. Blade too could feel his consciousness greying at the edges, awareness diminishing to a single vanishing point of survival. He fought the controls, trying to bring the carpet straight and level, but its motors were no match for the forces within which it was trapped. It tumbled again, slid sideways, flipped upside down, spun, sky and ground interchanging, and then the ground was rushing towards them.

Impact.

Hard.

The bomb was a bastard, a typically lashed together prototype in which the user interface had clearly been a late, barely thought about add on, with a heaping of paranoid security layers dumped on top. Personally, when dealing with a device designed to go bang in a manner that would cause unpleasant and permanent consequences for everyone within a rather large radius, Presto would have gone with the option of a big obvious button marked "Stop". But the git who'd designed this abomination had obviously disagreed.

Presto was more than four minutes in, and he was still picking his way through the security systems, his spells probing at the bomb's outer workings. To be fair to Jaquenta, she'd warned him that the interface's creator was someone she considered eccentric in the extreme, but a mixture of haste and arrogance had caused him to discount that warning.

"How's it going?" Dani asked, with just a trace of tension evident in her tone.

Presto gave her a vaguely noncommittal grunt in reply, and carried on probing – and then, yes, in!

A glowing interface appeared in the empty air between them and the bomb.

"Okay, I'm in," he told her.

At the top of the interface were the words "Countdown Initiated" in bright red lettering, with the countdown itself next to them.

00:01:20.

00:01:19.

00:01:18.

He quickly scanned over the rest of the user interface seeing only readouts of the bomb's status, which basically amounted to a collective declaration that the bomb was fine, and that in just over a minute it was going to go bang.

What there wasn't, was any kind of button marked stop.

"So how do you turn it off?" Dani asked.

"That's a very good question."

"Really? I was kind of hoping it was a stupid one."

"Sorry to disappoint you."

Presto cast another link spell, hooking into the UI, digging around to the procedures behind it, searching for a stub procedure unused by the UI, or hidden perhaps.

Nothing.

He pushed in further, working his way into the very heart of the main control spell, very much aware that a wrong move here might trigger the bomb into detonating early, either through an overly defensive piece of programming, or someone in the control room upstairs noticing what was happening and pushing some kind of manual override. The bomb itself was silent, the only noise he could hear being a dripping of water somewhere and the sound of Dani's breathing. So many routines, layer upon layer of functionality, and crappily written at that.

00:00:33.
00:00:32.

And then, yes, there – the emergency stop routine. All he had to do was call it directly, and—

Password.

Bugger. Bugger. Bugger.

"The emergency stop routine requires a password."

"You're fucking kidding me?"

"Nope."

00:00:19.
00:00:18.
00:00:17.

"Only one thing to do really."

"What's that?"

"Crash the main program."

"And what will that do?"

"Well, the exception handling might gracefully suspend it, or it might just detonate straight away."

00:00:09.
00:00:08.

"Do it."

No more gentle probing now. Presto took his link and drove it into the heart of the main control program, zeroing a whole section of the program's control code. The user interface froze, then disappeared. For a horrible awful moment, the red flashing light set into the bomb's side stopped flashing but stayed solid red – then it too blinked out.

The seconds ticked by.

Eventually, what had to be more than eight seconds since Presto had crashed the main control program, Dani looked at her wrist-dial. "T+5 seconds. I think we can call that a result."

Presto took his first proper breath in what seemed like an awfully long time, feeling his body start to shake as a post-adrenalin crash took hold.

The grifter put a hand on his shoulder. "Come on. Hop onto the flatbed. Let's get this thing onto the platform and out of here."

The wait at the top of the shaft had been tense. With no way for Dani and Presto to communicate with them, Darick, the Storm, and Jaquenta could gauge the success of their compatriots only by the

253

absence of any conventional explosion at T-30 seconds, and the subsequent absence of instant vaporisation at T-0 seconds. At that point, Darick had relaxed slightly, but only slightly; they were all still deep in enemy territory, with success still a long-distant objective.

And then, at around T+7 minutes they heard the whine of the platform approaching. Darick peered carefully over the edge and saw Dani and Presto below, sat in the driver and passenger seats of a flatbed, with a large egg-like object laid on its bed in a tubular steel cradle.

Thirty seconds later the platform rose into view. As soon as it locked into place, Dani began edging the flatbed forward, motioning at Darick and the others to climb on. Darick helped the Storm transfer their equipment from the wagon to the flatbed, then scrambled up after Jaquenta, followed by the Storm.

"You're late," Jaquenta told Dani and Presto. "You were supposed to be back by T+5."

"Well for starters, the platform's controls got scrambled," Dani told her. "Presto had to bypass the main start routine and jump start it."

"That would be the wild mana from below breaking through?" said Jaquenta, holding up the dosimeter at her belt to reveal that it was flashing amber-red, as was – Darick realised with a shock – his.

"Yeah."

Jaquenta tapped the younger woman on the shoulder. "Perhaps we should get going."

"Before our dosimeters turn black?" Darick asked her.

She gave him an apologetic smile. "With the security system down, the colour of your dosimeter should be the least of your worries."

"Why?"

"It wasn't just the wild mana that the force-wall was keeping out."

Darick waited for her to elaborate on exactly what it was that was now about to flood through the complex, but she was already turning away to converse with Presto.

Whatever it was she was referring to, Darick figured it probably wasn't something that he could do much about, so he instead muttered a silent prayer to the SkyFather and took up a position just in front of the bomb.

The flatbed pulled away.

It was only due to blind luck and the gods' kindness that the carpet's first impact was right-way up; had it not been, Blade, Laliana, and Rej's mortal existence would have ended there and then. That first impact was hard enough to trigger the carpet's safety systems; airbags exploded from the dashboard and a roll bar swung up and over their heads. The carpet bounced, flipped, tumbled. Somewhere along the way, Blade managed to cut the lift, figuring that all they could do now was keep their heads down and hope, pray, and then hope some more.

And then they were impacting again, bouncing end over end, their trajectory driven not just by their momentum, but by the unnatural gale force winds blowing across the skyport. Enveloped as he was in the airbag's embrace, Blade couldn't see a thing. But finally they stopped, upside down, the carpet rocking gently on its roll bar.

Blade had one of Pete's field knives in a holster on his belt. He forced his hand down between the airbag and the seat, found it, pulled it out, and forced its point into the airbag – which deflated with a pop loud enough to be heard over the surrounding storm's fury. He hooked a foot underneath the console, thumbed the belt release free, then spun-dropped to the concrete underneath the carpet. Beside him, Rej and Laliana were already trying to wriggle out from the airbag. He pulled the dog free, then helped Laliana down.

"Come on," he told her, twisting round only to find himself facing the now familiar features of the blond-moustached officer who'd arrested them in the forest, and who was now crouching down to peer under the upturned carpet. Behind him a squad of soldiers armed with two-handed longbolts advanced warily, bracing themselves against the wind; behind them, a combat wagon rocked on its suspension as the storm's repeated gusts smashed into its slab-like sides.

The officer pointed a shortbolt straight at Blade. "Don't try anything stupid, Mr Petros."

Chapter Thirty-Nine

Dani had the flatbed's motor gunned up to maximum, its continuous high-pitched note echoing around the tunnel's tubular interior. Jaquenta was saying something from behind her, shouting to be heard against the whine of the vehicle's motor. "The ferry's round the next bend. Once we ride that across, it's just the final stretch up to the surface."

Dani nodded, gripping the vehicle's steering wheel tightly as the tunnel eased into a sweeping curve.

"It's supposed to be kept on this side of the river when not in use," Jaquenta continued. "As a security precaution."

Above them, the tunnel's lights stretched away around the long, seemingly endless, curve. Then the tunnel straightened, to reveal a gap in the lights up ahead. An echoing roar emerged, clearly audible above the noise of the flatbed's motor.

It was the underground river Jaquenta had told them of, Dani realised; the last obstacle between them and the surface. She eased off the power as the roadway emerged from the tunnel into a huge, floodlit cavern. Ahead of them was a soil and rubble levee several metres high, with a gap in the middle through which the road passed, only to end abruptly at the river's edge, its continuing route marked by twin chains that disappeared into the raging torrent.

And somewhere over there, on the opposite bank, where it was not supposed to be, floated the ferry, a flat slab rocking gently in the foaming waters.

Dani was already braking when bolts of crystal-green mana spat out from somewhere across the cavern. She reacted instinctively, in the way you tend to do when people start shooting at you, wrenching the wheel sideways to send the flatbed into a long, only semi-controlled skid that had all four of its wheels and at least two of its passengers screaming.

She fought the skid, overcorrecting, sending the back end sliding out the other way, in a manner that would have been highly unpleasant even if she hadn't had a bloody great bomb strapped on the back. The wheels drifted off the roadway, caught on some grit, gripped, tipped, gripped again, then slid as more bolts of mana stabbed above and around them. Finally, the flatbed skidded to a sideways halt against the levee, just a few feet away from the carved gap that the roadway passed through. She twisted round, finding Presto already springing up from the bed behind her.

"We need to get across," the wizard shouted.

"Yeah. But how?"

Presto hurled himself off the flatbed's rear bed and began to claw his way up the levee, figuring that with events moving this fast his best course of action was to act now and democratically discuss things with the rest of the team later. He reached the top of the levee and peered cautiously over the edge, finding Dani beside him, one of Pete's hand-and-a-half assault bolts clutched in her hand.

A fresh spread of mana fire erupted from the other side of the bank. Presto looked closer and saw the running and crouching figures of black uniformed troops; lots of them. Still the beams stabbed out, deadly and beautiful, but also frayed and drifting. Some beams smashed into the levee below them; others curved away to harmlessly explode against the cavern wall behind them or plunge harmlessly into the river.

"The wild mana!" he shouted. "It's causing the bolts to malfunction. That's how they managed to not kill us when we drove straight at them."

"Right," the grifter replied, hesitantly. "There's still a shitload of them, and they're still laying down a shitstorm of beams, even if they aren't going straight." She shifted up onto one knee, shot a long sweeping burst at the figures across the river, and then dropped back down just as the return volley emerged. "Can you teleport us across?"

Presto was already thirty seconds ahead of her with that thought. He shook his head. "Not with this amount of wild mana, not unless you're happy to arrive inside out. And besides, there's no way I'd get the flatbed across. Way too much mass."

"So there's pretty much no way out of here that doesn't involve going across on that ferry?"

"Not that I can see."

"You got any idea how we might get it back over here?"

Presto pointed down to where the roadway plunged into the river, beside which was a small box mounted on a post. "Do you see the box there?"

"The ferry controls?"

"Yes. Fire a few bursts from your bolt, and then get down there. See if you can work out how to get it back over this side of the river."

Dani looked dubious. "And what are you going to be doing?"

"Covering you."

Dani shot another long burst across the river, not aiming at anything or anyone in particular, then skidded forward off the levee into a scrambling descent of its far side. If she'd ever done anything stupider or more risky than this in her life thus far she couldn't offhand recall it, but right now it didn't seem like she had much choice but to act like that guy in a crystal war flick that you know hasn't got a chance in a thousand of making it to the end credits.

Behind her, Presto was screaming Sorcerac, combat-wand in hand; for an instant the wizard was silent, and then a dozen or so long foaming streams of red-blue-green mana shot over her head at the soldiers across the river, who scattered for cover behind the various boxes and crates collected along the far bank. Four, maybe five sliding footsteps later, she reached the base of the levee and set off in a running crouch along the bank towards the control box, her barely controlled fear surging through a body that felt like like ice. Beam after beam of mana passed around her, in front, above, behind. Then, as she skidded into a kneeling halt beside the control box, a shimmering, pink-tinged wall a couple of metres across flashed into existence in front of her, just in time for three separate mana beams to obliterate themselves against its surface.

That had been bloody close.

The controls mounted on the box were mercifully simple: buttons marked "ON" and "OFF", with the off currently glowing red; and a lever that had two positions, one towards the far side of the bank, and one towards this side of the bank, with the far side being the lever's current position. She stabbed at the on button, waited for it to go green, then tugged the lever towards her side of the river.

With a whine that was just about audible over the roar of the river and the now near-continuous mana barrage, the ferry began to move towards her. She heard a shout from above and across: Presto.

"Get ready to cover me!" the wizard was shouting, the maelstrom of noise so great that Dani was more lip-reading than hearing him. Presto screamed more words of Sorcerac, threw a truly massive set of flaming, tumbling, rainbow coloured fireballs across the river, and then – at her nod – launched into his own scrambling descent of the levee.

Dani stepped around the edge of the force screen and shot a long continuous spread across the soldiers' positions, keeping her finger on the trigger until the cartridge beeped empty. She thumped the eject stud and was already inserting the replacement cartridge before its now useless predecessor hit the ground, trigger finger squeezing to send more stabbing beams at the soldiers opposite, until Presto stumbled in behind her and she was able to retreat, crouching, behind the shield.

"Good work!" the wizard said, slapping her on the arm.

"Thanks, but don't we still have a problem?"

"That would be how we're going to just drive the flatbed onto the ferry and travel across, without those gentlemen over there shooting us dead several times over?"

"Yeah, that's pretty much what's worrying me."

"Well, I'm thinking we could – dammit!"

Dani didn't need to ask what it was that had triggered the wizard's exclamation. The ferry, which had got about halfway across the river, had now abruptly reversed direction and was heading away from them.

"There's no one at the far bank's control box," Presto shouted. "There must be some other master control."

"Can you override it from here?" Dani screamed in reply. Normally, overriding someone else's control systems would have been her sort of thing, but with beam after beam smashing into the shield, she was happy to put her ego aside. The wizard spoke a few words of Sorcerac, then touched the box. His eyes unfocused as his consciousness worked its way into the box – then he screamed, and slumped down into Dani's catching arms.

"Trap," he stuttered out. "They just dumped a load of raw mana down the control circuits."

"Are you okay?"

"Just about. But the circuit's blown, both ends. Only way to control that ferry now will be from the ferry itself."

"The ferry that's headed back that way?"

"That would be the one."

More beams slammed into the force wall, a concentrated salvo this time. For an instant it flashed a tinge of green before returning to pink, but it was duller now, its shimmer not quite so alive.

Presto grimaced. "It appears that our friends across the water have got our range. We need to get out of here." He shrugged an apologetic shoulder. "Sorry, this is my fault for blundering down here without a plan."

"Don't worry about it. Can you walk?"

"Barely."

Dani wrapped an arm around the wizard's waist, feeling his greater weight slumping against her. "Come on." She set off, firing one handed, blindly, knowing that to attempt to climb the levee would be suicide, heading instead for the roadway's gap. But if the climb would have been certain death, this was probably a near second. Beams stabbed by them, death mere feet away, her feet pushing at the loose shifting sand, the wizard's breathing harsh and laboured.

And then return shots were streaking overhead, smashing into the river bank opposite. Long streams of energy, blindingly bright when compared with the far overhead flood lights. It was Jaquenta, she realised, casting from somewhere on the levee's crest above. And then they were around the gap and heading into the levee's lee, Darick and the Storm waiting for them, Darick taking Presto, while Dani found herself collapsing into the Storm as the worst adrenaline crash of her life swept over her.

"Now what?" the rock star asked.

"Fucked if I know," Dani told him.

Presto was already barking instructions before Darick had even eased him down into a makeshift seat on the levee's lee bank.

"We need to get moving," the wizard shouted through pain-gritted teeth. "The longer we give them to get organised, the more impossible this will be. We've got one more chance, and we need to take it now."

Darick said nothing; this whole situation was so far beyond his capabilities that he'd gone beyond uselessness into utter, mute, impotence.

It was Jaquenta who spoke. "What's the plan?"

"You and Dani get up on the levee. Lay down a covering barrage. Keep their heads down. Storm?"

The rock star looked to be just this side of screaming, gibbering terror. "Yeah man?"

"Get behind the wheel of the flatbed. Get it free of the levee, and be ready to drive round and through the gap and onto the ferry, when we give you the word."

"Okay. You got it."

Darick managed to force some words though his terror-constricted throat. "And what am I doing?"

"You're going with me."

"And what are we doing?"

The wizard reached over his shoulder to push his wand into the holder he wore across his back. "Well since I don't fancy flying into all of that, we're going to do something different that's right up your street, Father. We're going to make like prophets."

"Make like prophets?"

Presto gave him a faintly manic grin. "We're going to walk across the water."

Unlike his men, the blond-moustached officer wore no faceplate on his helmet, something presumably intended to either aid communication with his troops or mark him as a leader. It also, of course, was rather advantageous to anyone who might want to punch him very hard in the face, which, by a not too unremarkable coincidence, was exactly what Blade now did, sending the man staggering back, hands clutching his now-broken nose. Punch thrown, Blade scrambled out from beneath the upturned carpet and delivered a straight-kick to the groin of the already doubled-over officer, followed by a spinning, round-house kick, before pulling his Blade Petros XR-2000+™ sword – the special edition, titanium alloy model – from its scabbard with a free-flowing motion achieved through a lifetime of practice, just in time to find himself not quite face-to-face with three troopers pointing longbolts at him, their fingers already tightening on the triggers.

Commentators, journalists, and other astute followers of the game often said of Blade that it wasn't his combat skills, impressive though they were, that had turned him into an arena legend. He was a master swordsman, that much was true. But there were others who were equally adept with either weapon or fist. Nor was it, they said, his strength or his size or his agility that marked his greatness. He did indeed have an imposing frame that combined great strength with incredible agility, but there were many near-superhuman athletes in the arena, of whom he was just one. No, what set Blade apart, the astute observers said, what marked him out as perhaps the greatest AdventureSportsman who'd ever lived, was his speed, and not simply the speed of his body, nor even his reactions, but the speed of his thoughts.

Blade could think faster than perhaps any man alive, could think faster than might ever seem possible, could think so fast that it sometimes seemed as though he was bending either time or space, such was his ability to begin his evasion of an attack before it had even been launched, and to launch his counter-attack only instants later. Thinking at the speed of instinct, fired by reactive patterns formed by thousands of hours of practice, Blade was already diving into a roll as the longbolts fired, evading the beams, and moving so fast that he was upon the three troops before they had even the merest chance to respond. He was beyond human now, more than merely a mortal man, his sword weaving in a pattern too fast for the human eye to follow, spinning, slicing, cutting. Even as enraged and desperate as he was, he still didn't want to kill. But he was very much prepared to wound if necessary. The three men fell aside, one clutching a severed stump, two clutching at pumping cuts. Still, more troops were coming at him, trying to bring their long-bolts to bear on him, deterred from firing only by a fear of hitting their own comrades.

And then the storm hit again.

Slowly, silently, the combat wagon lifted off the ground and spun gracefully away, looking for all the world like some kind of lifting, oversized carpet – until you saw its wheels, and remembered that it wasn't. The wind plucked Blade from the ground and slammed him against something very hard, with all the ease of a mischievous toddler playing with its rag doll. Hail tore at him, razor sharp and hard as diamonds, hitting with the force of a blacksmith's hammer.

He risked opening his eyes just a crack. Around him was a scene of chaos. Skyships bobbing, rolling, writhing, with only the towers to which they were attached keeping them in some kind of order. As he watched, a tower ripped from its foundations and was carried away by the now-loose skyship to which it had been attached. The huge ship rolled upside down, crashed hard into the ground, then snapped in half, the two halves depositing a hazy, wind-blown trail of debris and wreckage as they tumbled across the skyport.

Then the wind began to ease. Blade found himself sliding down the side of a building against which he'd been pinned. He landed in a crouch, his sword somehow still in his hand. Two soldiers were picking themselves up beside him. He kicked one in the chest and punched the other in the face with his pommel, then looked around for Laliana and Rej, spotting them crouched in the lee of a low concrete wall. All the other soldiers had gone, taken by the wind. He quickly ran over to his two colleagues.

"You guys okay?"

"Ri rurt ry rreg!"

Laliana, displaying an inner steel that spoke well of her, was already hauling herself to her feet. "Which leg was it?"

The dog rolled over onto his back, and pointed at his back left leg with his front right paw. "Rat run!"

She grabbed the leg, planted a kiss on it, and then said: "Right, that's it kissed better." She looked back at Blade. "Okay, we're good."

Blade nodded, mentally mapping out a new route to their destination. The guys would be on their way back now and he didn't figure they'd be too pleased if he and Laliana weren't there waiting for them.

Chapter Forty

Some years back, when his faith still burned bright with the easy confidence of newly minted adulthood, Darick had attended one of the church's so-called "red-brick" seminaries, institutions built some decades earlier during a period in which rapid social and cultural change had combined with low interest rates and attractive government grants. Stretched across the rear wall of the entrance lobby of the otherwise plain and functional main building had been a huge mural, a depiction of the twin prophets Muroc and Merak leading five hundred of the faithful to safety across the River Thena. The mural had made water-walking look easy. The reality was proving to be anything but.

Darick's first step onto the water had triggered a stumble that nearly took him down, as his foot hit a solid surface several inches earlier than his brain had been expecting. He'd recovered from that, but then the river's waters were moving under him, the effect as though he were trying to walk sideways across a moving pavement driven by a dodgy, surging motor. He took one step, and then another, and then another, finding himself running just to keep on the spot.

All the while, his force-shield shimmered to one side of him, counter-turning with each of his turns, always keeping itself between himself and the far bank, turning his view of their destination a hazy purple. Bolt after bolt either screamed past or pinged off the shield, each deflection triggering a piercing whine that set his ears ringing. He had to stay focussed, he realised, had to keep his mind on the task of following Presto's scrambling figure a few feet ahead.

Concentrate, he told himself. *Concentrate.*

The river was a bastard. Presto had walked on water before, but save for one drunken escapade involving a chain-ferry and its twat of a captain, an episode punctuated by childish and obscene hand gestures from both sides, his previous water walking experience had been conducted entirely in, or to be strictly accurate on, swimming pools. It was all very good for the true believers to bang on about Muroc and his brother whats-his-face taking a group of refugees for a walk across the Thena, but what they never got round to mentioning was that, as rivers go, the Thena was neither wide nor deep nor particularly fast flowing.

Each footfall was treacherous, made onto a surface that moved as though alive, a writhing surface that ripped your feet away as soon as they were planted, so you weren't so much walking as stumbling.

Being shot at didn't much help either.

A little way ahead, sideways on as he crabbed towards it, a rock thrust clear of the surface, creating a sheltered area of water behind it. He edged in its direction, feeling the eddies swirling around his feet. But as he planted one foot into that sheltered area while his trailing foot was still being swept away by the current, he felt himself being twisted around. And then he was falling, plunging into the so-cold, dark waters, the spell useless now that he was no longer on his feet.

The river gripped him, pulled him down. He turned, once, twice. He'd never actually been that good in water. Panic surged through him at the hard realisation that, submerged and unable to speak as he was, casting was not an option. His face trailed over some gravel on the river's bed, then he bounced off something hard enough to wind him, paralysed all the while by the icy-cold of the water.

And then he felt a hand gripping his ankle.

Darick had been only feet away from Presto when the wizard's trip had plunged him headlong into the raging torrent. Darick twisted round, acting on instinct he'd not known he possessed. After steadying himself, he launched forward into a smooth dive that took him down under the water in search of his submerged comrade.

It could only have been the SkyFather's work. Only divine intervention could explain how his blind, desperate, underwater strokes had taken him to Presto. But take him they did. His hand struck something, he grabbed hold of what turned out to be an ankle and pushed hard for the surface, breaking though into the cool dark air and taking a long, shuddering breath.

Still the river swept them downwards. Darick reeled Presto in, grasping first belt, then arm, to draw the wizard toward him. Then he twisted, pushed down, and felt his feet gain purchase on a nothing-turned-something by Presto's still functioning magic. He pushed himself to the surface, rising up through the water as though climbing invisible stairs, ignoring the screaming protests of every part of his brain that knew what he was doing was impossible, and then hauled hard at the still flailing Presto to pull the wizard up.

They were now back on their feet, but facing one major problem:

that they were surfing downstream into the gloom, at the speed of the river, towards what sounded like one mighty set of rapids. The one saving grace was that, moving as fast as they were, the bolts were all now passing behind them; but as saving graces went, that wasn't one that he felt he needed to pay thanks to. Still grasping the wizard round the waist, their force-shields now locked together, he took a step, and then another, and another, trying to edge out of the fast moving stream in which they were currently trapped.

A rock loomed up, ahead and to one side.

Step, another step, a further step, yes—

The slam into the rock was brutal, but Darick ignored it, grabbing instead at a useful looking handhold and pulling the two of them into the lee formed behind the rock. For now, they appeared shielded from both the river and their opponents on the opposite bank. "Are you okay?" he asked Presto.

The wizard grunted. "I'll live. And thanks, by the way."

"Just glad to be useful," Darick replied.

Presto took a cautious step around the rock, but was immediately halted by four bolt-blasts on his force shield that were sufficiently strong to send him rocking back. He ducked back behind the rock. "They appear to have acquired our range." He held his wrist up to his mouth, and spoke into the glowing green dot that pulsed upon it. "We could do with some support."

The whisper spell cast onto Dani's wrist spoke in Presto's voice. "We could do with some support."

Dani raised the glowing green dot to her mouth. "On it. Hold on." She nodded at Jaquenta. "You ready?"

"I was born ready, darling."

Dani wasn't completely sure she could trust her, but right now she didn't have much choice. "On three," she said. She counted one, two, on her fingers, and then popped up above the crest of the levee on three, her hand-and-a-half assault bolt already coming to bear, her finger resting on the trigger. She shot a quick series of beams at the source of the most intense activity opposite, not particularly wanting to kill anybody, but figuring if they were too stupid to keep behind cover, that was on their heads, not hers.

A second or so later Jaquenta opened up with a truly spectacular fanned outpouring of raw magic that smashed into the far bank in a cascade of green-purple explosions. Dani kept shooting, emptying the cartridge as Jaquenta cast a second and then a third attack spell. From somewhere across the water, something big went boom – an industrial sized mana pod maybe; the storage unit of a wagon, perhaps.

The cartridge beeped empty. Dani thumbed the release as Jaquenta shifted to something else, something that produced a kaleidoscopic fog across the far bank, sparkling a thousand different shades of everything, and then pulsing a thousand more.

In the gloom down below, she saw Presto and Darick emerging from their cover, setting across the river, looking to be more confident in their movements now, leapfrogging from rock to rock. She rammed a fresh cartridge into the bolt and resumed shooting short neat bursts into the fog, aiming now to merely dissuade anyone from trying to venture through it. Jaquenta similarly shifted to short neat bolts of mana.

Shoot. Scan. Shoot. Scan. And then she heard a cry and a shout and the whine of an assault-bolt rapidly shooting from below and behind them. The Storm.

Trouble.

Once you got the hang of it, water walking wasn't so difficult: not as slippery as ice, less exhausting than sand. Presto skipped and slid in behind a rock, waited crouched for Darick to join him, then emerged from the cover to resume their scrambling, crabbed advance across the river, covered all the while by Dani and Jaquenta's collective barrage. Bolts still emerged from out of the magical fog enveloping the far bank, but shot blind they sailed past, an annoying distraction, but no more.

He paused at another covering rock spike, waited a few seconds for Darick to slide in behind him, and was about to push forward when both Dani's shooting and Jaquenta's casts ceased abruptly.

"What the…?" he muttered.

Darick had noticed too. "Why have they stopped shooting?"

Presto looked back through the gloom at the levee, but could see nothing and no one at its crest. "I have no idea."

And then something very, very big sailed past them and smashed into the levee's river-facing slope in a way that was most definitely physical, the blast strong enough to send sand flying twenty or thirty feet in each direction and leave a crater perhaps five feet across.

"What was that?" asked a clearly panicky Darick.

"Something military that throws physical projectiles," Presto told him. "And the thing that really worries me is that those things usually come with sensors that can see through visual effects."

"Which means?"

Something truly huge hit the other side of the rock spike with enough force that Presto felt it through what must have been three or four feet of granite. He drew a shuddering breath into lungs that had been emptied by the force of the blast, and then replied, "Which means that they can see us through the fog and shoot that monster straight at us."

Another blast hit the rock, lower this time, sending a wave wrapping around the rock, first lifting them up, and then slamming them back down. Presto hung on.

"What are we going to do?" the priest asked.

"I don't know," Presto replied.

And he didn't.

Getting the flatbed free of the bank of sand into which it had embedded itself had taken a bit of back-and-forth manoeuvring interspersed with spots of hard revving, but the Storm had eventually got it lined up beside the gap, while still being behind the levee's shield.

And then he waited, his habitual feeling of uselessness that the task had temporarily dispelled returning. Driving the flatbed had felt good. He'd driven enough tour wagons back in the day to develop a muscle memory that was still with him. But this now was hard, waiting down below while above him on the crest of the levee Dani and Jaquenta fought a hard and bitter battle in support of Darick and Presto, who were out there in danger.

A rattle of claws on metal roused him from his thoughts. Crouching on the other side of the windscreen was something the like of which he'd previously seen only in late night horror flicks or during very bad herb trips. It was something that might once have been human, or animal; frankly, it was so far removed from what it might once have been it was hard to tell. Thick saliva dripped from something that was presumably a mouth, given that it came equipped with teeth, albeit multiple rows of them. Three eyes stared at him: yellow, red and green; two working, one flicking from left to right. A long, bony, two elbowed arm reached out to the Storm, and tapped on the glass.

Something in the Storm's primeval lizard brain switched into terrified auto-pilot. He lifted the hand-and-a-half assault-bolt Dani had left him with and, shooting one-handed, pulled the trigger. A bolt of pure green mana smashed through the windscreen and into the thing's body, sending it hurling off the flatbed's bonnet, landing hard several feet away. It screamed, a long, pain-filled scream, then died.

A little voice in the Storm's head informed him in matter-of-fact tones that he'd just killed someone. For a moment his inner monologue began to debate with his conscience. It wasn't someone, the monologue pleaded in defence. It was only a something, and something horrible at that. And then something very big landed on the flatbed's bonnet with a thump hard enough to set the vehicle rocking on its springs. It started punching at the already shattered windscreen, and this time when the Storm's lizard brain shot it right through the head his conscience's voice stayed mute. From the scraping sounds emerging all around, a bunch more things were landing; not just on the bonnet, but on the top of the cab and in the cargo area behind him. There were two of the things on the bonnet. He shot one, but then the second dived through the gap left by the now disintegrating windscreen and fastened its long beaklike jaws onto his left arm.

He shot it through the body, twice; desperately triggered the door release with his elbow; then tumbled backwards out of the cab, the dying, convulsing body of the mutated beast still clinging to his arm. He hit hard onto compacted sand on top of unyielding rock with an impact severe enough to wind him, threw the dying bird thing free, and began to scramble to his feet, only to be knocked back by something else that was half bird, half man, and all disgusting abomination. It forced him back down and began to push its face towards his, coming ever closer despite the Storm's desperate attempts to hold it away.

Then a bolt of mana seared through it, close enough to set the Storm's nerves tingling. It smashed against the flatbed's front wheel. A hand reached down and hauled the Storm to his feet.

"You okay?" Dani asked, pausing to shoot three quick-aimed beams, before looking back to the Storm for an answer.

"Just about," the Storm told her, trying to keep the shakes at bay. He looked up and immediately wished he hadn't. There were dozens of the things all around them. Behind the flatbed. On the flatbed. All shapes and sizes. Things with four legs. Things with wings. Things with eight legs and two heads. Skin, fur, feathers, scales.

A huge fan of fire sprayed over the top of them. It was Jaquenta, the Storm realised, firing from further up the levee. The things dropped back briefly, but then howled and began to edge back.

"What the fuck are they?" the Storm found himself screaming.

"The abominations you get after thirty years of an uncontrolled wild mana node, I guess, things the force-wall was keeping out." The younger woman switched her assault bolt to her left hand then reached up to the flatbed with her right. "Come on. We need to keep them off the bomb. Cover me!"

Up on the surface, the weather's magically fuelled fury had abated only slightly, the tornados gone, but brutal gusts of wind still ripping in from every direction. Blade finished his latest darting run into cover, and then waited for Laliana and Rej to join him.

"We nearly there?" she gasped, collapsing into a crouch.

Given how fit Blade was, and how hard he'd been running, she was doing well just to keep up, he realised. "Nearly," he replied. He pointed to his two o'clock. "Over there. That's the one we're going to take."

"Good job it didn't get blown away by the storm," she panted.

"Yeah." He laid a hand on her arm. "You okay?"

"Just about." She pushed herself to her feet. "Come on. We don't want to be late."

Blade nodded. Actually, it wasn't so much being late that worried him, as arriving late only to find some other bugger had got there first. He pushed that thought aside. This was a madly complex plan, which could only work if all the ducks involved lined themselves up. All he could do was drive through his part of the operation, and trust to fate for the rest. He peered past the display board behind which they were hiding, scanned for guards, then set off.

Nearly there.

Chapter Forty-One

Darick watched, helpless, as Presto shouted into the whisper spell cast onto his arm.

"Guys! Anyone!"

There was no answer. Another massive thump shook the rock they were sheltering behind, the force enough to nearly dislodge Darick from his hold. "They must be busy," he suggested.

"Clearly!" the wizard snapped. "Look, we can't stay here." He looked around, and then up toward the overhead floodlights, staring for a moment and slapping himself on the forehead. "Idiot! Moron! Twat!"

"What?"

"Have you still got your pair of owl-eyes?"

Darick fished into the pouch on his belt and pulled out the owl-eyes set that Pete had given him. "Yeah."

"Put them on. I'm taking out the lights."

"I thought you said that massive bombarding thing could see in the dark?"

Presto flashed him a devilish smile. "I did, but I'm guessing the guys who operate it can't. Long as it's under some kind of manual control we should be okay, least for a few seconds. Okay, get ready to go."

Darick pulled the owl-eyes over his face. The world instantly turned into a featureless blur of continuous, uniform, fuzzy green, leaving him blind. Too much light, he guessed. He left the owl-eyes on, hearing Presto already launching into the words of a spell, and trusting the wizard to know what he was doing. A ball of light lifted up from where Darick knew Presto was standing, light so bright that it showed even in his light dazzled display. The light split, a dozen or more jets streaming off – and then his fuzzy green display went a ghostly green-black, interspersed with scattered and blurred streaks of brighter green.

"That's the overhead lights destroyed," Presto told him. "Let's go."

Darick saw a blurred lump that might have been Presto moving out from behind the rock. "My owl-eyes aren't working so well."

"They're distorted by the wild mana. Don't worry about it. Just walk."

With Jaquenta covering them from above, the Storm and Dani managed to get back on the flatbed. The Storm was in a trance now, shooting beam after beam, reloading, then shooting more. His shots weren't particularly well aimed, but they didn't have to be, given that the ranges he was shooting at were pretty much point blank. When Pete had shown him how to load and shoot the bolt, back in his store's basement shooting range, the weapon had seemed alien, clumsy, and when his fingers had tried to switch the mana cartridge, they'd fumbled. Not now, not when his life quite literally depended on his ability to switch cartridges in less time than it took something to take the three paces it needed to rip his face off.

The creatures fell back under the combined barrage of two assault bolts and a rapidly casting wizard – and then the lights went out, turning the cavern blacker than the darkest night, a blackness so absolute that the Storm couldn't see the hand in front of his face.

"Owl-eyes!" screamed Dani.

The Storm reached into his belt pouch, tugged out Pete's own-brand owl-eyes, and pulled them onto his face. The silky black world was replaced by a fuzzy green one. He lifted his assault-bolt back up and started shooting at anything that was moving. Again the creatures fell back for a moment, but then they surged forward, even more numerous now. The wave hit the flatbed, breaking upon it only to surge around each side. From behind came the sounds of more furious casting, but when Jaquenta's spells erupted they flew now not over the Storm and Dani's heads but rather sounded as though they were hitting targets much closer to home.

The Storm spun round and saw Jaquenta shooting bolt after bolt from her fingertips at point-blank range, a horde of abominations threatening to overwhelm her. There was no creativity in her spells now, just desperate defence. Beside the Storm, Dani was shooting at Jaquenta's attackers, sending her bolts closer to the sorceress than the Storm would have dared. Jaquenta cast a final spell then dashed down the levee for the flatbed, the Storm hauling her on board with just split seconds to spare, as a sharp beak snapped down on the empty air her leg had just vacated.

"You okay?" Dani shouted.

Jaquenta gave her a ragged smile. "Just about, and thanks, by the way."

"Anytime," Dani told her, but the sorceress was already back up and casting now, sending out glowing nets that materialised from nothingness, then fell to the cavern's floor, each net catching a dozen or more of the mutated creatures.

But still the abominations came.

The sorceress's breathing was ragged now, the strain written upon her face. "I'm not sure I can do much more of this," she stuttered through pain-gritted teeth.

A flash of something burst above them, casting light across the cavern; it hung in the air, floating slowly downward, turning the blackness into day, and the Storm's owl-eyes' display a solid green. He ripped them off, and saw the creatures once more advancing, emboldened perhaps by being able to see again. Then, from the far side of the levee, a faint whine split the air, a whine they'd heard briefly several minutes ago.

"That's the ferry!" Dani shouted. "Presto and Darick must have made it to the far side."

The Storm's bolt chose that moment to run out of charge. He thumbed the mana cartridge free and reached down to his belt, but found the cartridge pouch empty. "I'm out!" he screamed back at Dani. The cavern was full of the creatures now, so many of them that it was hard to see the cavern's base beneath its carpet of writhing... things. The gap in the levee that led to the ferry's landing point was blocked; worse, the flatbed's cab looked to have been overrun. "How in all the planes of hell are we going to drive there?"

The grifter was still shooting, still had some mana charges left, had perhaps been more measured in her shooting than an edge-of-panic rock star. She shot some last beams, then nodded at the bags of equipment piled up against the flatbed's cab. "Your lute!"

"What about it?"

"Get it out and play!"

"Play what?"

"Anything!"

It took the rock star a few seconds to respond to Dani's command, but then he snapped into action, letting his bolt fall down on its strap, stepping over to the big canvas kitbag, and pulling out the combat lute and amplifier that Joe had given him.

Dani didn't wait for him to set it up and plug in. She was still shooting measured shots, still trying to keep the wave after wave of mutant attackers at bay, conscious that after this cartridge beeped empty she had one more and then that was that.

And then the Storm was plugged in and playing, standing in front of the bomb with his fingers on the lute, his legs planted, the amp by his feet. His fingers were dancing over the strings, weaving a tune that floated on the air and seeped into the souls of all who heard it. It rose, soared, increasing in pitch and tone, and volume, and intricacy, punching through mere perfection into something far beyond, to something that was better than any piece of music had a right to be. Men who'd heard the most wondrous of symphonies played by the finest of orchestras would still have cried deep tears had their ears heard this. Dani had been told tales of the bards of old who could weave melodies of such magical wonder that they dissolved the fabric of reality that separates the mundane from the mystical. Having once dismissed such stories she now knew them to be true.

Something within her was stirring, arousing a courage that she knew was in her but not of her. She moved now, with a precision and confidence she'd not previously possessed, the music pulsing within her, taking her to a level she could not have reached alone. She vaulted for the flatbed's cab, catching hold of the frame and turning her vault into a swing that carried her through the open driver's side window. Something had been inside, but her outstretched feet slammed it to the other side of the cab, the impact giving it no chance to react before she shot it. All around her the mutated beasts were falling back, driven away by the waves of music crashing down upon them.

And still the Storm played.

The motor was running. Dani rammed the drive lever into forward and hit the throttle, sending the flatbed slithering forward as its wheels fought for grip in the loose sand. In the rear view mirror she saw the Storm sway, but the rock star kept playing, the tilt of his head suggesting that he was somewhere else now, somewhere not quite of this world.

A couple of the creatures remained in place, paralysed. Dani crunched over them, telling her guilty conscience that whatever they might once have been, they weren't that anymore, and that in killing them she'd released them. She knew that one day she might have to revisit that lie, but this wasn't that day, not when she and her comrades were fighting for survival on the very edge of oblivion.

She wrenched the wheel round as she got to the gap, spinning the flatbed onto the roadway. Ahead, the ferry was just docking with the bank. Dani drove onto it, let the motor wind down, then braked, coming to a stop just feet away from the ferry's far end. For a moment there was stillness, and then the ferry started to move, heading back to the far bank. She flipped the door release and dropped out of the cab, only to find a bunch of bolts slamming past her, worryingly close. This clearly wasn't somewhere she wanted to be, so she bounced back onto the flatbed's rear cargo bed, putting the cab between herself and those firing, then stepped over to the Storm, making sure to keep down in a crouch. The rock star had stopped playing now, was slumped over, his eyes flickering as his consciousness faded in and out.

"Did I do okay?" he asked.

"You were awesome," Dani told him.

More bolts slammed into and around the cab.

"Come on," she shouted at the Storm and Jaquenta, who didn't look to be in much better shape than the rock star. She grabbed the two of them and dragged them behind the cover of the cab. Then, over the space of several drawn-out seconds, the bolts went quiet, the shooting ceasing.

"What do you think happened?" Jaquenta asked.

"Don't know," Dani replied. "Guess Presto and Darick managed to figure something out."

Presto and Darick were hunkered down near the far bank's ferry control panel, trying to keep behind what was left of their now merged force shields. Shot after shot thudded in from the cavern's far reaches, the shields growing a little dimmer with each hit.

Exhausted and outnumbered as he was, Presto didn't much fancy stepping out from behind the shields to send something back in reply. But he knew he had to, knew that if he didn't gain some tactical advantage in this battle raging around their bridgehead, the results would be catastrophic for the rest of the team when they attempted to bring the ferry and the bomb back across. Then, over a period of several seconds, the barrage weakened and died.

"What did you do?" Darick asked.

"Nothing," Presto replied, truthfully. It wasn't just the shooting that had stopped. Behind them, beyond the advancing ferry, burning aura-flares slowly descended, but no more were being launched to join them. He peered carefully around the panel. The air was hazy with the smoke thrown out by several fires, and the remains of Jaquenta's mist, but he could see men falling back from their defences in confusion, apparently unconcerned by Presto, Darick, or the advancing ferry. Some broke towards them, running past to throw themselves into the raging river. Others paused, overwhelmed by confusion. Meanwhile, from somewhere in the smoke behind them, screams were erupting, inhuman screams, beyond mere pain and terror.

And then Presto saw them, advancing out of the fog. Dozens of them. Walking slowly, remorselessly, devoid of thought or sense.

Or life.

Darick edged round to crouch beside him. "What are they?"

"I think," Presto told him, "it's more a case of: what were they?" He focused in on the nearest of the advancing horde, seeing a corpse of a man wearing the tattered remains of an orange fluorescent work suit. The man's body was rotting, with much of his scalp hanging loosely from tattered strands of flesh, but enough remained to show that he had once been pale, with red hair. His dead, sightless eyes looked towards Presto, and he turned slightly, adjusting his course to head straight towards the wizard.

"They're people?" Darick stuttered. "Dead people?"

"I think they're the former workers of the mana storage facility, the ones who didn't make it out when it went bang. It was too dangerous to go back in and retrieve the bodies, so the authorities just sealed the whole complex with a force-wall and left the dead where they'd fallen."

"The... the force wall we just... dispelled?"

"Apparently."

The priest sounded as if he was on the edge of panic, which was fair enough given that Presto wasn't far behind him. "But if they're dead, they should be in the Overrealm, or the Underrealm, or somewhere! Not here!"

"I guess there was a problem with their entrance tickets," Presto replied, trying to figure out which spell to key up. You can't cloud the mind of a creature that's dead, nor control it, nor paralyse it. Perhaps something more basic might work? He spoke a few words, then threw a jet of pure mana out of his hand. It smashed through the undead worker's chest, right where his heart should have been. The worker tumbled backwards, crashing to the ground.

For a moment he laid there, then he climbed remorselessly to his feet and resumed his advance, the blank expression on his face utterly unchanged by the huge smoking hole in his torso. Presto fired a second spell, taking the worker's head clean off this time. Again, the worker tumbled backwards; again he climbed, headless now, to his feet.

Darick was still struggling to comprehend their situation. "But the explosion was thirty years ago! You're saying they've been like this, all that time?"

"Yes."

Behind the now headless worker, dozens more undead followed, getting ever closer. Presto realised he wasn't the only one shooting. Those troops who'd previously shot at Darick and himself, those who weren't currently throwing themselves into the river, were shooting too, with similarly ineffective results. He saw one trooper go down beneath the advancing wave, followed by another comrade, and then another. Two undead caught hold of the first trooper and literally ripped him to pieces before moving on. A torn-off arm bounced across the ground, twitching; as Presto watched, its fingers began to pull the arm across the ground towards him.

Presto glanced to his rear, seeing that the ferry was only seconds away from docking, only seconds away from being overrun by the undead tide sweeping towards him. He took a third shot, blowing the worker's leg away, and was rewarded by the sight of the undead abomination hopping towards him, followed by dozens more of its fellow lifeless beings.

How can you kill that which is already dead?

He looked across at the clearly terrified Darick. "I'm out. You're up."

"What?"

Presto pointed at the advancing figures. "Those were good men. They don't deserve to exist like this. It's time for you to send them on to the afterlife."

"How? There isn't anything in the Book of Standard Worship that covers this!"

Presto gripped the priest hard by the shoulders and looked deep into his eyes. "Improvise!"

Darick edged out from behind the now anchored force-shields and took several steps forward on shaking legs. He reached deep into his soul, searching for his ebbing faith, but found only a dark, cold emptiness. What use was faith in a world that could produce awfulness such as this? Faith had to have meaning, else what purpose could it possibly serve? And yet still the poor, wretched creatures advanced towards him, while behind him the whine of the ferry ceased as it docked with a dull clunk. A deep desolation settled upon him. He and his companions would die here, and perhaps worse than that, die only to remain in the nether state in which those he faced were trapped.

And there was nothing that he, a failed priest with a broken faith, could do about it.

Something, a movement maybe, or a mannerism perhaps, caught his eye. A woman, her features too rotted to even guess at her age, dressed in what might once have been a business suit. Who had she once been? Had a husband mourned her loss? Had children grown to adulthood shorn of their mother's love? Had she left behind loved ones who even now might be leaving offerings on altars, imagining her soul sleeping safely in the Overrealm?

Whoever she was, she deserved better than this.

She deserved far, far better than this.

They all deserved far better than this.

Failed priest or not, broken faith be damned, he was here and the bishop wasn't, and if anyone was going to help these poor people it had to be him.

He took another step forward, on legs now made firm by a resolve he'd not known he had, and raised his hands to the cavern's velvet-black roof, and to the sky beyond. "SkyFather!" he screamed. "Hear this call, I beg of you! Hear this call, though I am unworthy! Pity we, your troubled children!" He felt something surging inside him, something that wasn't quite confidence and wasn't quite resolve, but was something else, something greater, something stronger.

Faith, he realised.

Genuine, untroubled faith. He could see now that what he'd once called faith was something far lesser, the shadow of true faith, clouded by doubt and dimmed by the harsh light of a blasphemous world. He felt strength flowing through him, firing every nerve, lighting every synapse. From somewhere he felt the pride his mother would have had in him now, were she here to see him, but it was a knowledge of that pride and not the pride itself, an awareness unsullied by any egotism or ambition.

He was the SkyFather's servant now, a mere vessel through which salvation could be delivered. He dropped the hands that had previously pointed at the heavens to point instead at the still-advancing undead. "SkyFather! Release these souls from their torment! Grant them the salvation they have been so cruelly denied! Not for me, nor my companions, nor even for the world we wish to save. But for those who I see before me, trapped in a fate they did not deserve. In the name of we, your servants, I beseech you! Release them!" His echoing words died away, leaving behind a silence broken only by the slow shuffling of undead feet and the screams of troopers dying deaths too appalling to contemplate.

An unearthly silence settled upon the cavern, accompanied by a presence that touched Darick's soul, a presence that was beyond words, beyond meaning, beyond anything that could be described in worldly terms – and then the undead exploded, all of them as one, each obscenely animated corpse turning into a puff of dust that fell gently to the cavern floor. Left behind was a silent cavern empty save for burning cargo containers, and his companions. Of the troopers who'd opposed them, no trace remained.

Presto slapped him on the back. "Nicely done, father! Okay, let's see if we can start that flatbed up and get out of here!"

Chapter Forty-Two

When the flatbed finally emerged from the main access tunnel, it was into a ruined landscape of endless dirt, punctuated by the occasional dead, twisted tree, and lit by geysers of wild mana spewing green wispy tendrils of raw chaos high into the night sky. The only thing that had happened in the ten minutes since that emergence was that dawn had begun to break on the eastern horizon, the first rays of the still-hidden sun transforming what had already been a nightmarish scene into the sort of twisted vista produced by artists long on talent but tragically short on humanity.

And Blade and Laliana were late.

The Storm took a look at the wrist-dial he'd grabbed from Pete's. Another minute ticked by.

He wasn't sure quite how much more of this he could take, this endless cycling not merely through rest, exertion, rest, and more exertion, but also through hope, despair, hope, and yet more despair. Then he heard the faint whine of an aura drive approaching from the direction of the spaceport.

"That's them," Dani muttered, pointing at a spot on the horizon.

The grifter's eyes must have been better than his, because the Storm couldn't see a damn thing. Unable to discern anything in the gloom he grabbed the owl-eyes that still hung around his neck and pulled them over his eye-sockets. As before, the world turned into shades of green, with a smudged something in the centre of it all that was the craft Blade and Laliana had been tasked with stealing. As it grew nearer, the smudge grew in size, the slowness of its approach gradually revealing its impressively imposing scale.

"Just how big a ship did they steal?" he heard Presto mutter from behind him, followed by, "I don't know, but have you noticed it's all white?" from Dani. And then the faint sound of the approaching drive was drowned out by the ear-shattering whine of two combat carpets dropping down hard behind them. Twin searchlights converged on them, producing a green flare inside the Storm's owl-eyes harsh enough that he was still trying to blink the dots away several seconds after he'd ripped them off.

An amplified voice split the night. "Any of you bastards move and we'll cut you to pieces."

The Storm turned to look at Presto. The wizard pulled his clawed fingers into fists and began to mouth a spell, but then something within him died, the light in his eyes dimming as he accepted defeat. "Sorry guys," he muttered. The wizard looked up at Jaquenta, confusion in every line of his face. "Tell me you didn't..."

"Did you really think I'd betray my new husband for my old, darling? Or fall for your absurd story about the end of the world? You remember when I snuck inside the security monitoring station to check it was all clear?" She laughed. "I wasn't checking. I was sending my husband a pre-arranged signal and activating a tracking function." Fake, exaggerated concern settled onto her face. "Oh, I'm sorry, I didn't mention that I'd remarried, did I?"

The first carpet bounced to a landing several metres away, its companion hovering a little above and behind to provide cover. A ramp dropped at its rear and troops began pouring out, like well-drilled emperor ants, their discipline and order lending an air of inhumanity to their movements.

"So why go along with it all?" Presto asked, the edge of pain in his voice matching the despair the Storm was experiencing. "Why help us steal the bomb? Why help us get this far?"

"To kill three birds with one stone, darling. Firstly, to have just one last chance to play with you. And secondly, to discredit and destroy two particularly inept and deserving individuals. Let's just say that tomorrow this project will have a new Head of Science, and a new Head of Security – and you're currently looking at the new Head of Science. Admittedly, I do have to take the slight shame of supposedly having you mind-spell me, but that's a small price to pay in the long term." She nodded at the approaching white skyship as it hove into view. "And talking about the new Head of Security, here he is."

The skyship descended to a landing, dropping heavy anchors that screwed themselves into the soil, before lowering a ramp from its belly. The surrounding troopers quickly moved to gag Presto and cuff his hands behind his back, before motioning them all towards the ramp. For just one mad moment, the Storm felt himself turning to run, but then reality and sanity both crashed in. Where would he run to? And just how many paces did he think he would make before he got cut down? He'd always figured it would be the herb that did for him, or perhaps a swimming pool, or even a carpet crash – the traditional exit options for those who'd chosen the path of the rock star.

Not an aura bolt in the back.

The mood as they boarded the skyship was grim, grim enough that even clad in the psychological armour of his newly renewed faith, Darick could feel his confidence ebbing. He'd thought that they'd averted the world's destruction; had they instead merely postponed it? They reached the top of the ramp, emerging into a spacious cargo hold, where they were then forced to pause while Jaquenta launched into a full-scale row with the troopers' leader over what to do with the bomb.

It was, Darick realised ruefully, almost insulting, the degree to which he and his companions had so quickly been relegated to mere footnotes in the story, albeit footnotes that still had an awful lot of weapons pointed at them.

"My orders are to secure the bomb and remain in place," the lieutenant was saying.

"Well, you can secure the bomb here, on this ship," Jaquenta hissed at him. "And then remain here in place with it."

"That's not what my—"

She took a pace towards him. "Right now, that bomb is out on the surface where anyone can grab it, and anything could happen to it. It's being bombarded by raw, wild mana. It took us two years to build this prototype, and every minute it stays here on the surface is potentially destroying it. This is the personal skyship of the Deputy Head of Security. We can have the bomb back to the spaceport and safely into storage within fifteen minutes. Or we can stay here, and I promise you I will make sure you take full, personal blame for any damage that turns out to have been done to the device."

She let the words hang in the air. The scriptures said that the SkyFather had a purpose for every human being, a purpose for which he had explicitly moulded them. Sometimes, Darick found it hard to see that purpose, and quite frankly right now Jaquenta was looking like a serious challenge to those portions of the scriptures.

After several long seconds of silent stand-off, the troopers' lieutenant nodded a reluctant assent and spoke into his throat-whisper. A few seconds later the flatbed trundled up the ramp and into the cargo hold, the bomb still in place on its rear. The lieutenant issued a last order to the troops remaining on the ground, then hit the close stud mounted beside the ramp. It lifted, sealing them in.

Seconds later, Darick felt a lurch in his stomach as the skyship lifted away from the ground. Something jabbed him hard in the back; the front barrel of a trooper's assault-bolt. A couple more jabs guided him to a row of struts that stood at the far end of the hold, to which Presto and Dani were already tied. For a moment, a desperate thought of resistance bounced through Darick's brain. From what Presto had said after his imprisonment aboard this very ship, it appeared to be run by a skeleton crew. Perhaps he could get away somehow and hide, evading the troopers. But a renewed jab in the back caused that thought to die a quick death. The trooper shoved him down hard against one of the struts, and roughly fastened his hands behind the structure. Other troopers, meanwhile, were attaching some sort of built-in chains to the flatbed with a practiced ease that spoke of previous experience.

The troopers didn't blindfold him. Darick knew that was a mercy to which he probably owed the SkyFather thanks, but right now he wasn't feeling very thankful. Especially when all this one minor blessing served was to allow him to watch a squad of troopers relaxing in the knowledge that their job was done, their enemies neutralised, the "cargo" rescued. The men sat down, their helmets now removed, their bolts down. It was almost strange to see the people behind the masks. Young faces set beneath blond and brunette hair. Laughing, joking. It was a strange kind of world, Darick mused, in which ideologies of the basest, most fundamental evil could ensnare those who, in their own way, were guilty of nothing save a desire to seek their dreams.

It was a strange kind of world. A dark world of lies, deceit, corruption and betrayal.

A woman dressed in grey coveralls appeared on the catwalk that lined the hold's upper area and began to descend the spiral staircase that led to the lower level on which they sat. Her arms were full of items of some sort. It wasn't until she reached the bottom and began to toss them to the troopers that Darick realised what they were: food packs. The troopers began to rip them open, exchanging a bunch of what were presumably private jokes as they did so.

The woman didn't bother offering any food to the captives, not that Darick particularly cared. Right now, even the thought of food made him feel sick. The thought of existence itself was making him feel sick.

Across the cargo hold, Jaquenta was stabbing at a comms button, her failure to share the troopers' good mood made clear by her hunched body language. "Call me mad, Davan, but I had actually thought you might be bothered to come down and meet me." She paused for a moment, waiting for a reply that never came, before mashing down on the comms button again. "Davan? Davan! So help me—"

A green aura bolt flashed down from above and blew the entire comms unit away from beneath her fingers.

A voice came from the catwalk above.

"If you so much as blink, the next one won't miss. And any of you soldier types fancy granting your loved ones a pension, make a move. I want you all down on your knees with your hands on your heads."

Blade. That was Blade. Darick felt a surge of joy within him so strong it brought tears to his eyes and a coughing sob to his throat. Thank you, SkyFather, he thought. Thank you.

Chapter Forty-Three

Blade watched from his vantage point above as Laliana first injected Jaquenta with a knock-out potion the two of them had found in the medical kit, before freeing the guys and helping the five of them bind the troopers with their own cuffs. Only then did Blade allow himself to relax and descend the stairs, a happy Rej at his heels.

He greeted Presto with a nod. "I can't believe this actually worked."

The wizard grinned a most un-Presto like grin back. "You should have had more faith in the plan, Blade."

Blade was spared the need to think of a snappy answer by a clearly upset the Storm erupting into a very angry verbal interruption. "Will somebody please tell me what the fuck just went down?"

Darick appeared beside the rock star. "I'd quite like to know what's been going on myself, actually. What plan?"

Blade looked at Dani, and Dani looked at him, and then they both looked at Presto. "You want to explain to them?"

The wizard was still grinning. "I probably should. But perhaps we should wake my darling ex-wife up first?"

After binding and gagging the unconscious Jaquenta, Laliana woke her up by pouring a bottle of water over her head. This was actually unnecessary, given that Presto could simply have woken her through a basic consciousness spell, but Laliana presumably didn't know that, and he thought it funnier not to tell her.

Jaquenta coughed and spluttered as her awareness returned. Presto knew from personal experience that right now she'd be suffering from the nausea and deep muscle fatigue that a suddenly interrupted magical anaesthesia leaves behind. She dry heaved a few times, sat slowly up, and then focused on Presto with a look of pure, utter fury. All the artifice was gone now, the layers of deception and manipulation stripped away. This was the real Jaquenta, the raw mix of ambition, contempt, narcissism, and hatred that lay at her very core.

It was oddly satisfying to see it.

He fixed a finger straight at her, then motioned with his other hand for Laliana to remove the gag. "Try anything and I'll aura blast you," he told Jaquenta. "And I'll put ten years' worth of hate into it."

She didn't nod, but the slight flash of fear that flickered across her eyes let him know that the message had been understood.

The Storm leaned into the conversation in a very literal way, twisting slightly to bring his face in front of Presto's. "Now will you tell me what the fuck just happened?"

Presto gave him a vague nod and wave, took a few seconds to light up one of Pete's combat cigars – smoking on a skyship was probably illegal, but frankly, who cared? – and then launched into an explanation, happily allowing himself to fall into the speech patterns and mannerisms of a smug crystal detective at the denouement of a one-hour special. "Well, let me first take you all back to the period immediately following our capture."

He waited until he got a terse nod from the rock star and a look of anticipation shot through with hatred from Jaquenta, and then continued.

"We needed to get out of our captivity, obviously, and then find a way to steal the bomb. But beyond that, we needed not just transport for us and the bomb away from Craagon's Reach, but transport with a high enough security clearance that we could then sail away unmolested. Frankly, it seemed like we were a few dozen miles though Shit Pass in a wagon a few mules short of a team. And then my darling ex-wife here turned up."

He gave Jaquenta a smile calculated to annoy the living crap out of her, but stopped when it became clear from the Storm's demeanour that it was annoying the living crap out of him as well.

"The thing you have to remember about Jaquenta is that she can't leave well alone, and it kills her to not be involved. Whatever the situation, whoever's doing what, she's always looking to figure out who she can manipulate, how she can somehow gain something for herself out of the situation. The fact that she appeared on the scene was itself a demonstration of that. And as soon as she did appear, I started to consider how I could use her desire to manipulate, against her."

He paused to puff on the cigar, giving Blade a chance to interject.

"Like in martial arts, when you encourage your opponent to attack so you can turn that attack against them."

"Very much so. And when I realised that she was romantically involved with the man who'd attacked us at the reservation, orchestrated our framing, and tortured me, I knew that he would be an additional pawn she would wish to use in her manipulations, thus creating one more element I could use against her."

It was Jaquenta who interrupted this time. "How did you know I was involved with Davan? We kept our marriage a secret."

"Let's just say that having been married to you, I know how you act towards a lover, how you treat them. The thousand and one ways in which you reveal the connection between you and them."

"But I only ever treated him with rudeness, contempt and frigidity when both you and he were present."

"Like I said, I know how you act towards your lovers."

A sudden look of concern flashed across her face. "Davan! Is he safe? What have you done with him?"

"He's fine," Laliana told her coldly. "We hid on the flight deck and jumped him and the pilot just after the landing. They're locked in a cupboard right now, and the autopilot's taking us due west. It was nice of you to remember him. Eventually."

Presto resumed. "So anyway, I knew that if I asked her to help us steal the bomb, there would be two possible outcomes. Either she would refuse, in which case we'd be no worse off than we already were. Or she'd say yes, in which case I'd know that she was going to try to help us to a certain point before betraying us in a manner that she calculated would be advantageous to her and her pet torturer, as well as damaging those who stood in their way."

Darick looked perplexed. "Did you not consider the possibility that reason and common decency might cause her to genuinely aid us?"

"No. That she would never genuinely aid us was the one factor in the entire plan that I was fully certain of. So, having reached my previously described conclusion, my course of action was clear, that being to make an impassioned pitch to Jaquenta in which I apparently entreated her to join our quest."

A cough bought his attention back to the Storm. "Okay. I get that. But how did you know that she'd go all the way through to getting the bomb to the surface and having this Davan cat come cruising over the horizon in his skyship? How did you know that she wouldn't shaft us earlier?"

Presto held up his hand in acknowledgement of good point, well made. "That's true, and to a certain extent, I didn't know. This was always a gamble, and a desperate one at that, with no real plan B. But for her to pretend to be captured by me involved a loss of status for her. For that to be worthwhile, she needed a big pay-off in return, and if she'd betrayed us prior to getting the bomb, she wouldn't have got that pay-off. And she needed it to go far enough that she could maintain the pretence that I'd genuinely mind-controlled her."

He paused for another puff on the combat-cigar.

"That meant that she couldn't rescue herself, but instead had to wait for Davan to come in and rescue her, preferably in an environment that he and she could control, to ensure that her true role remained unrevealed. Having us go all the way to the surface only to be captured by his skyship and a bunch of his troopers would both fulfil those requirements and play to her narcissistic sense of theatre."

Presto looked at Jaquenta, but for once she seemed utterly lost for words, bereft in a manner that would have made him feel sorry for her had she not filled him with such utter hatred.

The Storm still appeared to be having trouble taking it all in. "Right. So you gambled that she would tell this Davan bloke about it, and arrange for him to like, turn up at the surface and capture us all?"

"Yes."

"And she thought, like we all thought, that you'd told Blade to go and steal a ship and come to meet us, but actually—"

Presto waited for the coin to drop.

The Storm took a step towards Blade and pointed accusingly. "You knew, didn't you? You knew the whole point of the plan was that she'd shaft us? He'd told you all of this, some time when we weren't listening. You were never going to steal just any ship." The words were tumbling out now. "You were always going to find the white ship and sneak onto it and hide and wait for Davan to bring you to us?"

Blade smiled an embarrassed smile. "Erm, yeah."

The rock star waved a hand to indicate himself, Darick, and Dani. "And meanwhile the three of us stooges had no idea what was going on."

Dani coughed. "I did actually know too."

"Well, that's just fucking great!"

"What you didn't know," Presto pointed out, "you couldn't inadvertently reveal. The best way to have you and Darick play the roles of men who believed Jaquenta was on their side, was to let you think she was."

Darick moved into the centre of the space before the Storm had a chance to reply. "I think the main thing is that the plan worked. We did it! And you know what? I think that's worth a good set of claps on the back!"

Corny as it was, the line broke the ice. The Storm glowered for a moment more, then relaxed into a smile. "What the whatever. We did just save the world, right people?"

"We did," Blade told him, slapping him on the back. "All that's left now is to fly this baby back to Empire City and blow this conspiracy sky high."

And then Presto heard a voice from behind them. "I think not, humans."

Chapter Forty-Four

It was almost a voice from a thousand crystal flicks, but not quite; for where those voices were invariably spoken with a forced and laboured attempt at an alien quality, this voice had the smoothness of genuine speech. This voice was real.

Dani spun round and found herself staring into a beautiful chiselled face set between pointed ears, framed by hair of spun gossamer, and placed upon a tall, lithe frame that was easily a head taller than hers. A half dozen figures flanked him, dressed in perfectly tailored black combat suits and wielding hand-and-a-half assault bolts crafted to a quality that took the breath away.

The resulting silence was broken by the sound of the Storm's reawakened fury. "No one mentioned anything about fucking elves!"

"That's because we didn't know about any elves," muttered a clearly perturbed Presto through gritted teeth.

"Well, if you didn't invite them, then who the fuck did?"

The elf chuckled. "You humans are so typical. You live out your firefly lives driven by anger and hate. You fear that which you do not understand and you attack that which you fear."

Blade advanced towards the elf, stopping only when the raised bolts and stern expressions of the elf's guards made it clear that to continue would be somewhat of a terminal option. "Spare us the patronising fucking lectures, you pointy-eared bastard. No one invited you here, so why don't you all just fuck off!"

The elf smiled a smile made more annoying, rather than less, by his near impossible beauty. "Well, that's not quite true, is it, Amethyst?" He let those words hang for a moment, then slowly turned his gaze to fall upon Laliana.

Dani felt her knees weaken as thoughts crowded in. What had Laliana done, and why? A memory came to her. A woman, singing: *Their teeth are out, their tusks are up, they're setting us all a-shout.*

A beautiful woman, with pointed ears that poked through her blonde hair and a voice like the one that now spoke to her.

Dani found herself speaking aloud. "My mother."

The elf walked forward to stand just before her, and placed a hand on her shoulder. "Yes. Your mother. And my daughter."

Two of the elves shoved Blade over to one of the pillars and tied him to it with thin silk ropes. Presto was forced roughly down next to him, tied up, and gagged, followed by the Storm and Darick. Only Dani and Laliana were left untied, as the elf who was apparently their grandfather continued his speech.

Blade watched; he didn't have much choice given the way he'd been tied up, and it gave him something to do while he tried to get his hands free from the bonds.

"You must not be angry with your sister, granddaughter. She was merely following the role that the ancient prophecies laid out for her, as was your mother when she travelled to the human lands and met your father."

Dani gave Laliana a look that blended anger, hurt, and confusion, and got a very guilty look in reply.

"We contacted her when she reached adulthood, and revealed her heritage to her. She agreed to work with us, contacting us through a device we entrusted to her. We have been tracking her through the same device."

"I had to," Laliana cried. "They played me a message from our mother. She said that she'd given birth to us so that we could fulfil the prophecy."

"A prophecy," the elf added, "that the half-human daughters of the line of Kalwron would one day save the Elven race from destruction at the hands of the Sleeping Dragon."

A dark smile crossed Dani's lips. "Did the prophecy say how we were going to save the Elven race?"

The elf stuck a noble pose. "It did not say. But when our spies deduced the nature of the Sleeping Dragon, the meaning of the prophecy became clear. You would help us steal the mana bomb from the humans that had created it, so that we instead might wield it. Instead of them using it to destroy us, we could use it to destroy them."

"Grandfather, no," Laliana cried. "If you use the bomb, it will destroy everything, elf and human. Dani and I are to save everyone by preventing the bomb from ever being used. I told you that. You said you understood."

The elf shrugged, the noble air falling away to reveal the screaming narcissist beneath. "I lied. We have come here to take the bomb, and take it we will."

"You can't," she shouted.

A look of contempt settled onto the elf's perfect features. "Do you think I care about the concerns of a half-human abomination such as you? A half-human abomination that my daughter despoiled herself to conceive, carry, and birth? A half-human abomination my daughter then had to give her life for, merely to fulfil a prophecy?"

Laliana crumpled to the ground crying, crushed by the hammer blow of this harsh betrayal. Pissed off as he was by what she'd done and the consequences it would likely have, Blade still had it in him to feel sympathy towards her. Both she and Dani had been dealt bad hands by life's cruel dealer, but Laliana's hand had turned out to be drawn from a crooked deck. The thought of her and Dani's upbringing brought forth thoughts of his children, and that then conjured a surge of sadness at the seemingly imminent prospect of their lives descending into the worst of chaos. If the end did come, would he be there to protect them in the desolate new world? Or would he die locked in an Elven prison, as the lights went dark and the magical locks clicked forever shut?

Then something cold pressed against his hand. He paused his struggles to escape, and reached with his fingers. One fingertip touched the edge of a blade, another the rounded face of a handle.

Scissors, he realised.

There was a low growl from behind. "Ru rot rhem?"

It took Blade a bit of finger juggling to rotate the scissors to the correct orientation, but that done, the blades sliced easily through the silk ropes. The rings of pain that had been encircling his wrists dissolved; a throbbing sensation began to return to his numb fingers. He gave it just a few seconds for the throbbing to ease, then edged slightly to the side.

Presto had been tied to the same pillar as himself; it took only the slightest of shifts to manoeuvre the scissors across and cut through the wizard's bonds. The wizard wriggled in slight confusion, turned, looked at Blade, and then nodded as an unspoken understanding passed between them.

He counted a silent one, two, three, marking each number with a barely perceptible nod that only Presto would see, and then – on the count of three – exploded upwards. He bore no weapons, wore no armour, had no enchantments cast upon him, and was facing a half-dozen members of what were likely the Elven nation's most elite special forces, tooled up with the best weapons Elven craftsmanship could produce.

It didn't matter.
He was Blade.
He was the greatest A-Sport warrior of all time.
And this was for his kids.

Blade might have been exploding out of his captive crouch faster than any human being had a right to move, but Presto wasn't much slower; he'd already ripped his gag free and begun to scream his first syllable before his legs had straightened and his knees locked.

A fire was burning through him, and as high as the stakes currently were, it wasn't those stakes that were driving his actions now. This wasn't about his life, or the lives of his companions. It wasn't about the bomb, or humanity, or the future of civilisation. It was about more than that.

It was about the elves.

It wasn't just that they were smug, superior, specieist bastards who would have snuffed humanity out at the instant of its birth had their own lazy arrogance not led them to miss the moment. It wasn't that, having so failed, they'd instead spent the next several millennia interfering with the affairs of men like a cat plays with mice, before sodding off across the Western Ocean in the most epic of sulks. It wasn't the cold, cruel lack of empathy that they habitually mistook for wisdom. It wasn't even that they would live several lifetimes to his one, such that the elves he now faced would still be young when he was merely dust and bones in the ground.

No, this was something far more fundamental.

It was that the most precious thing in Presto's life – the thing that had fired his senses more than any herb could ever do, and had so enraptured his soul that set against it even a lover's embrace would pale – was a product of the elven peoples.

The elves had invented magic.

And Presto hated them for it.

Every Elven spellcaster Presto had ever met had been convinced that he was still the teacher, and Presto the human, the student. Every single one of the pointy-eared bastards had claimed to have a deeper connection with the ways of magic than any human could ever achieve. As he exploded out of his crouch, Presto was casting faster than he perhaps had ever cast. He had always been good, he knew that. But now, with the long-ago forging of his academic career now tempered by the events of the past weeks, he was better. He really, really wanted one of the elves to be a wizard, just so that he could have the satisfaction of beating him. And he didn't just want to beat him.

He wanted to make him grovel.

Dani barely had time to spot Blade exploding upwards before a pair of scissors came arcing her way. She caught them and dived towards the pillar around which the Storm and Darick were tied, popping up just in time to see Blade clubbing an Elven guard with the guard's own bolt, while a Sorcerac-screaming Presto was so engulfed in multi-coloured magic that the very air around him was shimmering. Across from the wizard, the elf who'd claimed to be her grandfather was also beginning to cast, his arms waving, and his lips forming syllables in the same Sorcerac that Presto spoke.

She quickly cut through the bonds that held Darick to the pillar, then moved over to the Storm. But as she lifted the scissors to the silken rope that bound the rock star's wrists together she began to experience the now half-familiar feeling of every hair on her body reacting to a truly massive surge of mana that was engulfing the cargo hold's interior as the duel between Presto and her grandfather erupted into an exchange of spells of truly epic proportions. And then she was sliding backwards down a floor that was somehow in the process of becoming a wall as the two wizards turned the three dimensions of the universe inside out. Gathering speed, she slid by the flatbed, which unlike her was held firm by a set of chains. Not wanting to hit whatever lay at the end of this drop, she reached out a hand and grabbed hold of one of the steps attached to the side of the flatbed's front driving compartment.

The sudden ceasing of her downward motion damn near pulled her arm out of its socket, but she managed to cling on through the pain. And still the tilt of the floor was increasing, so much so that the skyship's nose must now be pointing at the sky, a situation that while not impossible, was certainly undesirable. She felt her feet swinging clear of the floor as the cargo hold's orientation reached vertical. A screaming figure fell past her, then another. She tried not to think of who it might be. Right now, she needed to get herself to something that was a close enough approximation of safety for her to then be able to devote attention to others.

She tried to haul her way up the side of the flatbed, reaching for the door handle with her right hand, but missing, the sharp metal of the step all the while cutting into her left hand's fingers. She reached again, missed, swung back, reached again – and then felt steel-tight fingers wrapping round her wrist like pincers, pulling her upward, onto the front face of the cab, which now formed a ledge.

"You good?" Blade asked.

The warrior was crouched like a cat, balanced lightly on the balls of his feet.

Pain in her shoulder aside, she was, so she nodded, then looked around, trying to get some sort of handle on who was where doing what, with Laliana her first priority. After a few desperate seconds of searching, she spotted her sister high above her, wrapped around the same pillar to which Jaquenta was tied, her foot jammed into the sorcereress's head. The Storm was across from her, similarly hanging onto the pillar to which he was tied, flanked by the still cuffed human troopers. Darick, meanwhile, turned out to be far below Dani, crouched warily on a section of wall turned floor, Rej beside him, both apparently unhurt; they must have slid down early, she realised, before the slope went fully vertical.

And Presto? Presto was floating above the flatbed, in the centre of the hold, her grandfather similarly floating several feet away from him. Mana cracked all around them, reality itself fragmenting in a series of bizarre kaleidoscopic events, colours that had no right to exist blazing across a zone in which the regular three dimensions had acquired new competition.

She felt something being pressed into her hand and, looking at it, found it to be an Elven hand-and-a-half assault-bolt.

"Cover me," Blade told her.

Chapter Forty-Five

It was a good ten feet from the flatbed's upturned cab to the catwalk that had once run along the left hand wall but now ran up it, and a good forty-foot drop if his jump fell short, but a career's worth of sessions with the best sports psychologists money could hire had long ago taught Blade that the key to success was to visualise it.

He thought of the jump, imagining his flight, visualising the grasping of the catwalk, seeing in his mind's eye his momentum carrying him up and round to a perch from which he could jump again. And then he was exploding into the jump, guided by a programmed self-conscious free of doubts, the unfolding reality so matching his preparatory visualisation that it felt almost deja vu like. The base of the catwalk went sliding by; he reached out to grasp it, then pulled just enough to adjust his flight from a fall to a swing, his motion carrying him back and into the catwalk's side railings. His feet found a strut that they'd known would be there, paused for a moment as his knees absorbed the impact, then pushed hard, sending him sailing back towards the flatbed.

He hadn't needed to wait to observe, to plan his next move. When he'd been on top of the cab, he'd heard the sounds of movement from beneath, movement that a career's worth of tactical awareness had told him came from two individuals who weren't any of his comrades, who'd somehow got themselves into a position just below him, between the bomb and the flatbed's cab.

And now he was flying straight at them.

He hit the first elf square in the chest, smashing him back down against the bomb. The elf slid screaming off the egg's smooth, rounded surface, and carried on, screaming, until a sharp thud indicated that he'd hit the wall far below. But Blade was already spinning, launching a kick at a second elf, hitting him in the face while he was still trying to bring his bolt to bear, the bolt slipping from his fingers and falling away.

And then he felt a lurch in his stomach.

The world had just dropped several feet.

The elf was good, bastard good; so much so that Presto had a nagging suspicion that the pointy-eared shit had had a good dose of the combat mage experience that Presto, ex-academic that he was,

was largely lacking in. This was the basest, most fundamental kind of contest. Mind against mind, knowledge against knowledge, reactions against reactions, and sheer, damn, stubborn refusal to lose against equally stubborn refusal.

Presto had begun the duel with a bog standard aura-blast, a probing parry that he'd not expected to land, but which he'd hoped might establish the parameters of the contest. It had, though not in a manner he'd quite hoped, given the casual ease with which his opponent had blocked it. Presto had parried the return blast, with perhaps not quite as much ease, and then the two of them each launched into full spectrum attacks: physical, mental, and ethereal.

Aura-blasts and reality-shifts on the physical, mind-fogs and hallucination attempts on the mental; meanwhile in the ethereal plane their avatars wrestled. Somewhere along the way, their combined casting had begun to affect first the local environment, and then the skyship's systems, as its auto-pilot fought to comprehend a universe that now rotated not around objective reality, but around the two duelling mages located in the ship's belly.

Presto was only dimly aware of the ship's movement; he'd levitated himself in the first moments of the combat, removing the floor as an avenue through which his opponent might attack him. He was casting at his very limit now, channelling more mana through fragile human nerves and sinews than any sane healer would recommend, operating at a pitch so extreme that it seemed as though time had paused. And yet his every attack bounced off the opposing mage's magical defences, and every returning attack pushed his own defences to the very edge of destruction.

He switched tactics, going old school, throwing away centuries of academic theory, discarding every intellectual position propagated on the pages of peer-reviewed journals, falling back instead on instinct, raw talent, and the decidedly old-fashioned but still highly effective power of a pair of Kellen's Mighty Fists.

The first giant magical fist bounced off the elf's mana shield, setting up a slight shimmer that the second fist crashed into. The shield rocked as the fist-shaped lump of energy some five feet across impacted its smooth surface. It held, but for the first time the elf's expression held a look of slight unease. Presto threw in a swerving fireball, then immediately switched to the ethereal place to launch the cascading hoop-snake, mana-eating spell he'd created as part of his doctoral dissertation.

For an instant, the ethereal plane blinked as the spell self-destructed, triggering a blowback in the physical world that hit just an instant before the fireball collided with the elf's defences. Weakened, the shield yielded, keeping out the raw flame but letting through a blast of heat. A cry of pain emerged from the elf's previously tight-clamped lips, his head rocking backwards, his floating frame shaking.

Creaks of protest came from the skyship's structure as it dropped several feet before its lift field regenerated and caught it, but Presto's awareness had so shrunk that he was only dimly aware of such things. He threw a writhing Josepher's Tangling Net across the gap, the colour boosted variant, and saw it wrap around the shield-shrouded figure of the elf; it began slowly, inexorably, to tighten, Presto pumping mana burst after mana burst into it, feeling the fury with which his opponent was resisting it.

And then the elf was screaming, drawing in power, reaching further inside himself than he had previously in this combat, further inside himself than he had ever, perhaps. The net exploded into a thousand fragments, destroyed by a ball of raw, anger-driven mana that expanded out and crashed through the vehicle within which they fought.

The skyship's structure screamed a scream of tortured metal being pushed to its physical limits, the ship itself turning, rotating, falling all at the same time, in every currently existing dimension – the three that were supposed to exist and the bunch more that weren't.

From somewhere there was the sound of snapping chains, followed – an iteration and a bit of thirty-two feet per second later – by the dull thud of a loaded flatbed colliding with something hard. And then a loud, automated voice pierced the chaos that had engulfed the cargo hold.

"Detonation sequence resumed at emergency pre-set hold. Detonation in thirty seconds. Repeat—"

If the flatbed's fall and subsequent impact with the cargo hold's far wall hadn't stopped the combat, the bomb's bombshell that it had resumed its detonation sequence certainly did. As the skyship settled back onto an even keel, those elves still on their feet – their leader included – ran for the rear ramp, barely giving it time to open before throwing themselves into the void beyond, where they flew away using personal float-packs, super-warrior style.

Darick watched them go. Quite frankly, after first having his stomach wrenched every which way, and then having to roll frantically sideways to avoid a falling flatbed with a rather large cargo attached, he wasn't in a condition to do much else. And from the way that his companions had also merely watched the elves leave, they apparently felt the same way.

A few seconds later, a clearly exhausted Presto came dropping in beside Darick next to the upturned flatbed, underneath which the bomb was wedged.

"Detonation in twenty seconds," the bomb helpfully announced. A red light on its side was blinking.

"Can you stop it?" Darick asked the wizard.

"Don't know. But you'll have an answer within twenty seconds, I can promise you that."

"Detonation in fifteen seconds."

"Make that fifteen seconds."

Getting into the main control program the first time round had taken a few minutes and a good deal of careful manoeuvring. This time round, Presto just smashed his link spell in, hoping that the bomb's current emergency routine might lack the multiple security layers of its non-emergency predecessor.

But it had been a misplaced hope. The security was still there, still as opaque as it had been back when he'd had several minutes to get in, rather than several seconds.

"Detonation in ten seconds."

How can you attack a sealed system, running on internal mana stores, that's protected behind layers of physical armour and magical shielding, shielding that extends to all known planes? In desperation, he launched a huge ethereal assault on the bomb itself, hoping that he might blast something loose. It was a desperate hope, but right now he was all out of options save desperation and hope.

"Detonation in five seconds."

So much for desperation and hope.

Blade had at some point arrived on the scene. "Can you stop it?"

Presto looked up at the warrior. "No. Sorry."

"Detonation sequence initiated."

The wizard didn't need the bomb's calm announcement to know that it was detonating. He could feel it in his bones, in his nerves, in every cell of his body, in every spark of his soul. The chain reaction of self-replicating spells the bomb was casting in its heart were already pulling in mana at a rate that Presto had never before experienced. That part of his awareness still on the ethereal plane could feel the magical equivalent of a hurricane blowing over that normally death-still realm. And some of that mana was flowing into him; far, far more mana than his frail human body could ever have called through its own pitiful efforts, and as it did he began to experience reality at a pitch beyond anything he could ever previously have imagined.

Somewhere, a sensation in his inner ear told him that the skyship was falling from the sky now, its lift-fields depleted, but Presto didn't care. He felt as though his soul was everywhere and nowhere, as though he had both split into a million selves, and yet also ceased to exist. And he was casting, he realised, or at least the many parts of the multi-faceted being he'd become were casting.

Time was slowing, stilling, coming to a halt. Presto was outside of existence now, no longer bobbing along with time's flows and eddies. His magic reached out, wrapping around the bomb, taking hold of the now near-infinite number of self-replicated spells. In one single frozen instant that might have lasted a lifetime, he snuffed them out, one by one, and yet all at once.

And then he was back.

Him, Darick, Blade, and the bomb – its red light dim now, no longer blinking.

"What happened?" Blade stuttered, a look of stunned incomprehension on his face. "How? It was, like, the world didn't quite exist anymore – and then it did. What did you do?"

Presto took a moment, while his super-charged soul settled back into place. "I'm not sure I can explain. The detonation was pulling in so much mana that it was turning the world into something else, and I was within that, with access to more power and greater abilities than I could ever have imagined. For just that one moment, it was like I was a god, with the powers of a god. I could see all of creation laid out before me. I could sense every creature, every ray of light, every mote of dust. I saw the infinity of creation within which I exist."

"And did that make you feel insignificant?" Darick asked.

"No. Sorry, should it have done?"

And then a furry object was on him, a wet tongue washing over his ear. Through all his exhaustion he felt himself smiling. "Well done Rej. You did good."

Somewhere along the way, the skyship had returned to a level plane. He levered himself to his feet and on shaking legs walked over to where Dani and Laliana were standing, staring at each other, locked in a shared agony he couldn't begin to imagine. From somewhere in his perhaps now changed soul he felt a surge of empathy that was frankly unfamiliar. He grabbed them each by the shoulders, pulling them together.

Laliana looked up at him, her face tear-streaked. "I'm sorry. I'm so, so sorry."

He silenced her with a wave of the hand that was wrapped around Dani's shoulders. "Don't worry about it. You did what you thought was right, and you acted in good faith. In the end we were all prisoners of our prophecies. Now we're free, but only if we walk forward, and leave the past behind."

He flicked a glance at Dani, and was rewarded with a sight of the angry mask slipping off her face. The grifter reached out a hand to her sibling.

"Sisters forever?"

A relieved smile flooded onto Laliana's face as she reached out to take Dani's hand in hers.

A cough from behind them broke the moment, a cough which when Presto turned proved to have come from a smiling Blade. "Well if it's okay with you gentlemen and ladies, I think we should set course for Empire City, before our Elven friends notice the absence of any large bangs."

Chapter Forty-Six

Blade hadn't slept on the flight home. He couldn't really, given that he was — autopilot aside — the only pilot they had. But he doubted that sleep would have come easily anyway. Sure, they'd stolen the bomb and saved the world. But was that really the end of the story? When they'd left Empire City they'd left as criminals wanted for heinous crimes.

And nothing about that had changed.

So while his companions snoozed fitfully in the various couches scattered across the skyship's bridge, he divided his time between monitoring the autopilot, watching the scanners to make sure the elves really had sodded off, checking out the captives now locked in a small room behind the bridge, and pacing.

Lots of pacing.

But finally, the last of the long hours slid by, and the first of the several moments he'd been dreading arrived. He reached out and flicked the whispercast unit to transmit. "Empire City Control, this is Skyship Griffin Hammer requesting approach path to Central Skyport."

The response from sky traffic control was immediate.

Skyship griffin hammer, you're cleared for approach path six-niner and docking at mast seven-two. Welcome home. We've been expecting you.

He thumbed the transmit button without thinking. "You've been expecting us?"

Everyone's been expecting you. Look around!

Blade took a slow careful look through the encircling bank of windows that lined the forward half of the bridge, finding the formerly empty sky suddenly full of carpets, broomsticks, and assorted skyships, with more arriving with each second that he stared dumbfounded at the view. Some of the craft flying alongside them bore the blue and white checkers of the guards. At least three bore the logos of major news organisations.

"What the hell?"

Dani's head carefully eased its way in between his couch and Laliana's. "I might have a bit of a confession to make here."

"Which is?"

"When I was in the security office taking down the systems, I found a whole batch of documentation relating to the project."

"And?"

"I might possibly have sent it to a dead-letter server set to send it on to every major news organisation, plus the guards and the government, about five hours after we were due to steal the bomb. Together with a quick note explaining what the bomb would have done, had it gone off. Oh, and they had a copy of your dissertation in there, Presto. I put a link into that too, pointing out that you were actually the expert in this field."

"Thanks," came the wizard's dry reply.

A click sounded from behind them. Blade spun his chair round and found the Storm standing beside the large crystal set mounted on the rear-bulkhead. A 24-hour news channel appeared on its screen, the image on it that of their skyship taken from one of the flanking carpets.

—if you've just joined us, you're watching Blade Petros and his companions making their final approach into Empire City's Central Skyport, the final chapter of what is perhaps the biggest story of the century, carrying with them an illegal weapon stolen from what government sources are describing as a major criminal conspiracy involving significant portions of the intelligence, defence, academic, and business communities.

"Do you think that means we're okay?" asked Darick.

To recap, the Empire City Guard have announced that all charges against Petros and his companions, who of course include Northern Fire's the Storm, have been dropped. Arrest warrants have been issued for those members of the conspiracy thus far identified, and the government has already announced three separate judge-led inquiries.

Presto paused in the lighting of what was presumably a celebratory cigar. "I think that's a yes. All that's left now is for us to escort our captives off the ship and grasp the fame, fortune, and grovelling apologies to which I'd say we're entitled."

"I'm up for that," said the Storm. "Well, the grovelling apology bit, at least."

"I'd certainly like to see if I can get back to what I used to do," said Presto.

"And so would I," said Dani. "Like to get back to what I normally do, that is. So I'd rather not just walk out of here into fame and fortune, if you get my drift."

Laliana was nodding. "I'd probably rather stay out of it, too."

Blade nodded at the controls. "Do you want me to take us somewhere else?"

Dani shook her head. "No, you're good. Take us in, and we'll just slip away."

The Storm pointed at the crystal, which had now switched to a view of the thousands of people awaiting their arrival at the skyport; a throng that included a battalion or two of the news-slates' finest. "You think you can slip away through that?"

The grifter smiled. "Well, if I can't, I'm not the girl the spell thought I was."

The coffee bar on the skyport terminal's upper floor was packed to the rafters, its interior overflowing with the sort of excited buzz not normally associated with skyport travel. Dani weaved carefully through the throng and put the coffees down on the table she and Laliana had managed to snag, a table that offered a good view of both the exit and the large crystal on the far wall.

"Rrot arout re?"

Dani fished a bottle of water out of her jacket pocket, spun off the lid, poured some of the contents into a paper cup, and then placed it on the floor next to the dog's snout. "There you go, Rej."

The view on the crystal's screen changed to the doors of an elevator, the commentator's voice dropping into the portentous tone such commentators reserve for truly momentous occasions.

And there we see the elevator at the base of the docking mast through which Blade Petros and his band of world-saving adventurers are due to emerge. It's being reported that the guards have secured the skyship and its deadly, but now defused, cargo, and have taken several conspirators into custody. And... yes... here we go, the doors are opening.

On the screen, the doors slid open to reveal a sardonic Presto, a jumpy the Storm, a mildly bewildered Darick, and a clearly unsure Blade.

And can we see? Yes... yes we can – that's Blade Petros. He looks nervous.

"He'll be looking for Toozie," said Laliana.

"You reckon?"

The arrivals lounge was crowded to a point beyond chaos and nearing insanity, with only a thin line of guards and a rope barrier preventing a total breakdown of order. But the one person Blade had hoped might be there, wasn't. A thousand pictographic flashes went off over a single, staccato second, leaving him blinking back the dots now floating around his vision.

She wasn't there.

A man in a bishop's vestments appeared in front of the guard line, smiling the sort of oily smile issued by politicians, second hand car salesmen, and – it appeared – senior members of the Holy Church of the SkyFather. He made straight for Darick, his arms outstretched.

"Brother Darick!"

Darick dodged the attempted hug with a neat side-step and an outstretched hand. "Archbishop."

The Archbishop turned to address not Darick, but the floating camera that had appeared beside them. "We at the Holy Church are thrilled to welcome our brother priest home, after a vital mission in which he has so magnificently displayed the continued relevance of the church in this, the Second Millennium of the Third Age. Father Darick will shortly be assuming his new role as head of a multi-faith centre currently being built in—"

"No." Darick physically stepped in between the bishop and the camera, a neat move, if ultimately a pointless one, given that the camera quickly manoeuvred around him to poke its lens right back into the conversation. "When I was a nobody, with nothing going for me save a faith in the SkyFather that the majority of my fellow clerics appeared to lack, you wanted nothing to do with me."

"Well, I think you're over—"

Darick was in full flow now. "And if the events of the past few weeks have shown me anything, it's that if I have faith in the SkyFather, I have no need of worldly structures. I don't need the church, and I'm afraid that includes you."

The bishop turned angrily away, to be replaced in an impressively seamless fashion by a female reporter, equipped with the requisite blonde hair, white teeth, and sympathetic smile. "So what are your future plans, Father Darick?"

"I thought I might wander the land, meeting the people."

She frowned her serious frown. "Like Kasulu, in the *Way of the Wanderer* flicks?"

"Well, I actually thinking more of the Prophet Munu when he took the Word to the Northern tribes, but, well, I suppose your analogy is equally apt."

The Storm eased in beside Darick and in front of Blade. "While we're at it, if the boys in the band are watching this, I'd just like to tell them sincerely to go—" He paused, looked across at Darick and smiled, before resuming. "Let's just say I quit. From now on it's just me and my lute, and well, we'll see if I can write songs after all."

Blade was still searching for Toozie, and then somehow she was there at the edge of the crowd, fighting with a pair of guards. He stepped quickly over. "It's okay, she's with me," he told them. "At least, well, you know—"

"It's okay," Toozie told him. "I'm with you."

He reached across and lifted her over the rope, easing her gently down to the ground with a slowness that probably revealed how much he didn't ever want to let her go again.

"You did it," she said, smiling. "You saved the world."

A vague awareness told him that the camera was floating just to his side, but right now he didn't care who was watching. This moment was for him and Toozie, and no one else, save perhaps the kids one day when Mum and Dad were talking about the old times.

"I should never have let you go," he told her.

"I know."

"If I asked you to marry me again, would you say yes?"

"Why don't you ask and find out?" she said, in a voice whose amused tone was betrayed by the smile teasing at the edges of her mouth.

"Toozie, will you marry me?"

"Yes."

A roar erupted across the coffee shop, drowning out the commentary from the crystal until someone thumbed the volume right up.

—really is turning into a fairytale ending to a story so reminiscent of the old ages. Four men, heading into the wilderness with the fate of the world resting on their shoulders.

Laliana sighed. "They never mention the women, do they?"

Dani shrugged. "Well we did run away and hide."

"Rorr ra rogs!"

Laliana gave him a kiss on the snout. "I know, Rej. They don't mention dogs either. But don't worry. We know what you did."

Blade, Toozie, Darick, and the Storm were edging forward now, heading down the tunnel formed by the guard-flanked rope barriers that led to their post-adventure futures. Presto followed in their wake. The events of the last few weeks seemed to have fundamentally changed each one of his colleagues, but he himself felt pretty much like the same person he'd been before.

It might perhaps have been a deep strain of arrogance streaked with narcissism, but deep down he'd always believed that he was special, a man who had destiny riding alongside him, and frankly, the events that had just transpired had certainly done nothing to dissuade him of that. The only trouble was that he was still unemployed, homeless, and had – in the course of saving the world – broken pretty much every magic-related law going.

A man in a formal academic toga emerged from the guard lines. "Dr Tannarton?"

Presto reached into his coverall's pockets and found a last, final combat cigar. Might as well get a last bit of law-breaking out of the way. He stuck it in his mouth, and put his finger to its tip.

Flame.

It lit and he sucked deeply, before turning his attention back to the man. "That's me."

"I'm Denalo Trant, the Vice-Chancellor of Empire City University. We'd like to offer you a job."

"At ECU?"

"Our Department of Magical Studies is increasingly well-regarded, and we're moving up the league tables for student satisfaction, exam results, and resulting employment. The position of departmental head is currently vacant, and we think you're the man to fill it."

Presto took another suck on his cigar. "In case you hadn't noticed, I don't actually have a license to practice magic."

A confused look settled upon the Vice-Chancellor's face. "Did no one tell you? Your license was restored by emergency proclamation three hours ago, backdated to three weeks ago to absolve you of any legal liability for all and any magic you were required to cast when fighting the conspiracy."

"Really? That's nice." He thought for a moment. A job was a job, and the gods knew he needed one. But ECU? The city college?

"I know what you're thinking, that ECU would be something of a come down after the Imperial University. But I think you'll find that we're something special."

Presto laughed, a laugh that betrayed the sadness he still felt at the loss of his former life. "No offence, but when it comes to the practice and theory of magic, it's very much Imperial University first and daylight second."

"Now, perhaps. But we think that with you in charge, we could change that."

The man's words hit Presto with the force of a thunderbolt served neat, save for a side slice of truth. He was bigger than Imperial University, and he was far more than Imperial University. He didn't need them. The answer to the question "Which is the best Department of Magic on the planet?" was always going to be "The one that's run by Presto Tannarton". He stuck out his hand. "I accept."

"Thank you, thank you. You won't regret this, I promise." Trant leaned in. "But you had better put out your cigar."

"Why?"

"It might not have been illegal for you to use magic to light it, but this is a no-smoking zone."

On the crystal screen, the flash-lit figures walked away through a distant doorway towards a fleet of waiting cars. Laliana took a sip of her coffee, and then looked back to Dani. "So what are you going to do now?"

"I really don't know. I was thinking I'd go back to what I did before, but, well, it all seems a bit pointless really. There has to be more to life than just hustling to survive."

Then a man popped a chair down beside their table, which he then proceeded to slide onto. "Ms Xanare?"

Damn near no one knew Dani's real name. Once, before all of this, such a situation would have terrified her. Now though, she felt strangely calm. She took a sip of her coffee and shrugged. "Could be. Who's asking? And why?"

"Let's just say I'm with an organisation that was supposed to stop conspiracies such as the one you and your companions have just destroyed. An organisation that recent events have proved is in need of a woman of your skills. Would you be interested?"

"You realise my methods of working are somewhat unorthodox."

"Unorthodox is what we're looking for, Ms Xanare."

Dani looked up at her sister, the only moral barometer she'd ever needed. "What do you reckon, sis?"

Laliana shrugged. "Got to be better than flogging Sir Ethelded's statue for the fifteenth time."

"True enough." Dani put out her hand. "Job offer accepted. I'll take myself a two week holiday, then report for duty." She pushed herself out of her chair. "Come on, sis, Rej. Let's go."

"Ms Xanare?"

"Yeah."

"I haven't told you how to find me."

Dani gave him the full thousand-Kellen smile. "It's okay. I'll find you."

THE END

Dear Reader,

Thank you for purchasing and reading *The Sleeping Dragon*. All of us at Wild Jester Press hugely appreciate it. We hope you enjoyed the read and, if you did, we would ask one small favour of you: that you take some time to write a short review in the online location of your choice.

Online reviews are hugely important for independent and small-press publishers like us. We don't have marketing budgets. We can't pay to be prominently displayed in bookshops. We sell by "digital word of mouth", and reader-produced online reviews are the means by which that happens.

Thank you!

Out now from Wild Jester Press

Looking to read something else by Jonny Nexus? Then check out his ENnie-nominated first novel, *Game Night*.

Six Gods Sit Down to Spend an Evening Roleplaying. Badly.

In an anachronistic realm at the far end of creation, five adventurers near the climax of an epic quest, upon which hangs the fate of their world. Sadly for them, however, they are but pieces in a roleplaying game being played by a group of bickering gods.

Epic events will unfold, only to then unravel. Secrets will be revealed and then forgotten. A much-abused reality will warp, mutate, rewind, and – on occasion – capitulate. Stupidity will birth tragedy; mischief will spawn chaos; malevolent arrogance will conjure forth genuine evil.

A story of myth and legend twelve thousand years in the making is heading towards its final chapter.

It's game night.

"The best novel ever written about gaming. One of the funniest novels ever written about anything."
– *Steve Darlington, gaming writer*

"A Pratchett-esque debut novel of gods, roleplaying, and game-night kerfuffles. Buy Game Night. It's a fun, fresh, irreverent read that'll ring true to any gamer even if, unlike the protagonists, you happen not to be a god."
– *John Kovalic, Writer & Artist (Dork Tower, Munchkin)*

Alternatively, check out Jonny's second novel *If Pigs Could Fly*, the first book in an offbeat urban fantasy series.

"West Kensington Paranormal Detective Agency. Dr Ravinder Shah speaking. No case too weird, no problem too bizarre. Strangeness a speciality. How can I help you?"

London Social Worker Rav Shah moonlights as a paranormal detective, aided by one of his clients and a Border Collie he rents by the hour. It was supposed to be a bit of fun: a search for truths out there; a quest for a life more interesting than the one that fate, destiny, and personal apathy had granted him.

But then a case involving a Yorkshire farmer and a herd of flying pigs leads him into a world darker and more dangerous than he'd ever dreamed.

The truth is indeed out there.

And it's got Rav square in its sights.

"Jonny has a nice eye for detail and the plot buzzes along bedecked with Pratchett-esque observations. If you liked the Dresden Files but longed for the occasional cup of tea and better manners, or Rivers of London but found the good guys just a bit too competent, then this should be right up your street."

— *Steve, Goodreads*

"Jonny Nexus has a genius for setting his weirdness firmly in Britain, with what feels like first-hand local detail and a marvellous deadpan delivery of Ravinder's mishaps, whether at the hands of supernatural entities and their minions, the local constabulary or his boss."

— *Becky Ottery, Goodreads*

Made in the USA
Lexington, KY
01 July 2018